I0636142

When God's Wind Blows

Stewart Bint

When God's Wind Blows

Stewart Bint

Copyright © 2023 Stewart Bint

All rights reserved, including but not limited to the right to reproduce this book in any form; print, audio, electronic or otherwise. The scanning, uploading, archiving, or distribution of this book via the Internet or any other means without the express written permission of the Publisher is illegal and punishable by law. This book may not be copied and re-sold or copied and given away to other people. If you are reading this book and did not purchase it, or it was not loaned to you or purchased for your use, then please purchase your own copy. Purchase only authorized electronic or print editions and do not participate in the piracy of copyrighted materials. Please support and respect the author's rights.

This is a work of fiction. Names, characters, places, and incidents are the products of the author's imagination or are used fictitiously. Any resemblance to actual events, locales, or persons, living or dead, is entirely coincidental.

Paperback ISBN 978-1-77400-058-8
Ebook ISBN 978-1-77400-059-5

www.dragonmoonpress.com

For my dear friend Doreen Donoghue

Acknowledgements

This is the most important page in the book, because there wouldn't be a book at all, without the people named here.

My sincere thanks to everyone who helped with the extensive research that was necessary to add realism to this fantasy/paranormal tale.

While it's a work of fiction, many scenes required as much accuracy of the real world as possible, to nudge the unbelievable towards being believable. Even so, I've still employed a touch of artistic licence here and there for dramatic purposes, but if anything is completely wrong, that's down to my mistakes, and not to anyone here, who provided me with fully accurate information.

So, here we go.

Thank you to Stuart Ross, Stephany Martin, and Dominic (Danny) Williams, for sharing their horrific experiences of COVID and Long COVID. I hope I've done justice in portraying some of the unthinkable anguish they've been through, and I pray they're now recovering well and their lives are returning to some semblance of normality. Whatever normality is nowadays.

Thank you to Dr. Jamie Breakwell for describing the workings of a hospital medical ward during the early stages of the COVID pandemic. And thanks to Dr. Ron Daniels for details of how a COVID Intensive Care Unit functioned at that time, along with the step-by-step process of proning COVID patients. But what really hit me during my time with Ron was how scared medical staff were for their own safety. We definitely owe a huge debt of gratitude to everyone in the health sector around the world.

My dear friend Doreen Donoghue gave me a vital insight into her out-of-body experience, and also inspired a powerful and moving scene towards the end of the book. Without Doreen's input, When God's Wind Blows would lack much of the emotion I hope it portrays. So, not only many thanks to Doreen, but hugs and kisses, too. I love you, my friend xx.

Although I'm a former radio broadcaster, studio equipment nowadays bears no resemblance to the desks I used in the 1970s and 80s. Thank you to BBC Radio Leicester presenter Jo Bostock who explained how modern radio desks function, and how radio stations adapted to new working practices during the pandemic.

I needed background on police procedures. Thanks to Jude Markillie for explaining what I had to know, and for introducing me to the concept of the Holmes police computer.

There is an impassioned speech in chapter 20 about the environmental crisis our planet faces. The words of my fictional character Jasmine Foster-Brown were provided by climate activist Grace Maddrell, who had already written a powerful guest post on the subject for my blog a few years ago.

Then there are my Twitter friends, Adam (from Barton on Sea) and Hayley Clowes, who talked their way into being named in the book. Happy to oblige. Even though they're murdered in the opening paragraph, they have a nice little backstory told in flashback, which I hope will convince you, the reader, to invest your time reading the book to see the reasons behind their murder take on global proportions.

As always, my thanks and much love to my dear wife Sue, son Christopher, and daughter Charlotte.

Last, but very much not least, profound thanks to Gwen Gades and her team at Dragon Moon Press for putting her faith in me once again. Dragon Moon Press published my debut novel, In Shadows Waiting, where we first meet Simon Reynolds. That book is set in 1982 when he's 18. When God's Wind Blows is the sequel to that, and takes place in 2020 and 2021 when he's 56 and 57. It's good to get back inside his head after all these years of being away from him.

So, I reiterate my thanks to everyone named above for helping me bring Simon back to life.

Stewart Bint, Leicestershire, England,
Monday, 14th November, 2022

Part One
MURDER

1

Vaccination

Poolswood, England, February 20-21ˢᵗ, Hayley

Hayley Hampshire lay dead on her drive, gunned down alongside her husband just a few seconds earlier. The echo of machine gun fire and the squeal of tyres rang through the air as the blacked-out BMW sped away along Clowes Road.

Excitement and relief had flooded through her when she took the phone call several days previously. The phone call that ultimately led to them getting out of their car at that particular time.

And on the landline, too. Not her mobile.

"Either Auntie Pat... or Michael," she said to Adam when the distinctive high-pitched trilling began in the hall during breakfast, knowing that her aunt and Adam's friend were the only two who still rang the house phone.

She put down her piece of toast and cast a backwards glance over her shoulder as she headed towards the kitchen door. "A fiver says it's Michael."

"Done," said Adam. "He won't be up at this time. Eight o'clock on a Friday morning. The money's in my pocket already."

"Oh." Hayley had arrived at the phone alongside their broadband router on the hall table and was looking down at the caller ID displayed on the small screen. "It's not Michael," she called. "It's the doctors."

Her tests had only been three days ago...surely not. *But they wouldn't be ringing me if all was well.* Her heart skipped a beat, then started thumping in what felt like double time to Hayley. Which, given her condition, was not a good thing.

"The doctor?" said Adam, from the kitchen. "What can she want?"

Hayley picked up the handset. "Hello." A tiny, barely discernible, tremor in her voice.

A slight pause. Then: "Hello, is that Hayley Hampshire?"

"It is."

Adam appeared behind her. "Is everything okay?" he whispered. Hayley mouthed at him to shush, and waggled her hand.

"Good morning, Mrs Hampshire. This is Evelyn at the doctor's surgery." Unless... *Yes, please let it be that,* she thought, *please let it be that.*

And it turned out it was.

"Mrs Hampshire, Doctor Beresford would like to invite you for your first COVID vaccination."

A palpable sigh of relief escaped her lips. "Thank you." Her heart was more stable now; beating slower. "That's made my day, Evelyn."

Evelyn was speaking again. "You're aware that because of your congenital heart condition, you would be more at risk than other people of your age if you were to contract COVID-19?"

"I am. I had a full check-up on Tuesday following a heart scare, and they warned me again of the increased risks. My husband and I have both been shielding at home since lockdown began last March. We've literally only been past our front gate once since then, and that was for the hospital check-up."

She paused, then continued: "I thought for a moment you were ringing to tell me the test for pulmonary hypertension was positive."

"I do have those test results as well, Mrs Hampshire. Doctor Beresford asked me to tell you they're negative. She's writing to confirm that today."

Another sigh of relief. "A real double whammy," said Hayley. "No pulmonary hypertension, and I'm getting my COVID jab. Mum and Dad only had their jabs a couple of weeks ago, too."

"Don't feel you're jumping the queue, Hayley." Hayley now, not Mrs Hampshire. "Because you're regarded as being clinically vulnerable, we'd like you to have your injection now."

Hayley smiled. "This is the first time my atrial septal defects have been anything but a curse," she said.

"The surgery has a vaccination session at the Poolswood Leisure Centre next week, Thursday the 18th, if you're able to make that," said Evelyn.

"Oh, not at the surgery itself?"

"No, we don't have the amount of refrigeration equipment necessary to store the Pfizer vaccine at the surgery."

"I'll be having the Pfizer jab, then?"

"You will. Nothing to worry about. I've got a slot at two o'clock if that's alright for you?"

"It is. I'll put it on my calendar now."

"Just take some form of photo ID with you—a passport or driving licence—don't be late or you may lose your slot. Also, try not to be too early, it's important not to have too many people there at any one time. And be sure to wear a mask."

"I will. And a visor as well."

"So, two o'clock on Thursday, February 18th," said Evelyn. "You're all booked in."

"Thank you, Evelyn."

"When you get there, you'll need to queue outside, social distancing of course, and marshals will then guide you inside where you'll have the vaccination."

"OK, that's fine. Hopefully, it's the start of things getting back to normal for me."

"While I'm on the phone, Hayley, is Adam there, please?
"He is. Would you like to speak to him?"
"Yes, please."
Hayley turned to Adam. "Evelyn, from the surgery, would like to talk to you."
"Thanks." Adam took the handset from her. "Hello, Evelyn."
Hayley could hear Evelyn speaking, but the words were too indistinct. She made her way back to her breakfast in the kitchen, where she could still hear Adam's side of the conversation.

"That's perfect," he was saying. "The same time as Hayley. Yes. Thank you, very much. As she said, we've both been shielding from the start of the first lockdown last year, so this is very welcome news."

Hayley could guess what was happening. Adam will be having his vaccination next Thursday, too, she thought. She looked at him and smiled as he came back into the kitchen. The earlier comment to Evelyn about this being the first time her atrial septal defects were anything but a curse, wasn't strictly true. She wouldn't have met Adam without her congenital heart disease, let alone getting together and marrying him.

August 2005, Hayley

Just as it would do years in the future when she took Evelyn's phone call, 15-year-old Hayley Martin's heart missed a beat. But this was for an altogether different reason. As she looked across the cardiology waiting area to the boy about 20 feet away on the other side of the central aisle, he caught her eye and smiled. Hayley felt her face flushing and looked away quickly.

Angela Martin hadn't missed her daughter's brief encounter. "Go and have a chat with him," she whispered.

"He's probably getting his results today as well."

"Mum! Don't."

"You could both do with cheering up. I'm sure he doesn't like hospitals any more than you do."

I bet, thought Hayley. Nothing in the waiting room to cheer us up in any way, or even to make us smile. We'll have to rely on ourselves to do that.

Posters showing the heart's inner workings and the cardiac cycle, along with its place in the full vascular system, adorned the wall to her left. The opposite side showed myriad imperfections and diseases, and any number of ways to maintain good cardiac health, including the so-called 5-A-Day campaign launched by the Government a couple of years ago. The one that saw her Mum start laying down the law about broccoli and spinach. Hayley hadn't minded the oranges, bananas and grapes, but when it came to the greens, well, just yuck.

The anticipation of what may lie ahead when they got in to see her consultant, Dr Kamal Nagaraj, was stoking some jitters and led her to believe that maybe striking up a conversation with that good-looking lad might not be such a bad idea after all.

She risked a glance back in his direction. His eyes were still locked on her. *Shit.* Instinctively she looked above his shoulder at one of the wall posters. Any one. It didn't matter which. She wasn't registering what she was looking at.

"Mum," she said loudly, feeling her cheeks burning, and realising that meant they'd be going red. "Isn't that what they've tested me for?" She pointed at the poster behind the boy, showing several images of various parts of the heart's anatomy.

"Which one, dear?" asked Angela.

Hayley squinted. "Cardiovascular disease," she murmured,

reading the words across the top.

"No, they didn't think it was that, did they?"

"Didn't they?"

"Hayley, your tests have all been for congenital heart disease, which isn't the same thing."

"Oh." She fully intended to scan the other posters, but somehow her gaze became entangled with his again. This time he winked one of those pale blue symmetrical eyes. And stood up.

Shit, shit, shit, he's coming over.

The boy perched astride the chair in front of her, resting his arms across the back, and leaning towards her a little. A hint of aftershave wafted into her nose.

"Hi," he said. "Are you waiting for your results?"

Hayley nodded. "And you?"

"Yeah. 'fraid so. But I guess it'll be better to know what we're up against, whatever it is. Whether I'll be able to play for Arsenal, or if it'll just be a lifetime of shouting at them on the TV."

"Football?" *Ouch. What made me state the bloody obvious?*

"Hey, you're quick. Really on the ball, you might say."

Hayley rolled her eyes but couldn't resist a wry smile. "Arsehole," then "Ow," as her mum's elbow nudged her sharply in the side.

"Hayley!"

"Well, he is."

"Yep. That's me," he said. "Everybody's got one, so I guess that makes me part of a not-so-exclusive club. I don't know why you're wasting your time talking to me."

"You do talk a load of what comes out of one, too."

Hayley noticed how he tilted his head away to the left and down slightly while maintaining eye contact with her, and she hoped the amusement flashing across his eyes was with her rather than at her.

"Anyway," she said. "Arsenal? Tossers."

More facial muscles came into play as his smile progressed to a grin, and Hayley found herself wondering what it would be like to run her tongue over those white, almost perfectly straight, teeth. Just one, towards the right side, was slightly snaggled.

He said: "I wouldn't say no to playing for them one day if my heart lets me."

"Like that's ever going to happen."

"You never know. I've been with The Saints' Youth Academy since I was seven."

"Shut up!" *Her beloved Southampton FC.*

"No, it's true. Right on the verge of getting into the First Team squad as well." He winked again. "They need someone like me to get back into the Premier League. Now Crouch has gone to Liverpool I'll take his spot as the top scorer and then be lured away to Arsenal. You see, they need me as well, only coming second last season. What a comedown."

"So why are you here? At the hospital, I mean. What happened?"

"I had a heart attack during a training session. We were..."

Hayley gasped. "What? That's awful."

"Tell me about it."

Hayley stared at him, numb from his words.

"We were in the middle of training. I was just going for a ball, and my chest suddenly felt like it'd been rammed by a bull. Don't remember many of the gory details. The medics looked after me at the training ground, then got me carted off here. Been through so many tests over the last week, and getting my results today.

"But enough about me. What about you?"

"Oh my God. What do they think it is?"

"Could be any one of a number of things. They tested me for shitloads of stuff. Come on. Your turn. I hope your heart wasn't already broken before you met me."

"Arsehole."

"Hayley!" That was her Mum again.

February 20-21ˢᵗ, Hayley

Now, 16 years on from that day they met, Hayley and Adam were finishing breakfast after Evelyn's phone call, before going into their home gym, converted from the garage; a ritual they followed as husband and wife on an almost daily basis.

Hayley cast appreciative eyes in Adam's direction, taking in the muscles and six-pack rippling beneath the surface of his Team-GB vest top, and ran her gaze from the top of his powerful legs emerging from black Man Waistband shorts, down to his Under Armour fitness shoes.

Adam described her as a classic beauty; pretty, with striking blue eyes and high cheekbones. Her moderately high forehead denoted intelligence, and was framed by sleek, pale blond hair parted in the middle, the bottom ten inches painstakingly curled into corkscrews where it cascaded around her shoulder blades.

As always for their daily gym sessions, she wore a combination of tight blue tracksuit bottoms and a long-sleeved top. This not only failed to leave any curves of her five foot ten willowy frame and pleasingly slender legs to the imagination, but also accentuated the long fingers of her well-manicured hands, and her pedicured bare feet. Such was her standard gym wear, which she knew was also the underlying reason behind another of their rituals—the transfer of their heavily-sweating post-gym bodies into the bedroom for half an hour before a cleansing shower.

It was one of those gym sessions, though, a couple of weeks ago, that had led to days of worry which were finally relieved by Evelyn's phone call.

Adam had been 15-minutes into weight training, and Hayley was on the running machine when she felt her head start to spin and her lungs suddenly couldn't take a refill, no matter how desperate they were becoming for air.

"Adam!" Her voice reflected the fear and panic engulfing her.

Her normally carefully controlled breathing took on a life of its own...the lack of air getting into her lungs perhaps made it think its host had been transported into the vacuum of space. Each desperate, crackling inhalation became a supreme effort, as if dragging air into her lungs was the most unnatural thing in the world. A tightness right across her chest felt like it was pushing air out and not letting any back in.

An unwelcome thought flashed into her mind. *COVID. But surely not. How? I always insist we're so careful.* Neither of them had been out since the pandemic lockdown started last year. She'd been furloughed by the travel agency, and Adam had worked from home for the last three years anyway. *We haven't even used click-and-collect for our groceries. Order online and home delivery. Every time. Thoroughly clean all work surfaces, and hand sanitise as soon as everything's away. So, it can't possibly be COVID, can it? Surely it doesn't come on this quickly.*

While those thoughts flashed along her network of synapses almost in a millisecond, she saw Adam start to climb off the weight-lifting bench, which appeared to be floating away to her left. With fading control over her facial muscles, her panicked expression lost some of its rigidity, becoming quite slack as she saw the gym equipment all around her losing its orientation and perspective: the punchbag hanging away to her right looked to be miles away, and she gradually became aware of a faint hissing, then whooshing sound, which developed into a distant ringing. The rack of adjustable dumbells on the back wall swayed and shook, and the rowing machine undulated like a sheet in the wind. She saw her medicine balls lurking in the far corner through the depths of an unfocused fog which claimed her full range of vision. The words and tune of Ariana Grande's Motive coming from the Bluetooth speaker on the wall lost all sense and meaning to her, sounding muffled and distant as if she were underwater.

And all the time, the invisible arms clasping her chest in a relentless bearhug increased their intensity.

Her eyes came back into focus for a moment. But it *was* only a moment, as the treadmill's digital dashboard appeared to start swimming away. The mental autopilot which kept her legs pounding along the never-ending road was fading, and she felt herself wobbling dangerously. Instinctively, she reached out to grab the handlebars on either side of the screen to keep herself upright.

Confusion became the norm inside her head as she struggled to grasp why air was apparently now alien to her system. The world beyond her bubble was speeding further and further away from her new insular reality. Her hands, now gripping tightly around the front bars, felt cold and clammy, and she sensed, rightly or wrongly, that time was running out. She fumbled for the stop button but missed it, and as her bare feet lost their grip on the treadmill running board she was thrown off balance, falling forward and cracking her head with a sickening thud on the handlebars.

The treadmill continued its endless revolving journey at six miles an hour, pushing her legs behind her, allowing gravity to take control of her flailing body. Hardly before she had time to register what had happened, a thousand woodpeckers were unleashing their beaks above her right eye which had taken the full force of the impact. Continuing in one fluid movement, she fell face-first onto the running deck, which flipped her backwards off the machine. Stars spun merrily around her head, and another laboured drag of air immediately followed an agonised gasp of pain.

Adam was over like a shot, easing her into a sitting position.

"Hayley, what's happened?"

"I...I...can't breathe," she managed to gasp after a few seconds. That much would have been clear to Adam, as the sound of his wife's grating, crackling attempts to pull air into her lungs filled the garage.

He picked up his mobile from the shelf. "I'm calling an ambulance."

"Emergency, which service?" asked the operator who answered his 999 call almost immediately. He opened his mouth to tell him, but at that same moment, Hayley's tortured breathing caught in her throat, irritating it to the point of a full-blown coughing fit, doubling her over.

Adam dropped the phone, slapping Hayley sharply on the back.

"Don't," she gasped. Adam ignored her, and a second slap seemed to clear the irritation. Spittle flew from Hayley's mouth onto the gym floor, and the coughing eased.

"Emergency, which service?" repeated the operator, his

voice tinny and faint from the mobile. "Do you need police, fire or ambulance?"

Adam scooped it up. "Ambulance, please. Quickly. My wife's having trouble breathing."

"Is she breathing at the moment, Sir?"

"Yes, but with difficulty. Hurry, please. 44 Clowes Road, Poolswood."

"Just a moment. I'll put you through."

Adam barely had time to switch the phone on to full speaker before the ring tone stopped: "Poolswood Ambulance Station." A female voice this time.

"My wife's having real trouble breathing. We were in..."

"Is she breathing at the moment?"

"Yes, but she's really struggling. Can you send...?"

"What address are you calling from, Sir?"

"44 Clowes Road, Poolswood. Please hurry."

"What's the patient's name, please?"

"Hayley Hampshire."

"Hamshire?"

"No. Hampshire. With a P, like the County. Look, can you please just send an ambulance?" His voice rose, part in frustration, part in anger.

"Just a few seconds now, Sir. We need to make sure the paramedics are as fully briefed as possible. How old is Hayley?"

"She's 31."

"Thank you. Could you give me your phone number, please...in case we get cut off, I'll be able to call you back."

After Adam had given his number, the operator told him an ambulance was on its way.

"I'll stay on the line until they arrive," she said. "I just need to ask you a few questions so you can help Hayley if you need to.

"First of all, what's your name, please, Sir?"

"I'm Hayley's husband, Adam Hampshire."

"Thank you, Adam. I'm Jan, and I'll be with you every step of the way at the moment. How's Hayley now? Is she fully conscious?"

"Yes. She's sitting up on the floor with her back against the wall."

"It's good that she's conscious. Let's assess the situation before the paramedics arrive. Does her skin look blue at all?"

Adam looked closely at Hayley. "A little, around her lips."

"Does she have any chest pains?"

"No," said Adam.

Hayley waggled a hand at him. Her face contorted as she struggled to draw more air in. "I do," she gasped. "Everything's tight. And it hurts."

"Oh, wait a minute. She does have chest pains."

"Hayley, this is Jan, from ambulance control. Can you describe the pain to me?"

"Weird. It's quite sharp. And tight." A pause of several seconds between her words, as she tried to draw in enough air to speak. "In the middle of my chest, if that makes sense."

"Hayley, are you sweating."

"Was already, from gym." She struggled to get her words out. "But since this started it's different. Cold, clammy."

"Do you feel sick, or dizzy?"

"Not sick, but dizzy, yes."

"Adam, so that Hayley's not using up too much air by talking, can you describe her breathing to me."

"Very laboured and noisy. Here, listen for yourself." Adam held the phone a couple of feet from Hayley's face.

"Yes, I see. More of a crackle than a wheeze, is that right?"

"I'd say so."

"Does she have any symptoms of COVID, such as a high temperature? Has there been any change to her sense of taste or smell? Any signs of fatigue or new aches and pains, a sore throat or headache?"

"No, none of those. We're taking extensive precautions against COVID. Both my wife and I have congenital heart conditions, so we've been shielding since the first lockdown last year."

"Oh, I see. What condition does Hayley suffer from? I'll alert the paramedics about it so they know what to expect."

"She has atrial septal defects—basically a hole in the wall between the upper chambers of her heart."

"Thank you, Adam. I'll make sure the paramedics know that before they arrive. Can you tell me exactly what happened just before the attack started?"

"We were in our home gym. We do a session daily. Hayley's supposed to exercise regularly, but cautiously. Well, so am I, for that matter."

"And you were following your routine today...nothing out of the ordinary?"

"Yes, everything was normal."

"Has there been any change to her condition while we've been talking?"

"She had a coughing fit just before we started speaking, but that seems okay at the moment. It's just her breathing that's so bad. How long will the ambulance be?"

"Not long now. Clowes Road isn't far from the station, and they're coming with lights and sirens. Just keep checking her breathing, okay?"

Hayley nodded to Adam. "I'm alright." She was able to draw a little more air into her lungs now. And the flow seemed easier, too. Not right, she thought, but less strained than a few moments ago.

"Adam, the ambulance will be with you shortly," said Jan. "We won't ask Hayley to wear a mask under the circumstances, but could you ensure you are, please? For your safety as much as the paramedics'."

During the few moments it took the ambulance to arrive, Hayley felt air going into her windpipe in a calmer, more controlled way. The panic that had been coursing through the oxygen-starved blood in her veins and making her heart pump faster (but just as ineffectively in terms of keeping her organs supplied with their life-giving nutrition) was diminishing by the second.

"Let's check your blood pressure," said the female paramedic, while her male companion took Adam aside to ask what had happened. She strapped the sleeve onto Hayley's upper right arm and began to pump.

She looked down at the reading. "140 over 90. A little high, but..."

"Beyond the starting line for stage one hypertension," said Hayley.

"Yes, we've been told about your atrial septal defects. This attack started during your gym session, didn't it?"

"Yes. The cardiology unit drew up my exercise regime. I'm always careful not to exceed my limits with it." Hayley shuffled a little. Her buttocks were starting to go numb, and her back was aching from the gym wall. "This is the first time anything like this has ever happened."

The paramedic seemed to notice her discomfort. "Do you feel up to moving? Perhaps get you to a chair?"

"Please. That would be good."

When the range of tests was over, the paramedics agreed

that Hayley should be taken into the specialist cardiology unit at Poolswood General Hospital (she baulked at the name, at the thought of yet another interminable visit there—she'd certainly not been a stranger there over the years) for further tests, in particular for pulmonary hypertension. "There's no need for you to be admitted immediately. It's passed now, and all indications are that there's no damage to your heart. It may have been an extremely powerful panic attack, but we do need to get you checked out. We're sending a note to your doctor now. Ring this afternoon, and she'll refer you to the hospital."

Thursday, February 18ᵗʰ, 2021, Hayley

Hayley leaned closer to the mirror in the ensuite, puckering her lips before dabbing the excess lipstick off the surrounding skin. Then she tightened them. And relaxed. Perfect. She wanted to look her best as always, even if she was only going for her first COVID vaccination.

"Ready, Adam," she called, as she made her way downstairs to where he was waiting in the hall. "And take that look off your face. We'll be there in plenty of time. If you remember, Evelyn did say not to arrive early."

"As I remember, she said not to arrive *too* early."

Hayley flicked her arm to activate the Fitbit screen on her wrist and glanced down at the time. "We've still got half an hour. Stop panicking."

Adam pulled the door shut behind them and they got in the car.

"You know," he said, as they turned out of Clowes Road onto the main artery into town, "I finally feel the world's waking up again. Our world, anyway."

Hayley's mind wandered back over the past 12 months or so to when Coronavirus disease 2019—the name shortened to COVID-19—increasingly gained attention. Like the rest of humanity, she and Adam had watched as news of the Chinese Government imposing a lockdown in Wuhan was dismissed by many people as something happening on the other side of the world that couldn't possibly affect them.

Newspapers and broadcast journalists were screaming about the forthcoming pandemic with such fervour and lack of concrete evidence that she regarded it as media hype. Even when news emerged of the UK's first confirmed case towards the end of January after a university student in York fell ill with a fever, dry cough and muscle pain, and the student's mother who had flown to the UK from Wuhan a week earlier was also feeling unwell with a fever, cough and sore throat, the UK still seemed to be sleepwalking into the future. Over the coming days people were being stranded on cruise ships, and some international air travel restrictions were put in place. Tension and unease were mounting, but it still seemed a million miles away from her and Adam's little corner of the world.

Reports in some quarters of the media quoted specialists in infectious diseases as saying just a handful of cases were to be expected in the UK. Hayley remembered saying to Adam: "They may get it in big cities, but I can't see it affecting us here."

It didn't take long for her to realise how wrong she was, and for the last 11 months, she and Adam had been cut off from outside life beyond the protection of their 1970s detached house.

Now, as Adam had said, their world may be opening up a little.

"Yes," she said. "The vaccination'll give us our freedom back."

Adam turned left off the road onto the drive leading to the leisure centre and followed the parking marshall's instructions to pull into the bay next to a blacked-out BMW 5 Series M Sport.

Pulling on their masks and clear plastic visors, Adam and Hayley crossed the car park and walked past three men in sunglasses and blue medical facemasks who were standing at the start of a short footpath. The path widened out to become a paved area in front of the leisure centre's doors where they were greeted by a marshall.

Two socially-distanced short queues—only around ten people in each, all looking to be in their sixties—snaked around to the doors. "Good afternoon," said the marshall. "Can I ask which surgery you're with, please?"

"We're both from School Lane surgery," Adam replied. "With Doctor Beresford."

"Thank you. Could you join the left-hand queue, keeping to social distancing? You'll be inside in a couple of minutes."

"Thank you. How many of us are being done today?" Adam looked down at the line of footprints imprinted onto the path at two-metre intervals.

"Around 2,000 today," said the marshall.

"It must be like a military operation."

"It is," the marshall agreed. "I'm sure you were asked to be on time, but not too early. We're only allowed to have so many inside at once, so the timing's vital to keep everything running smoothly. If anyone gets here early or late it'll have a knock-on effect on other patients."

"Okay," called another marshall, from the front of the queue. "A few more inside, please."

He guided everyone in front of Adam and Hayley in the left-hand queue and two behind them, through the door and down a corridor to the main sports hall, where volunteers—Hayley assumed they were volunteers—sat at four desks with vaccination paperwork in front of them. Behind them, rows of uncomfortable-looking plastic chairs stretched across the hall and down to the far wall, each chair separated from all its neighbours by three metres.

Adam and Hayley were sent to their seats, and only had to wait a few moments before the vaccination team reached them. Hayley felt two things when the needle pierced her skin. Firstly, the faintest prick, more of a scrape, really; and secondly, a sense of relief more powerful than she could ever remember. Even more powerful than when she had taken Evelyn's phone call.

The rest of my life starts today. Right here. Right now.

While waiting the statutory few minutes to ensure there were no side effects, she looked proudly at the NHS card showing the batch number and the fact that she'd had her first Pfizer vaccination on 18.2.21.

She attached the circular 'I've had my COVID vaccination' sticker depicting a white crown inside a teal and red heart onto her purse and followed Adam outside.

Yes, today really is the first day of the rest of my life. She felt so happy.

Hayley took Adam's hand as they walked across the car park back to their Peugeot. It would be the last time she'd ever touch him.

The BMW was still parked next to them, the faces of the three men inside barely visible behind their sunglasses and blue medical masks.

As Adam pulled out of the bay the BMW inched forward.

At the bottom of the drive, Adam had to pause to let four vehicles pass, before turning right onto Priory Road. The

BMW waited patiently behind him and also turned right.

"Out twice in less than a fortnight," said Hayley. She smiled. "Another momentous day."

The traffic lights at the junction with Broadhaven Road changed as Adam drove through them. Behind him, the BMW accelerated to squeeze through on red, eliciting a long horn blast from the car whose path it had crossed. Adam looked in the mirror and smiled. He shook his head. "That guy's probably gained two minutes by shooting the lights. Wonder what he's got to do that's so important."

A few moments later Adam parked on their drive.

The BMW pulled up against the kerb on the opposite side of the road.

"I just need to make a couple of phone calls first," said Adam, closing the car door.

The BMW's passenger and left-hand rear doors opened.

Hayley closed her door and looked at Adam over the Peugeot's roof.

The BMW's front and rear seat passengers got out.

"I'll get my tracksuit on while you're doing that," she said.

Both passengers silently reached back into the BMW.

Adam's grin seemed to indicate to her what a good idea he thought the tracksuit was.

And emerged holding light Kalashnikov RPK machine guns.

Hayley caught their movement out of the corner of her eye and turned to look at the two men in sunglasses and blue medical face masks. She barely had time to register what they were holding before the deafening and repetitive clatter of more than 100 rounds of bottlenecked 7.62 mm cartridges exploded from the barrels of both guns, shattering the peace of Clowes Road.

And shattered Adam and Hayley.

The steel-cased cartridges tore through flesh and bone, the sheer force whipping them to the ground.

Their bodies arched and writhed, organs were torn apart and bone smashed to pieces as the relentless stream of ammunition swam in rivers of blood, pulverising everything in its path.

Wave after wave of murderous metal thudded into soft, forgiving skin, muscle and sinew.

The Peugeot was instantly dotted with red, and its bodywork was peppered with holes. Sticky pools of blood spread across the drive mixing with fragments of glass from the car's shattered windows.

Even before the jerking bodies subsided into mere twitching, reminiscent of St Vitus' Dance, the two men jumped back into the BMW and it sped away with the echo of Kalashnikov fire fading into the February sunshine.

2

Infection

Late December 2020, Simon

Sometimes, as a radio presenter, people say I just prattle on about nothing of consequence. Sometimes, what I've got to say is important. Sometimes it's not. But I think what's important right now, is that I stop saying 'sometimes.'

Sometimes, though, you just have to repeat certain words for effect. Like to reinforce your message. Get the point home. Make sure your audience is in no doubt. Because sometimes, they're not, are they?

And for me, that's always important. Not sometimes. Always. And effect. That's important, too. I like to convey my message clearly and concisely. Of course, I do.

But my over-inflated ego demands I use words for effect, too. That didn't just spring up overnight, either. I've carefully cultivated the combination of communicating both effectively and for effect since my media studies degree at uni. Which is where it all started.

'Simon's exam paper was a bit of a disaster. He writes too much for effect at the expense of simplicity.' Yes, thank you, Ms Lovell Stanley, you may have been the best lecturer in the journalism module but I could have done without that comment at the time. Looking back, though, the many hard-nosed journalistic radio interviews I've done over the years have benefited from a dash of simplicity. But my penchant for effect came well and truly into its own during the interviews with showbiz luvvies.

As I say, it's a combination: Effect and Simplicity. A

winner all the way.

I guess the secret is for you to separate the wheat of my sincerity from the chaff of my prattling. But I can tell you categorically there was no chaff about my near-death, out-of-body experience. That was definitely wheat.

It happened earlier this year. I tried writing about it a couple of times, first on the laptop at my desk, then with a pen and notebook sitting in my favourite armchair, but this vicious Long COVID sabotaged both of those attempts. Even writing short snippets for my journal proved to be difficult at first, so the task of producing the thousands of words needed to fully explain what happened would be no more than a pipe dream, even now.

It's been getting a little easier, though, bit by bit. At least I can function for a few hours each day now, meaning I'm back behind the microphone, albeit for a curtailed show. I'm only doing the phone-in section, and from home, too.

Isn't modern technology wonderful? I have a professional-quality microphone plugged into my laptop and a wi-fi link to the studio. My producer, Olivia, feeds the show down the line to me and manages all the phone calls. All I have to do is talk.

In the early days of my recovery, even that would have been beyond me, thanks to the relentless and constant fatigue, wandering concentration and memory issues (my family say I tended to forget things and repeat what I said just a few moments later, slurring my words, sometimes the first time I said them, sometimes when I forget I've said them and repeat them. See. I do need to stop saying 'sometimes').

Olivia is glad of the chance to be on air herself for the hour on either side of the open line, but I'm feeling stronger all the time and looking forward to the day when I can reclaim all three hours. I feel fit enough to give it a go now, but the top brass at Poolswood Sound say not yet, mumbling phrases filled with 'duty of care,' 'don't want you collapsing in the middle of a show,' and 'may invalidate our insurance.'

I suspect that the latter point is the overriding factor in their decision.

The slightest exertion used to leave me breathless, with my heart racing. I'm half imagining I can still feel its relentless grip even now, as I sit quietly on my sofa, watching Boxing Day television on December 26th 2020.

As it is, I have a slight throbbing behind my eyes which I know will get considerably worse as the evening wears on; my fingers have been aching all day—I could probably manage that by itself, but it's the combination of those joint pains with all the other symptoms that's been the real bugger (this combination is negative, not like the positive combination of effect and simplicity. I'd, really, like this combination to cease, go away, disappear, fuck off. But I know it won't).

Oh, where was I? Dozed off for a moment there. Probably because I'm still hardly sleeping at night. Or maybe it was a little COVID-induced blackout where my concentration goes, and I forget things? Fortunately, they're getting fewer and further between, now. Did I tell you my mind wanders and I forget things? If I didn't, my concentration sometimes goes, and I forget things. One moment I can be saying something, and the next (the next moment to me, anyway—in reality, ten minutes could have passed) I don't have a clue what's going on.

Actually, I should be used to blackouts by now. I've been having a very different type of blackout on and off ever since my sister, Helen, died in 1982. Such a strange feeling, I'm in the middle of doing something, then the next thing I know I'm waking up in bed the following morning with absolutely no recollection of what's happened since. And, even stranger, this is where you need to hear The Twilight Zone theme music in your head, because I functioned normally all the time, right through every blackout. Doing what I was supposed to be doing, but I couldn't remember it. Examples are my very first therapy session after Helen's death, Grandma's funeral, even my fucking wedding day for goodness sake (and night—par for the course, as usual, I didn't remember anything until waking up the next morning. Oh, don't tell Janice—that's the only blackout I've kept from her. She'd kill me if she knew I had no recollection of saying my vows to her at the time); and, perhaps the most devastating one, the time we discovered she had cancer.

All those years, all those tests, all the shaking of heads by experts, and no one could fathom out why. But now I know. When the answer finally came, it was a real doozy, I can tell you. My journey to enlightenment began with that out-of-body experience eight months ago, in April 2020.

But we need to start a couple of weeks before that...

Late March 2020, Simon

"But, John, that's exactly what the budget has set up." I shook my head in frustration, raising my eyebrows at Olivia, who grinned back at me from the production room, through the studio window.

A cheeky grin. Hhmmm. I'll wager more than evens that she'd guessed he was going to turn out like this—I'd seen her talking to him at length before putting his call through to me on air.

"Yes, Simon, I know. I know," John continued in my headphones...the headphones which only covered my right ear so I could listen to the on-air feed and anything Olivia needed to tell me on talkback, while still hearing natural sound in my left. "But it's how they're going to implement it that's so wrong. I mean it's the most important thing about Brexit, isn't it? They've got to get it right for holidaymakers."

The dry tickle irritating my throat on and off throughout the show today was now making its presence increasingly felt with a mild burning, and turning my voice slightly hoarse. A glance at the studio clock told me there were less than three minutes to the news at the top of the hour. Keep going. You'll make it.

I grimaced a little as the throbbing headache behind my eyes that I'd originally woken up with this morning, poked its finger through the defensive paracetamol barrier. The painkillers had done a sterling job for the last four hours, kicking in shortly after taking them when I arrived at the radio station at half past nine, but their shields were now starting to buckle and crumble as the headache's battering ram ground them down.

"Most important? Sorry, John, did you just say that duty-free allowances are the most important part of Brexit?"

"It said on the news last night that this consultation that the Government's having will look at bringing allowances back. But that's not what we want, and it's not right. We should be able to bring any amount of booze and cigarettes back from holiday, shouldn't we? There shouldn't be any restrictions. No allowances. Just as much as we want."

I smiled, swiftly working out an intelligent, measured and civil response geared to take the conversation forward in both an informative and entertaining way. Calls like this are exactly what I love about the open-topic phone-in section of my daily programme. Keeping me on my toes, making me think. It was a good job I'd read the background briefing notes from our chief political correspondent this morning, looking in detail at the Government's latest Brexit update about possible ways of taking duty-free legislation forward. Keeping abreast of all the day's news is a vital part of preparing for the show (it also makes me a whizz—and greatly sought-after team member—at pub quizzes) because there's no telling what rubbish the great unwashed will throw at me. And it's great to be able to give as good as I get without repercussions.

Well, when I say without repercussions...I'll never forget the station manager's thunderous face when he called me into his office after I'd told one caller I wished her mother had been on the pill. That had been in my early days. With age and experience comes the wisdom of knowing where to draw the line. I still fire both barrels when necessary, but it's a different technique nowadays and involves passing the buck.

"Some people might argue with you there, John." (See what I mean about passing the buck. It's not me arguing with the caller, is it?). "I think they'd tell you several other things have formed a long queue ahead of duty-free allowances on the list of important..."

"I'm sorry, Simon, but you don't know what you're talking about."

That tickle in my throat was getting worse. Not long now until I cue Tamsin in with the news. No. Can't wait that long. It's got to be now. I muted my microphone and let rip with the type of expulsion that only a pent-up, dry cough can generate.

And that's when the sore throat kicked in. *Probably ruptured a blood vessel. That cough was a real doozy. I* swallowed, scrunching my face up in a grimace at the unexpected stab of pain, and coughed again. A single push this time, hopefully, enough to give me an unhindered voice to the news.

Too much dead air already. Microphone back open.

"I think you'll find I do," I said, perhaps a little over-gingerly, so as not to aggravate that cough, which I could feel was simply lurking beneath the surface, waiting for an opportune moment to pounce again. *And take a hike, headache, I need to concentrate.* "Let's just take a look, shall we? First off, John, we're back in control of our own affairs. No interference from Brussels. Secondly, we've saved more than £8.5-billion in EU budget contributions in one year alone. Three, we're no longer skivvies to the EU's immigration policies, we can control who we let into the country now. We can also trade with who we like, and employ more of our own people." *Ouch. It hurt having to say this on air. Sometimes (that word again!) the Devil's Advocate can be such a nasty piece of work.*

"Come off it, mate," John's tone sounded scornful to me as it stabbed into my fully covered right ear. "None of those are as important as duty-free, apart from maybe kicking the foreigners out, of course."

Damn. Why hadn't he said this at the start of his call? I could have opened fire with all barrels, instead of having to go against the grain and defend the indefensible. But, hey ho, that's the nature of the job. Sometimes I sound like a Tory politician, sometimes a Labour politician, sometimes even LibDems and the Greens. At least I get accused of being biased every which way, depending on whether there's a Y in the day.

"You're all heart, John, aren't you?" I said, with another glance at the clock and slid the phoneline fader shut.

"Unfortunately, that's where I'm afraid we must leave it. Time's beaten the phone-in again, as it always does. All good things must come to an end. For today at least." I told you people say I just prattle on about nothing of consequence. But what they don't know is that I'm often watching the second-hand flow over the clock face, just as I'm doing now, talking right up to the precise second I need to stop.

Just a few seconds to two o'clock. "Stay tuned for the final hour, when my studio guest will be Poolswood author Imogen Lambert, telling us what inspired her latest thriller, When Crime Does Pay, and playing four of her favourite pieces of music.

"You're listening to the Simon Reynolds Lunch Break here on Poolswood Sound. It's now two o'clock; time for the news with Tamsin Mcilroy."

I eased my microphone fader to its closed position and glanced up to make sure the red 'on air' light was off. I hit the talkback button. "Liv, could you bring me a couple of paracetamol in, please? I'm starting to struggle with that headache again, and I've got a sore throat now as well."

She nodded through the glass but brought my guest in before heading to the medical cabinet. I stood up and hugged Imogen at the edge of the desk. "Imogen, lovely to see you. Congratulations on publication day yesterday."

"Hello, Simon. Thank you."

"Come and sit down, you know the drill."

The left side of my curved control desk blossomed out into a wide semi-circle, containing the guest mic. Imogen sat in front of it, on the opposite side to me. "I should do by now," she said. "Breakfast, and all that?"

Laughing tickled my throat, threatening another cough. "Yeah, give me a sec." I glanced down at one of four screens in front of me, which displayed the programme's audio database and running order, and showed that Olivia had lined up a James Blunt track to kick off the final hour of the show. "We'll start with the new book—the fact that it was published yesterday, and all the gubbins about where your ideas for it came from. Then we'll take your first piece of music, and I'll ask why that's so special to you."

Olivia came through the studio door with my tablets. "Here you go, Simon."

"Thanks, Liv. These should kick it into touch again." I downed the paracetamol, grimacing as the simple act of swallowing them felt like fingers brushing a graze.

"A heavy night on the Malbec, Simon?" Imogen asked.

I looked at her over the top of my glasses. "Huh-uh. I wish."

"Seriously, though, Simon, I heard you ask for the tablets and say you'd got a headache and sore throat. Are you okay?"

I grinned at Imogen. "I'll be fine." I'd last seen her a couple of weeks ago at a party she'd hosted at her home, just four doors down from mine, to celebrate the new novel. Janice and I took two bottles of Malbec. Janice had had a few of her favourite rhubarb and ginger Edinburgh gins and I'd devoured the Malbec. All of it. Both bottles. I had a feeling Imogen wouldn't let me forget that any time soon.

The clock showed the news would be ending in a few seconds. I slipped the headphones back up from where they'd been resting on my shoulders. "Let me get underway, and then you can divulge your breakfast secrets."

"...top temperature 7°C," Tamsin was saying in my headphones, "dropping to around three degrees overnight. Starting overcast tomorrow, staying dry and mostly cloudy. That's all for now. The next news and weather here on

Poolswood Sound is at three o'clock."

I drew down the fader disconnecting the studio from the news booth adjacent to the newsroom on the floor below and played the station identity jingle. Then slid up my microphone fader and was ready for the off. "Welcome back to Friday's Lunch Break with me, Simon Reynolds. In the final hour, we're talking to local author Imogen Lambert about her latest novel in the Michael Peacefire series, When Crime Does Pay.

"Now, from his 2019 album 'Once Upon a Mind,' James Blunt's feeling rather 'Cold.'

Imogen watched the red 'on air' light wink out before she spoke. "I hate this song," she said. "It's just not like James Blunt at all. Too fast."

I glanced down at the screen behind the mixer unit, looking at the four music tracks she'd chosen to be part of her hour with me this afternoon, which Olivia had lined up on the running order. "I'm not keen, either," I said. "I'm not keen on him, full stop. Glad you've not picked any of his stuff.

"Anyway, sorry, Imogen, we need to get you ready." I looked at how far she was sitting from the mic and judged how loud I'd need to set it. I hit a key on the console and asked her my standard question to test her sound level.

"So, what did you have for breakfast this morning?"

"One of these days I'm going to shock you, Simon, and say a toy boy. But, until that wonderful, gloriously utopian day is upon me, I'll have to settle for muesli and fruit."

I tweaked the pre-set volume slightly, and sat back, satisfied she wouldn't either deafen our listeners or be too quiet when we started chatting.

As much as I was enjoying the chat, as the hour wore on, I found I was increasingly sweating, and then I lost focus on what Imogen was saying.

"...so there could have been two possible outcomes. Michael Peacefire may have decided on a couple of different ways forward..."

What she said on either side of that was a meaningless, distant echo. And my vision was equally affected. Her face swam in and out of my sight, from where she sat on the other side of the desk next to the BNCS screen which showed me the studio's status regarding transmitter and DAB feeds. Not that that mattered at the moment.

And it seemed that what my guest was saying didn't matter either. This hazy, abstract feeling left me completely detached from both my studio and Imogen. Which never happens. I pride myself on always being totally in control (even when a well-known politician told me the question I'd just asked him was irrelevant, saying "...with respect, Mr Reynolds, the question you should be asking me is," brought up a totally different question and proceeded to answer it. No, he didn't get away with that one).

Here, with Imogen unaware of my growing turmoil, I wondered for a couple of terrifyingly horrendous moments if it was a new way of my blackouts starting. When they come on normally, it feels as if an editor has cleanly sliced a chunk out of my life. There I am, for example, one moment shaking hands with the Prime Minister who's about to present me with a radio award, and the next moment (to me, anyway) waking up the following day in a hotel bedroom.

My proudest professional moment consigned to...well, to goodness knows where as far as my memory of it goes.

As my head spun (metaphorically, of course—I'm not doing an impression of Linda Blair in The Exorcist, even though it felt like the green vomit may be on the verge of putting in an appearance) I braced myself now to wake up next to Janice.

But it didn't happen. I stayed in the here and now, albeit feeling some distance from reality. While the paracetamol had taken the edge off the headache, it hadn't dulled the pain completely, only reducing it to a nagging presence. I was left somewhat light-headed, with a feeling of pressure trying to push its way out of my skull. Combining that with the hollow, empty pit at the base of my stomach, I wondered if my body was crying out for chocolate, cheese or a glass of Coke sugar and carb rush.

The hour passed excruciatingly slowly, but at least I was able to contain that dry cough until each music break and the promo jingles both for my show and a full station ident. During my early broadcasting days, I learned a trade secret to subdue a cough while I'm in full flow, which I've successfully used a great many times. It's simply a case of lightly pressing the Adam's apple. I've never understood the physics (or biology, whichever) behind it. But it works.

"Imogen, we're now coming to your fourth and, unfortunately, the last piece of music. You've chosen Max Ehrmann's iconic and, indeed, legendary, poem, Desiderata. So, why this?"

"I discovered Desiderata in my teens, and've tried to live my life by its teachings ever since. It shows that every single one of us on this planet has a right to be here, and gives great advice about living our lives to the full.

"It's a very powerful spiritual force to me, guiding me on a daily basis. I'd go as far as to say it's helped me every step of the way on my journey, both as an author and as a human being."

A palpable sense of relief washed over me as I closed Imogen's microphone and began my final link. "Inspiring stuff, indeed. Many thanks to Poolswood author Imogen

Lambert for taking time out of her busy schedule to tell us about the latest novel in the Michael Peacefire series. *When Crime Does Pay* was published yesterday by FieldBlue Books. It's available online and from selected bookshops."

I was scanning that sweep hand on its relentless journey around the studio clock face again, to ensure I started playing Imogen's fourth track at exactly the right second for it to end precisely at 3 o'clock.

"And now, to play us out, Les Crane's beautiful 1971 version of Desiderata."

The red on-air light winked out, and I flopped back in my chair. Now the coughing came.

Imogen's furrowed brow and hooded eyes showed she was worried about me. She didn't need to say so.

"Simon, I'm getting you home straight away," she said.

Normally I'd brush it off. But today. This. This was different. It was becoming more of an effort to do anything. And even my thighs were starting to ache now.

"Thank you. Would you mind? That'd be good. As long as you were planning on going straight home. I don't want to put you out."

"I am. No worries."

"If you're aching that much, have a bath rather than a shower," my wife suggested after Imogen had driven the 28 miles back to the village. I hoped I'd feel up to Janice taking me to the studio tomorrow to pick up my car. It'd be safe enough in the underground park at the radio station, but I hated being without it.

"Put plenty of muscle-soak in," she said. "And take your time. Dinner will be another hour."

I couldn't decide about food. Part of me was hungry— notably that hollow pit in my stomach, but the raw and jagged walls of my throat baulked at the idea of anything touching them on the way down.

"What have we got?" I asked. Don't get me wrong. Janice doesn't cook every night. No, no, no. We take it in turns, but she was in charge of the kitchen tonight.

"Prawn curry," she said. My favourite. I swallowed again. Quite raw, but I'd put up with the soreness for a prawn curry.

The bath didn't help with the aches, but my throat felt a little better in the steam, and there was plenty of that because on the rare occasion I bathe instead of showering, I like the water almost scaldingly hot. The headache had been reduced to feeling slightly distant—the paracetamol having locked the pain away again.

While lying back with the water over my chin, almost to my bottom lip, I'd wondered at how fast this cold or whatever it was had floored me. I'm prone to chest infections and hoped I could shake this off before it took hold. I didn't want it to get to the stage it had a couple of years ago, when lying flat triggered the cough, and I had to sleep sitting up in a chair for ten nights.

Afterwards, dressing gown on, I headed downstairs to the extensive open-plan kitchen diner. "Is it nearly ready?" I asked, "or have I got time to pour us a gin?"

Janice turned to face me from where she was transferring the pan from the hob to the island unit. "Just dishing up. There are beers in the fridge, though."

I looked down at the sizzling curry, full of juicy king prawns. Something struck a chord with me, though, as not being quite the same. Not sure what. Perhaps it was just my brain trying to play catchup after its on-and-off cat-and-mouse fighting with the pain throughout the day.

Normally I'm a wine person, as my previously declared

love affair with Malbec can testify to, but the strength of Janice's powerful curries would drown the flavour of even the sturdiest wine. So my regular accompaniment for those meals is always a bottle or two of premium strength lager.

I retrieved them from the fridge and poured them into two glasses, while Janice spooned the curry onto plates. *What is it that's not right? Something's amiss.*

I took a sip of beer. Hhmmm. Bland. Then a bite of king prawn soaked in the Madras curry. I could sense spice, something hot, but nothing else. No flavour.

Four dry red chilli peppers guarantee that Janice's Madras curry is always right up there, scoring four out of five on the curry heat scale. But today was more like a minus-one.

That appetising golden brown colour was right. The rich consistency was spot on. So what had she done to make it so bland, so tasteless? And there was no smell to it. Smell! That was the difference I hadn't been able to put my finger on a few moments ago.

For fuck's sake.

The answer hit home with all the subtlety of a runaway express train. My brain's definitely playing catch-up. I didn't need to Google what was behind all this. I'd read enough about it while preparing for a couple of recent interviews and a phone-in.

I should at least have thought about it with the headache, the sore throat, the aching muscles, and the dry cough. Not being able to taste or smell anything sealed it.

"Janice, I think I may have COVID." My God, that sounded stark, even to my ears, and I knew it was coming. What on earth must it have sounded like to Janice?

She put her fork down and looked at me, with wide, shocked eyes.

"What? Because of the aches and pains? That could be a bad cold or even flu."

I shook my head. "No. It's not that. I thought something was wrong as soon as I came into the kitchen and couldn't smell the curry. I can't even taste it. I've got COVID, Janice."

All thoughts of the meal gone, I stood up, moving away from the table.

"Oh, God," she said. "Should we call the doctor?"

"They won't come out. I'll have to get a test done."

Janice pushed her chair back and started to come towards me.

I took a step backwards. "No. You can't come near me."

Tears welled up in her eyes, and I felt mine getting watery, too. "I'll sleep in the spare bedroom," I said.

Now those tears were trickling down her face. "I just want to hug you."

"I know," I said. "But you can't. It's too dangerous." Jumbled thoughts flashed through my mind, each scrambling to get to the front. Who I've seen today, who I've touched, what I've touched, Imogen—that hug in the studio and the kiss on the cheek when she dropped me home—her car, the studio door handle, the desk, the chair, the mixer and broadcast control decks. How many people have I passed it on to today?

Janice's voice broke through the jangling confusion. "You go up, I'll disinfect thoroughly throughout the house."

"Okay. I'll get the laptop from the study and take it up with me. I want to order the testing kit." The tickling, dry cough punctuated those words, and I felt a slight resistance deep in my chest as I tried to draw a breath afterwards.

To say my night was restless would be something of an understatement. Once I'd ordered my COVID test online and phoned the radio station manager and Imogen to tell them what had happened, I tried to focus on escapism TV, but couldn't settle. The cough became more persistent when I lay down, and even though I propped myself up on pillows, three o'clock came and went, and I hadn't had a wink of sleep.

My chest felt hot to the touch, and I gradually noticed it tightening enough to restrict my breathing a little more. It became a tad harder than usual, first to draw a breath in fully, and after a few moments to exhale as well. This shallow, quickened breathing exacerbated the cough, which completed the circle, attacking my air intake again.

I believe it must have been sheer exhaustion which eventually took me into an uneasy sleep at around four o'clock. At some point during my restless tossing and turning, I caught an indistinct glimpse in my dream of a young girl concealed in the shadow of a tree. She stepped forward into the moonlight. The dreadful white pallor of her skin contrasted starkly with the deep ruby-red lips which slowly gaped open to reveal a black tongue that snaked out to rest on her chin.

Flicking back her lank, greasy hair, she raised her arms, turning to point them in my direction and I felt a strange tug deep in my chest, as if the air in my lungs had given up fighting COVID in my respiratory system, and was trying to find an alternative way out. Two thin white strands emerged from my body, and the pulling sensation increased as the strands flowed through the girl's outstretched arms and into her mouth. With a final tug, the strands connecting us pulled free of my body and wormed their way over to her, disappearing down her throat. A long, slow sigh escaped her lips and the lustre of her pure white skin became just a fraction brighter than it had been moments earlier.

A renewed sheen gave her hair a richer tint and added glow, and it even looked a little thicker and longer than a moment ago.

As she dropped back behind the tree, seemingly satisfied and replenished, that strange, brooding forest dreamscape changed, and I was back in a nightmare I remembered having once before, long, long ago, when I was 18 on that dreadful night my sister Helen died back at our old family home, White Pastures. Our beautiful red setter, Titus, who'd died a couple of days before I had the nightmare the first time, was in it.

He'd sprouted wings of flaming orange and a tail that ended in a wickedly sharp blade resembling a scorpion's stinger. He was chasing a giant green-winged cat, as Helen's smiling face drifted into view. Before I could smile back, it dissolved into a snarling, spitting tiger, which in turn became Helen's boyfriend, Mark Brody, who'd been staying with us.

In my dream, both on that awful night, and its rerun now, Mark was humming softly to himself. A soothing, melodious tune. The sound was heavenly, totally out of this world and I listened entranced. It was the music of angels. The humming grew in pitch and intensity, and as I lay spellbound Mark's face transformed into a clock, its hands showing a quarter past four.

Another explosive cough tore me from the nightmare's grip before it could take me any further down that horrific path I still remembered so well from 1982. Air was dragging in and out of my lungs in shallow, panting gasps. I looked across at the bedside clock. Quarter past four.

The rasping, dry cough coupled with my lungs struggling to draw in air, unleashed a wave of panic. "Janice," I called. But my voice was barely more than a whisper.

And I needed to pee.

Pushing back the duvet, I swung my feet to the floor and eased myself up to standing with legs that felt as if they were made of strawberry jelly. Where on earth did that thought come from? I don't even like strawberry jelly.

I flopped back down onto the bed, and that's when it hit me. A small sun burned in my chest and went supernova in my head. My last memory was summoning up the energy from deep within me to scream for Janice. This time it was more than a whisper, it was loud and long.

3

Crime Scene

Detective Chief Inspector Stephanie Ingram swung her legs out of the white 18-month-old Kia Stinger GT S and bent to slip on the standard Bermond Life disposable overshoes before alighting completely, hooking her facemask straps behind her ears and making her way towards where the two bodies lay.

"What have we got?" she asked of the six-foot-two, 112-kilogram man-mountain, who was holding up the blue and white tape instructing people that this was a 'police line do not cross,' for her to duck beneath.

It cordoned off 60 metres on both sides of 44 Clowes Road to keep residents and the first journalists to arrive, well away.

"Steph! What's happened here?" She turned briefly to face the Poolswood Recorder hack who'd called to her. "Give me time, Darell, I've only just got here."

"But what have you been told? Come on, Steph, my deadline's coming up. We've had reports of what sounded like machine gun fire. Is that right? Is anyone dead?"

"Sounds like you know as much as me."

"Just a quick comment," the journo pleaded. "Come on. Please."

Reaching metaphorically into her mind, Stephanie plucked out a standard holding response that she'd picked up on a media training course. She knew it would keep her in the Recorder's good books if she needed to make a public appeal on this one: "All I can say is we've been called to a house on Clowes Road following reports of an incident. It's understood there are casualties. Nothing more is known at this time."

"Thanks, Steph."

She nodded and set off with the man-mountain towards number 44.

"So, Kit, what do we have," she asked when they were out of Darell Bostock's earshot. Looking down the street, she saw a black Dancover 6 x 4-metre crime scene tent erected on the drive.

"Two bodies, Ma'am," Detective Sergeant Kit McGrath told her. "A man and woman. Bob Easton's with them now."

"Do we know who they are?"

"Formal identification's going to be tricky. They're pretty much shredded, especially their faces. But neighbours say it's likely to be the husband and wife who lived here."

"So the initial report of machine gun fire was right?"

"Certainly looks like it, Ma'am."

"You've got the tent up quickly," she said. Her call had only come 15 minutes ago.

"Couldn't have the neighbours seeing this. As I say, they're pretty much shredded. The plods have told everyone to stay inside."

Stephanie looked up and down the street. A few faces peered out through windows, but only uniformed officers were to be seen outside, within the cordon. "Good work, Kit."

McGrath held the flap open for her and she stepped inside the tent, shuddering at the sight greeting her.

"Oh my God."

Not much fazed her as a police officer with 27 years of experience. If truth be told, it never had, right from seeing that very first dead body in 1995 when she was a rookie cop.

But the sheer amount of blood, organ fragments and other matter covering these two bodies lying on either side of a red Peugeot 208 elicited a heave from her stomach, and she struggled to keep down the chicken mayonnaise sandwich she'd eaten for lunch. This took murder on the UK's streets to a whole new level, she thought. *McGrath wasn't kidding when he said they were shredded.*

"For fuck's sake." Her exclamation was as spontaneous as her second heave.

Doctor Robert Easton looked up from where he was crouched over the female body sprawled by the passenger door. "If you're going to throw up, kindly go outside. I don't want your lunch mingling with hers."

That killed off any chance Stephanie may have had of keeping her half-digested sandwich, which rose alarmingly fast from her stomach into her throat and tried to climb even higher. Clasping a hand to her mouth she pushed the flap aside and just made it to the kerb in front of a neighbouring house in time.

McGrath peered out at her through the flap, thought about going to her, thought better of it, and disappeared back inside.

"Right," she said briskly, returning to the Dancover a few moments later. "Sorry about that."

"Hmmm," said Easton. She saw him glance at the tissue she had used to wipe her mouth, which was now soiled with regurgitated sandwich remnants. "Here." She took his proffered plastic evidence pouch, dropped the tissue inside and sealed it before putting it in her handbag.

"Thanks, Bob. Sorry about that."

He nodded sympathetically. "It is pretty bad, I'll admit."

"I take it there's no doubt as to the cause of death?"

"None whatsoever. Blood poisoning from insect bites.

Both of them."

She saw McGrath stifle a grin.

Easton walked round to the other side of the car. "I've not counted the bullet holes. In fact, there's so much damage to their bodies I doubt if we'll ever get an accurate number. But, yes, it's safe to say one or more of them would have inflicted the deadly blow that saw them over the rainbow bridge."

Light cast by a portable Samalite lamp on top of an extended tripod in the corner of the tent glinted off numerous bullet casings on the ground and gave an eerie glow to the pools of blood.

"Gangland execution, maybe," she mused to herself. Then, to McGrath: "Did the neighbours see anything?"

"Apparently a car sped away immediately afterwards. The plods are doing door-to-door and seeing if there's any footage from CCTV or doorbells."

"Who saw the car speeding off?"

"A woman just along the road," McGrath told her. "She was cleaning her landing window."

"Right. I need to talk to her. Show me."

As Stephanie followed her up the stairs, she reckoned Mrs Susan Wilson must be in her late seventies, which would perhaps account for the throwback decor. The black and grey tartan-style carpet grated on her eyes, as did the dark grey flock wallpaper.

Mrs Wilson had been sitting in her living room with a blanket around her, being comforted by a woman police constable and a cup of tea when Stephanie and McGrath arrived at the house. And still visibly shaking.

"Do you mind if we ask a few questions about what you saw?" Stephanie had said.

Frightened, almost haunted eyes looked back at

Stephanie from behind thin-rimmed oval glasses above the medical facemask. "It was awful. Such a lovely couple." Her voice cracked.

"Did you know them well?"

"Only to pass the time of day. And I haven't seen them at all since lockdown started."

"Perhaps you could show me where you were cleaning the windows and tell me exactly what you saw."

Mrs Wilson turned to face Stephanie when they reached the window at the top of the dogleg staircase. Grey hair pulled back into a traditional bun shone in the sunlight streaming through the newly polished glass. Stephanie saw window cleaner spray and a cloth discarded on the floor.

"I was standing here when I heard that awful noise."

"Can I take a look?"

Mrs Wilson moved down the landing to make room for her at the window. Stephanie leaned in to peer down the road. She could only tell where number 44 was, around 50 metres away to her left, by a constable standing at the bottom of the drive.

"What did you see, Mrs Wilson?"

"I saw Adam and Hayley's car turn into their drive, and then a big car pulled up and two people got out. One from the front and one from the back."

"Which side of the road was it?"

"The other side. That's why I could see it so well."

"Did the cars come past your house?"

Mrs Wilson shook her head. "No. They came from the direction of the main road—from Pinchbeck Road."

"Were they men or women?"

"I couldn't tell," said Mrs Wilson. "They were both wearing sunglasses and COVID masks."

"You said the big car stopped almost as soon as Adam and Hayley got here—that's their names is it, Adam and Hayley?"

Mrs Wilson nodded.

"So, the big car stopped straight after you saw Adam and Hayley pull onto their drive?"

"Yes. Then... then... Sorry." Tears glistened through her lenses.

"Take your time, Mrs Wilson. It's alright."

"I couldn't see their car after it turned onto this side of the road and onto their drive." The hesitancy in her cracked voice showed the pain. "But after the two people got out of the big car they just shot them."

Stephanie grimaced, trying to understand what this woman was going through.

"Then the car sped off down the road," said Mrs Wilson.

"It didn't turn round?" Stephanie's question was almost rhetorical. She knew it wouldn't have turned around, but needed official confirmation from the witness as to which way it had gone.

"No. It went that way." She pointed to the right.

"Okay," said Stephanie. "Thank you. Do you know what type of car it was?"

The old woman shook her head. "No. It was quite big."

"Can you remember the colour?"

"Yes, it was grey. And the windows were all black."

"Now, Mrs Wilson, it doesn't matter if you don't know the answer to this. But do you know the difference between a hatchback and a saloon?" Stephanie looked down from the landing window to the small three-door red Toyota Yaris parked on the old lady's drive.

"Oh, yes. It was a big saloon car."

"But you didn't recognise the make."

"No, I'm sorry."

"Don't worry, Mrs Wilson. You've been extremely helpful. Thank you."

As Stephanie and McGrath made their back towards number 44, they heard the tinny, piano riff strains of her mobile's ring tone.

She pulled the phone from her pocket and looked at the caller's I.D. "It's the Chief," she said, accepting the call and hurrying away from McGrath. "Good afternoon, Sir." A brief pause while she listened. Then: "Yes, I'm here at the house now."

A few moments later, after the call ended, she caught up with McGrath who was talking to the plod at the bottom of Adam and Hayley's drive.

"The Chief Constable wants to brief me personally on this one," she told him. "I'm going in to see him now."

"Very good, Ma'am."

"Take charge here while I'm gone, and can you set up a full team meeting back at the shop for ten o'clock tomorrow morning?" She strode off towards the Stinger without waiting for his reply.

Friday, February 19th, 2021, Stephanie

"Morning, everyone," she said as she breezed into the Homicide and Serious Crime Command office at precisely one minute to ten, dressed simply but impressively, in a navy blue double-breasted jacket, pencil trousers and John Lewis & Partners Angela Platform Court shoes.

Several officers acknowledged her from where they sat at their desks, while another raised a hand from the coffee machine in the far corner. McGrath stood by a large writing board at the front of the room, on which he had already set up several photographs and timelines. Alongside, a projector screen suspended from the ceiling displayed the words 'no signal' on a blue background.

Stephanie called to the detective at the coffee machine. "Bring me one, please, Pat. Cappuccino, no sugar.

"Now, before we start, I spoke to the Chief Constable about this yesterday," she said. "Our first thoughts are that the style and ferocity of the killing could link it to rival gangs or drugs. He's asked me to keep him informed of everything we find out, so I'll be reporting directly to him twice a day. And, needless to say, he wants it wrapped up pretty quickly.

"The media are all over this like a rash. We've given them a basic holding statement, but Public Relations have arranged a press conference for mid-day. I've got to face the cameras, so by then, I'll need to be fully up to speed on what we've got, and what we still need to know. Kit, fill us all in, please."

"Yes, Ma'am," said McGrath. He gestured towards two photographs fastened to the top of the board.

"The victims were Adam and Hayley Hampshire, shot with over 200 rounds from Kalashnikov hand-held machine guns. No criminal record for either of them. Not even a parking ticket or speeding fine. Clean as a whistle. So, unless they've been kidding the world rotten, I can't see that they're linked to serious crime. But, stranger things have happened, I guess. Max has been researching the Hampshires."

He looked across at Detective Constable Max Carver, sitting to the left, towards the back of the office. "Max?"

"Thanks, Kit," said Carver, standing up and coming to the front. "So, Hayley Hampshire." He pointed to the pretty blonde smiling out of the photograph. "Thirty-one years old. Travel agent at Shrinking World Travel's Poolswood branch. Worked there for eight years, but was furloughed for the last 11 months. Married Adam in 2010. No kids.

"She and Adam had been shielding rigorously throughout the pandemic, as they both suffered from heart conditions. Hayley's is known as atrial septal defects, and Adam's..."

"What's that when it's at home?" Stephanie wanted to know.

"According to her mother, it's a hole in the heart, but there's more to it than that. Apparently..."

"You can skip the finer details, Max. Hole in the heart's good enough for me at the moment. I'll read the medical reports if they're relevant."

"Okay, boss. On to Adam Hampshire. He was 34, and he had an inherited condition, Hypertrophic Cardiomyopathy." He saw Stephanie's mouth open, and continued quickly, anticipating her question: "Enlarged cardiac muscle cells. Basically, it means abnormally thick heart muscles. Most people who've got it don't have any issues, and lead normal lives. They probably don't even know they've got it. But Adam was one of the unlucky ones. He developed complications which gave him a heart attack when he was 18.

"As a teenager, he'd been a promising footballer on the verge of making it big time, but the heart problem put the kybosh on that."

"How's he been earning his living since then?"

"He was a software engineer, writing code for a company supplying computerised prototyping solutions for electric cars."

"A bit of a boffin, then?" said Stephanie. "And very different from the footballing career he chose originally. Was he furloughed?"

"No," replied Carver. "He'd been working from home since starting the job in 2018. It was home-based from the beginning.

"They had a wide circle of friends who they used to meet

regularly for meals or drinks before COVID. But, according to Hayley's mother, before yesterday they'd only been out once since the first lockdown began last year. That was for a hospital appointment after Hayley was taken ill a couple of weeks ago."

"Why were they out yesterday?"

"Because of their heart problems they're classed as medically vulnerable to COVID and were getting their vaccinations at Poolswood Leisure Centre earlier than their age group. They'd just got back from having the jabs when they were shot," said McGrath.

"No one we've spoken to has a bad word to say about either of them. Seems they were the perfect, well-liked couple."

"So, who'd want them dead, and in such a spectacular fashion?" mused Stephanie. "What was Hayley doing while she was furloughed? Any type of new activity on her phone or computer while she's been at home? Anything that might indicate she'd started a new venture that could have brought her into contact with people who've got access to such weapons? And, more importantly, that could have got her on the wrong side of them?"

"Nope," piped up Detective Constable Paula Bowen from her desk halfway across the office, to Stephanie's right. "Nothing that we've found yet. I spent most of yesterday afternoon and evening going through their phones, along with their laptops and Adam's work computer. Just the normal stuff you'd expect. Nothing out of the ordinary at all. Not that I understand anything on his work computer. It's mainly programming G-code and correspondence with his office."

"Get his boss to take a look at it, Paula. See if they can spot anything odd. And see if he'd been working on anything that could be regarded as a major breakthrough in the industry."

McGrath cast a quizzical look at Stephanie. "Are you thinking it could be related to his job?"

"Just looking at all avenues, Kit. The automotive sector's always been a cut-throat business, with manufacturers trying to outdo each other. Even more so now, I shouldn't wonder, with the race to develop cheaper, longer-range electric cars. I know it sounds like a long shot, and it depends what he was working on, but if he was on the verge of a breakthrough in something, it could just be possible that he was killed to stop it from going any further. At least in the short term, to give another company the chance to get ahead. See what you can come up with, Paula.

"Now, about the gunmen's car. Do we have anything on that?"

McGrath pointed to a timeline on the writing board. "We do, indeed. A BMW 5 Series M Sport, on fake number plates. And this is where it gets particularly interesting. We've got a fair bit of CCTV footage and a few recordings from digital doorbells which show it following the Hampshires home."

He turned to a computer nestling on a trolley pushed up against the wall. "But you won't believe where it first crossed paths with them." He woke the computer up and pressed Enter. The ceiling-mounted projector sprang to life, displaying a paused video image of a car park on the screen.

"Look at this." He set the video rolling. All eyes in the room watched as the parking marshall guided a grey BMW 5 Series M Sport with blacked-out windows into the first available bay. Stephanie noticed that the date and time stamp in the video showed 1.50 p.m., yesterday, Thursday, February 18th.

"This is CCTV footage at Poolswood Leisure Centre,

which is currently being used as a COVID vaccination hub," said McGrath. They watched as three people alighted—difficult to tell if they were men or women, given the distance, and that they each wore tracksuits, baseball caps, sunglasses and medical facemasks.

But Stephanie judged they walked like men as they passed out of shot to the left of the screen.

"Keep watching," said McGrath.

A red Peugeot 208 appeared a few seconds later and followed the marshall's pointing finger to park next to the BMW. "Adam and Hayley," said McGrath as the couple got out.

He brought up a second file on the computer, and the view on the projector screen switched to an image looking across the front of the leisure centre towards the car park. "This was taken from a camera at the far corner of the building. If we zoom in a little..."

The picture became considerably more pixellated as it moved beyond where a short queue led down to the doors with everyone standing on the socially distanced vinyl footprint markers, and picked out three people waiting at the start of the path leading to the car park. The three people from the BMW.

"Here come Adam and Hayley," said McGrath, as they walked past them on their way to join the queue. One of the trio took something from a pocket and raised it to eye level.

McGrath hit pause and zoomed in even closer. The picture quality deteriorated further, but it was just possible to make out that BMW-man was holding a phone.

"Is he...is he, taking a photograph?" asked DC Patrick Whitmore, who had made Stephanie's coffee at the machine a few moments ago.

"That's what we think," confirmed McGrath. "Unfortunately we can't get the image any clearer, but it certainly looks as if he's taking a photograph of the back of Adam and Hayley. Watch what happens next."

He pulled the image back to full distance and hit play again. It showed the three men returning towards the car park.

Then he switched back to the first CCTV camera and the detectives watched them get back in the BMW.

"Now, fast forward around 25 minutes." Time in the car park sped up, punctuated by several horizontal bars across the screen until he brought it back to normal speed when Adam and Hayley were seen returning to their car. They pulled out of the parking bay, and the BMW eased out just a few seconds afterwards.

"We've got a few more minutes of footage from traffic cameras showing the BMW following them home if you want to see it. But every sighting's marked here." He indicated the timeline on the writing board.

"Thanks, Kit. We don't all need to see any more. But I want someone to go through every second of the footage frame by frame. Pat, could you do that for me? Don't let anything get past you. We've got to catch these bastards. And quickly."

The team sat in silence for a few seconds. Stephanie wondered if, like her, they were trying to come to terms with the implications of what they had just seen. The thoughts flying through her head seemed impossible. Unthinkable. And yet, there they were. The unthinkable being thought.

Let's just see, shall we? Anything to put off what's looking more inevitable by the moment. "Have we got anything from the traffic cameras showing both cars arriving?"

"We have. All taken care of."

"And?"

"Ma'am?"

"Do I have to spell it out for you, Kit? Were the cars seen

together on the way to the centre?"

"No. We've checked all the cameras between Clowes Road and the leisure centre. The BMW isn't on any of those roads. The only time it's on them is following the Hampshires home."

"Where do we first pick it up."

"On the Blackthorpe Road, coming in from the motorway. We can follow its progress on several cameras after that, right up to arriving at the centre."

"But nothing before? Nothing on the motorway?"

"Afraid not."

"So it approached Poolswood from the North, while Adam and Hayley came from the South of the town?"

"Yes. There was no contact between the two until the Hampshires parked next to it."

Her disturbing theory was gaining more ground by the second. *Tell me it's not true. If it is, just what the fuck are we dealing with?*

"What do we know about its escape route?"

"The neighbour, Mrs Wilson, told us it carried on along Clowes Road." McGrath moved to an Ordnance Survey map of Poolswood on the wall. "It must have gone through the estate and onto the main road at the Copwood roundabout. Traffic cameras picked it up again heading back towards the motorway, and it was last spotted at the end of the average speed check section on the bypass."

"Doesn't it come up again anywhere? Not even on any of the motorway cameras?"

"Not a thing. It's just as if it disappeared into thin air."

"Establish a boundary of the nearest traffic cameras in every direction, with the bypass speed check in the middle. It's got to be in there somewhere. And find me a motive. We're fumbling in the dark until we get even a hint of one.

"Mike, I take it you've pulled an all-nighter on this?" Michael Keeling, the slightly-built Holmes Reader/Receiver from Operational Support, had indeed pulled an all-nighter. But from what he'd just heard, his immediate findings wouldn't take their investigation much further forward, although it did offer a possible new line of enquiry on the car.

He peered over the top of his uncharacteristically stylish Dolce & Gabbana glasses at her. She felt his somewhat earnest expression, barely existing chin which sloped alarmingly into his neck, his eager-to-please quick manner of speech, and 'Life Would Be Boring Without Badminton' T-shirt were a true giveaway of his geeky nature.

If there were any obvious connections, or even similarities, between the Hampshires' murder and other crimes, she knew Mike would have already found them by scrupulously cross-referencing nationwide information stored in the key IT system known as Holmes 2. The Home Office Large Major Enquiry System single application, used by police forces throughout England, Scotland, Wales and Northern Ireland, would have thrown up all cases involving, for example, Kalashnikov automatic weapons or the type of BMW used by the Hampshires' killers.

"Early days, Ma'am, but we're narrowing the field regarding known criminals, particularly in the drugs business, who have a BMW M Sport."

"Sorry, Mike," said McGrath. "Obvious question, but have any BMWs fitting that description been reported stolen in the last 36 hours?"

"No. The car seems clean, which is why I've used an algorithm to isolate criminals nationwide with that car, and then a separate category for all owners—not just criminals—within a 25-mile radius. That may help draw up a priority group of people to be interviewed inside the boundary from where the car was last caught on camera."

"Good work, Mike," said Stephanie. "OK, everyone, carry on with the tasks Kit assigned you yesterday. And somebody, anybody, please find me a motive."

She looked around the office. *You know, don't you? You all know.*

It was Paula who eventually broke the ensuing silence. "Boss?"

"Paula."

"I hope to God we do find it's linked either to Adam's job, or that Hayley got into something over her head that's not readily visible to us yet from her phone or computer."

Stephanie nodded. *Yes. Here it is. They're on the same wavelength as me.*

"Because if it's not..." continued Paula.

"Then they were simply in the wrong place at the wrong time," Stephanie finished for her, feeling a chill run down her spine as she said it: "Picked out entirely at random and murdered for no apparent reason."

The word she was sure was in all their minds remained unspoken. Terrorism.

4

Funeral

Late March 2020, Simon

The next thing I remember clearly from the real, waking world in the here and now, was seeing the paramedic's masked face above me. Then I was being wheeled out of the house towards a waiting ambulance standing on my drive. I heard the gravel crunching as we moved.

Janice must have been nearby. Although her voice floated into my ears, the words were muffled and indistinct.

But memories from long ago had filled the intervening time since I blacked out, swirling together, one after the other. There was nothing jumbled about them, though, they streamed through my consciousness (or should that be unconsciousness?) in the right order. Christ on a bike! They say your life flashes before your eyes at the moment before death.

No. Panic over. Nothing was flashing about these memories. They seemed full, long and well-defined, and must have taken hours to retrace those particular steps of my life. Or maybe time runs slower when you're not processing it properly. Or maybe I'd been hallucinating.

Whatever.

They were still clear and specific as I approached the ambulance where another paramedic waited at the bottom of the hydraulic ramp to get me inside.

I could feel the oxygen mask strapped over my nose and mouth, and realised my breathing wasn't so laboured now. Each intake of air still appeared to come in stages of small incremental breaths to fill the remaining space in my lungs, but that powerful sense of suffocation had gone. Air was getting in.

This blackout wasn't of the same ilk as those I've had on and off since Helen's death in 1982. During those, it's just as if my mind's been unplugged, only reconnecting when I wake up the next morning, with no memory of anything in between. This had been altogether different. My body in the real world may have been away with the fairies, but my mind had still been aware and functioning.

Immediately after flopping back down on the bed with those strawberry jelly legs, I was 18 years old again and in my bedroom at White Pastures, when the spirit—which we'd all seen clearly just once, but had felt its presence in our house throughout that long-ago summer—took Helen on the night after her 20th birthday. The official cause of death had been a heart attack, but I'd seen time come around again across the years as the spirit claimed the reincarnated soul of its own true love, killed 40 years previously at White Pastures, and eventually reborn into our family.

There I was, back again in 1982 at the time I somehow witnessed events from the Second World War, when German bombs fell on the house and village. It had begun as a dream, with Helen's boyfriend, Mark Brody, humming softly to himself. A soothing melodious tune. The sound was heavenly, totally out of this world and I listened entranced. It was the music of angels...

The humming grew in pitch and intensity, and as I lay spellbound, Mark's face transformed into a clock, its hands showing a quarter past four. Suddenly I was looking at my bedside clock radio, which showed the same time. The humming was getting louder all the time, developing steadily into a terrifying siren. I wanted the noise to stop.

Across my bedroom, I could see another bed that wasn't quite solid but, instead, was wispy and transparent. Two people, who also weren't quite solid, were sleeping in it. I looked around feverishly. This wasn't my bedroom. The curtains that were drawn tightly across to prevent even the slightest shaft of light from lancing out into the darkness weren't my curtains. The carpet on the floor wasn't my carpet. The wardrobes weren't my wardrobes. None of it seemed quite real or solid. There was something ethereal about it, and I could see the wallpaper through everything quite clearly. But it wasn't my wallpaper.

Apart from all that, it *was* my bedroom.

How it could be.

How it might have been once.

How it *was* once.

The siren droned on outside but not loud enough to drown the sound of aeroplanes high above. Suddenly the girl in the bed opposite sat bolt upright, her back to me as she shook the man's shoulders violently. I watched with incredulity as he too sat up, his face obscured by the girl. She put her hands to her ears, clasping them tightly to kill the interminable row of the siren. She shook her head from side to side, hands still at her ears, her long blond hair tumbling in uncontrollable cascades around her shoulders.

When I tried to leap out of bed to comfort her I realised I couldn't move. I was sitting up in bed in my room—*no. Not my room*—and I couldn't move a muscle. All I could do was watch helplessly as the scene played out around me— and it was real. This was no stage-bound drama and I the audience. It was happening before my very eyes. I saw the girl jump out of bed and run in her nightdress to the door. By the time I looked from her to the man, I could only see his back as he fled after her into the corridor. I'd learned soon afterwards, that his name was Jim Roberts, and the girl was his young wife, Heidi.

The instant the door swung shut behind them I was free of whatever unseen chains held me immobile against the bed. With one spring I was across to the door, my hands gripped the handle, twisting, pulling, pushing, turning—but I couldn't get the door to yield. It was shut firmly and stayed shut as if locked. I tugged for several seconds but the door wouldn't budge. I was trapped in my bedroom. *No. Not my room.*

And the noise. The intolerable noise. The humming had become a high-pitched whistling. I ran to the window and pulled back the curtains. Flames streamed before my eyes. The whole sky seemed on fire, one huge mass of orange and smoke. The village itself appeared to be ablaze, and over the treetops I could see the flames as they leapt into the night sky, casting an eerie glow on everything around them the night the bomb fell on White Pastures in the final days of the war.

The whistling became more intense, nearer, and louder as the bomb fell lower and lower. I hammered on the window, desperately trying to shout a warning to the girl who by now was running across the lawn. But she gave no indication of hearing me. I tried to open the window, but it refused to move. It was shut firmly and wouldn't give an inch. I looked up and fancied I caught a glimpse of the falling shell glinting against the moon. There, below, the girl in her nightdress was running to her doom. And I was helpless in my bedroom—*no. In her bedroom*—unable to stop her.

By now her husband was on the edge of the lawn, his head raised heavenward as he too saw the falling bomb, which was only a few dozen metres above the trees at the bottom of the garden. His garden. My garden.

Then the bomb was down and everything else was up. High up in the air. Trees, or rather torn shattered fragments of trees, were up in the air, grass and earth were up in the air. And the shrill, penetrating whistle was replaced by the roar of a deafening, ear-splitting explosion.

Somehow that terrible scene from long ago was being replayed in front of me. The drama had almost reached its conclusion. The young girl, Jim Roberts's bride, was about to meet her death in the grounds of White Pastures. The whole house shook around me as I watched Jim Roberts throw himself to the ground, his hands protectively around his head.

The last thing I'd seen before my bedroom window shattered in front of my eyes was the girl being flung in the air like a rag doll. In mid-flight, the force of the impact whipped her around, and her horrified face turned agonisingly towards me in the last split seconds of her life. And I saw her features for the first time.

Her face, her broken, smashed and bloody body had spanned the years from World War ll to 1982 as she tumbled and twisted. The explosion rang in my ears and as I threw my hands up to protect my eyes from the thousands of shards of flying glass, I was knocked backwards by the force of the blast.

But that fraction of a second when I saw her face was enough. There was no doubt I had been looking straight into the terrified face of my sister, Helen.

The sound died away. The silence, the overwhelming quietness, echoed unnaturally in my soul. I lay there for a few seconds on the floor where I'd been blown by the force of the explosion before I heard the door open, and a scream stung my ears.

My younger sister, Sarah, stood framed in the doorway,

the very doorway that only moments earlier had refused to yield to me. She must have touched the switch because light instantly flooded the room. I looked around tentatively. The curtains were drawn back, waving erratically, and the window lay in shattered glass fragments on the floor. The curtains' dancing movements stilled. Nothing stirred. Sarah didn't move. Her hands covered her nose and mouth. Eyes wide open. She was rooted to the spot.

Then I realised that hers hadn't been the only scream. Before she'd torn down the passage to my bedroom, I'd been aware of a more agonised scream from elsewhere in the house.

I hadn't been able to hear the girl outside when she screamed, although I'll never forget the sight of that silent cry working its way up to her lips when she felt the deadly breath of the explosion. But it was Helen's voice that had screamed the horrible, unnatural death knell as I was blown backwards onto the floor. And the scream came from the depths of White Pastures. From Helen's bedroom.

Mum suddenly appeared in the doorway beside Sarah. She was hysterical, her hands, too, were up to her face and she was stamping each foot in turn in a sort of peculiar little dance. When she saw me there, amidst the splinters of my window, her hands slid slowly down her cheeks and over her chin, and her legs buckled beneath her before she dropped onto the landing carpet.

I hardly had time to get up and start tiptoeing carefully through the glass before Dad appeared.

"What the devil's going on?" he yelled, seeing the devastation in my bedroom.

"Helen. See to Helen. See that she's alright," I shouted as I navigated through the maze of glass splinters that threatened my bare feet if I misplaced a step.

Dad didn't come back. I was still comforting Sarah and Mum when he called my name. Until that moment only Sarah's sobs broke the stillness, and I realised that the house had been insanely quiet. One second I was at the window looking out on a scene of long ago, then that scene had been obliterated, overtaken by events in the here and now.

"Simon! For God's sake! Simon!" The agony in Dad's voice was unmistakable as it rang out from Helen's bedroom.

Leaving Sarah to look after Mum, I ran down the passage to find Dad kneeling on the floor beside Helen's bed, his hand gripped tightly around hers, pressing it to his lips, his head bowed. He turned towards me, his whole body trembling. I looked down at the form lying motionless beneath the rumpled bedclothes.

Tears rolled down Dad's cheeks. I had to listen carefully to make any sense of the listless, whispered words that were coming between his wrenching sobs.

"My God, Simon...my God. She's dead."

Immediately after hitting me with those awful words again, that distressing scene faded and I found myself walking up the ramp to the medical centre in the neighbouring town, heading towards my first blackout. Dad had insisted I see a therapist to help me process and overcome what we'd been through in the previous months.

You know the old saying, 'I'll be there in spirit'? The opposite was true during my first appointment with her. While my body had apparently been there during the consultation, my spirit had gone awol. I reached out to open the surgery door and noticed several small cracks radiating out from a thin piece of tape on the vertical glass panel next to it. I remembered thinking someone must have smashed it, and immediately after that, I woke up the next morning. The fact that I was now reliving that strange, incredulous feeling with the hindsight of experiencing so many similar blanks in my life after that, didn't make this latest memory of that first one any easier or less weird.

I'd simply laid there looking at the ceiling for a few seconds, unable to comprehend what was happening. I'd been opening the surgery door. And now I'm here. In bed.

What? I sat up. Looked at my clock. Quarter to eight. But...how did I get here? I'd just said goodbye to Dad who was waiting in the car for me, outside.

Everything seemed normal as I looked around my bedroom. Unlike that night of the bomb when it was my bedroom but wasn't, this was. The loosely-drawn curtains were letting in sunlight. Just as they did yesterday morning. The carpet on the floor was my carpet. The wardrobes were my wardrobes. But it should be two o'clock in the afternoon and I'm at the medical centre in the nearby town of Merebrook, telling the receptionist I've got an appointment with a counsellor. So why am I in bed?

The empty, hollow pit that had been eating away at my stomach since Helen died hadn't left me—it was always there as soon as I awoke, and that day was no different—and the tears were welling up again now as I eased myself out of bed.

Although my subconscious seemed to recognise that this was a memory and wasn't happening for the first time, my mind still turned the same somersaults it did that afternoon in 1982, which would have won first prize in any mental gymnastics competition.

I pulled on my dressing gown and made my way downstairs. Mum and Dad were at the dining table having breakfast. No sign of Sarah yet. She'd taken to sleeping in even later. Everything appeared to be normal.

"Morning," I said from the doorway.

Their response came in unison: "Good morning, Simon." Mum pushed her chair back and stood. "I'll put some toast on for you. Two rounds?"

"Yes, please." I looked at her face in vain for any indication that something was out of kilter.

But it seemed the only thing out of kilter was me. Let's try something.

"Dad," I began when Mum had gone to the kitchen. "You know what I said in the car after seeing Anna?"

"Yes."

Hhmmm. That's more than I know. What would I have said? I've gotta take a punt on this. "Do you think she can help?"

"I'm sure she can. She's an experienced counsellor. And you said everything went well."

"I know. It's just that..." *What could I tell him?* "Something really weird's happened."

Dad's eyes widened a touch, and his brows rose, before pulling down almost immediately into a frown. "What? Is everything okay?"

"Honestly, Dad? I don't know."

"What's happened?"

I took a deep breath. "That's just it," I began. "I don't know what's happened since I went to the medical centre."

"What do you mean, you don't know?"

"I can't remember anything after standing at the surgery door yesterday going in for my appointment with Anna, until I just woke up."

He simply stared at me. I can't blame him. I wouldn't know what to say to myself, either.

"I've no idea what I said to you on the way home

yesterday, or whatever we did last night. I can't even remember seeing Anna. Everything before that was crystal clear, but everything after that was blank until I woke up.

"It's just as if I blacked out."

"You were perfectly normal," said Dad. "Maybe a little quieter than usual, but I put that down to talking to Anna. You said you told her the whole story."

"So, why can't I remember it? Dad, I'm really worried."

I think it was the American critic Dorothy Parker who said actress Katharine Hepburn ran the gamut of emotions from A to B during a stage performance. Well, I'll go 24 letters better. My gamut of emotions was running right through to Z.

"You seriously can't remember anything?" asked Dad. It seemed he didn't know what to do or say.

"Not a thing."

"Maybe your mind's stopped trying to process what happened, and shut it out." I sensed he was floundering. "Perhaps talking to Anna wasn't such a good idea. It brought it all back too early before you were ready."

"No, I'm more than ready. I think it's just..." And that's when the flashback ended. I may have known 38 years ago what I was thinking, but it had completely gone in this memory.

I'm now walking along a cracked concrete path, looking down at occasional weeds sprouting through. Mum and Dad are ahead and Sarah's alongside me. I shudder as the open grave comes into view beyond the trees. Another memory from another time, another place, another blackout.

Another few moments and I know I'll be waking up in bed the morning after Grandma's funeral. What did I remember from this? The vicar wasn't the Reverend Hubert McBeil. He retired a couple of years before Grandma died.

What was his name, now? It's on the tip of my tongue. He stood on the other side of the grave, the coffin resting above it on cross stick poles, with the lowering straps running underneath and through the handles, then folded neatly on to green cloth surrounding it.

He waited until around 30 of us had made our way from the church service to this final graveside committal.

"Today we are gathered together to say goodbye to Rosemary Paulina Reynolds, beloved mother of Robert and David, and Grandmother to Simon and Sarah, and also to Helen who has gone on before. On behalf of the family, I'd like to thank all of you for coming today.

"Death reminds us that we live in a fallen, imperfect world. We are reminded of our failings, flaws and limitations. Anytime we stand at a graveside, we're reminded of the shadow that has been cast over humanity because of Adam's sin. Paul tells us in Romans Chapter five, Verse 12, that through one man, sin entered the world, and death through sin, and thus death spread to all men.

"But death doesn't merely remind us of the universal nature of mankind's problems. God did not leave us in the valley or under a shadow. We realise that God has a solution for us. Through the power of Jesus Christ when I walk through the valley of the shadow of death, I shall fear no evil.

"We are told in Thessalonians, Chapter Four, verses 13 to 18: 'But I do not want you to be ignorant, brethren, concerning those who have fallen asleep, lest you sorrow as others who have no hope. For if we believe that Jesus died and rose again, even so, God will bring with Him those who sleep in Jesus.

"'For this, we say to you by the word of the Lord that we who are alive and remain until the coming of the Lord will by no means precede those who are asleep. For the Lord Himself will descend from heaven with a shout, with the voice of an archangel, and with the trumpet of God. And the dead in Christ will rise first.

"'Then we who are alive and remain shall be caught up together with them in the clouds to meet the Lord in the air. And thus we shall always be with the Lord. Therefore comfort one another with these words.'

"We shall always be with the Lord. There will be no isolation in heaven. We will not be separated from each other. Heaven, for us, will be a place of perpetual reunion.

"Just as Rosemary Paulina has now gone on before us, others in the family have gone on before her, and even now are waiting to greet her as she moves forward in her journey."

Hearing that, made me wonder if Helen was waiting there for her. As either Heidi or Helen, with or without Jim Roberts.

"When a dearly loved mother and grandmother is suddenly no longer with us it can trigger many questions. We are here today as the people of God to find comfort in the truth of Scripture, and to surround Rosemary's family with our love, our faith and our prayers.

"No matter how eloquent the words that are spoken today, there is still a very genuine sense of sorrow and loss that a loved one is no longer with us. We're no longer able to enjoy Rosemary's company, her friendship, and her fellowship.

"May the God of peace, who through the blood of the eternal covenant brought back from the dead our Lord Jesus, that great Shepherd of the sheep, equip you with everything good for doing His will, and may He work in us what is pleasing to Him, through Jesus Christ, to whom be glory forever and ever. Amen.

"Oh, death where is thy sting? Oh grave, where is thy

victory?

"Rosemary Paulina is not here. She stands in the presence of the Lord, the same Jesus who said to the dying man on a cross 'today you shall be with me in paradise.'"

He gestured to the oak coffin resting over the grave, ready to be lowered in. "The body that lies before us is but the earthly tabernacle, the house in which Rosemary lived among us for a time."

The coffin bearers stepped forward, each taking hold of one of the lowering straps.

"Tenderly and reverently, we commit that house to the grave, to God who gave it, waiting for the day when both the spirit and the body shall again be united at the coming of the Lord. And we rejoice in the fact that her spirit is even now with you, the Father of spirits. In the face of death, we thank You for Your gift of eternal life."

The funeral director bent to adjust the fitments of the cross stick poles holding the coffin in place over the grave.

"In Jesus's name, Amen."

As the coffin bearers started playing the straps slowly through their hands, the casket inched its way down into the Earth.

Almost before I recalled that the descent was my final memory of the funeral ahead of the blackout, the scene faded and darkness hit.

Instead of the darkness of oblivion, though, this was night-time darkness. The three-quarters moon and some of the brighter stars reflected across the water in front of me. The rear lights of a departing car shone red for a few seconds before disappearing from view. I'd driven down here often enough with Janice in the dark, during the early days of our relationship before we moved in together, to recognise that bend which led beyond the trees to the main road. Our night-time excursions hadn't involved getting out, apart from climbing in the back, which was easier than trying to scramble over the seats in the brown Mazda 626 coupe I had at that time.

For all that Janice and I managed to generate our own heat, we usually made sure the blower was turned up as well, which meant I'd never been cold down here by the lake, until now.

And, boy, was it cold.

Which is hardly surprising as it was around three o'clock in the morning on the shore of Orangebow Lake in early March and I was stark naked. I briefly wondered if this memory would take me right up to the time the blackout began, as it had with Grandma's funeral and my first counselling session.

No time to dwell on that now. Twenty-four-year-old Simon was already making his way gingerly across the gravel drive to where the grass bordering it would be kinder to his bare feet.

All these memories felt strange to me. They were more than simple reminders or thoughts. It's almost as if I were actually back there reliving them.

But why make me go through that awful night of Helen's death again? And what's with these memories leading up to my first three blackouts? COVID is playing nasty games with me. A little part of my mind wandered briefly to where I lay in reality, on the spare bedroom floor, with Janice's frantic voice cutting through the Orangebow darkness. It wasn't the Janice I'm marrying tomorrow, but the Janice I've been married to for 32 years. "Simon! Oh God, what's happened?" I opened my eyes and looked up at her. Instantly my tortured lungs reminded me that I could barely breathe.

"Janice, help me," I managed to gasp, each word separated by a hoarse, desperate pull of air.

"I'm getting an ambulance," she said.

A pale layer of mist danced before my eyes, separating me from Janice, dragging me back to when my stag night had ended with my friends stripping me naked, dumping me at the lake car park and speeding off, just eight hours before my wedding.

"Shall we leave him his shoes?" Jonty Taylor had asked, as they were bundling me out of the car. Remind me to buy him a drink for at least caring a little bit.

"No," my Best Man, Trevor Aimes, told him. "Definitely not."

"What about his wallet?"

"No, he's having nothing. Let's see how resourceful he is out here, seven miles from anywhere, as naked as the day he was born."

Oh, I was resourceful that night. I'd made sure of it earlier. They may have taken every stitch of clothing I had, my wallet, all my cash, my keys, my watch, and even the St Christopher medallion I was wearing, but they didn't know about a couple of coins I'd shoved up my arse (yes, literally up my arse!) before the stag pub crawl had started.

"That's disgusting," Sarah had told me earlier in the day when I asked if she'd be my emergency rescuer should the need arise.

"I know," I laughed, "but I'm terrified they'll strip me and tie me to a lamppost or something. At least I'll have some money to ring you to come and get me."

I could vaguely remember there was a phone box at the Blackthorpe Crossroads along the main road. It was probably at least three miles away, but at least all I'd got to do was get there and ring Sarah. As soon as I stepped off the painful gravel track onto the grass, though, I realised the choice between the rock and hard place I was in the middle of wasn't going to be easy.

The glittering, frosty sheen covering the grass made it almost impossibly cold to walk on, and I guess I'd also have been bitterly cold even fully dressed. So, given the fact that I was naked and exposed to this cruel March night must have increased the risk of hypothermia.

Can't hang around.

I alternated a brisk walking pace with a slow jog to try and keep my feet off the frozen surface for as long as possible during strides. I reached the end of the lake's grounds and turned left onto the main road which led back towards the town. The tarmac was easier going than the grass because it wasn't as cold, neither was it as sharp as the loose gravel, and I quickly developed a natural rhythm at a speed that, if not keeping the cold entirely at bay, at least took the edge off the rawness.

The thought crossed my mind that I'd have to either press myself into the hedge to hide if a car came along, or I could try and stop it and explain my predicament. Fortunately, I wasn't called on to make the decision.

Eventually, the phone box came into view. I opened the door and went inside. Now all I had to hope for was that it hadn't been vandalised or was out of order. All was well, the dialling tone was the most beautiful sound to my ears as soon as I picked up the receiver to check it out. It was probably a touch warmer in there than outside, and what a relief it was to put the directory on the floor and stand on it, to protect the soles of my feet from the cold concrete base.

Then came the unpleasant task of retrieving the coins from their hidey hole, and wiping them on the frosty grass.

My sister answered on the seventh ring. "If that's you,

Simon," she said, sleepily, before I even had a chance to open my mouth, "you'd better not be in Edinburgh."

"Not quite," I replied. "I'm at the phone box at the Blackthorpe Crossroads, near Orangebow Lake."

The giggle in her voice was unmistakable. "I assume a lack of certain items of clothing is stopping you from getting home by yourself?" *Yes, alright, there's no need to sound so amused by it.*

"A lack of any items of clothing," I retorted. "And a lack of keys, wallet and money."

"I ought to just leave you there. You do know that, don't you?"

"And have to face Janice's wrath when I don't turn up for the wedding?"

"You're only a couple of hours' walk from home," she said. "You've got plenty of time. I'm going back to sleep."

"Sarah. No!"

"Give me one good reason why not." A hint of another giggle. *She won't really leave me out here. Will she? Not after agreeing to be my saviour. No. She's only kidding.*

"I could freeze to death, or get frostbite at the very least. I nearly froze solid getting down here from the lake."

"I suppose Janice wouldn't like it if any bits broke off."

"She wouldn't be the only one. Now, are you coming, or not?"

"Stay there. I'll be as quick as I can." The phone went dead.

As did that memory. The moonlit night phased out of existence and Janice and I were being ushered into Dr Caroline Horton's office.

Wait, though. COVID is playing some seriously strong mindfucks here, and nothing's consistent. What's it trying to tell me? First, it showed me Helen's death, then just a few seconds before my very first blackout—ahead of my appointment with Anna—and on to my first memory immediately after that, along with the awkward conversation with Dad.

I saw several minutes of Grandma's graveside service at her funeral right up to when oblivion hit me, but nothing afterwards. I went straight from the funeral to being naked on that bitterly cold morning, and now I'm at that awful moment when we heard about Janice's breast cancer. So, I haven't relived everything right up to the blackout before our wedding. I've always remembered what happened until Trevor and I went into the church.

This is another quick one, though. It's only a few seconds until we hear the bad news. "I'm very sorry, Mrs Reynolds," Dr Horton was saying. "The tissue sample you gave us indicates the presence of cancerous cells in your breast."

What the fuck's happening to me? Fuck you, cancer. Fuck you, COVID.

Part Two
COVID

5

Investigation

Friday, February 19th, 2021, Stephanie

Stephanie didn't intend to waste any time in utilising Mike Keeling's information from his all-nighter. "Forward the addresses of all those BMW owners inside the 25-mile radius to Kit and me, please," she told him.

"Kit, I'm popping upstairs to let the Chief know what we're doing. While I'm up there with him, prioritise which you think could be the best ten owners for us to start with. As soon as I've got this press conference out of the way, you and I'll get out there."

"Yes, Ma'am."

Stephanie heard their two phones ping as Mike sent details from the Holmes file to them.

She strode over to the glass panels at the edge of the third-floor walkway and looked down on the assembled journalists in the large open-plan lobby beneath her. She counted 15. It was almost as if the Chief Constable read her mind. "A few more than usual, Steph. But this isn't a usual crime. Public Relations tells me we've got a couple of the nationals here, as well as BBC and ITV."

"Only to be expected, Sir. I'd better go and get it over with. I want to get out there and crack this case."

She followed him down the staircase and they both walked to individual lecterns in front of the blue police backdrop.

Even after nine years of handling press conferences, Stephanie still felt a little intimidated, never knowing whether the questions would simply be aimed at gathering factual information or be deliberately barbed to try and trip her up. At least she wasn't in London, though, with the Metropolitan Police. She gave thanks daily to whatever higher power prompted her to reject their overtures to her in 2018.

She glanced around the faces seated in front of her, glad that she knew so many of them, including the ever-present Darell Bostock from the Poolswood Recorder; Ayesha Patterson, Poolswood Sound's senior reporter; Lizzie Moses, the Evening Telegraph's crime correspondent, and the rather young and inexperienced Jason Manning from the county's online news service.

"Good day, ladies and gentlemen," began the Chief Constable. "Thank you for coming this morning. As I'm sure you know, two people were murdered on the streets of Poolswood yesterday.

"Because of the particularly brutal way in which this double murder was carried out, and some other rather disturbing aspects of the case, I'm taking the unusual step of appointing myself as Senior Investigating Officer..." a murmur went around the journalists..." with Detective Chief Inspector Stephanie Ingram running the day to day operations. For all intents and purposes, DCI Ingram is in charge, but she's reporting directly to me.

"I'll now ask her to bring you up to speed on what happened yesterday and what we know so far. DCI Ingram, the floor's yours."

"Thank you, Sir. Good morning, everyone. Yesterday, at around 2.40p.m. an incident occurred on Clowes Road, Poolswood, which left two people dead from multiple gunshot wounds. They were 34-year-old Adam Hampshire and his wife,

Hayley, who was 31. They'd just got out of their vehicle after returning home from Poolwsood Leisure Centre where they'd received their COVID vaccinations. Both were shot several times. Two gunmen escaped the scene in a grey BMW.

"The victims' next of kin have been informed, and are receiving specialist assistance from our family liaison officers at this very difficult time. We have a little information about the couple which we can share with you. Adam Hampshire was working from home as a software developer, and Hayley had been furloughed from her job at a local travel agency. They didn't have any children.

"We're following several lines of enquiry, initially to try and establish a motive and to find out more about the car. If anyone saw a grey BMW 5 Series M Sport with a fake personalised number plate of TBW 781 at any time yesterday in Poolswood or beyond, please let us know. We'd be particularly interested in any dashcam footage showing the vehicle. We know it came into Poolswood along Blackthorpe Road and left the same way. It was last seen in the average speed check area, heading towards the motorway."

She looked across at the Chief Constable. "Unless you have anything, Sir...?"

"Thank you, DCI Ingram. No, I've nothing to add." He turned back to the journalists, many of whom now had their hands raised. "We'll take one or two questions. As there are some new faces here today, could you please identify yourself before you ask your question?

"Stephanie, do you want to chair this?"

"Yes, I will, Sir. Darell, I think your hand was up first."

"Thank you, Steph. I'm Darell Bostock, Poolswood Recorder. You said the victims were shot multiple times. Can you confirm the rumours that machine guns were used?"

"You've known me long enough to know I never comment on rumours," replied Stephanie.

"Let me rephrase. Were they shot with machine guns?"

"They were killed with weapons which were capable of firing several rounds in quick succession."

"So that's..."

"You can draw your own conclusions, Darell. I can't go into any more details, for operational reasons. Now, anyone else? Yes, Jason?"

"Thank you, DCI Ingram. Jason Manning. County Online. Do you have a motive for the killing yet?"

"Not yet. This is actually one of the disturbing aspects of the case the Chief referred to in his introduction. It's very early days in the investigation and we're working hard to establish any possible reasons why Adam and Hayley Hampshire were targetted in this way. But at the moment, there's no indication of what the motive could be.

"The Hampshires both had underlying health conditions and had been shielding since the start of the pandemic. Before yesterday they'd only left their home once in the last 11 months. And to confirm what we said earlier, they were only out yesterday for their COVID vaccination."

"Are you saying it's a random attack?" That came from one of the faces she didn't recognise.

"All we're saying at this stage is that we don't have a motive yet, Mr... er?"

"Nathan Powers. ITV News."

"Well, Mr Powers, because we don't have a clear motive yet, we need the public to be extremely alert. Especially if they see the gunmen's car. They shouldn't approach it, but we'd ask them to contact us immediately."

"In that case, can you give us a full description of the car?"

"As we've mentioned, it's a grey BMW 5 Series M Sport with a fake personalised number plate of TBW 781…"

"When you say 'fake,' what do you mean?"

"It looks like a traditional personalised number plate, originally from the 1960s when three letters and numbers were standard. That particular number was in use at that time but is no longer registered.

"The other thing about the car," added Stephanie, "is that it looks from the CCTV footage we have of it, as if the windscreen and front side windows are illegal. They're blacked out to the same level as the rear windows. The law states that windscreens must let in at least 75 per cent of light, and front side windows 70 per cent. So that distinguishes the car at first glance."

Stephanie acknowledged another journalist who raised her hand.

"I'm Ayesha Patterson, from Poolswood Sound. Were the gunmen waiting for the victims when they arrived home or did they follow them there?"

Stephanie had discussed with the Chief Constable just how much information to give the media about this particular aspect. "I think we keep some of this to ourselves at this stage," he'd told her during their briefing session that morning. "I agree, Sir," she'd responded. "If we can get any suspects to admit where they first saw the Hampshires without that part of the story being public knowledge, it'll help strengthen our case with the Crown Prosecution Service."

"My thinking exactly," he'd said.

"We have CCTV footage showing the BMW behind them at Broadhaven Road traffic lights, and at a couple of other locations," she told the gathering. "And a witness on Clowes Road said it pulled up immediately after they'd turned onto their drive.

"That's all we can say at this time, but we do have a little pack for you all." She indicated Jackie from the Public Relations department, standing to the left at the back. "It contains our full statement and pictures of Adam and Hayley. We'd ask you to respect their families' privacy at this very sad and traumatic time."

Ayesha Patterson raised her hand again: "Steph, could we have a separate interview with you for the radio, please?"

"And me?" asked the BBC and ITV reporters in unison.

"Stephanie nodded. "We'll use one of the side rooms."

An hour later she guided the Stinger out of police headquarters and glanced over at Kit. "It's probably too much to hope that we'll strike gold at the first go, but this does look rather promising, given the computer software connection."

While Stephanie was briefing the Chief Constable and holding the press conference, Kit had had no hesitation in putting Frederick 'Fritz' Chikatilo at the top of his list, for two reasons. Holmes showed he had strong, but unprovable links to organised crime and was also Chief Executive Officer of a computer software company now specialising in electric vehicle technology.

"He's certainly a good starting point, Ma'am. On the surface, he appears to be squeaky clean, but the intel on him says very different, and makes him well worth a look." Kit scrolled through a file on his phone.

"He's 34, with a reputation for being one of the most feared hard men on the South coast drugs scene, even though he's only got one conviction to his name. He appears at the edge of investigations time and time again, but then the trail goes cold. The drugs squad have pumped hundreds of hours into trying to bring him down, but he always manages to stay one step ahead."

"What was his conviction for?"

"Possession of a couple of bags of cocaine. They found it in his car during a stop-and-search operation last year. He played merry hell about it, according to this footnote. Claimed he was only stopped because he was black and driving an expensive car. Spouted racial discrimination, and all that. He lodged an official complaint against the police but didn't get anywhere with it.

"A top lawyer got him off the possession charge with just a hefty fine, but it meant he was finally in the system after years of staying under the radar officially."

"A bit of an Al Capone character, would you say?"

Kit frowned. "I think Al Capone was a bit before my time, Ma'am. I've heard the name, but..."

Stephanie glanced away from the road and locked eyes with him for a second. But a second was all it took for her to see the twinkle. *Damn. He's done it again.*

"Ah, I remember," he said. "He was a character in that film, The Untouchables, wasn't he? I saw it on some TV channel that shows old movies and black and white programmes."

"Fuck off, Kit."

"You must have seen it the first time round, did you? When it first came out?"

"Kit. Fuck off."

Turning right at the Blackthorpe Crossroads when heading away from Poolswood takes you through the village of Meriton and brings you out in the market town of Merebrook. But if you hang a left instead, you'll soon be able to look down on the spectacular Orangebow Lake country park. A mile or two beyond that, just over the river bridge, a winding country lane forks off from the B road and quickly becomes too narrow for vehicles to meet without both having to manoeuvre onto the grass verge.

Which is exactly what Stephanie was having to do before she and the mud-splattered Range Rover facing her could go their separate ways. The Stinger wouldn't be quite so white, either, after this little adventure, she thought.

She acknowledged the other driver with a quick raise of her hand as they pulled by each other.

A couple of moments after they bounced back off the grass, Kit pointed to a gap in the trees bordering the road. "I think this must be it."

He opened Google Maps on his phone, toggled to the aerial view and clicked the arrow so the screen spun to point in the direction they were facing. "It looks as if Chikatilo's house is just up here on the left. It's called Larkwise Lodge."

Stephanie pulled into the gap and discovered it tapered to become a short drive leading to a set of ornate black aluminium double swing gates with curved tops, connected to matching flanged posts. The same style of horizontal bars formed a security fence sitting immediately behind the trees and high hedgerows which shielded the large L-shaped, almost flat-roofed, house and grounds from passing motorists' prying eyes.

She inched the car towards an intercom set at window height on an aluminium stand and pressed the silver button above a speaker and keypad.

A few seconds later, a disembodied female voice came from the speaker: "Hello."

"Hello," said Stephanie. "I'm Detective Chief Inspector Stephanie Ingram. I'm here with Detective Sergeant Kit McGrath. We'd like to ask Mr Frederick Chikatilo a few questions, please."

There was a slight pause before the response came. Not too long, just three or four seconds, but Stephanie knew it had been thinking time. "I'm sorry, but he's extremely busy this afternoon with back-to-back Zoom calls. If you'd like to make an appointment for tomorrow?"

"And you are...?"

"I'm Mrs Chikatilo."

"Well, your husband has a choice in this. You tell him now that he can either spare us some time to answer our questions between his Zoom calls, or we'll take him to the station and he can spend the afternoon there talking to us. Tell him that now, please, Mrs Chikatilo."

There was another pause. A little longer this time. "Give me a moment. I'll see if I can interrupt him."

"You do that."

They waited longer than a moment. It was more like two before Mrs Chikatilo's voice came from the speaker again. "He'll see you. Come up to the house."

The double gates swung open, and Stephanie eased the Stinger through.

As they drew nearer to the house she took in the vast amounts of glass, steel and concrete. The first storey of the striking, modern-looking property comprised four sets of six bi-fold doors—two on each leg of the L—overhanging the ground floor at both ends, appearing to be suspended in mid-air. A balcony spanned the full width, above a wooden-decked terrace extending into a walkway to what she assumed was a swimming pool. Being February, the pool was still protected by a winter safety cover.

She and Kit both spoke at the same time. "Beautiful," said Kit. "Dreadful," said Stephanie. They looked at each other and grinned.

"It's like a set of glass-sided storage containers," she said.

"Philistine," said Kit.

Ground floor bi-folds stretched away on both sides of the front door—also glass—in the angle of the L. "I hope they don't throw many stones," he muttered.

Stephanie stopped the car alongside the house, where the drive gave way to a sloping lawn stretching down to a hedge bordering open countryside. As they alighted, she became aware of a figure wearing grey tracksuit trousers with a more formal starched white shirt standing in the entrance, arms folded. His slightly narrowed eyes above the blue medical mask reflected suspicion and open hostility.

Aggressive, she thought. *What's he got to hide?*

Having a name like Frederick Chikatilo, and the Fritz nickname which the Holmes file said was used throughout the emobility industry and the underworld, she wouldn't have automatically thought of him as black. Reading his body language she could readily understand why he'd accused the police of racial discrimination when he'd been stopped. *How will he react to us?*

His build was similar to Kit's, tall, powerful-looking, and well-proportioned. There's probably a home gym here, as well as the pool, she thought.

"What do you want?" he growled at them. *The voice was definitely in keeping with his hostile stance.*

She pulled out her identification card and opened it to show her photograph and badge. "I'm DCI Stephanie Ingram, and this is DS Kit McGrath."

"I didn't ask who you were. I asked what you wanted." He didn't even glance at their warrant cards.

"It's just a routine enquiry to eliminate you from an

investigation we're currently undertaking, Sir," said Kit.

Chikatilo maintained his stare straight at Stephanie, ignoring Kit. "Make it quick. I've had to cut short an important Zoom call for this, and I've got another one in a few moments."

Steph smiled inwardly. *Hence the formal shirt, but comfortable legwear.* "We'll try not to detain you long." By now they had reached the door, and Chikatilo did not attempt to move.

"Can we come in, please?" she asked.

"No. You're not wearing masks, and you won't be staying long."

"We have masks, Mr Chikatilo," she replied, fishing two from her bag and passing one to Kit.

"I said no. You can ask your questions out here. You've got two minutes before I'm going in to prepare for my next meeting."

"Look, Sir..." the tone of Kit's voice when he extended Siiiir, rang alarm bells with Steph. *We can do without allegations of racial harassment here.*

"It's okay, Kit. If Mr Chikatilo can tell us what we want to know, we'll be away in no time."

"I'll ask you again. What do you want?" His icy stare hadn't wavered from Steph throughout the exchange.

"We're trying to eliminate owners of a particular motor vehicle from our enquiries. We understand you drive a grey BMW 5 Series M Sport. Would you mind telling me where you and the car were between one and three o'clock yesterday afternoon?"

His response to her question also answered an unspoken one. *So, he can laugh.* It was a harsh, ironic laugh, but still a laugh. Well, of sorts.

"There's a pandemic on, if you hadn't noticed. I was here. And the car's not been out of the garage for days. Where do you think I'd be?"

"Can anyone vouch for that?"

"My wife. We were both here all day."

"Was anyone else with you?" asked Kit.

Chikatilo still didn't look at him—his eyes continued to bore into Steph's face. "Not in body, no. We were alone. But, you said between one and three...?"

"That's right."

"I was on Zoom calls. The first between one and two o'clock, and a second between two and three. My camera was on all the time. At least half a dozen people will vouch for that."

"We'll need their names, Sir." Stephanie didn't have to worry about Kit extending into a sarcastic Siiiir on this occasion.

Chikatilo now looked at Kit for the first time. "Wait here." He retreated a few paces inside before shouting out: "Aamina, print the attendance sheets from yesterday's calls with Elektrica and PowerCrate. Include email addresses and phone numbers."

When he came back to the door, Stephanie told him they needed to look at the car. Silently he disappeared back inside the house, returning a moment later with a keyfob

"Follow me." He led the way along the wooden-decked terrace by the covered pool, and round the edge of the house to the back. Steph and Kit saw that the property was even larger than it appeared from the front, with several split-level rooms, invisible from where they had been standing, angled into the hill, and a triple stone garage jutting out from the side.

Chikatilo pressed a button on the fob, and the wide grey

door slid upwards, rolling back inside the roof. Sandwiched between a white Lamborghini Huracan and a deep blue Audi SQ7, the grey BMW was the poor relation there. Trying to keep her eyes off the other two cars, there was ample room for Steph to walk around the BMW. It was the same colour as the one used in the murder, and while the back windows were tinted to the same degree, there was nothing illegal about the front ones and windscreen.

"Satisfied?" snapped Chikatilo.

"I think so. For now," replied Steph. "But we will be checking with the people on your Zoom calls from yesterday."

"I'm sure you will."

Stephanie wondered which had come first, the gangland activities or success with his software business. She knew the overall type. What probably started as self-assurance would have turned to the arrogance and contempt she now saw before her, as he grew richer and seemingly more untouchable.

One of these days, Mr Chikatilo, it'll all come tumbling down. Yes, you'll make a mistake and we'll be waiting for you. "From what you say, Sir, and once those people have confirmed it, we'll be able to eliminate you from our enquiries, and you won't hear from us again about it." *Maybe not about this. But don't get too complacent.*

"I should hope not, DI...er, sorry, what's your name again?"

"Ingram, Sir. Stephanie Ingram. And it's DCI."

"Well, DCI Ingram, I should hope not. You've wasted enough of my time, and yours. What am I supposed to have done, anyway?"

"No one's saying, or even thinking, you've done anything. A grey BMW like yours was involved in an incident in Poolswood yesterday. We're simply eliminating all local owners from our enquiries as quickly as we can."

"Is it about that couple who were shot? There was something on the news last night and this morning regarding that."

"I'm afraid I'm not at liberty to say."

That laugh of sorts rang out again from behind his mask. "No, of course you're not. Ah, my wife's got your list." As they approached the open front door, a slim young woman in a yellow sleeveless floral dress, but no mask, stepped outside. She held out two sheets of paper. Chikatilo took them both quickly, but not before Steph noticed two purple bruises on the outside of her left forearm.

"Back inside, you've no mask on," he snapped at the girl, who Steph judged to be at least ten years younger than him. Her cheekbones looked like they might have once been finely carved from polished ebony which had now warped a little, pushing her prettiness into a slightly gaunt and tired category.

"Here," he said, holding out the papers to Steph, but Kit snatched them before she could react. "Everyone who was on the calls yesterday."

As they walked back to the car she released the electronic lock and cast a glance over her shoulder back towards the house. Fritz Chikatilo was still standing in the doorway, his glare as intense as ever.

She got in and shut the door.

Kit began scrolling through Mike Keeling's file again. "There's another guy on the list who lives fairly close by," he said. "How about we see him next, instead? He's only a couple of miles away."

Stephanie started the car and they moved off, the gates swinging open as they approached. She saw Chikatilo in the mirror, still in the doorway. "Who is he? Is he in your top ten?"

"No, but I hadn't realised he was so close. Some religious nut, John-Luke Matthews, who owns Batchelors Farm, near Dagglethorpe. He's the self-styled head of a spiritual cult that's based there. Calls himself Reverend, but according to Holmes, that's not an official title. The cult came to prominence a couple of years ago when a family from Bournemouth accused him of brainwashing their daughter. He was charged with kidnap, but they couldn't make it stick."

"I remember that," said Stephanie. "It went to court not long after our local celebrity author, Imogen Lambert, brought out a book with a similar storyline to that. The press dubbed it 'life imitating art.' Okay, yes, let's go and see him. We may as well keep the mileage down." She saw the dashboard's digital clock showed 1.35 p.m. "We'll still have time to pull a couple more in afterwards."

Kit started to enter the postcode for Batchelors Farm into the satnav, when the car became filled with the piano riff of Stephanie's mobile ringtone, and the screen changed to the phone display, showing DC Paula Bowen was trying to get in touch.

Stephanie accepted the call. "Yes, Paula."

"Boss, are you near a radio, or have you got the Poolswood Sound app on your phone?"

"We're in the car. I can put the radio on. What's happened?"

"Tune in to Simon Reynold's show. This murder's just gone into the stratosphere. I've never heard anything like it. New developments are unfolding right now, and they're absolutely fucking stellar."

6

Panters Club

Late March 2020, Simon

"Can I come with him?" I heard Janice ask through the haze.

"I'm afraid not," the paramedic replied as he strapped my wheeled stretcher into place in the ambulance. "You won't be able to visit him, either. The regulations are very strict now, because of COVID."

Since the paramedics hooked me up to the oxygen cylinder, the skin of the bubble I felt I was in, had faded a little and the light of the world no longer seemed to be as blurry or distant as it had been. The fog which I was trying to peer through became more of a mist, and the insular envelope around my ears that rendered voices indistinct and fuzzy appeared to be diminishing. Their words, while still sounding a little muffled, were clear enough for me to understand. And to instill a new sense of unease in me. I needed to stay strong for her, though.

"I'll be fine, Janice," I wheezed. But I wondered how much of my weak voice she could make out through the oxygen mask. I looked up at the paramedic. "Can I take my phone with me?"

"Of course." He turned towards the open door at the back of the ambulance, which is where I assumed Janice was. "Have you packed it in his bag?"

"No. I never thought about that," I heard her say. "Let me get it."

"Don't forget the charger," he reminded her.

My stretcher had me in a half-upright position, and a few moments later I saw Janice pass my overnight bag to the paramedic. "You'd better say goodbye," he told her. "It's unlikely you'll see him again until he's discharged from the hospital."

Well, that's hardly fine and dandy, is it? Am I going to be stuck in hospital with this horribly uncertain virus, cut off from Janice and the girls? Those thoughts turned the pangs of unease into a full-blown panic. I was in two minds now about going to the hospital. The oxygen was getting me through the crisis, so maybe if the paramedics left me a couple of cylinders and all the gubbins to get it into me, I'll be as right as rain in the morning.

Yeah, right.

You know the phrase, a meeting of minds? Well, those two minds I mentioned have just had a meeting. And the upshot is, I'm going into hospital.

Fuck you, COVID. You can mess with me all you like. But you ain't gonna win.

Janice's sobs were enough to break my heart. I could still hear them as I called "I love you," while the ambulance doors swung shut.

I hope she heard me. The click of the doors latching sounded awfully final.

On the first part of the journey to hospital, I realised there was one thing COVID didn't seem to affect, and that was my sense of feeling. The paramedics weren't riding on the siren—I guess there wasn't much traffic around at that time of the morning. I did hear it briefly a couple of times, perhaps when they approached junctions, but every time they accelerated and slowed down, or navigated a roundabout, I was pulled against the safety straps on the stretcher. It didn't hurt—my point was that I was conscious and fully aware of what was going on around me.

One paramedic sat with me and kept checking my

oxygen intake. "You're doing fine, mate," he said when I asked if passing out and not being able to breathe properly were normal symptoms of COVID. "It must have been frightening for you. But we'll soon have you at hospital."

I'd thought suns could only go supernova once. But I was suddenly engulfed with the same feeling I'd had in the bedroom. For a moment it burned brightly in my chest before that bubble surrounded me again, separating me from reality.

A piercing buzz filled the air, jolting the paramedic upright. He checked some instruments alongside me and adjusted a valve on the oxygen equipment. Immediately I felt the cool flow of oxygen increase against the skin of my face.

For the rest of the trip I vaguely heard the siren, and the ambulance was going faster now.

There was no hanging about when we arrived at Poolswood General Hospital, either. A couple of staff—I don't know if they were doctors or nurses—were all over me immediately.

"I'm worried about his oxygen saturation levels," the paramedic told them as they trundled my wheeled stretcher down the ambulance ramp. "They were pretty low when we first got to him, but they stabilised, although a little low, at 91 on the way here, before plummeting again."

I heard one of the hospital staff ask what they were now. "They dropped to 83," the paramedic replied. "We increased the oxygen flow and they've stayed at around 88 for a few moments."

"Thank you. Let's get him in."

Every breath I took inside the oxygen mask was still an effort. *I don't want to die. This is a shit way to go. Why me? I hope Janice remembers where the will is. I love you and the girls, Janice.* At least my life wasn't flashing before my eyes, so I guess that's a good thing, yes?

But what have I achieved? Is it enough? It may have to be. *Yes, of course it's enough. But I don't want it to be enough. I want to do more. I've had a reasonable career in radio.* Stop it! *HAVING a reasonable career, not HAD. I've still got millions more words to say on the airwaves.*

And the girls, of course. Our two wonderful daughters, Hannah and Claire. They're my finest achievement. *I need to see them again. I've got to get through this. When I do, I'll tell them I need grandchildren. Stop hanging around and get on with it.*

The ceiling lights started moving, indicating to my befuddled brain that my stretcher was being wheeled at a fair old pace along a corridor. I tried to look around for the paramedics. I needed to thank them. No sign of them.

We came to rest somewhere. I assumed it was a side room and not a ward, as I couldn't see any beds. I think there were at least four people around me, poking, prodding, connecting me with wires to a machine full of knobs and dials, jabbing something into the back of my hand, and then slotting a tube into it. Goodness knows where the other end of the tube went, and I felt too weak to turn to look.

I awoke, half remembering a dream I'd had since COVID knocked me for six again. Hang on, though. Have I just had it here in the hospital, or am I remembering the one I had at home when I finally got to sleep earlier this morning? No, this was different. When the young girl concealed behind the tree in my forest dreamscape stepped out into the moonlight I saw it was Grandma. She wasn't young, either. Strangely, though, she wasn't particularly old. She was Grandma as I remembered her as a child...perhaps my very earliest memory of her.

Flicking back her hair—it wasn't lank and greasy like the young girl's in my earlier dream, Grandma's was a rich golden brown with a shining, lustrous glow—she, as the young girl had done, raised her arms, turning to point them in my direction.

This time, instead of the thin white strands emerging from my body and going to her, they came from Grandma's arms and flowed through the air towards me. Instinctively, I threw my own arms up to protect my head and watched as they acted like lightning rods. The white strands hurtled across the space between us, painlessly piercing my hands and I felt a cross between tingling and itching as they sped up inside my arms and into my body.

Grandma smiled at me. Suddenly, I remembered she had spoken in the dream, and her words now hit me like the proverbial thunderbolt. "We'll meet again soon, Simon." *No, no, no, no. What does that mean? I've already decided I'm getting through this. So, come on, Grandma. As much as I love you, and still miss you so much, there's no way I'm seeing you for a good many years yet.*

As my waking mind struggled to hold on to the image of the dream, I fleetingly wondered if it was my subconscious reacting either to COVID invading my body or to the drugs the machines were putting into me through their tubes.

Then I imagined that whatever Grandma had sent me turned into Captain Caveman. I hadn't thought about Captain Caveman for an eternity, not since watching him in cartoons as a child. And yet, there he was, running around my bloodstream pounding and smashing the virus with his club.

"Morning," said a quiet voice away to my right.

The face looking down at me when I opened my eyes was partly concealed by an oxygen mask with a tube snaking out of sight.

"I thought you were awake," whispered the face behind

the mask. "The sound of your whole breathing pattern changed. The others went back to sleep after the early morning drugs round, so we'll need to be quiet for a bit longer. I'm just on my way for a pee before breakfast. Back in a moment."

He moved out of my line of vision, and I didn't feel like looking where he went. Not yet, anyway. I wanted to get my bearings first. Actually, I guess he's as good a place as anywhere to start, on that score. He was slowly heading towards a door marked 'Toilet' a few paces away. A long tube trailed behind him connected to a white panel on the wall alongside the bed next to mine.

I was in the middle bed of three, with a mirror image of that arrangement directly opposite. The beds each had a chair alongside and were separated from their neighbour by curtains, which were now pushed back to the wall. I felt it was rather a grim sight, as everyone, including me, was connected via tubes and wires to several machines on multi-tiered trolleys.

The man facing me wore an oxygen mask similar to the one I'd had in the ambulance, and which my neighbour, now in the toilet, was also sporting. But the patient next to him was receiving his oxygen through a nasal cannula clipped inside his nostrils, which made me realise that the inside of my septum felt a little pinched. I gently put my hand to my face, expecting to feel the plastic oxygen mask. Instead, however, I felt the two prongs of a cannula in my nostrils, and followed their path with my fingers behind my ears and down to where they met at the base of my throat. From there, they curled over to be fed oxygen via a flow meter plugged into a white oxygen wall panel.

Two sets of clear liquid in bags hung from hooks on a portable pole stand, dripped into me intravenously, one through the back of my hand, and the other a couple of inches below my elbow. As if I weren't extruding enough tubes and cables, a clip on the end of my left forefinger was plugged into another machine on the bottom shelf of the trolley.

The background hum of the machinery alongside all six beds was suddenly competing with the sound of the toilet flushing, and my neighbour emerged slowly through the door.

"So," he said, after shuffling his way back and plonking himself down on the foot of my bed, just before another door at the end of the room opened. The nurse who walked in looked straight at my visitor above her medical mask.

"Alan, back to your bed, please, until after breakfast," she said. "Mr. Reynolds, how are you feeling now?"

I'd barely had time to consider that since waking, so took stock for a moment before answering. Alan raised his eyebrows at me, winked, and sat down in the chair next to his bed, pushing the tube trailing from his oxygen mask over the arm. Gingerly I started to test every inch of my body.

Headache: check. Not overly painful, just that nagging throb in the background which seemed to have taken up residence.

Sore throat: check. My mouth felt dry, and swallowing even the tiny amount of saliva in there made me wince.

My breathing was a little laboured, but at least air was getting into my lungs through the cannula.

Arms and legs were a little achy.

Despite just having woken up, I still felt tired.

Just thinking about the cough manifested a tickle in my throat. I guess it's not psychosomatic, though, COVID's really inside me, working its evil magic, despite the best efforts of Captain Caveman.

"I guess I'm okay," I said. "Better than in the night, anyway." I looked at the name badge above her right breast pocket. "To be honest, Julia, I don't remember much about it. What happened to me?"

"The doctor'll be doing his rounds mid-morning. I'm sure he'll be able to tell you then."

According to the clock above the nurses' station on the side wall of our six-bed bay, the breakfast that Alan mentioned arrived shortly after seven. The guy wheeling the trolley introduced himself as the ward host, Michael, which was confirmed by his name badge.

"They told me you'd joined us in the night," he said. "So I've brought you some breakfast. We couldn't have you going hungry, now could we? If there's anything you're not keen on, I can change it for you." He tapped the side of his nose. "But I've brought you the best."

The ubiquitous face mask made it difficult to guess his age, but the spiky blond haircut with its textured top and short tapered fade on the sides put him anywhere from late teens to late twenties.

He took a selection of plates and bowls containing Greek yoghurt, mixed berries with melon, and whole wheat toast, along with coffee, off the trolley and placed them on my bedside table ("The coffee's decaf," he informed me. I informed him what he could do with his decaf. He laughed, and said he'd pour me a proper one from the pot. I said I'd have it black, please).

"The lunch menu's there," he indicated a sheet and pencil he'd left on the table alongside my breakfast. "I'll collect it when I come for the pots later."

Alan and my fellow patients wearing oxygen masks took them off for breakfast, but I could see they couldn't breathe too well without them. It was a tiny bit harder than normal for me to swallow with the cannula pushing oxygen up my nose all the time. And, of course, my lack of taste and smell meant I may just as well have been eating cardboard.

After breakfast, Julia asked if I'd like to get up and sit in my chair for a while, although she said I would need to be back in bed when the doctor called in on his rounds at about 10 o'clock.

Once I'd got my dressing gown on and was in the chair I rummaged around in my bag to see what Janice had packed for me. Yes, she's put my Kindle in, and remembered the charger.

But I didn't get the chance to lose myself in fiction. All six of us were now in the chairs next to our beds, and Alan seemed keen to pick up the conversation which Julia had stopped after just one word earlier.

"So," he repeated, "as I was saying before I was so rudely interrupted." He cocked his head towards Julia sitting at the nurses' workstation. "Welcome to The Panters Club."

That rather took me aback. "The what?"

"Just listen to us." He held his upright forefinger to the outside of his mask in front of his lips. All I heard was the hum of machinery and all six of us drawing noisy breaths.

"Ah." Realisation dawned. "The Wheezers Club would probably be more appropriate," I said.

"Name's already gone," he said. "The Florence Ward downstairs took it."

Julia spun around in her chair. "Don't encourage him. We haven't even got a Florence Ward."

"Spoilsport," said Alan. "Anyway, panters we are, each and every one of us."

"Are you sure Wheezers has gone?" asked the guy directly opposite me. "That sounds better than Panters."

"Aye, it does," came a strong Scottish brogue from his neighbour. "I think I'd rather be a Wheezer, too. More power to your elbow, son, and lang may yer lum reek."

That made me smile. I hadn't come across that good old Scottish expression for years, and the first time I heard it, as a 12-year-old, Mum had to explain it literally translated as 'long may your chimney smoke,' and was the Scottish way of wishing someone a long and healthy life. We were on holiday in Cornwall and befriended an elderly Scottish couple staying at the same hotel. He said it to us as we were leaving at the end of the holiday. On the button at that time, but just a tad ironic now.

"I'm Jock, by the way. Well, I'm not, but that's what these bawbags call me on account of my fine North of the border heritage."

"Let's pretend we're all on a training course," said Alan. "You know those childish introductions the trainers always make us play? Jock's already nibbled my biscuit on that one, so we can leave him out. And you know I'm Alan, because Julia nibbled my biscuit about that, too. So, let's start with Iain over here." He indicated the patient in the end bed, opposite his. "Iain, tell our new Panter your name."

I can see my time here's going to be a laugh a minute if my breathing can handle it. Oh, and 'nibbled my biscuit'! I love that. Never heard it before, but I'm so going to nick it.

"I hate going first," said Iain. "I'm going to pass the buck to Mohammed."

"Don't tell him your name, Mohammed," quipped Jock.

"Don't worry, I won't. I'm too shy," said the man in the bed to my left. "I'm staying in the background. Which just leaves Adil." Adil, opposite me, raised a hand. "Hello, fellow Wheezer."

"Good to meet you all, Wheezers and Panters alike," I said. "I'm Simon."

"Says who?" asked Alan, with a 'come on' waving of both hands, reminiscent of a football manager encouraging the crowd to get behind his team.

Four voices spoke in unison: "Simon says."

"Simon says 'put your hands on your head.'"

This was going to be a long morning.

Just before quarter to ten Julia unlocked a cupboard and started putting tablets into small, clear plastic cups.

"Aye, aye, it's the mid-morning drug squad," said Jock.

"And not a moment too soon," said Adil. "It's been four hours since you woke me up for the last lot and I'm starting to feel withdrawal symptoms. I need my fix."

"You do realise she only woke you to give you a sleeping pill," Alan told him.

Julia passed a cup to Alan. "You be quiet and take your medicine for me like a good little boy." She went on to give medication to the other four, but there was nothing for me.

"What about me?" I asked. "I guess I'm not as important as the others. Is that it?"

She laughed. "Don't you start. You've only been here five minutes and already these reprobates are rubbing off on you."

"That's one of the symptoms of COVID," I told her. "It's highly contagious. You only have to be around someone for a few moments to catch their humour."

She looked at me over the top of her glasses. "Is that so?"

"It is so," said Alan. "And I'll tell you why. Simon says. That's why."

Jock put down his cup after swallowing the medication. "Simon says 'you will all laugh.'"

"You'll all be laughing on the other side of your faces when we add a daily enema to your medication routine."

"Don't give me that shit, Julia. You know you love us really."

"You know what they say, Jock—you hurt the ones you love."

We made a good team and I was determined not to be

outshone. "Is that why you're not giving me any medication, because you love me?"

"You'll get yours soon enough," she told me with a complete poker face.

Hhmmm. Which way do I take that?

"The doctor will be with you soon. I'm sure he'll explain everything."

Julia was right about that. She got us all back in bed for ten o'clock when Dr. Dean Nicholls led an entourage of four into our bay.

He pulled the curtains all around my bed and unclipped my notes from the rail at the bottom. "Good morning, Simon, how are you feeling now?"

"Morning, Doctor. A little better than last night, thank you. At least I can breathe easier now."

"Good to hear that." He studied the notes for a moment. "We were a little concerned when you came in because your breathing had changed twice. You were struggling for breath at home, which eased when the paramedics put you on oxygen. But you had another flare-up in the ambulance and they had to increase the oxygen level.

"Once you were on the ward we decided to start you off on the standard nasal cannula that you're using now. It's delivering an oxygen concentration of 35 percent at the rate of five litres a minute. If you start struggling again, there are a few options open to us—we can switch you to a high-flow cannula, or a variety of oxygen facemasks. But you're stable now."

I wanted to ask for how long, but it could only ever be a rhetorical question. Health professionals are many things and can seem to work miracles sometimes, but gazing into a crystal ball isn't one of them. COVID seems to affect different people in different ways, and I guess there's no way he could predict anything.

What he could do, however, was tell me their plans for keeping me as safe as possible while my body fought off the virus. So I opted for a different line of questioning and hoped I didn't come over too much like a journalist.

"What's COVID doing to my body, and what's going to happen to me while I'm in here?"

Doctor Nicholls raised his eyebrows. I wish I could see his facial expression behind the medical mask. "COVID-19's predominantly a respiratory illness," he began a little hesitantly. Maybe I'd thrown him off his well-rehearsed track. "In a nutshell, during your time in hospital, we'll be supplementing your oxygen intake to give your body time to build up resistance to the infection and fight it off."

He looked down at my notes again. "You don't have any known underlying health conditions, such as lung or heart disease, diabetes, or conditions that affect your immune system, so that's all on the positive side."

Doctor Nicholls ran through my treatment regime and showed me how to see for myself what my oxygen saturation levels were on the wall panel. "The paramedics stabilised you at 88, and we've got you up to 95 now," he said. "We're a little concerned that they dropped quickly to what I'm afraid to say was a worrying level in the ambulance, so we'll be keeping a close eye on them, but if you start to feel ill again, or see the level drop, press your emergency button straight away."

As soon as Doctor Nicholls opened my curtains and moved on to Mohammed I FaceTimed Janice.

When her face appeared on my screen her red-rimmed eyes showed a hint of puffiness beneath them, and I could tell she was trying to hold back tears.

"Morning, my darling," I said.

"It's horrible here without you." No preamble from her. Just straight in. But, that's Janice for you. "I love you, and miss you so much. How've you been in the night?" Now her tears came.

This was going to be harder than I thought.

"Love you, too." My turn to try and hold back the tears. "It's not so bad in here. I'm doing fine. You should have seen the breakfast I had. Not that I could smell or taste any of it. And the other guys on the ward are great. We're going to…"

A laugh cut through her sobs. "Now you're gabbling. Have they given you double the dose of medication?"

I laughed, too. They say it's the best medicine, even though it may have been more for Janice's benefit than mine. "I've seen the doctor and he said my breathing's stabilised now. Look." I pointed to the cannula. "I'm not even on a full oxygen mask. And the doctor said I can take it out when I need to go to the toilet. Some of the guys in here have to be hooked up to it all the time, except when they're eating. They've even got an extra long tube so they can keep taking oxygen in when they go to the toilet."

Several days passed with the same routine: I awoke, ate, joked with the lads, FaceTimed Janice, FaceTimed Claire, FaceTimed Hannah, and was constantly poked, prodded and checked (well, not literally poked and prodded—much of the checking was done by the nurse inspecting the readouts on the machines, but by now my whole body was aching all the time), and I was so tired I almost felt like I was sleeping even when awake.

And then, shortly after England waved goodbye to March 2020—the month COVID really made us all sit up and take notice—I died.

7

Buddies

Late March 2020, Andrew

Doctor Andrew Moore needed a quick break from the time-consuming task of proning COVID patients in Poolswood General Hospital's Intensive Care Unit.

As soon as he entered the staff coffee lounge he scanned the room slowly and deliberately, seeing the same look on everyone's faces. Haunted and drawn, with naked fear etched into that locked expression and lurking behind their eyes. It was regular and expected nowadays, and had been for the last four weeks.

He hadn't thought today would be any different. But there was always hope.

In the early days, it had never been anything more than a somewhat embarrassed, almost surreptitious, glance. And he told himself at the time that this was before the floodgates were due to open and the predicted wave of seriously ill patients would push the already under-resourced National Health Service to breaking point. He recalled the first time he noticed a powerful sense of trepidation amongst his colleagues. He'd just come from another afternoon dry run with his 'buddy' in the special station set up outside the ICU. It was part of COVID operational plans drawn up for the hospital with the help of the military. When the time came, and sure as God made little green apples the time would come, they needed to be ready.

The lounge had seemed quieter than usual, perhaps too quiet. Normally it would be alive with a variety of conversations, some conducted in the same hushed tones they'd have used to arrange secret assignations, and some far more raucous and loud as if discussing the outcome of previously attended trysts. Today there were no huddled groups. Hardly anyone was talking. They simply cradled coffee mugs or raised slices of cake or biscuits to their mouths with mechanical, robotic movements.

Furrowed lines blemished pale foreheads, and the beginnings of dark circles were visible around the eyes. Had any of that been there on his colleagues' faces before, and he simply hadn't noticed?

Sky News was on in the background, the presenter talking about the oncoming COVID storm. While some of Andrew's colleagues stared blankly at the wall-mounted TV screen, no one appeared to be really watching or taking it in.

As he looked around the small, tight-knit group who had grown to be more than just colleagues over the years, and who he now regarded as friends, the lounge positively oozed worry, and he wondered if his face reflected the same. He told himself he was simply checking that his colleagues were coping. Or not, as the case may be. The nagging feeling at the back of his mind hinted, though, that perhaps it was more for his own mental health, to know that everyone else was starting to struggle, too, and that he wasn't alone in this fight.

Originally he thought the 'buddy system' instigated under military guidelines by the hospital's Chief Executive, Maggie Bricknell, was a waste of time. She's only been in the job six months, he thought when he read her email. What does she know about anything, sitting up there in her ivory tower on a salary of £121,000? And that was another thing. An email. A fucking email. She didn't even afford him and the team the professional courtesy of telling them face-to-face. Not even a phone call, or via the technological wunderkind of Zoom that was fast making its mark amongst the corporate wallahs.

He was proud of the fact that all 19 years of his NHS career had been spent as a front-line doctor. After all, that was why he'd chosen this path, to help people, and he always spoke directly to them face to face, whether he was delivering good news or bad news. He didn't hide behind emails. In his experience administrators and bean counters, particularly in the NHS, were as far removed from reality as it was possible to be, and more concerned with spreadsheets and targets than about patient welfare. His friends working in the commercial sector told him it was the same everywhere, profit before people every time. It drove him absolutely batshit, and he vowed he would always oppose bureaucracy and its pointless directives which appeared to only be there to keep pen pushers in work.

But each time they rehearsed the scenarios, the more he began to realise there may be some value to Maggie Bricknell's buddy decree. The clincher came when he spotted that his buddy, nurse Emma Grassmere, hadn't taped her glove properly.

It had been the first day back on duty for both of them after some much-needed rest time. "Did you see those awful pictures coming out of Wuhan on the news last night?" she asked, as she pulled on her long-sleeved fluid-resistant blue gown.

"Awful," he said. "And Lombardy's getting bad, too."

Next came her white FFP3 respirator mask, goggles similar to those worn on factory floors and building sites, and full face shield visors capped by flexible head protectors. Finally, she hitched up the long-cuffed gloves and started taping the left one to her sleeve.

"Andrew," she said, somewhat hesitantly. "Can I ask you something?"

"Of course. But you do know I'm married? And you've missed your Leap Year chance. February 29ᵗʰ has been and gone." Before the World Health Organisation declared COVID-19 a pandemic a few days earlier, Doctor Andrew Moore had not been known for his humour, but recently the team of critical care nurses, advanced practitioners, physiotherapists, support technicians, and ward clerks saw a whole new side to him.

He wouldn't call his transformation into a budding comedian a Road to Damascus moment, as it had been building for a while, but thinking about it, he could perhaps trace its origins back to the day when he first noticed the worried faces in the coffee lounge. He started to become more aware that the laugh or cry syndrome—the distant relative of the fight or flight release of adrenaline—needed careful attention. For years his stiff-upper-lip approach kept him at arm's length from the only way many front-line medical practitioners could get through their regular package of death and despair, which was laughing and making jokes. The light slowly dawned that humour between medical professionals wasn't disrespectful or sacrilege, but was a necessary coping strategy for sound mental health, especially in the face of what was forecast for the coming weeks and months.

"Damn," said Emma. "Do you mean to say I've got to wait until 2024? COVID may have got us by then. If so, then let's eat, drink and be merry, for we know not what rigours the slings and arrows of COVID's outrageous fortune may inflict on us. And in that sleep, if we perchance to dream will we awake nobler in the mind?"

"Ay, there's the rub, methinks we're bastardising Shakespeare too much now, though." Andrew fell silent then.

Even though her eyes were only visible through the goggles and visor, he knew the pain they would be reflecting. Sometimes you didn't need to see through them to look into someone's soul. Sometimes you just knew. It was the pain they were all feeling ever since COVID started knocking Brexit and, indeed, everything else, off the news agenda, and the ICU staff quickly realised they were going to be on the front line of a battle, the likes of which had never been seen before throughout the world.

"How many of us will still be here in three months, Andrew? In six months? In a year?"

Even though that very question had been bubbling away in his own mind for some time, a shake of his head was the only answer he could give. Was the Hippocratic oath really intended to cover something like COVID? He and his colleagues had responsibilities beyond the hospital. They had loving and caring families, who should surely come before the words of an ancient parchment. In this time of a worldwide crisis, wasn't family more important?

He'd asked himself time and again whether they were doctors and nurses first, or sons, daughters, partners, mothers and fathers first. The answer was the same every time, just as no doubt it would continue to be, no matter how many times he asked. Doctors and nurses. Always doctors and nurses.

"It's in the lap of the Gods, Emma. All we can do is our best for the patients, and stay as safe as we can ourselves. We owe it to the patients, but we also owe it to our families to keep them safe, too."

This may have been a dry run, but as Emma started to move towards the door to the ward, he threw up a silent prayer of thanks for Maggie Bricknell's buddy system where suiting up was always done in pairs to ensure each other's PPE had been put on correctly.

"Emma, you've not taped your right glove."

These makeshift hazmat suits are only as good as how we don them, he thought. His words of a few seconds ago rang again in his ears: We also owe it to our families to keep them safe, and to do that we've got to keep ourselves safe. We can't afford to give COVID an inch, or it'll take a fucking mile.

And now, fresh from proning just a third of the unit's patients to begin 16 hours on their stomachs, he looked at his nine medical colleagues sitting around the tables with the strain clearly showing on their faces as usual, and recalled that conversation with Emma.

Indeed, he thought. How many of us will still be here in three months? In six months? In a year?

Resuscitation

April 1st, 2020, Andrew

Andrew was dreaming of a COVID-free world.

Not a world where COVID had huffed and puffed and blown many people's houses down before disappearing as quickly as it came, but a world where COVID had never existed. A world that slipped from 2019 through January, February, and March 2020 without the phrases 'Coronavirus disease 2019' and 'severe acute respiratory syndrome coronavirus 2' ever appearing in news reports or instilling unease, anxiety and fear in most of the world's population.

He hovered above Poolswood General Hospital, looking down through the roof into the Intensive Care Unit as if he had X-ray vision (it suddenly dawned on him in that strange way it often does in dreams, that an X-ray machine was floating alongside him and he was looking through it into the ward). Every bed was empty. He turned the machine to look into all the other wards in turn. They, too, were empty. No patients. No staff. The hospital was deserted.

He smiled, thinking of the disease and illness-free zone that Poolswood had become. Flying higher, he focused the X-ray machine on other hospitals throughout Britain. All empty. Then higher still, until the curve of the Earth was clearly visible beneath him. Now he was looking into houses, apartments, hotels, offices, and factories across Europe. All empty. Empty of people, anyway. Dogs, cats, parrots, budgies, gerbils, hamsters, and rabbits all stared back up at him from their homes.

Horses, cows, pigs, sheep, and other animals roamed the fields.

He flew to the other side of the world, where the X-ray machine showed him the same picture. Had every human being disappeared off the face of the Earth? Was this COVID's legacy?

Now he was back above Britain and dropping towards Poolswood Hospital again. The animals all called to him in their own language, but he clearly understood that their barking, meowing, neighing, bleating, squawking, and mooing were saying the same thing: "Aprilfool, Aprilfool." The words combined into one note. Then another and another. The repeated note became an insistent ringing in his ears.

Yes, it was an April Fool, he mused. The thought of a COVID-free Earth was just that: an April Fool. COVID existed outside his dreamworld. It was there, in reality. Just as real as that repeating sequence of notes assaulting his ears. Which he realised was the shrill tone of the emergency 2222 internal call.

Snapping awake, he reached out for the receiver. "Andrew Moore."

A voice came loud and urgent down the line: "Medical Emergency Team to Marie Curie Ward. Patient going into cardiac arrest. I repeat. Patient going into cardiac arrest."

"Stand by. We're on our way."

He looked across to where Emma had been catnapping in the chair opposite, and saw she had also been dragged awake by the phone. At least they'd managed a few moments of sleep during their break. "Cardiac arrest on Marie Curie Ward," he told her.

They donned their full set of Personal Protection Equipment within moments, in the special station set up just outside the ICU, and were heading to the door when the emergency phone rang again. Emma went to pick it up, but Andrew beat her to it: "ICU."

"My patient in cardiac arrest is now flat-lining." It was the same voice as before. "Urgent assistance required immediately in Marie Curie Ward."

"We're kitted up and on our way," he told the caller. "We'll be with you in two minutes."

He turned to Emma who was holding the door open for him. "Marie Curie Ward again. Their cardiac arrest patient's flat-lining."

The first thing he saw when they burst through the door into the six-bay ward were two patients standing outside the fully drawn curtains around the middle bed on the left. "In there, Doctor," one of them told him, somewhat needlessly.

Andrew pushed his way through the curtains to where he saw April Karinski pumping on Simon Reynolds' chest. "Keep going while I get the defibrillator set up," he shouted to her.

She mouthed a number with each compression. "27. 28. 29. 30." Then she reached for the Ambu Bag Valve Mask again, placing the clear plastic face covering over his mouth, and squeezed the self-inflating bag connected to it. Air was forced into Simon's lungs.

"Very little response," she called to Andrew.

Andrew and Emma fetched the ward defibrillator over to the bed, pressed the green button to switch it on, and removed the pads from the bottom of the device. While April continued to pump Simon's heart, Emma peeled the sticky label off the first pad and fastened it to the upper right side of his chest. She placed the second pad on his stomach below the left armpit and stepped back. The ECG readout analysing his heart told Andrew a shockable rhythm was present.

"There's enough," he said. "You've brought him back from flatlining. Carry on compressions, April. Charging to 150."

Then: "Clear. Shocking." And pressed the shock button. Simon's body arched for a second or two, and an automated, robotic voice came from the defibrillator: "Shock delivered," followed by a short bleep, and: "Begin CPR now."

"Straight back on the chest, please," Andrew instructed April. "Thirty compressions to two ventilations for a further two minutes."

He had carried out this routine literally thousands of times during his career, and many people walking the Earth owed their lives to him, but he was acutely aware that his success rate had plummeted since the pandemic struck. Some patients couldn't be resuscitated during CPR, while many who had and were taken into critical care in induced comas, later died in ICU. The death toll was rising.

At the back of his mind, he wasn't hopeful about this patient, but perhaps that was just natural weariness and an impending sense of doom which he felt may be facing the entire planet.

He looked across at April's pathetically inadequate PPE— the flimsy plastic apron, which he thought quite frankly was much like someone would wear if they were selling fish in a supermarket, and the standard disposable blue surgical mask of the type that was becoming ubiquitous everywhere. And that was it. At least intensive care staff had sturdier equipment which would provide a little more immediate protection. He glanced at April's profile as she continued to count while pumping: "15, 16, 17."

If we're still terrified, with our higher grade protection, how must medical ward staff like April be feeling? he wondered. *Especially when we swan in, intubate a patient and whisk them off to ICU in what are almost HAZMAT suits? We're operating with the grace of God. They're working with just hope and a prayer.*

"Emma, after the next shock can you take over the compression cycle, please? April, ring 2222 again and tell them we're running the Advanced Life Support algorithm and need the rest of the Medical Emergency Team here. We may need to intubate the patient and put him into an induced coma."

He wasn't counting the number of resuscitation rounds they carried out, but it must have been at least five before he felt a faint pulse, indicating they'd shocked Simon's heart into beating again and blood resumed its journey around his body.

"He's back, but still not breathing. We need to intubate

immediately."

Andrew stood back while anaesthetist Dr. Hilary Sutton administered muscle relaxants into a vein through one of the cannulae that had been feeding a constant cycle of medication into Simon's arm for the last few days. Now, it acted as a swift entry point at the start of the procedure to induce a coma. Again, bread and butter work for the experienced critical care team, but, watching her in action, Andrew felt, as he had every time they'd performed it recently, that it was now a world away from pre-COVID hospital life.

He rolled Simon's bed away from the wall and stood behind it. Emma opened Simon's mouth and inserted a plastic guard, slotting it into place over his teeth, before switching on the laryngoscope's light and pressing down on Simon's tongue with the blade, clearing a pathway for Andrew to gently guide the tube into his throat, and advance it further into his airway.

When the tube was perfectly situated to force air from a mechanical ventilator into Simon's lungs, he inflated a small balloon that would secure it in place and prevent air from escaping. Where the tube snaked out of Simon's mouth, he fastened it to his skin with tape and connected the end to the ventilator.

"He's ready," said Andrew. "Let's get him to Intensive Care."

Four hours later Andrew was in a small office next to the ICU with Simon Reynolds' medical records pulled up on the computer screen in front of him. After reading them he concluded that this case was one of those mysteries of COVID-19. A relatively fit and healthy 56-year-old, he mused. The fact that he was permanently on blood thinners after a dangerous blood clot on his lung a few years ago should be offering additional protection; only a touch overweight, and no underlying medical conditions that may have accelerated the COVID virus. And yet, there he was, having gone into cardiac arrest after Hypoxia deprived his body of an adequate oxygen supply at the tissue level.

He picked up the phone and dialled Janice Reynolds' mobile number.

"Mrs. Reynolds," he said when she answered on the fourth ring. "I'm Doctor Andrew Moore, from Poolswood General Hospital." There was a sharp intake of breath at the other end.

"Oh God," she said. "What's happened? Is Simon alright?"

"He's stable now, but his condition suddenly deteriorated overnight and we've placed him on a mechanical ventilator to assist with his breathing."

"Oh God," she said again. "Can I talk to him?"

This was always the difficult part, he thought. "I'm afraid you're not going to be able to speak with him for a while." Do this as gently as possible. "As you know, he'd been responding well to oxygen flow through a nasal cannula. He was a little breathless, but it hadn't been getting worse. Unfortunately, though, his oxygen levels suddenly dropped considerably overnight, and he went into cardiac arrest."

That elicited the Oh God hat trick from Janice, and then she asked: "He's had a heart attack?"

"No, he hasn't. And it's important to remember that."

"But you said..."

"Simon's heart malfunctioned and suddenly stopped beating unexpectedly. That's cardiac arrest. We got his heart going again with CPR—cardiopulmonary resuscitation— almost immediately. But a heart attack's different. That happens when blood flow to the heart is blocked. You could say a heart attack is a circulation problem, and sudden cardiac arrest is an electrical problem.

"All this happened because he wasn't able to breathe properly, and that was caused by an escalation of his COVID infection. So to help his body recover while he's on the ventilator, we've deliberately put him into a surgical coma."

A sob now from the other end of the phone. "What does that mean? How long will he be in it for?"

"I can answer your first question easily, Mrs. Reynolds. The second one isn't so straightforward, though. What it means, quite simply, is that Simon's body isn't having to do so much work while he's recovering. The machine's breathing for him, so he's focusing all his energy and strength on shaking this virus off and getting better.

"As to how long, though, I like to think it'll just be for a few days, but possibly two to three weeks at most. Generally, we bring someone out of an induced coma as soon as their condition allows for it. We'll keep you informed how he is twice a day."

"But..." She paused. Andrew didn't try to fill the gap. It was a lot for her to take in, out of the blue like this. Especially as Simon's records on the screen in front of him showed he had been making good progress in the few days he'd been on the Marie Curie Ward. She must have thought he was taking the first steps towards recovery and going home. Then this shock. Andrew waited for her to gather her thoughts again.

"How will you bring him out of it?" she asked. For years, he regarded the order they asked the questions to be a good indicator of their state of mind, how they were coping, and perhaps more importantly, how they may cope in the future. Psychologically, he saw this question as showing that Janice Reynolds was already fast-tracking the difficult time her husband faced and was looking ahead to the worst being over.

"We'll bring him out slowly, by reducing the sedation and drugs he's getting. It's a gradual process, so he won't wake up instantly as he does after a night's sleep. It might take a few hours, or even a day or two, depending on how long we need to keep him in the coma, for the drugs to be washed out of his system."

"What treatment is he going to have while he's in the coma? Will he know anything about it, or feel any pain?"

He was used to hearing relatives' words tumble out in this way, almost falling over each other as her brain tried to process everything he was telling her at once. The longer their conversation lasted, the more he expected she'd absorb what he said. "Simon will get the best possible round-the-clock medical care, and we'll monitor him constantly.

"One part of his treatment I should explain in more detail, though, is that we'll be proning him for several hours every day."

She started to say something, but he carried on quickly, anticipating her question. "It means we'll turn him to lie on his stomach, in a 'prone' position, which is better for his lungs than lying on his back. More of the lung expands when a patient's on their stomach, so the ventilator can push more air in with each breath." He paused, waiting to see if she had any more questions about that part of the treatment, then continued, to fill the silence: "Many patients say they don't remember much, if anything, about their stay in Intensive Care," he told her. "So, I don't think he'll know anything about it until we bring him round. And you were asking about pain; while the main purpose of inducing a coma is to give his body time to heal, it also serves to ensure he's free of any pain and discomfort."

"Is it because Simon's seriously ill, or would you normally do something like this?"

Time for more reassurance. Well, he thought, to offer hope anyway. Even if it turns out to be false hope. That earlier feeling about this patient still nagged at the back of his mind. "It's normal practice when we intubate someone, Mrs. Reynolds. It helps to..."

"Sorry, Doctor, what was that word you used? Incubate?"

"No. I said intubate. It means we've put a tube into his mouth and down his airway. It's part of the mechanical ventilation process. The tube's connected to the ventilator which is breathing for him at the moment. If he weren't in a coma he wouldn't be able to tolerate the breathing tube in his throat."

He glanced down again at Simon's notes on the screen. "In a nutshell, the coma will help his recovery by buying time for his body to cope with the infection. The ventilator is doing what his lungs would normally do, which means they have time to heal and massively improve his body's ability to fight off COVID, ready for them to start working on their own again. It's important to remember, though, that this is supportive therapy—it's not a cure in itself—by blowing oxygen into Simon's lungs through the tube that goes through his mouth and into his windpipe. It's keeping him alive long enough for his lungs to get better."

"Can I come in to see him? Would it help if I held his hand and spoke to him?"

Before the first week of March, Andrew thought it must have been at least 18 years since he felt such emotion at a personal and human level when talking to patients or their loved ones. Delivering bad, or simply unpalatable, news with a calm, aloof authority was part of his job, but he always made sure to handle such conversations with empathy and courtesy.

But with more COVID-related deaths mounting up in recent days, and ever more people like Simon Reynolds being placed in induced comas, the deeper essence of what made Andrew human began to take over. The inner humanity that lay at his very core tugged just a little harder at his heartstrings each time he had to pass on bad news. In the nine days since lockdown started, the strain of denying relatives the chance to hold their loved one's hand just one last time, to be with them as they took their final gasping breath so they didn't have to die with only a nurse comforting them—and only then, if the nurse weren't needed somewhere else—was becoming intolerable. Not only for Andrew but for Emma, for April, for Julia, for Hilary. For all front-line staff at the hospital.

And here he was, about to deny another distraught wife the basic human right of being with her critically ill husband at a time when they both needed each other the most. Each time he told a partner, parent, son or daughter, the extent of their loved one's condition, he could see how overwhelming, frightening and scary it was, with numerous questions running through their minds. Some questions were more pertinent than others. Some were harder to answer than others, especially now with COVID lockdown restrictions biting.

Janice Reynolds had just asked one of those questions. Normally Andrew would have said to come in and sit with Simon, hold his hand, and talk to him, just as she'd asked. He always used to tell patients' relatives: "We often hear that while they don't remember any details about their time in a coma, they have a sense that someone had been talking to them and touching them. They knew they weren't alone. So be with them, even if they seem to be totally unconscious."

He couldn't now, though. And that hurt. Death was part of his job (too big a part, if truth be told), but the fear of spreading COVID made it even harder on front-line staff now and was adding emotion to the equation in bucketloads.

"I'm afraid COVID regulations mean you can't, Mrs. Reynolds," he said as gently as he could.

The thought was always there as to how many more families will be devastated by not being with their loved ones as the pandemic picked up apace. Especially at the end. *Let's hope to God it doesn't come to that with Simon. But if it does, there's only one way she can 'be there' with him.* By video; just as he'd been inspired to use video to let novelist Imogen Lambert's family say goodbye to her.

Less than 24 hours after Imogen was rushed in it became clear that her lungs were damaged beyond repair. He'd never seen such a quick and devastatingly powerful attack. He hadn't been on duty when she was admitted and settled into the Alderman Branning room which had been set up as an additional Intensive Care Unit, but just hours later he could hardly believe he was looking at X-ray images and data of a woman who was completely fit and healthy the previous day.

"We don't have a lot of hope that Imogen's lungs will be able to recover from the extremely severe damage they've suffered in such a short time from Coronavirus," he told her husband and son when he made his initial telephone call to them. "She's on non-invasive ventilation, which means a ventilator is feeding oxygen into her through a mask fastened around her face, but that's only helping slightly, and is very much in the short term. The problem is, that her lungs haven't collapsed," he said. "They're become very stiff, rather like an old sponge that won't work anymore, so no amount of oxygen is going to sustain her.

"We're trying last-ditch efforts right now to give her some high-dose steroids to see if we can make her lungs any less stiff. Unfortunately, if they don't work, there's nothing else we can do to help her. I really would suggest that, unfortunately, as a family, you should now be preparing for the worst."

He braced himself for the inevitable question, and here it was, from her son: "Can we come and be with her?"

"I'm so sorry, Mr. Lambert, you can't. Because of the risk of contagion, the Government's regulations mean family members aren't being allowed into the Intensive Care Unit."

Two days after that conversation Andrew had looked around the small ward, fully understanding how distressing it must be for Imogen. As a novelist, her imagination would be running riot with what was going on around her and in her own body. The fear in her eyes was almost tangible as if she realised (and something told him she probably did) that the dragging, rasping sound accompanying every hard-earned, laboured breath indicated the final one wasn't too far away.

He'd only ordered the latest Michael Peacefire novel a few days ago from Amazon after hearing part of her interview with Simon Reynolds on Poolswood Sound while driving to start a new round of sleeping-in shifts at the hospital. His wife told him later that a package had arrived for him, which would be waiting unopened on the hall table at home. And now both were under his care, critically ill; Imogen at death's door, with Simon probably not far behind. Reading her book would hold its own special poignancy for him.

Speaking was almost impossible for her, but she'd still be able to hear the constant beeping and whirring of the machines keeping the four patients alive in the small room. He had already explained she wouldn't be placed in an induced coma as it couldn't help her lungs recover, but seeing the other three were intubated meant she'd be aware she was the only one not being placed in a coma. He wondered if that would tell her just how ill she really was, or would it throw her a lifebelt of thinking she wasn't as bad as they were?

The end of her life was fast approaching and would be spent apart from her husband and son. Alone, except for the medical staff who could provide the best possible physical care to ease her passing, but couldn't give the love and emotional comfort of her family. There'd be no one to hold her hand, to tell her they love her and they'll all be together again someday in the next world. No one to talk about cherished holidays, birthdays, and anniversaries, or those wonderful days when her son was born, his first day at school, grazed knees, and bringing his first girlfriend home. Those memories made up her family life, but she'd still need to hear the stories about them from her loved ones to ease her final moments.

The nurse currently changing an intravenous drip on one of the other patients in the bay, was, like him, in full PPE, as were all staff in both the original ICU and hastily set-up makeshift units. He knew that would be another frightening element for Imogen, as the scene of complex medical equipment could almost have come from a horror sci-fi movie where fully suited-up alien space travellers conducted experiments on their abduction victims.

That image in his mind from some long-forgotten video triggered a thought. *Video.* Maybe there was something he could do, after all, to let her family be there...not physically in the flesh, but the next best thing. A video call.

He went through into the small office adjacent to the ward. A few moments later he looked across at his colleague as they viewed the latest data together, and shook his head. "The steroids aren't working at all."

"I agree," said Dr Abayomi Mansour. "I'm afraid she's only got hours left, if that."

Andrew sighed long and loud. "I'll tell the family. But let me run something past you first."

Tears streamed down Allan Lambert and his son Christian's faces as Andrew positioned his iPad on Imogen's bed table so she could see them both onscreen.

Allan's hand covered his mouth, then he lowered it. "Hello, my darling."

It tore at Andrew's heart as Imogen weakly tried to wave. "Hello," she managed to croak. "I love you both." He realised from the data he'd been looking at moments earlier that the physical effort of producing those words would have been extremely difficult for her.

"You're a warrior, Mum," sobbed Christian. "I miss you so much already."

"We're here for you, my angel," said Allan. "My beautiful Imogen, we're both begging to God to bring you safely through this."

A slight movement from Imogen's hand. "No." It almost sounded like a door creaking open in an old-fashioned haunted house horror movie. "I'm done." Her three words fired up a torrent of coughing, and it was a full minute before she was able to conjure more words and make herself understood. "Going. Love you. Goodbye, my treasures. Want to hug."

"Mum." Christian's lip trembled as more tears came and he sniffed hard to try and quell the lump in his throat. "I want to hug you, too, and kiss you. Hold your hand and touch you when I tell you how much I love you."

"My wonderful angel." Fighting his emotions, Allan

screwed his face up with a faint shake of his head.

No one should have to go through this on video, Andrew thought violently to himself. This is all wrong. It shouldn't be happening like this. He was a hardened medic and knew such conversations happened the world over, all the time. But not on video. These final precious moments should be a private, personal time, full of touching and hugging, maybe tears dropping from faces hovering above the patient onto their hands or the bed.

COVID wasn't only stealing lives, it was stealing dignity and comfort from the dying, while feeding their relatives the guilt of not being there in their loved ones' final moments. This meagre solution was all he could offer, but he vowed to himself he'd offer it to every end-of-life patient in his care until the pandemic was over and humanity in death could be restored.

Imogen's wheezing became louder while every breath slowed even further, as if being pulled from the rarified atmosphere of mountain tops, the air thinning with each ascending step, heading towards a total vacuum.

Andrew made sure his iPad was secured in place and wouldn't move. "I'll leave you to it," he said and quietly slipped out of the bay knowing he'd be back within minutes to gently close Imogen's eyes and convey his sincere condolences to Allan and Christian.

His thoughts about Imogen and her family dissolved and he snapped back to the present, aware that Janice had just spoken. "Sorry, Mrs. Reynolds, what did you say?"

"I said I'm happy to take the risk of catching COVID. I just want to come in and be with him. I'll wear whatever protective clothes I need to."

It sounded so reasonable when she put it like that, but nothing could prepare anyone for the sheer horror of what he knew COVID is capable of. If she'd seen the fear in patients' eyes as they struggled to draw a breath—if she knew how fast it could devastate a fit and healthy woman like Imogen Lambert—if she'd experienced the trauma that even hardened critical care staff had faced in recent weeks, would she still be prepared to take that risk?

The decision was out of his hands, anyway. Which was perhaps just as well, because left to his own devices he may have been tempted to say yes.

"Unfortunately it's not that simple. You could be carrying the virus yourself and spreading it in the hospital. We just can't afford to take the risk. That's why the regulations have been brought in. I'm so sorry, but I've got to say no.

"When we bring him out of the coma and he's able to talk, I'll set up a video call for you. I'm sure he'd like that."

Let's just hope we get to that stage.

For the first time, he thought about the connection between Simon and Imogen. Both were fit and healthy, both middle-aged, so not in what the Government classed as a vulnerable group. They'd been together in what he assumed would have been a confined studio with no natural airflow when Simon interviewed her about her new book. Maybe they both caught COVID from someone else there. Maybe one already had it and passed it to the other.

It seemed to him like another twist in the steep learning curve COVID was bringing to bear on the world—nothing about it is the norm. So many maybes, so many terrible possibilities.

8

Coma

April 1st, 2020, Simon

Before April Karinski saw I was going into cardiac arrest, I lay in a wonderfully warm, comforting state for a few moments, drifting in and out of sleep, only partially aware of my surroundings but becoming increasingly mindful of how clammy and sticky I was, and how much I was sweating. On top of that, a dull ache deep in my ribcage bubbled closer to the surface with each rasping breath.

As the raft on which I was floating through the sea of slumber gently sloped further and further, tipping me towards the edge, I couldn't hold on to the arms of Morpheus any longer and tumbled into full wakefulness with a metaphorical bump.

But 'full wakefulness' these days isn't what it used to be in the time before COVID. Until March 25th 2020 I'd positively bounce out of bed, frequently well ahead of the alarm, much to Janice's...not annoyance, but definite chagrin, and was downstairs making toast and singing along to the hits belting out on Poolswood Sound's breakfast show when she finally emerged.

Since coming into hospital, waking up reminded me of trying to get my first car started on cold, drizzly October mornings. The manual choke on the ancient Austin A35 enriched the fuel mix in the same way I guess the oxygen fed through the cannula kept my blood count stable, but the spark plugs were always damp, meaning ignition was unpredictable, and even when the engine finally fired up it was accompanied by a cacophony of coughing and spluttering.

That's as good as it's been for the last few days.

My watch showed we were three hours and 58 minutes into the new month, but if I'd expected to wake on April 1st[st] and find COVID was just a cruel hoax, timed to end today with the world screaming that the whole thing had been an elaborate April Fool trick, I was sorely disappointed.

Looking around at what had been my home for the past week, the night light showed everything as it had been when I'd dropped asleep. All six of us in the bay were still hooked up to oxygen, and the background sounds of mechanical whirring and the occasional beep spoke of the wide array of machines at the business end of tubes snaking out of us like tentacles.

COVID was real. I, and the rest of humanity, really had been having a two-month waking nightmare; the world hadn't been playing a trick on us. How I'd have laughed—both with humour and relief—if dear Mother Earth had taken a leaf out of the Poolswood Recorder's book from a few years ago and shouted April Fool at us this morning, and everyone's lives had been rebooted to the default pre-lockdown position.

Although I'd never been much good at biology, I'd take an educated guess that it was my lungs where the hesitant and reluctant breaths were feeding the ache.

That didn't stop me from smiling at the memory of the newspaper's renowned April Fool prank which had been 26 weeks in the making. (Well, I don't have anything else to do, or the energy to do it, even if I did. Memories and thinking comprise the entire Simon Reynolds world right now). It started six months before April 1st[st], in October the previous year actually, when deputy editor Ciaran Weaver published the first of a series of features which he said would look at one village in the county each week in alphabetical order. They started with Aynesbrook and went on to Brastock the following week, then Calerton.

It proved to be an interesting feature over the months, looking at life in those villages, and talking to residents, their local councillors, shopkeepers and pub landlords.

As the weeks wore on, readers were wracking their brains over where they'd go for X and Z. It turned out they cheated ever so slightly for X, featuring Exington, but I guess no one really minded.

So we turned our attention to wondering what they would do for Z in the final feature. Not only were there no villages in the County starting with Z, there weren't even any with that letter in them.

The answer, when it came in the April 1st edition, was a real doozy. There, across the centre page spread, was the village of Zanyness. The 'photos' showed roads and paths going nowhere, and some of the village landmarks were pictured as the Eifell Tower, Hogwarts and the Sphinx. Interviews with residents included Ebenezer Copperfield, Marylou Poppups and the landlady of the Mad Hatter pub, Alicia Wonderhand.

Oh. We'd all been had in the most outrageous way, and readers loved it. I even had Ciaran on my show, talking about how they came up with the idea.

It was certainly more elaborate than the best April Fool trick I'd pulled over the years, and I thought I'd put a bit of effort into that. Since 2013 I've had my own column in a monthly magazine circulating throughout the County. And when the publication date fell on April 1st in 2016, I treated my readers to a little bit of fun:

A new nightclub with a twist is coming to Brastock.

Pranksters will open during the day, to cater for night workers. In other words, a dayclub. What a great idea. I love it. During the early part of my broadcasting career, my hours were 5.30 a.m. to 1.30 p.m., reading the news in the breakfast show, and then the hourly bulletins through to the 15-minute lunchtime programme. But I occasionally had to cover the night shift from midnight to 6 a.m. How I'd have loved to leave the studio and head straight for a dayclub. I was a real raver in those days.

Revelling on the dance floor at a local Brastock venue in the daytime has always eluded those who have to work regular nights. In the past, they've been beavering away to earn a crust while many others are out having a good time at a nightclub.

Instead of spending their off-duty hours watching daytime television, they will now be able to do what day workers have always taken for granted: let off steam and sink a pint or two after a hard day's (OK, in this case, a hard night's) toil.

Local workers are already looking forward to strutting their stuff to their heart's content, anytime in the 12 hours the club will be open from 7 a.m. to 7 p.m. six days a week.

Fears that the club would make too much noise and disrupt lessons at the neighbouring Brastock Primary School have been dismissed by club officials. DJ Mikey James says strict guidelines govern how loud he can play the music—especially as the club has been given permission to keep its windows open on hot summer days.

Only 65 decibels will be allowed to emanate from the building.

Otherwise, if the sound level is higher than that, all

residents within a 100-metre radius of Pranksters will be entitled to a year's free membership, plus unlimited half-price drinks. And it's coming soon.

Look at the first letter of each paragraph in this column to see the date Pranksters will be throwing its doors open for the first time.

The waking brain fog should have started to dissipate by now, but it hadn't. If anything, it was getting thicker and enveloping me in some kind of apathy. I flexed my fingers, but they were clammy and numb, as were my face, neck and arms. And I felt lightheaded. Was it just brain fog? No. That hadn't been too bad this morning. I'd looked at my watch, hadn't I? Seen it was April 1st. Remembered the Poolswood Recorder's brilliant April Fool prank.

Was that today? Or yesterday? I can't focus. Everything's blurry. But I can tell it's not my bedroom. Unfamiliar. Where am I? Where's Janice? Ah. I remember. I've got COVID and moved into the spare bedroom. But those beds opposite me aren't in the spare room.

It's not brain fog. Worse than that. Much worse. Not felt like this before.

Then a harsh ringing begins in my ears. The noise doesn't stop me from drifting off towards sleep again, though. Something deep inside says this isn't right. It shouldn't be happening. The numbness, the sweating, it's all wrong. I flinch and catch my already labouring breath as strong, ghostly fingers suddenly squeeze my chest, sending agonising spasms shooting through my body.

Maybe not my lungs. Maybe my heart.

But at least it snaps me awake. My stomach's churning. Nausea pulls bile up into my throat. I half swallow, half cough. For fuck's sake, what am I doing?

Hospital. Suddenly I remember I'm in hospital. Try to reach out for the emergency button. No need. Julia's pushed her chair back from the nurses' workstation and is rushing over to me. No, not Julia. She's finished her run of night shifts. This is...oh, who is it? What's her name?

Pain radiates along my left arm which falls uselessly off the bed, flopping limply. Each breath's an effort again. Like before. Like at home. Like in the ambulance. Why didn't I spot before that the ringing in my ears isn't in my head? It's coming from the white wall panel controlling my flow of oxygen. Some sort of alarm.

Julia-not-Julia looks down at me above her medical face mask. Then she's back at her desk. Picks up the phone. Punches a four-digit number.

"Medical Emergency Team to Marie Curie Ward. Patient going into cardiac arrest. I repeat. Patient going into cardiac arrest."

I baulk at her words, desperately trying to look around and see which of my fellow patients she's talking about. We can't lose one of the team, Simon says we're all going to survive COVID. Alan, Jock, Adil, Mohammed, Iain and me. The three musketeers times two. All for one and one for all, and all that jazz. No, whichever of them's going into cardiac arrest will simply have to pull through.

It may be the combination of pain and rasping effort to draw every breath which is making me a little dim this morning, but I can't see that any of them are in distress. They're all sleeping like babies, even through the penetrating alarm. The powerful drug in the sleeping pills they gave us at midnight is probably still surfing the wave of blood in their veins.

So why isn't it still doing that in mine?

My befuddled mind's really struggling here. Then a voice pokes through the alarm. Through the fog. Except it's my voice. But only in my head. 'Because they're not having the heart attack, you fuckwit,' the voice tells me. 'You are.'

As if to reiterate what the voice is saying, the paralysing pain in my chest starts to take that crippling metaphor too seriously. Julia-not-Julia's back from her phone call, her face hovers above me, peering down into my eyes. "Simon, can you hear me?" I try to tell her yes I can, but no words come from my mouth. I try to nod, but no movement comes from my head. She reaches for my neck. What's she doing? Is she going to fucking strangle me? My brain tells my arms to stop her, to grab her hand. But it's like talking to a brick wall. My arms apparently don't get the message, as they remain stubbornly still.

Then realisation dawns about her motive. I said I was no good at biology, but at least I know where the carotid artery is, and even though this pain in my chest is exploding like that fucking volcano in Iceland a few years ago—the one which spewed ash into the atmosphere that went halfway round the planet disrupting air travel for days—I know what she's doing. She's not strangling me, she's feeling for a pulse.

Now she's raising my left arm from where it was hanging loosely over the bed and checking for a pulse in my wrist. I can't even move my eyes to look at her. They continue to stare straight up at the ceiling.

An intense tugging sensation begins where the pain is worst—right around my heart, then quickly spreads throughout my body. I feel it everywhere, from my scalp to my toes. Thinking of my toes makes me wonder if the paralysis has hit my legs. The message fires off from my brain, but my legs don't get it. They, too, remain stubbornly immobile. But the sense of tugging continues to pull upwards from them, just as it does from my arms, my chest and my head. It feels as if my face is stretching towards the ceiling.

For the first time, I start to hear a slight slurping noise which increases in intensity as the tugging becomes stronger. It sounds like a wellington boot being pulled out of a gloopy mass of mud on a country walk.

The tugging becomes unbearable, as does the pain. Something's got to give.

I break free with a sudden jolt, and the slurping finishes with a loud pop, reminding me of a childhood pursuit of putting my finger inside my cheek and flicking it out again pretty sharply.

The pain disappears in an instant, and I realise I'm floating freely in the air looking down on my own body, with Julia-not-Julia still feeling for a pulse in my wrist. My body is the epitome of peace and calm lying beneath me in the hospital bed. But nothing else is calm.

My fellow three-times-two musketeers stir, no doubt agitated awake by the relentless alarms on the machines connected to the other me. Julia-not-Julia rushes back to the phone and punches in more digits.

Above her workstation the clock shows 4.10 a.m.

Is this a dream or an hallucination? I'm starting to worry that it may not be. But if that's the case, Julia-not-Julia's next words into the phone should surely be throwing my mind into a panic. "My patient in cardiac arrest is now flat-lining," she said. "Urgent assistance required immediately in Marie Curie Ward." But they don't. Even though she's saying I'm either dead or dying, all I feel is a strange ethereal calmness. There's my body on the bed, and here I am floating in the air, just like in those wonderful flying dreams I love so much.

I feel real. I feel whole. But if the newly released me is up here, what's happening to the other me down there? I really don't care. It's as if I no longer have any connection with the flesh, blood, bone and sinew that's carried the real me, the true essence of Simon Reynolds, through 56 years in that fragile mortal coil.

In the air, I turn and float a little way towards the nurses' workstation hovering almost at ground level now, and pivot to a standing position, with my feet just a couple of inches from the floor.

Julia-not-Julia replaces the phone receiver and rushes back to the me-in-bed, passing straight through the floating me. Whoa! How weird was that? I didn't actually feel a thing, and she showed no indication of being aware of what had just happened, either.

"What's going on?" Alan asks from the next bed. "Is he alright?"

Floating me turns to look across at him as he swings his legs over the edge.

"Stay there," instructs Julia-not-Julia, pulling the curtains all around, cutting the me-in-bed off from my fellow patients' concerned eyes.

She pushes her way back out and gathers up an armful of medical equipment from a cupboard. As she returns to my bed I catch a glimpse of her name badge: April. Surely that's got to be the universe having a laugh. April, trying to save my life on April 1stst. And yet, I watch with a detached fascination, not caring if she's successful or not, as she removes my cannula. This place just seems so right. So peaceful. There's no pain, no feeling. Do I really want to go back into that shell?

She starts pumping fiercely on my chest, counting each one in a whisper. "One, two, three." My body jumped with every compression, and I swear I heard a crack. She's broken a fucking rib. Floating me feels no pain from it, though. No emotion except that peaceful calm.

When she reaches 30, she pulls a contraption out of a bag marked 'Ambu' which reminds me of a large blue lemon attached to a pipe at one end, and a clear plastic mask at the other. She places the mask over my mouth, gripping it tightly, and squeezes the flexible 'lemon,' forcing air into my lungs in a long, slow stream.

My chest rose and fell in time to the airflow. Then it's back to the compressions. 'One, two, three.' Crack. There goes another rib. And I still didn't care.

If it hadn't been for a faint shimmering away to my right, near the door, I'd have probably watched her go through this resuscitation cycle several more times. However, the movement in the air was far more interesting, growing, as it did, to form a large oval around three metres in height and two metres at its widest point. Pale bluish strands of energy radiated out around the edge, but my attention was held rather more by what was inside the oval. It appeared to be the entrance to a tunnel disappearing into the distance, cutting straight through where the wall and door should be. As I floated nearer to it, I heard a faint whooshing sound coming from inside, which got louder as I passed through the rim.

As soon as I was inside, the gravity which I'd been defying in the ward took control again and I immediately dropped down, my feet hitting the ground. The whooshing instantly intensified into a powerful wind, as if some sort of invisible membrane over the entrance had been muffling it.

I stared along the muddy-grey walls of the tunnel as

they stretched away into the distance, trying to see what lay at the end. A tiny pinprick of white light showed through the darkness, drawing me irresistibly towards it. Did I want to go? Or would it be better to stay?

All I know right now is that despite the wind, I've never felt so calm and at peace. I take another step towards the light, fully aware that I'm leaving my Earthly life behind.

Janice's face appears in my mind's eye. Then Claire's. Then Hannah's. Looking back through the pulsating oval doorway into the ward, I see April still pounding relentlessly and rhythmically on my chest, then squeezing the oversized blue lemon to push life-giving air into my lungs. All this makes me want to stay. I turn to face that white pinprick again, and this time I swear it's bigger and nearer, now the size of a coin. The irresistible pull's drawing me away from my family. The white light is calling from afar.

I've never been in a wind tunnel, but I imagine this must be the closest thing to it. The swirling gale seemed to be channelling all around the walls, giving me the feeling that I was standing in the eye of a storm. And I know one thing, Toto, we sure as hell ain't in Kansas anymore.

The maelstrom is slowly pulling the grey walls together behind me, narrowing the portal to cut me off from the ward. Just before the hospital disappeared from view the ward door flew open and an astronaut burst in. At least, that's what the figure resembled in the short time I saw it, with goggles behind a full face visor, a beaky-looking white mask, and a blue gown.

And that was it. The ward blinked out of existence as the grey tunnel walls pulled together like curtains closing on a stage performance. If I were an actor in a story about intrepid explorers being trapped in a tomb by a stone rolling across the entrance, I'd have probably rushed over, hammering on it before adopting the more logical pursuit of looking for a hidden lever or button to open it. As it was, my tranquil sense of mind was clean out of fucks for giving, about the fact that there was no way back, and I simply turned away and started walking towards that mesmerising white light, which was no longer a coin, but now a trashcan lid perhaps only a hundred metres away. Even the wind rushing past my ears had switched to a soothing, rhythmic flow, drawing me along in its wake.

"Welcome, Simon." The soothing voice seemed to come from all around me, accompanied by faint musical chimes in the wind. An intense feeling of pure love flooded through me, just as a number of small glowing orbs materialised ahead, performing an aerial display of synchronised acrobatics, swirling and darting before settling into two regimented lines alongside, almost as if they were a guard of honour guiding me home. Not that I needed much guidance. I increased my pace down the tunnel towards the light.

Vaguely flanking both walls, I saw faint outlines of dimly-glowing figures, also matching my pace. None had form or features, and just for one horrible fleeting second, they evoked memories of when we first began to catch glimpses of the entity back at White Pastures all those years ago. The entity that grew in stature and power, and eventually took my sister.

The feeling passed as swiftly as it came, swallowed in a cocoon of peace and love emanating from the figures and orbs. Each step brought me closer to the realm of white light until I was actually there at the threshold. It was as if I were standing at the edge of a cave which opened out onto a vast brilliantly white cavern of cathedral-like proportions.

The powerful glowing white light illuminated the

extensive depths ahead which stretched out infinitely both to my left and right. But the focal point of its origin appeared to be several hundred metres ahead. From this distance, it looked as if the source itself came from an area roughly the size of the shimmering doorway which I'd passed through moments earlier out of the hospital ward .

The orbs broke away from their regimented ranks alongside me and began circling my head, the ones at the back inching nearer on each orbit, as if trying to urge me forward, out of the grey tunnel. They resumed their linear guard of honour as I took a couple of tentative steps into the new white light realm, and the figures flanking me moved forward in unison.

"Welcome, Simon," the same soothing voice came again. If I'd rated the earlier overwhelming sense of love at ten, the feeling was off the scale a hundredfold now. The powerful spiritual aura surrounding me was all-embracing and closing tighter. I was totally enchanted. Briefly, Janice's face appeared in my mind's eye again before exiting stage left. The vision prompted me to turn and look for the end of the tunnel I'd just come through. It had gone. There was no way back now, even if I'd wanted to. I was discarnately wandering here in this white glowing spiritual haven with only shimmering orbs and formless beings for company, showered in the most amazing love, peace, calm and tranquility I'd ever experienced—certainly nothing like anything remotely possible in the mortal coil on Earth.

Two more things surprised me. The first was that despite being the brightest, whitest light imaginable, none of it hurt my eyes. Maybe pain was banished in heaven's waiting room. Because, make no mistake, that's what this place has to be. No way is it connected with the downstairs destination. I felt the love flooding through me must come from a higher, unifying power.

Unconditional acceptance of this white light realm consumed the new me. Was I glimpsing God, the spirit of Jesus, or formless angels? What spiritual teachings, messages or knowledge lay beyond that light? I picked up speed as I moved closer to it. If this new me still had a beating heart, I have no doubt it would be racing at the anticipation of mystical revelations, messages, new knowledge and perhaps even a prophecy of future events.

The second surprise were the two figures silhouetted against the source of light. I swear they hadn't been there a moment ago. Far from resembling the formless beings which continued to float alongside me, these had definite mass and were becoming more recognisable with each step. Holding hands. One was Grandma, looking as she did in my recent dream, as young as she had been in my childhood. The other figure was much younger. Also female. Silky blonde hair tumbled past her shoulders. Impish eyes. Smiling mouth. Her cheeks showed a trace of blusher and her eyes a hint of misty blue. My long-dead sister, Helen.

Their faces reflected beautiful smiles which lit up my very essence, and peace and love emanated from them in thick waves, washing over me. The initial wonder at seeing them passed almost instantaneously as if being with my two dead relatives was the most natural thing in the universe (I won't say 'in the world' because I'm sure I was no longer in the world but had moved on to a higher, spiritual, plane of existence).

Different laws of physics must rule space here, because I was impossibly closer to the light source now than before Grandma and Helen materialised out of nowhere. When I'd stepped through the gateway into this realm I reckon that shining beacon must have been at least 500 metres away and I'd only taken 100 steps at most.

Now, as preposterous as it would have sounded to my mortal mind, I found myself a mere ten metres from it, with just Grandma and Helen between me and those final few steps to the beginning of my afterlife.

I started to move towards them, but Grandma raised her hand. "Welcome, Simon," she said. Or did she? I heard her words clearly, but her lips hadn't moved at all. That wonderful loving smile was still beaming from her face. "You have much to learn and a lot to do." This time I focus more on where her words are coming from, and I don't think I'm hearing them in the normal way, through my ears. They seem to be directed straight to my consciousness, and I asked myself if it was perhaps some form of mental telepathy.

Grandma's shining eyes locked on mine. "That's exactly right," she told me. "We have no need of the physical ways here."

"You heard my thoughts, my question?" I asked aloud.

Once more, her reply seemed to beam directly to my understanding. "I did." No physical words passed through my ears. Whatever method she used to convey them, her words were certainly hitting home. "Grandma, Helen," I began, again out loud. But what could I say? I should have had a thousand other questions, but I sensed all the answers were inside the light. I just had to cross into it.

All I really wanted to do was rush forward and hug Grandma and Helen, but the next words implanted into my mind stopped me in my tracks.

"Now is not your time to be at one with the cosmos, Simon. You've been summoned to receive a spiritual gift to take back to Earth. You have work to do there. Important work."

Dismay hit me. The sensation of not wanting to go back was overwhelming. I wanted to stay, embrace, be absorbed and merge.

"It was destined long ago that you and I should meet again after I passed over," Grandma told me. "The first was one week ago when I forewarned that we'd be seeing each other again soon."

My dream, I thought. The night I went into hospital.

"That's right, my grandson, except it wasn't a dream. It was a spiritual projection onto the astral plane, to prepare your subconscious for this visit and your gift. Powers are at work that you don't yet understand, but you will."

Those beautiful musical chimes from the tunnel still rang faintly as she spoke, and I realised it was impossible to tell if I heard them in a physical sense or if they were coming directly into my mind as well.

"Your gift will use you, before you can use *it*," she said. "When it comes to you the first time, it'll begin to provide you with one of the answers you've been seeking for many years. The second time, it will bring you to me again. Then, you'll learn more about the questions you've faced across the years, and what you still need to do on Earth."

Even though I wanted to stay here, a calm acceptance descended upon me, which also suppressed another question that had leapt into my mind: why couldn't Grandma tell me now? Why did we have to wait for our next meeting?

"Time to go, Simon," she said.

"Grandma, can I hug you both before I leave? It's been such a long time." That was one yearning that these waves of peace, love and calm, couldn't suppress.

I started to feel a slight tugging at my back. The darting

orbs formed two lines alongside me again, and the formless figures reappeared. The tugging increased a little, but not in a harsh, aggressive way, more of a gentle pull, simply lifting me off my feet until I floated a few inches above the ground. For the first time, I actually noticed what I'd been standing on. It was exactly the same as the walls and roof. But were they really walls, a roof and ground? There were no joins where anything met because there were no corners, just this dazzlingly white spiritual realm of immense brightness, where my ethereal essence was meeting two long-departed souls (could it be that this was my soul, too?).

Slowly and smoothly I started moving backwards.

"I'm afraid you can't," Grandma's words came into my mind. "If we were to touch, it would break the link holding you to your Earthly body and you wouldn't be able to go back."

"Would that truly be a bad thing, though?" Despite accepting that I had to face a destiny which was yet to unfold, the warm, comforting embrace of this spiritual domain still drew me inexorably to it, to Grandma, to Helen. Suddenly a jumble of thoughts and feelings from Mum and Dad hit me. It was like the eerie sensation of someone watching you, that makes the hairs on the back of your neck stand up. Very different from Grandma's words which I could hear in my head; this was as if they were close by, maybe waiting just on the other side of that bright, shining portal and sending me love. Perhaps a different form of mental telepathy. And Titus. He'd be there, too, along with the two cats Janice and I had loved during our marriage.

Somehow I know that everyone from my family who'd gone on before, was there, close by. I yearned again for that forbidden touch but had no control over my movement, or I fear I may have rushed forward to embrace Grandma and

Helen.

"The wheels of your destiny have been turning since Helen's death," said Grandma. "But you have to start them rolling yourself soon. I'll be there to help you."

More riddles.

I'd have to wait longer for that touch.

Helen hadn't spoken once during my time here, but she didn't need to. All the sibling love denied to us since she passed into this realm 38 years ago flooded from her, washing over me in powerful, rhythmic cascades. I guess there was no need for me to tell her how much I loved and missed her. As I simply thought it and sent love from deep in my heart, her smile widened. She got my message.

The pull on my back increased, moving me a little faster, like a train pulling out of the station.

"But wait," I thought. Yep, I'm getting the hang of this telepathy. No need to speak this aloud. "Grandma, my gift?"

Both she and Helen raised their hands in a farewell wave. "You've already got it, Simon. You've already got it." Even though they were both receding into the distance as I picked up speed, Grandma's words still sounded just as loud in my head. "Goodbye, my darling. God speed. It won't be too long until our next meeting."

Already got it? What did that mean? Even more riddles. More questions than answers.

And with that, they disappeared from view as I moved out of the brightness back into the muddy grey tunnel. The rapidly shrinking white doorway gave an indication of the speed at which I was travelling backwards, as it diminished through the trashcan lid to the coin stage and finally the pinprick.

Just as space in this astral realm didn't appear to obey

Earthly rules, it seemed time didn't either. Seconds, minutes, or even hours, may have passed as the formless figures and glowing orbs escorted me back, and all the while the wind whistled past me, accompanied by the musical chimes.

Other sounds began to cut through the rhythmic whooshing. These weren't being fed directly to my mind, this cacophony was definitely assaulting my ears. As the volume rose it was possible to pick out individual sounds. One was the interminable beeping of medical equipment. Another was a mix of human voices, although it was impossible to decipher individual words.

The next thing I knew, I was no longer surrounded by the muddy grey walls of the tunnel but was back in the ward, hovering above my curtained-off bed. Four figures huddled around my mortal shell, and I could see how I'd mistaken that first one who'd burst into the ward for an astronaut. It was clear now that, like space suits which fully insulated astronauts from the rigours of a vacuum, the protective clothing comprising blue gowns falling below their knees, medical masks inside face shields which in turn were topped by flexible caps, and gloves tucked into their sleeves, was designed to protect them from the COVID virus. Not an inch of their skin was exposed.

As they stepped away from me I saw my body clearly for the first time. Had I really come back from that spiritual utopia to this? A mass of tubes and white sticky tape obscured much of my face, with one wide corrugated pipe disappearing into my mouth. Two intravenous drips trailed into both arms, and my skin looked so pale and somehow just wrong.

I was staring at death warmed up. Perhaps I could get back down the tunnel to Grandma and Helen, touch them, embrace them. Ignore what Grandma had said about setting the wheels of my destiny in motion. I didn't belong here anymore. Now I'd glimpsed the other side I wanted to cross the threshold and be part of it for eternity, starting now. I'd finished with this body, and had no further use for it.

I feverishly scanned the room, looking for the entrance to the tunnel, but it no longer existed. All there was, were the four walls of the ward.

The tugging sensation in my back started drawing me towards my body. My mortal coil was reclaiming me. Anxiously, I resisted, but slowly and inexorably I was inching towards it, and couldn't stop myself.

"He's ready," said one of the four medics. "Let's get him to Intensive Care."

They started to wheel my bed and the machines I was connected to, out of the little curtained bay, towards the door. I felt myself being jerked along above it, as if I were tethered to it. In fact, that's exactly what it was. Some invisible psychic cord must still be connecting me. The tug at my back increased, quite sharply this time, and I found myself floating immediately above my body, moving at the same pace that I was now being wheeled down the corridor outside the ward.

Another tug.

Even stronger.

And suddenly floating-me became one with in-bed me.

The sun in my head went supernova for the third time.

Blackness.

9

Janice's Letter

April 3rd, 2020

My Darling Simon,

We're a little old-fashioned, you and I, aren't we? We resisted Facebook and Twitter until Hannah and Claire bullied us into joining, and now we both love social media. Maybe it's because we don't like change or coming out of our comfort zone for anything new, but once we settle into something we're fine with it and embrace it with the same fervour and passion we have for each other.

We still watch broadcast TV more than Netflix and Amazon Prime—although I did see that you'd watched all episodes of the Lost In Space reboot on one of the on-demand streaming services. We've only recently started using the ePassport lanes at the airport, we prefer taxis to Ubers, and eating out at restaurants instead of home deliveries.

Once you found a niche with your show on Poolswood Sound, you threw your early ambitions of making it on national TV out of the window. And I can't say I'm sorry. Despite my wild days at school, I'm a country girl at heart, and wouldn't want to swap village life for the bright lights of any city.

So...old-fashioned? Yes, we are. Do you remember when we first got together around the time of dear Helen's death, you said my Dad's hardware shop meant you'd always think of 'hardware' as the type of ironmongery he sold, rather than being what you called 'the gubbins' of a computer.

What I'm trying to do there, is explain why I'm writing a

letter to you instead of recording a video. Well, apart from not knowing how to switch on the laptop camera, a letter is more personal, more intimate, and more loving.

You've said many times we're the forgotten generation when it comes to technology, and therefore, we'll always be old-fashioned. That suits me fine, just as it does you. And yes, I know exactly what you mean. Growing up in the late 1960s and 1970s we both remember the days before technology ruled the world. For us, it was an exciting, almost futuristic time, with that first home computer, first mobile phone, and satellite TV. You said we had to change and adapt to that new way of living, while children coming up behind us had a distinct advantage because they were born into it.

Dinosaurs we may be. Old fashioned we may be, but writing a letter seems to put me in touch with you in a way that no video ever could. And I want you to feel the same wonderful warmth when you read this as I do writing it at this moment.

My love for you is still as marvellous and fresh as it was right back in those early days in Meriton. When I woke up this morning, everything was fine for just a few fleeting seconds. Then I turned over to kiss you, only to find an empty pillow, and my sorrow returned with the memory that you're lying in a hospital bed on the third day of your coma.

When you wake up and come back to me, you'll have beaten this dreadful COVID. But until that moment comes, I miss you so much and just wish I could press a magic button that would enable me to turn the clock back a few days and let time stand still for us. I know what I'm writing is a little muddled, but, so am I.

I feel so depressed and lonely without you, and just want to roll myself into a ball and cry. I love you forever, my darling, and know how lucky I am to have such a super, caring, and loveable husband. The only thing I'm looking forward to is the day you come home and I can hold you in my arms again. The words I want to say to you right now are that I will love you for the rest of my life and promise to take care of you forever.

Please forgive the clumsy way I'm trying to tell you how much I love you in this soliloquy, and let me simply tell you straight—I love you. Those three words sum up everything even the most romantic poet could write in the most beautiful sonnet. I pray for God to speed up the days until you're with me again. I live for the time when you will whisper those same words to me, as they're always the match that puts a flame to my heart, lighting my path across the rainbow to you, my pot of gold, at the end of it.

Do you remember our first proper date, when you took me to the autumn fair in Merebrook? I do. For me, it was like a burst of sunshine on a desolate landscape, like torrential rain in the desert, like the first light after months of darkness. How truly blessed I am to have you walk the roads of life with me. I simply can't imagine life without you, because you mean everything to me.

And all this time, you've truly been my international man of mystery. Where do you go when your brain takes a hike and your body goes on to autopilot? I don't even know you've gone and neither do you until you come back. So, in the words of the Peter Sarstedt song, 'where do you go to, my lovely?' But the mystery remains—if only we could see the thoughts that surround you, and look inside your head.

Do you remember how scared I was when you told me about these blackouts, or, as you call them, your 'holidays in the fog'? We were actually on holiday at the time, weren't we? It was our first holiday together, and the first time we spent more than a couple of consecutive days with each other. We'd decided on the spur of the moment to go to a disco in that big pub on the waterfront at St Ives—well, I seem to recall *you* decided. You saw a poster for it while waiting for me to come out of the toilet.

'Hey, Janice,' you said. 'Look at this. We'll go tonight.'

You were so strange the next morning and asked if we'd been to the disco. I laughed and said you were drunk, but I didn't think you'd been that far out of it. Then you said the last thing you remembered was showing me the poster and saying we'd go. I don't think I could've been more freaked out if you'd told me you were an alien from a far distant galaxy grooming me to have children to help save your dying race.

We sat and talked about it for hours. By then, you'd had about half a dozen such episodes, but many more were to follow over the years. I was scared shitless of what they'd find when you had that first brain scan in 1986, but I didn't know whether to be relieved or even more worried when the result came back negative. You put such a brave face on it, and it was a long time afterwards before you finally admitted to being as frightened as I was, but you'd been staying strong for me, lol. It should have been me staying strong for you.

So, my man of mystery, I wonder what's going through that brain of yours now, while you're in the coma? They tell me you won't know anything about it, but who's to say? Your brain's not like anyone else's, is it? It does its own thing, often when we least expect it. Perhaps it's gone on another holiday in the fog, wherever that may be. But it's got to come back from whatever place that is, when you wake up.

I hope I've been as big a comfort to you over your foggy holidays as you were to me during my cancer treatment. We talked long into the night after Dr. Horton told us I had breast cancer. You sat with me in the hospital after my mastectomy holding my hand, and during all my chemo. I honestly don't think I could have got through it without you being by my side.

And that makes what's happening now all the worse. I can't be by your side, and neither can Claire or Hannah. I can't hold your hand, neither can Claire and Hannah. We can't see you, we can't touch you, we can't hug you.

But know this, my sweet darling: I love you, Hannah loves you, Claire loves you.

We all thought you were doing so well and fighting this awful virus off. This is only a setback, and I'm sure you're not going to let it keep hold of you for long. Your body's healing every hour, every moment, every second you're sleeping. You'll soon be back with us, in my arms where you belong.

Oh, I must tell you this. Olivia told your listeners what's happened—she asked if I'd give permission, as people kept phoning the station to ask how you are. I didn't think you'd mind. When your fans knew you were in a coma the phone-in lines went mad. Everybody's rooting for you, my darling, just as I am. They can't wait for you to be back behind the microphone. Poolswood wants its shining star back from wherever you are in the heavens.

I told you this letter would be all muddled, didn't I? And it is.

I'm going to close now, my darling. Hurry back to me.

All my love, now and forever, dear heart.

Janice xxx

10

Monsters

April 6th, 2020, Andrew

He pushed open the anteroom door and stepped aside, holding it for Emma to go through into the Intensive Care Unit ahead of him, for the start of their 3 p.m. to midnight shift.

Fully kitted out in their fluid-resistant long-sleeved blue gowns with cuffed gloves taped to their sleeves, white FFP3 respirator masks, goggles, and full face visors, they resembled actors in any number of medical contagion thriller movies. But, as he told himself every time he'd started a shift over the last month, this was no movie, this wasn't fiction, this was real life. Scriptwriters' ideas which they had never dreamed would become true, were now fodder for news anchors on every bulletin, every day. Life was imitating art. And it was more Edward Munch's Scream than John Constable's Hay Wain.

Nurse Jim Rice looked up from the workstation as they came in.

"Afternoon," he said.

"Hi, Jim," they replied together. Andrew and Emma tended to do most things in unison since Maggie Bricknell instigated the buddy system. It meant they were on the same shifts, along with other buddy pairings. So whether it was this late one, the 12-hour overnight stint from 9.30 p.m. to 9.30 a.m., the 8.00 a.m. to 5.15 p.m. day shift (and what about the extended killer shift from 8.00 a.m. to 9.00 p.m.?), or 10.00 a.m. to 7.00 p.m., each pair stayed together now.

Given Andrew's new-found humour, he could have joked that he saw more of Emma than he did his wife, except it wouldn't have been a joke.

All things considered, as time wore on from the start of the pandemic, he saw further benefits of Emma being a permanent buddy, in addition to ensuring they were suited up properly. Communicating during tasks became almost telepathic. It wasn't mind-reading, at least not as he'd always imagined it to be, it was more as if they instinctively knew what each other was going to do and carried out the work in perfect harmony, rather like a glove moves with the hand.

"Four more patients have been admitted today, and two have died," the extended day shift doctor told them at the handover meeting before they embarked on their quick whistle-stop tour of the unit where Andrew would see the patients and their monitors for himself.

Pre-COVID, Andrew would have simply nodded at that and waited to be told which two they were. But his professional detachment was wearing thinner by the day, eaten away by what the virus was doing to so many families; to the Reynolds and Lambert families in particular. Imogen had gone in the prime of her life. Would Simon be next?

Each time he thought of Simon he remembered that final radio interview with Imogen, and the emotional maelstrom running through his head intensified. Imogen's book remained unopened on his bedside table. He couldn't bring himself to read it yet, while everything was still so raw after the heartbreaking video call to her family where she took her last breath. But he would read it eventually. He owed her that much, at the very least.

"Who?" he asked, and realised from his colleague's quizzical look, that his tone may have been a little sharp.

"Our two oldest patients," said Doctor Douglas Moss. "Reuben Jacobson and Doris Mitchell. Both were to be expected, as they'd deteriorated overnight. We carried out tracheostomies, but their lungs were just too badly damaged."

Andrew found himself inwardly sighing with relief. It was a tragedy of course for the two families who had each lost a parent, grandparent, and at Reuben's age of 91 and Doris at 87 quite possibly a great-grandparent, too. Would it have been more of a tragedy, though, if Douglas told him they'd lost Simon instead? Simon's medical records showed he was born in 1964, but who's to say he has any more right to live than Reuben and Doris? He worried—in fact, *worry* is nowhere near strong enough—he *agonised* over where that question would lead him if the pandemic took as firm a grip on the world as experts predicted.

They'd been told there were enough ventilators at the moment for everyone who needed mechanical help with their breathing while they fought off the severe acute respiratory syndrome. He'd also seen news reports about UK-based Formula-1 motor racing teams bringing their fast, accurate, design and manufacturing skills to the table by managing a range of companies outside the medical industry to ramp up additional ventilator production.

Inevitably, though, there'll be more patients needing ventilators in time than there are machines. What mental anguish will he and other doctors face when they have to play God and choose who lives and who dies? Would he choose the Reubens and Dorises of this world, or the Simons?

What about when those life-or-death decisions need to be made between the Simons? Or between two people even younger than Simon's 56? What then? Would his palpitations start when his heart beats faster, when he's trembling, sweating, and his fingers are numb? When anxiety rages through doctors and nurses on the front line, what then?

It was at that moment he heard Simon's name spoken aloud. Had he really heard it, though, or were his ears playing tricks? He was thinking about Simon, and there it was, the sound of his name. Actually, no, there were no tricks. He had heard it. He'd heard words on either side of it, too, but had been too busy exploring his own thoughts instead of paying full attention.

He did hear Douglas's last few words, though: "...so I'll ask Emily and Karen to get him ready, but I thought you may want to be there when they do the test. We can start the proning straight after."

"What? Sorry, Doug, I was miles away then. What were you saying about Simon Reynolds?"

If old-fashioned looks ever become the height of fashion, Douglas would be in Savile Row. He pushed his glasses to the end of his nose and stared over the top of them. The strain on Andrew's face was plain to see.

"It's getting to us all, Andrew. The deaths are awful and nothing like any of us have ever seen before."

"We should know better, Doug," Andrew said. "We should *do* better. We're medical professionals, taught to stay aloof from our patients. What good are we if we become emotionally involved?"

"You know we all experience high levels of work stress, even under normal circumstances. COVID's going to get a hundred times worse before it gets better, so there's no shame in admitting the additional pressure's getting to you. Christ, Andrew, you wouldn't be human if it didn't. And every member of staff at this hospital knows you're more human than many of us, after what you did for the Lambert family.

"Which reminds me, Bricknell's sent an email round this morning about that."

"What? Using my iPad to let them say goodbye?"

"Yes. You'll see it when you log on. She's telling us all to do the same—to use our devices to let dying patients say goodbye to their families. It's become official hospital policy. That single act of kindness didn't only make a world of difference to the Lamberts, but will make many more patients' last moments so much easier to bear. Christ almighty, it was an incredible gesture."

Andrew waved the compliment away. "It seemed the most natural thing to do at the time. The Lamberts were so grateful afterwards that I decided straight away I was going to carry on doing it. It's the least we can do for patients and their grieving families.

"Anyway, you were saying something about Simon Reynolds?"

"Yes." Doug turned to the computer and pulled up his records. "We noticed a small degree of movement when we were getting him onto his back this morning after his proning session."

That commanded all of Andrew's attention.

"His eyelids flickered when we'd got him settled," said Doug, "and he raised his hand a couple of inches, and said what sounded like 'Grandma.'"

"What?" That shook Andrew to the core. "Was he starting to come out of the coma?"

"No. All readings stayed exactly the same. There was absolutely no change. We'd literally just finished reverse proning and were moving away when it happened. It was all over in a second. Just the one hand movement, a slight flicker of his eyes—not enough for them to open—and that one word. If he'd simply been asleep, it would have been a natural movement, and just as if he were talking in his sleep."

"Was he still getting the same amount of anaesthetic? There wasn't a fault on the delivery?"

"Everything was as it should be." Doug pulled his glasses back to the bridge of his nose. "But we've arranged for him to have an EEG this afternoon just to double-check brain activity. That's what I was saying about Emily and Karen getting him ready. Physiology are sending someone up at four o'clock."

When they reached Simon's bed a few minutes before the physiologist was due, the humming, whirring, and occasional beep from the machines connecting him to artificial life all sounded normal to Andrew, and every readout was within regular parameters. He looked at Simon lying on his back, the corrugated tube from the ventilator passing through the clear plastic mask covering the lower part of his face, and disappearing down his windpipe. Oxygen level, heart rate, and blood pressure indicators showed no abnormalities, the IV lines continued to provide fluids, nutrition, and medication, and the drains and catheter were performing as they should.

All data indicated he was still in the comfortable medically induced coma, showing no reason for anything different. *Something must have triggered that movement, though. Coma patients simply don't raise their hands and call for their grandmas.*

April 6th, 2020, Simon's COVID Monsters

There's fog all around me. At least I think it's fog. I can't see anything. Then I know I'm dreaming because I'm in a forest. I've been here before—there's that young girl behind the tree again. Or is it Grandma, as it was once before?

I raise my hand in a wave. "Grandma," I call.

It's not Grandma this time. As she emerges from the

shadows into the moonlight which makes skeletons of the thin, spindly branches of my dreamscape trees, I see the lank greasy hair and bloodless white skin. And, yes, the tongue's still black, as she thrusts it between those almost luminescent red lips.

But what's this between my own lips? For fuck's sake, where did that come from? It's like a white, ribbed snake. I can feel it deep in my throat, but, surprisingly it doesn't hurt. Even more surprisingly, it doesn't make me gag. It trails from my throat into the trees. In fact, it disappears *inside* a tree.

More plastic pipes are coming out of me, going into trees. Small red and green birds sit on the branches, but instead of chirping or singing, they're bleeping.

I have to get away from here. From the girl, from the pipes, from the bleeping birds. That thought burns through my mind to the exclusion of all others, but why do I need to get away from the pipes? I don't really understand that, because something's telling me they're my friends. It's the unknown COVID monsters lurking in the trees that I should worry about. Where's Captain Caveman when I need him?

The COVID monsters are stirring. But I'll be okay, won't I? The pipes are helping me kick COVID's ass.

The monsters are moving. I can hear them getting close.

Suddenly I'm running. The pipes have gone and I'm plunging headlong through the thickly-packed trees, their spindly branches intertwining high overhead, growing denser all the time, blocking the moon and bringing ethereal dusk to the forest floor.

My clothes have changed. All I'm wearing is a simple cotton and polyester mixed fabric Lapover gown, rather like a loose tunic. Branches lash at my face and arms, and small, sharp stones and twigs bite into the soles of my bare feet as I hurtle on through the oppressive half-light. Then memories come flooding back and the land no longer seems quite so unfamiliar. The shattered remnants of a once tall and mighty Oak whose trunk has been cleft in two by a lightning bolt, stand directly in front of me.

Somehow I know the geography of this forest and realise I've been here before. Only in my dreams, of course, and recently. I remember walking peacefully along the forest trail, only occasionally being aware of something moving parallel with me through the trees.

That had been disturbing but not frightening. It was just a deer, I'd told myself confidently, just a deer. Not this time, though. This was no deer I was running from. These were COVID monsters and they wished me immeasurable harm. That's why I'm running. But now, my newly-recalled knowledge of the forest may be able to help.

I know that just a few metres to the left of the shattered Oak a clearing will open up in front of me, stretching away for about a hundred metres in all directions. There's something in the centre of the clearing that will help me escape my ever-nearing pursuer. And it's not Captain Caveman.

If only I can get there in time, but it'll be a close-run thing. I can hear the COVID monsters slithering through the undergrowth close behind. Too close. Gaining. How far to the clearing now? How far to the centre of the clearing and safety?

I burst through the blanket of trees into achingly bright moonlight, and there, 50 metres away, stands the craggy three-metre-high monolithic rock which will be my salvation.

Halfway across the intervening space, I risk a glance over my shoulder. After emerging into the glade from the dimness of the forest, my eyes were still getting used to the sudden onslaught of harsh moonlight, but almost as if my nightmare wanted to ensure I could see my pursuer in all its malevolence, the light swiftly adjusted to compensate. And I saw the COVID monster for the first time, which sent a thrill of pure terror coursing through my dreamscape persona, opening the floodgates for adrenaline to swamp my bloodstream.

Two pulsating grey orbs three times the size of medicine balls, pitted and pockmarked like the surface of the moon, tower 20 feet above me. They're connected to necks at least two feet in diameter which merge into one much wider trunk about halfway to the ground. Around 100 red structures resembling broccoli florets grow from the indented surface of each orb, slowly undulating as if a light breeze were washing over them. The creature didn't appear to have eyes, but it certainly had teeth, dozens of them and wickedly sharp, in rubbery-lipped mouths just below each orb.

I imagined a gigantic Captain Caveman clubbing these COVID monsters. But it didn't happen. Despite belonging to one snake-like body, each orb seemed to be acting independently, because they both struck at the same time, colliding with each other. Knocked off their target, the two sets of fangs flashed harmlessly past my neck, which gave me the few seconds I needed to reach the safety of the monolith. I don't know why I'll be safe here, I just know I will be.

Flinging my arms out to grasp the rock, I found myself soaking wet, crawling out of a river that flowed along a valley floor. Dozens of tiny needlelike teeth in the mouths of hundreds of small fish swarming towards me, snapped at my heels. The fish's heads comprised the same grey orbs and waving red florets of the bigger COVID monsters.

After scrambling up the bank I turned to look back into the water. The fish were emerging onto the land, the split at the end of their tails getting longer and turning into a pair of short stubby legs. Suddenly a fish launched itself at me, latching onto my shoulder and burying its teeth deep in my flesh, while the florets caressed my skin with the gentle touch of a mermaid's finger.

Gasping with the pain inflicted by the dozens of tiny pinpricks I instinctively lashed out at it, shaking my shoulder as I desperately tried to throw it off. Its teeth were firmly embedded, though, making my wild jabs at it futile. Grabbing its head I squeezed with all my might, pulling upwards at the same time. The teeth came clear of my skin, dripping with blood, and in the next instant, the head exploded in my hand, showering my face in wet, sticky, stinking goo.

I struggled further up the bank, my feet slipping in the mud. There, some distance in front of me, stood the shattered Oak, meaning the protective monolithic rock was nearby.

If only I could get there in time, but it would be a close-run thing again. The fish waddled after me, surprisingly fast on their squat tail-legs. Getting closer. Gaining. How far to the Oak now? Would I see the rock when I got there? How far to the rock and safety?

Time after time the COVID monsters caught up with me just seconds before I grasped the rock and was catapulted into another frantic chase. Sometimes I surprised myself at the speed I was running. My bare feet flashed unerringly across the land, carrying me mile after mile just out of reach of my pursuers. I looked desperately for the broken Oak, and every time it was almost, tantalisingly, just within reach, they finally caught up and teeth sank into me, or claw-like hands with twisted, rasping nails would start to pull me down into the very depths of a COVID hell.

Sometimes my legs would be heavy and leaden, and try as I might, I could barely move them, as I looked frantically in each direction for the first sign of the horror which could only be seconds away.

My sole emotion now was fear, sending adrenalin coursing through my dreamscape persona. And then the horror suddenly reached its climax. The fangs drooled mere inches from my heels. The disembodied hands, with small orbs and florets in place of fingernails, clawed at my back.

Spiders dropped with a sickly plop onto my head. These were no ordinary spiders, but were grey, red-floreted orbs, each with eight legs. They crawled through my hair, into my ears, up my nostrils, and forced their way into my mouth. Their tireless legs pried at my tightly clamped eyelids. I could smell the hot, fetid breath of the owners of myriad red eyes as they surrounded me, cutting off all avenues of escape, closing in slowly, slowly, slowly. They're biding their time, waiting for the precise moment for the ribonucleic acid of single-stranded genomes to swamp my lungs with every aspect of their SARS-CoV-2 makeup.

Then I'm lying on my back, feeling every rut, twig, and stone of the forest floor through the thin gown, with that white corrugated pipe snaking from a tree and coming into my mouth again. The red and green birds sit on the branches beeping rhythmically. There's also something else sitting in the tree. A person. A cartoon character, covered from head to foot with brown hair and an ankle-length beard. A pair of eyes and a nose peep out of the hair, and although his mouth is completely masked by the beard, I know he's smiling.

He lovingly patted the large wooden club he was holding. "Time I went to work," Captain Caveman told me.

EEG

April 6th, 2020, Andrew

The physiologist, Abraxas Khalifa, took a small unit with 20 electrodes plugged into it, across to Simon's bed. Then, using a paper measuring tape, he pinpointed around 20 positions on Simon's scalp representing particular points in his brain and marked them with a wax crayon. He scrubbed each one with a mild abrasive, before attaching the electrodes with collodion glue and gauze, and drying them in place with a quick blast of air.

Then he used a syringe to fill each electrode cup with gel and cast an experienced eye over the data acquisition computer screen to ensure all the electrodes were properly connected and sending back a powerful signal.

Horizontal lines moved across the screen, representing information collated from each electrode. They were all perfectly calibrated, and the EEG test began with a sequence of flashing lights over Simon's head.

As the test progressed, Andrew and the physiologist watched the blue lines waving their way from left to right.

"It's certainly a little abnormal," said Abraxas, tracing his finger across a couple of lines. "The temporal resolution's crystal clear—there's a degree of brain activity going on in there that we wouldn't really expect, given the amount of sedation he's getting. I'd like to have seen what it was doing when he moved and spoke."

I bet you would, thought Andrew. *So would I.* With the electrodes picking up around 1,000 data points every second, the EEG was the perfect window into Simon's electronic soul. When describing an EEG scenario to a layman he'd initially compare the brain to a still pond with

70 sensors placed all around it to pick up information. And then you lob a pebble in. Ripples start to go out and hit the sensors sending information back. He'd go on to tell his audience: "Instead of the flat surface of the pond, I've now managed to take a globe of water and chuck the pebble into the middle of that globe. The ripples start to come out and hit the sensors on the edge. Now, instead of one pebble, I've thrown 1,000 pebbles into it. The ripples go off in all different directions, hit each other, and make new ripples. The sensors have to pick up all this information at a very fast rate. This is what an EEG's doing, every second, so there's an awful lot of data to measure."

Abraxas frowned as he analysed the montage of data from each electrode moving across the screen. "The alpha activity is far more pronounced than I'd expect, even more so than if he were in a light sleep. It's almost as if he's awake but daydreaming or meditating. Look at that spike; the duration of the abnormal wave is less than 70 microvolts. It'd definitely hurt if you sat on that. I've never seen anything like this in a coma patient."

"What parameters have you set?" asked Andrew.

"Everything's set up at normal rates; 7.5 microvolts with a low-frequency filter at 1.0 Hertz and high frequency of 35 Hertz."

"Thank you, Abraxas," said Andrew at the end of the 35-minute test. "This has really thrown a spanner in the works. I'm wondering if we should think about bringing him out of the coma. With brain activity like that, I'm worried he may be aware of what's happening around him to some degree."

He was thinking of the number of patients he'd treated over the years who faced a long uphill journey after coming out of a coma. The weight of their emotional experiences of having a ventilator breathe for them, and not being able to walk or talk, along with the life or death crossroads they'd stood at, often preyed heavily on their minds. It was no surprise to him and his colleagues that the psychological effects on recovering ventilator patients were more pronounced than the physical ones.

Those symptoms could quickly rachet up to a diagnosable mental illness such as anxiety, depression, or even post-traumatic stress disorder.

Even worse, though, the thoughts going through his mind hinted that if Simon may be partly conscious and aware of what's going on around him, but unable to move or talk, it could possibly be Locked-In Syndrome. Andrew only had limited experience of patients with that neurological disorder but knew that EEGs usually revealed normal brain activity, not unlike the results he was now looking at on the data acquisition screen.

But that didn't account for Simon raising his hand and the single word. Could the movement have been a reflex, he wondered, as it happened immediately after the reverse proning? Had the staff really heard "Grandma?" Could it have been an involuntary body reaction such as a fart, which just happened to sound like "Grandma"? Something was definitely out of kilter here.

An hour later Andrew stood with five colleagues at the bottom of Simon's bed getting ready to prone him. After running through the preparatory checklist, he assigned himself to take the head position, managing the air tube and ensuring it didn't dislodge. "Emma, take his feet. Doug, Jim, his right side, please." Which meant Julian Marsh from the ICU education team who'd been seconded to the daily proning tasks, and nurse Karen Spencer were delegated to the left side.

A few days earlier Maggie Bricknell had rung to ask if he'd give an interview to Poolswood Sound about proning. He could barely believe it when her name flashed up on the screen. Bricknell *ringing,* actually speaking to someone instead of emailing, which he regarded as the cowardly scourge of the corporate wallahs. Must be important, he thought.

He picked up the phone. "Maggie."

"We've got a PR opportunity," she said without preamble. "Poolswood Sound wants someone to explain why we prone COVID patients—the whys, whats, and hows."

So, an hour later he found himself answering a Zoom call from Poolswood Sound's senior reporter, Ayesha Patterson.

"We're looking for a fairly simple explanation that's not going to confuse our listeners," she told him. "Try to avoid medical jargon if you can."

"OK. I'll do my best."

"What I always say is to imagine you're talking to a friend in the pub...when we could go to pubs before lockdown, of course. Your friend has never heard of proning, so you're explaining over a pint what it is, why you do it, and what the benefits are to the patient. I'll probably record a lot more than we'll be able to run on the news, so it'd be great if you could keep each answer fairly short and self-contained."

He nodded. "That's fine."

"OK, I'm now recording the call, so let's begin by you telling me, very simply, please, what proning is."

"Basically, it's a manual handling procedure where a medical team carefully manoeuvres a patient onto their front, face-down, in a 'prone' position. The aim is to change the way the patient is resting, going from their back to their front for several hours, and then we turn them on to their backs again."

"Why do you do this? How does it help the patient?"

He caught himself just in time. *No jargon. How do I describe this without using medical terms?* "I think we need to take a step back first, to help you understand what's going on when we prone a patient."

On the screen, Ayesha nodded.

"Normally, when someone takes a breath," he said, "their chest wall expands to create a vacuum inside their lungs, which draws in air. COVID attacks the lungs, making them inefficient, so there isn't enough oxygen getting into the blood, meaning their oxygen saturation levels fall dangerously low.

"When this happens we put patients on a mechanical ventilator to blow oxygen into their lungs for them. The machine can do all or just some of their breathing, depending on their condition. COVID attacks the lungs with such severity that in many cases patients have to be put into an induced coma to help their lungs, and indeed their whole bodies, recover and fight off the virus.

"Because of how our lungs are positioned, lying on our stomach reduces pressure on them from our heart and diaphragm, meaning we use parts of the lungs that we wouldn't when we're on our backs. This significantly increases oxygen saturation levels. Basically, lying face up squashes the back of the lung, so air disappears from that part of it. But gravity takes blood which needs its fill of oxygen, to the area that's squashed and doesn't have air in it. I hope you can see that picture?"

"Yes, certainly. That's very graphic. But how...?"

"Sorry, can I just add that turning a patient on to their front means blood goes to the areas of the lung which are well aerated—where there's more air—and picks up its oxygen. So, by proning the patient, their blood can take in more oxygen from the air being pumped into their lungs by the ventilator. But they can't stay like that all the time, or the front part of the lung would get squashed and we'd have the same problem."

"Oh, I see. So you're saying that this technique increases the oxygen level in their blood by using different parts of the lung?"

"Exactly."

"You said they're on their stomach for several hours. Roughly how long?"

"We currently prone them for 16 hours a day, and then turn them on to their backs again for eight hours."

"How did you discover that proning works so well?" asked Ayesha.

"Proning's not new. It's been around since at least the 1970s and has been used with unconscious patients in intensive care for many years."

"Is it dangerous?"

"I'd say it's more of a delicate procedure than dangerous, but, yes, there are potential hazards, such as long-term pressure sores and ulcers. There's also a possibility of dislodging the ventilator tube while we carry out the proning process," he conceded. "Having said that, though, the benefits outweigh the dangers, and it's very carefully controlled and managed. For example, the minimum number of trained medical staff needed to prone a patient is five. Here at Poolswood General Hospital, we make it a rule to have six. And we communicate with each other fully all the time, so there's absolutely no danger of doing anything wrong.

"In the few weeks of the pandemic we've already seen proning improve blood oxygen levels in a large number of patients."

"That's perfect, Andrew," said Ayesha. "Thank you very much."

11

Counselling

I recognise this place. Actually, I guess it could be any completely white void with the volume turned off. It really was as quiet as the grave. But, no, it's exactly as I remember it. But from when? When was I last here?

Nothing to see but white in every direction. Just as it was before, when I'd arrived here from the windy, noisy tunnel. Ah, yes, that stirred a memory, somewhere deep in the brain fog, scrambling to get to the surface and break through to total recall.

There hadn't been any tunnel this time, though. Straight here from my hospital bed. Well, I assume I'd come from my hospital bed. But was it yesterday, the day before, or perhaps last week?

When I was here before (yesterday? last week? last month, even?), that bright light had been straight ahead, but there's nothing now. Just the same shade of white everywhere.

Captain Caveman had been here, too. Ah, brain fog. No, he hadn't, not here in my white oasis. He was just a dream, wasn't he? But I hadn't dreamed of Grandma and Helen. I *had* seen them, I was sure of that. I'd come out of my body and travelled here. Peace and calm enveloped me as I looked around, half expecting to see them again, but I was alone this time.

Wait, though. If I'd gone back into my body, what happened after that? I remember a powerful feeling of belonging here and wanting to stay, but floating-me had been sucked back into in-bed me. Then I was in that forest, and the young girl had been there again, hadn't she? Yes, her of the lank greasy hair, bloodless white skin, luminescent red lips, and black tongue.

And I'd been chased by COVID monsters. I smiled at that thought. My brain fog must have gone into hyperdrive to turn microscopic Coronavirus cells into huge monsters in my dream, making the envelopes grey, and transforming the Glycoprotein spikes into red florets. Broccoli florets, at that. It had to be a dream, especially as Captain Caveman was there.

I tried to poke through the brain fog to look at it logically. Firstly, cartoon characters don't come to life, even in some strange phantasmagorical realm between worlds. Secondly, Coronavirus cells aren't part of huge two-headed snakes, the heads of walking fish, clutching fingernails, or spiders. I shuddered at the memory of the COVID spiders forcing their way up my nose, and into my eyes ears, and mouth. That dream had been fucking vivid.

Then logic hit back. Was it logical to come out of your body and travel down a tunnel to a stunningly beautiful and compelling white light where your long-dead sister and grandmother were waiting? Had the horror and supernatural activity at White Pastures all those years ago been logical?

I shivered. Not through cold, the temperature was pleasantly neutral, but because I was dead when I was here before, and I didn't want that to happen again. Or did I? I felt stirrings of the powerful attraction emanating from the light again, drawing me inexorably towards it.

Or is this something different? If I'm having another of those blackouts that have plagued my life, this one's not the same. They always finish with me being in bed, never starting there.

So, what now?

Oh.

My hand's reaching out towards a blue-framed glass door. Where did that come from? I didn't move for a few seconds as my fingers hovered inches from the handle. Tentatively I pulled my arm back, and turning to look over my shoulder I saw I was at the top of a wheelchair ramp alongside a set of steps. At the bottom, a path ran parallel to the building and through a gap in a row of trees, beyond which, was a car park. In the blink of an eye, I'd gone from being surrounded by a white wilderness of nothing, to standing outside a large redbrick building, identified by five words above the door as being Merebrook Surgery And Medical Centre.

Then I noticed several small cracks radiating out from a thin piece of tape stretching around 18 inches down the vertical glass panel next to the door. Recognition came flooding back, with the full memory of being here in that flashback while waiting for the ambulance to take me to hospital when COVID floored me. This was where my first blackout happened, on my way to the appointment with the therapist in 1982.

My heart pounded as I braced myself to wake up again, but nothing happened. I was still here. *Should I open the door and go in? Would that trigger the blackout?*

Inching a little closer to the door, I peered through the glass. And nearly jumped out of my skin when a voice spoke close to my ear. "Excuse me, please, mate."

I whirled around and saw a man standing a few feet from me. He must have come up the ramp from the car park while I was dithering there at the door. "Oh, sorry." I moved aside to let him pass, and when he was inside the foyer he held the door open for me to follow.

As I blankly crossed the threshold my thoughts swirled, making no sense whatsoever, performing the same mental gymnastics they had when I woke up in bed after reaching for that handle the first time. *How did I suddenly get here? Am I going to have another blackout? But I've already had a blackout here, so why am I back?* Now my heart's pounding in my ears as well as my chest.

Two receptionists sat at a long curved desk behind a glass screen. One was welcoming the man who'd just come in, while the other smiled up at me. "Good morning, Sir. How can I help?"

What do I do? Do I answer her, or am I just a passenger here, watching and listening to my younger self? Is the me from long ago going to step in? Am I going to know for the first time what happened during this session?

My heart beat faster at that thought. *Thirty-eight years later. Am I finally going to see what I did, hear what I said?* The therapist told me at the second session that I'd done really well, and come a long way. *Perhaps now, I'll know why.*

"Sir?" The receptionist called again. "I'm ready for you."

Come on, Simon, where are you?

I wasn't going to come, was I? I'd better get on with it.

"Sorry," I said, stepping forward. "I'm Simon Reynolds. I've got an appointment with your therapist, Anna Goodchild."

She looked through what appeared to be neatly displayed medical records on the desk between her and her colleague. "Yes, here we are, Mr. Reynolds. Take a seat, please, she won't be long."

Passing up the opportunity to skim through the pile of out-of-date magazines on the table in front of me—I noticed the top one, Titbits, was dated January 10th, 1981, and featured Joan Collins on the cover, with the tagline 'how to be a hit with younger men'—I tried again to make sense of what was happening.

How did I get from my hospital bed in 2020 to Merebrook Surgery And Medical Centre at an appointment I know I kept in 1982, but have no memory of? And now I seem to be reliving it.

Another thought struck me: my clothes. I was in pyjamas back at the hospital, but now I'm looking down at blue jeans and navy Adidas trainers with three white diagonal stripes on both sides.

I felt my hair. Much longer and thicker than it should be. Then ran my hand over my face. Smooth. No carefully cultivated designer stubble goatee which I'd had for years.

None of my thoughts were reaching logical conclusions. Fuck it, there was nothing logical about any of this, so how could they?

I looked around for the toilet sign and spotted it on a door at the far end of the half-filled waiting area. Several years ago…I can't remember exactly when…I'd started to notice it was more like my Dad staring back at me out of the mirror, rather than my own face. We haven't reached the stage of it being my grandad yet, but I reckon now I'm 56 it won't be much longer. Gingerly I went into the toilet, half expecting what I'd see, but I couldn't possibly have been prepared for the shock when it actually came.

Instinctively my eyes widened and my eyebrows shot up as I stared at the young fresh face. In the mirror, 18-year-old Simon did exactly the same. My mouth dropped open. So did 18-year-old Simon's.

My stomach churned and flipped, and although I couldn't see it in the mirror I knew that 18-year-old Simon's must be doing it, too, because it seemed that somehow I was now him, but with all 56 years' worth of my memories.

Given the nature of my career, words have always been second nature to me. I've never been short of them, nor had any difficulty putting them in the right order. But as I stared incredulously at the young face I'd only seen in old photographs for the last goodness knows how many years, that skill completely deserted me.

I guess having those mental blackouts on and off for years has made me a little more understanding and accepting of the weird and wonderful, but it could still mean I'd gone crazy, just snapped, and this wasn't actually happening. I really can't string any words together right now to describe how I feel. So let's just throw a few individual words out there and leave them to stand alone. Hopefully, they'll convey some idea of the emotion coursing through me: astonishment; bewilderment; confusion; perplexed. But let's save the grandpappy of those words 'til last: shock.

We've all seen at least one body-swap movie such as Vice Versa or Freaky Friday...or if we haven't seen one, we all know what they are: those films where characters swap bodies. This isn't quite the same, though. Fuck it, it isn't even remotely the same. I've not swapped bodies. I'm still Simon. It's just that I'm 56-year-old Simon inside 18-year-old Simon. At least, that's what it looks like.

Suddenly I needed to pee again, but I was in the right place this time.

I'd just got back to my seat when one of the consulting room doors opened and a woman in her mid-thirties with shoulder-length dark hair parted in the middle, emerged. Eighteen-year-old Simon probably wouldn't have noticed her age, but 56-year-old Simon did. She scanned the room, her eyes resting on me briefly, in passing.

"Simon Reynolds," she called.

"Take a seat, Simon," she said when she had guided me inside and closed the door. The room was a little larger than I'd anticipated, and light and airy. Five comfortable-looking high-backed chairs spread out in a wide, shallow semi-circle directly in front of me, with an oval, heavily-grained teak table alongside. The gentle sound from the small waterwheel fountain standing on it instilled a sense of calm and peaceful tranquility. If I'm honest, a couple of potted plants on both sides of her desk looked a little like bookends to the neatly stacked files and typewriter.

The pale green carpet and even paler wallpaper completed the appearance of being outdoors in nature.

I sat down in the chair second from left and she pulled the far right one around to face me, while still giving me plenty of space. Again, probably something 18-year-old me wouldn't have noticed.

"I'm Anna Goodchild," she said. "First of all, Simon, can I say how sorry I am for your sad loss? I'm hoping I can help you get through it, and your Dad thought it would be a good idea for us to talk. Do you think it's a good idea?"

I was ready to fire off a broadcaster's response (a 56-year-old broadcaster's response) but then realised I need to try to get inside my head of 38 years ago. This isn't going to be easy. Dead air on the radio is a complete no-no, but sitting here listening to that water gently trickling, there didn't seem to be any need to rush.

"Yes," I said after a few seconds. "I guess it's good."

"You guess. Sounds like you're not completely sure."

"No. No, it's definitely a good idea." *I'm told I did really well in this session, so I guess I'd better make sure I do. Stop saying guess!* "Let's do it."

"OK. Before we start, do I have your permission to record our talk today on tape?"

I could hardly refuse that, could I? "Of course."

"Thank you, Simon." She crossed to a shelf behind her desk and returned with a portable reel-to-reel tape recorder. It was a Uher. I smiled inwardly. As an 18-year-old I'd never seen one of those, but I went on to use them regularly during my university media studies course, and for the first couple of years of my broadcasting career. Obsolete now, of course. To edit our interviews we used to cut the physical recording tape with a razor blade, take out the bits we didn't want, and splice it back together with special sticky tape. All done on computer now, of course.

She placed it on the table, running the microphone cable across the neighbouring chair to an extendable tripod which she positioned close to my seat.

"We're recording now, so let's start with you telling me about yourself."

"I'm 18…" I began. *I just had to get that in, didn't I?* "…I recently finished my 'A' Levels and hoping to do media studies at university."

"Media studies. Interesting. Do you want to be a journalist?"

"A broadcast journalist. I'd love to have my own talk show on local radio." *One day Ms. Goodchild will be able to say he told me he was going to do this. And he has done.*

"You'll need a sharp mind for that, able to interpret things quickly and ask the right questions. Do you do that now?

"I like to think so. A little like you, I guess."

She smiled at that. "No need to guess. You're spot on. Now, what's your interpretation of what we're going to do today?"

A big ask for an 18-year-old, but not so big for a 56-year-old who believes he came to terms with Helen's death and understands she may possibly be with her soulmate. That thought kept me going over the years. Yes, the memories are still painful. Of course they are. Perhaps I'd smile more if they weren't. I still miss her terribly, even after all these years. I often wonder if Helen's boyfriend, Mark Brody, who was staying with us at White Pastures, on vacation from university where he was studying law, when it happened, still misses her. We lost touch with him after her funeral.

Despite the sadness, the vicar gave us hope that she may not be completely gone. I guess I'd better tell Anna all about it.

"How much did my Dad tell you about what happened before Helen died?"

"Nothing. All I know is that the family had a difficult time in the few weeks leading up to it. Can you tell me about that?"

Where to start? I guess the first time Helen and I saw our unwelcome visitor is the best place. OK, here we go, in for a penny, in for a pound. At least I've had 38 years to process what happened, not just a few days like the Simon I am now. I don't know if I'll be able to remember the minute-by-minute details after all this time, though.

"First of all, Anna, do you believe in ghosts?"

"It doesn't matter what I think, Simon. Do you believe in them?"

"I didn't until a few weeks ago." I paused, waiting for her to ask what led me to change my mind. She didn't.

Better plough on, then. "I genuinely believe Helen was killed by a supernatural spirit." I looked hard at Anna's eyes, the colour of wonderfully creamy milk chocolate. No reaction. Not a flicker.

"We started to notice something going past the window, in the garden. The first time it happened was when Mum and

Dad were out, my younger sister, Sarah, was dancing in her bedroom, and Helen and I were watching a film. I just caught a glimpse of it out of the corner of my eye." *It might have been the flicker of a cloud scurrying in front of the sun's dying embers that sent the sudden dark shadow past the window.*

"I saw it again a few moments later. Helen had dozed off..." *I remembered thinking at the time thank goodness she did, or she would probably have seen the face at the window before it vanished as quickly as it had come. It had been too indistinct for me to make out any features. It was more of a shape than anything, but it was the shape of a figure, nevertheless.*

"Between us, we saw it again several times over the next few days. It was...well, nothing definite or distinct. Just that glimpse, which made us wonder if we'd really seen it or not." Was this how 18-year-old me would describe that unnerving time? I guess it didn't really matter. As the memories came flooding back, I just felt the need to let Anna know as much as I could. And that included when I saw it properly for the first time...

Darkness had descended swiftly once dusk took a foothold, and the night shrouded the house like a veil, seemingly deeper and closer than usual. I knew in my soul that whatever was watching us was simply biding its time. I risked a quick sideways look towards Helen and saw that she too had fixed her stare on the window. She seemed to have sensed my glance because she cast a reassuring smile in my direction. Suddenly a single bark rang out from the kitchen where Titus had been stretched out on the floor. Helen jerked her head towards the window, and I involuntarily looked across at her. It was at that precise moment she screamed.

Instead of looking back at the window as I should have done, my gaze remained locked on Helen. Her hands flew to her face, covering her mouth, gripping both sides of her nose; her eyes were wide with a look of pure terror as if she were witnessing the ultimate horror.

It's strange the things that pass through your mind in a crisis. I remember how time seemed to stand still while obscenities circled my vocal chords waiting for me to give them life. I'd done what it—whatever IT was—wanted. Somehow, it had caused me to look away and then appeared as soon as I was distracted.

I knew it was too late, but turned to the window nevertheless, a shiver still tingling my spine. Again, just a hint of a dark shadow seemed to kill the moonlight, but I was aware of something—just for a split second—looking in, waiting to devour us with its evil.

At least, that's how I felt. It was the feeling of intense horror—deep, penetrating, and powerful—that engulfed me so suddenly, rather than the sight of the thing that was so terrifying and loathsome. It seemed an eternity before I could shake it off sufficiently to regain control of my senses. Titus barked furiously. We could hear him scratching frantically at the door.

The darkness at the window had disappeared as swiftly as it came and the next second I was heading for the door. I ran through the dining room towards the kitchen where Titus was still in a frenzy. For an instant the door refused to yield to my pushing, conjuring up all sorts of visions—it was in the kitchen, waiting. It had come inside to get us.

I was now more determined than ever to see this thing, whatever it was—burglar, shadow, menace—and I battered the door with all my strength. A squeal of pain and muffled thumping gave me a quick sense of satisfaction as the door met with resistance, connecting with whoever was in there.

As I burst inside my hand snaked up the wall toward the light switch giving life to the overhead fluorescent strip. Realisation dawned on me immediately, partly because of the silence and partly because of the sight: I had slammed the door into poor Titus who had been leaping up at it. Sad brown eyes looked out from the tangled mass of head, legs, and hair as he rolled over and scrambled to his feet.

"Oh, sorry, Titus. Sorry, old boy." He whined and licked my outstretched hand. Then, suddenly, he snatched his head away and turned to face the door that led out into the garden. A wave shuddered along the hair on his back and a low growl was born in the pit of his stomach.

"What is it?" I asked myself as much as the dog. His answer was to shoot away from me, skidding to a halt at the garden door. As he stared up at it, his growling became more urgent and insistent. As soon as he saw me reach for the handle he started pawing at the door. It was hardly open more than a crack when his nose poked through, and he sent the door flying from my grasp with a deft twist of his head.

As I followed him out into the moonlight, I caught sight of him disappearing round the side of the house towards the back garden, barking more frantically all the time. An eerie light washed over the stretch of lawn giving rise to the illusion of a rippling lake, a lake of grass flanked by elms and sycamores with a copse at the end.

On rounding the corner of the house, I finally saw it. Titus was chasing a running figure that was partly blending in with the moonlit shadows of the trees.

Although it seemed to be running, I couldn't actually see its legs moving. Its speed, though, told me it must be sprinting. As my eyes grew more accustomed to the darkness, I saw the figure stop and turn to face Titus, who by then was only a couple of metres behind it. All I could make out was a black shape advancing slowly, threateningly, menacingly, towards my dog. Titus drew himself up as if he had hit an invisible wall and a howl of horror wrenched from his body. Turning tail, he hurtled back towards me across the lawn. His pursuer came rapidly out of the shadows but was too far away for me to discern any of its features. I could still only make out a vague black shape.

Almost at once, I sensed that it saw me because it glided to a halt. There we stood, forty metres of lawn between us like two duelling cowboys at high noon. A faint moaning came from its direction, then without warning, it rose about ten feet up into the air and began to grow, both in height and in width. It moved slowly through the darkness, expanding constantly like some huge, obscene balloon until I felt sure it meant to engulf me. I stood frozen to the spot, as if my feet had taken root, my eyes locked on the shadow.

I'm not seeing this, I told myself. I can't be seeing this. It isn't happening.

The spell holding me paralysed was broken by a piercing scream from the house. I spun to face the lounge window and saw Helen's terror-stricken face framed in the glass staring out into the night. A faint rustling came from above me and when I turned back to where the shadow had been hovering there was no sign of it.

Sweat poured down my forehead as I ran back to the house and slammed the door behind me. Titus was under the table whining. Not far away from him was a wet pool where he had been sick on the floor. Helen rushed into the kitchen and fell into my arms sobbing. "What was it?" she cried.

I clasped her to me as tightly as I could. "It was nothing," I lied. "Only a shadow. That's all."

She pushed me away angrily. "That was no shadow. You know it wasn't. You saw it. It was a...a...a..." Her words refused to come. Like me, she could find no reasonable explanation for what we had just seen. My senses as well as my eyes told me this thing was not of this world. No mortal could have instilled the sense of horror that the faceless dark shadow, that growing thing, had. The only evidence we had was that of our own eyes and our own feelings. I began to wonder whether we would have to rely on feelings and intuition alone in our future dealings with this unwelcome visitor. Whatever it was.

Was it that intuition or some eerie compulsion that had awoken me a couple of nights later, then made me get out of bed and wander to the window? Poking my head between the curtains, I peered into the moonlight and saw the garden stretching away into a mass of trees and bushes. At first, all was quiet and still. Not a sound anywhere. Then I saw a patch of darkness appear. With the moon overhead, the night was quite bright. My eyes focused on the bottom of the garden, the place where traditionally fairies have always played. There were no fairies now. Instead, a dreadful feeling of unease washed over me, ignoring all my attempts to dispel it.

Something stirred in the bushes. Only faintly, but there was a definite movement. It was then, when my eyes were trained like those of a hawk into the very heart of the bushes, that I saw a dark shape flit through the moonlight. For just one agonisingly fleeting second, I glimpsed the shape of a man running, then it was gone without a trace even though there was nowhere for it to go except into thin air. In that same second, the eerie feeling also disappeared, just as if it had been his all-embracing cloak and he had taken it with him to keep him warm in his abominable lair.

Over the next few days, I came to accept—and indeed expect—our visitor. He appeared each evening just as the sun began to go watery and sink behind the treetops. I suppose I was a trifle blasé about it but it no longer frightened me. It hadn't hurt us and seemed content to flit harmlessly past the window and roam amongst the shrubs and trees.-

Oh, dear. If only we'd known.

My mind's eye must have blotted out my physical eyes while I was relating this part of our tale because I suddenly realised I was holding Anna's somewhat inscrutable gaze.

"Helen's boyfriend, Mark Brody, was staying with us, and he was the first to see it quite clearly," I continued to tell her. "Even when we still couldn't. Mark saw an actual face peering through the window at us while we were having dinner. As usual, the rest of us only saw a shadow going past the window. That happened on a couple of nights."

This feels so strange. My mind from 2020 now seems to inhabit my body in 1982. I'm describing something that happened over the last few weeks. But to me, it's from 38 years ago. *Is this what actually caused that first blackout? Am I responsible for it? Am I responsible for them all? If so, will some future me go back to each one I've had over the years and live through them for the first time?*

"Are you alright, Simon?" Anna's gentle question snatched me out of the memory and away from my pointless ponderings, back into the present. Well, into the present that was really my dim and distant past. Oh, fuck it, you know what I mean. I had no idea how long I'd stopped talking. It could have been seconds or minutes. I guess it was more like minutes as she'd obviously felt it necessary to break the silence.

"Sorry," I said. "It's just hard, with what happened next."

"Do you want to stop?"

I shook my head. "No. I need to tell you."

"We could do it next time if you'd rather."

I didn't even consider that. "No. I want to carry on." Aiming for strength and confidence, but perhaps coming across as just a little petulant

"Okay. In your own time. When you're ready."

I probably didn't need to tell her about every incident. Just the ones that truly shaped that awful climax.

"Really strange things started happening in the house after that. Dad couldn't find his car keys one morning. They eventually turned up in the car with the engine running. Saucepans disappeared from the kitchen. Presents for Helen went missing just before her birthday." I smiled as I recalled one incident that had been rather funny, but chilling at the same time, and was the first of the more deadly attacks that were to come. Helen was enthusing over dinner about their day out...

"It was lovely," she said. "We cut across country through the Isle of Oxney and parked at Camber. We walked along the beach for ages towards the Wicks."

Dad smiled. "Too many people about for my liking at this time of year. I bet it was packed."

"It was rather busy," admitted Mark. "The only reason we walked so far along the beach was to try and find a place to spread our towels without disturbing anyone."

"Fibber," laughed Helen, pulling playfully at his meticulously combed blond locks. Mark gently gripped both her wrists.

"Now look here," he said with mock severity.

Helen giggled, looking happier than I had seen for the

last couple of weeks. Mark taking her out for the day was the best therapy she could have had.

Her eyes shone as she peered into his face. "Yes, sir, I'm looking."

He let go of her left wrist and, speaking infinitely slowly, wagged his forefinger at her in rhythm with his words. "If you don't leave my hair alone, you'll be in very serious trouble."

From the corner of my eye, I spotted a swift movement outside the window. Even the split second it had taken to whirl my head in that direction was too long and it was gone by the time my eyes came to rest there. No one else seemed to notice it; they were all grinning at Mark and Helen playing out their charade.

When I looked back at Helen, a frown was creasing her brow and her eyes registered pain and surprise. "Mark!" she squealed, trying to prise his fingers off her wrist with her free hand. "Stop it. You're hurting me."

Suddenly Mark's arms shot up in the air and his chair tipped backwards, sending him crashing sickeningly to the floor. What happened next was shrouded in confusion and I'm sure was over too quickly for my mind to register it properly. What I thought happened was that as everyone leaped up, Mark's plate, laden with cold chicken and salad, raised itself into the air and smashed down onto his face.

By the time my senses recovered Helen and Sarah were both laughing at the sight of him lying on the floor covered with mayonnaise, lettuce, and tomato. But Dad looked angry. "What on earth are you playing at?" he snapped.

Wiping some of the thick creamy liquid away from his eyes Mark looked around bemused. "I don't know," he mumbled. "I thought someone grabbed my hand."

"That was me, silly." Helen was still giggling at him.

"You started to squeeze a bit too much and you were hurting me, so I pushed your hand away."

Mark was examining the back of his fingers. "You scratched me hard enough, didn't you?"

The laughter died in Helen's throat. "I didn't scratch you. I pulled your fingers off my hand, that's all."

"Then who did this?" demanded Mark, stretching out his hand to reveal several deep gouges across the knuckles. Helen stared at the wounds, her eyes widening at the sight of blood oozing its way across the torn skin.

"I didn't do that," she gasped.

"I didn't squeeze you, either." Mark scrambled to his feet. "I felt you bending my fingers back and the next thing I knew you'd knocked me off my chair."

"I only tried to get your hand off when you started hurting me. I certainly didn't push you off the chair."

More mayonnaise trickled into Mark's eyes. He wiped it away and picked the plate off the carpet. "How did my dinner get down here?"

"Your arm caught it as you fell," I lied quickly, hoping the others hadn't seen it suddenly lift of its own accord and home in accurately and fiercely on Mark's head.

Dad's severe expression began to crack as yet another dollop of mayonnaise trickled off the end of Mark's nose. "Let that be a lesson to you both. No more horseplay at the table. It's a wonder you didn't break anything."

The memory of what happened after that killed off any hint of a smile that may have started to creep over my face.

12

Reminiscence

April 7ᵗʰ, 2020—Attacks of August 1982, Simon

This was the first time in 38 years I'd spoken in such detail about what had happened, recalling each incident step by step, and reliving it moment by moment. This is what I should have done in 1982. What I was now doing in 1982.

We'd spoken about it as a family many times, and as Janice had been at Helen's birthday party when it seemed that all hell was let loose, she and I had discussed it endlessly. But I'd never simply sat down and told it as a story to anyone.

Anna had sat in silence again while I related that episode.

She looked at me, still not saying a word. The only sounds were the slight tinkling of water falling from the small wheel into the copper bowl, then being pumped to the top to repeat its journey, along with the barely audible whirring of the tape recorder.

"By now we'd begun to realise it seemed to be targeting Mark," I continued, a little apprehensively. We were reaching the nasty bits.

"And it was getting dangerous. A couple of days after it had attacked him at dinner, Mark, Helen, and I went to Brighton for the day. I hadn't really wanted to go and play gooseberry. But they insisted…

I daresay the water temperature was quite high as the sun had been glaring down on it mercilessly for twenty-two days, but when a renegade wave swept over my trunks it still came as quite a shock.

"It's gorgeous," gasped Helen, thrusting forward into the

rippling blue. I decided that as the ice was already broken, so to speak, there was little point dawdling any further. I took a deep breath and threw myself into the depths. The water stung my skin like a thousand tiny needles for a few seconds before turning into a soothing relaxant. A few determined and fast-moving strokes of the front crawl became a gentler breaststroke, and then I turned lazily in the water and floated on my back.

Helen and Mark were already about twenty-five yards further out, happily splashing each other. I turned over again and started to tread water; I could barely touch the bottom.

Suddenly, as I looked on, Mark's head shot under the surface. Even from a distance, I could hear Helen giggling as she slapped the palms of both hands sharply against the surface of the water like I had taught her, to make loud pops in the ears of underwater swimmers. It must have been twenty seconds before Mark came up for air, coughing and spluttering, and appeared to be trying to shout. His words were lost amidst a gurgling as he went under again. Helen was still laughing, but her arms were windmilling through the water as she backstroked away from the area of Mark's playful fooling.

I kept my eyes on the spot where he went under for the second time and saw him rocket upwards like a cork from a bottle. Whoa! He came clean out of the water, body arcing over, and then tumbling back heavily with an almighty splash. I watched in total disbelief as he sank for the third time.

There's absolutely no way he could do that, I told myself. *He's too far from the shore to launch himself that high.* My stomach knotted, telling me something was wrong.

"Helen," I cried at the top of my voice. "Where's Mark?"

She didn't seem to hear me and continued to swim away

from him, parallel to the beach.

"Helen! Go back to Mark!" As my cry died away a pair of arms reached up from the sea, flailing frantically. Then Mark's head broke through the surface. The air was rent by his screams for help. Then he was under once more in a cloud of spray, his helpless cries lost amidst a flurry of gurgling.

I sucked in as much air as my lungs would take and dived into the underwater world. My eyes swiftly grew accustomed to the strange perspective and I was able to see Mark struggling vainly to reach the surface. He was in an upright position, kicking wildly with his left leg. The other leg was stiff, pointing straight down, and before I could reach him he bent low and was bashing at his right ankle with both fists as if trying to free it from the grip of some unseen vice. A mass of bubbles escaped from his mouth, making their way to the surface. As I drew nearer, I could see his eyes bulging in their sockets, his blond hair streaming upwards as if vainly pointing him in the direction he needed to take.

He continued beating at his right ankle and started rubbing his left foot up and down his calf. *What was he trying to kick away?*

I arrived within a few inches of his writhing body, and, taking hold of his arm, tried to steer him upwards. It appeared he was doing his best to go with me but it was like pulling a ten-ton weight. I yanked for all I was worth until I was afraid I would tear his arm from its shoulder, but he remained rooted to the spot. As I released him, he grabbed my wrist and pointed to his leg. I nodded, indicating I understood he wanted me to haul him up by his legs, and I dropped down to the seabed.

His right leg was utterly and completely immobile. No

amount of pulling or pushing could move it, but nothing was holding it there. Nothing that I could see, anyway. Putting both hands around his ankle, I tried to channel all my power into the relevant muscles. Nothing happened for a couple of seconds. I might as well have been trying to push a mighty oak over. Then all resistance suddenly vanished. We both shot forward at least two yards. Before I could drag myself to a halt, I felt both my wrists being grabbed and torn away from Mark's foot.

I spun backwards and the watery void danced around me in a circle.

My head and heart were pounding, my lungs burning like fire, screaming for a fresh supply of oxygen. I saw that Mark had now pushed through the surface. He'd been down much longer than me, but I didn't think I could survive another second without taking an immediate breath.

I broke through into the air, gulping in a mouthful of salty water in the haste to replenish my lungs. Coughing it out, I managed to splutter a few words. "Are you okay?"

A torrent of water spurted from his mouth, rendering him unable to speak. By now Helen had arrived.

"What happened?" she cried, reaching for Mark's arm.

All I wanted to do at that moment was draw in huge lungfuls of beautiful, sweet, life-giving air. "Get him to the beach," I managed to gasp between coughs.

Helen's swimming expertise gave her the confidence to take immediate command of the situation. "Float on your back, Mark." He weakly complied, and she cupped a hand under his chin and began a powerful sidestroke towards the shore, pulling him effortlessly behind her.

My tortured lungs rattled and grated but began to feel a little more normal as the air started to expel any water left in them. On turning towards the shingle, I could see the water's edge was crowded with people who'd witnessed part of the drama and were on their way to help us. By the time I could feel land beneath my feet and managed to wade ashore, a tall, powerfully-built man had whisked Mark back to our towels and was slapping him hard on the back. I hurried over as fast as the unforgiving shingle would allow and found Mark spluttering his thanks to the concerned crowd standing over him.-

"But that wasn't the end of our horror that day." Still no reaction from Anna. I wish she'd show some emotion about our suffering. Or maybe it's just because I'm used to talking with people, not to or at them.

Anyway.

"Mum had lent us her car, and Mark had driven to Brighton," I said. "But his ankle was badly bruised after he was held down underwater, so we decided I should drive home. And that's when it tried to kill us again."...

I kept strictly within the speed limit, even on the open B road between Ringmer and Cross In Hand when I was tempted to see exactly what the Nissan could do.

I craned my neck a couple of times to catch a glimpse in the mirror of Mark and Helen who'd fallen asleep in the back. Their gentle rhythmic breathing grew slightly deeper as we crossed the county boundary back into Kent.

It was a good feeling, purring along, sometimes being overtaken by speeding cars, even occasionally overtaking slow ones myself. I'd only driven short distances previously, and as we swallowed up the miles, I needed all my concentration to combat the drowsiness creeping into me. I'd had the driver's window half-open for the last few miles but now wound it down fully, enjoying the refreshing blast of air. I could still feel my eyes closing, though, and it was a real effort to stop them from shutting.

Even shaking my head violently only brought me back to full alertness for a few seconds before the weariness was back.

As if something were telling me that it was okay to go to sleep.

Gentle.

Soothing.

Join Mark and Helen. Asleep, it seemed to be saying.

Sleep. Sleep. Sleep.

It was like being pleasantly merry. Half of me kept fighting the feeling.

Wake up, for fuck's sake, insisted one inner voice.

But the other half of me...

No, said another, much more soothing inner voice. *Go to sleep.*

You know you want to.

You're drowsy.

You want to doze.

It's okay. Doze.

If only for a few seconds.

You'll wake refreshed.

Shaking my head, I raised my eyebrows as high as they would go in an effort to stop my eyes from slipping shut. I tried to read the speedometer but the dial swam crazily around the dashboard. The road was now hurtling beneath the windscreen at a frantic pace.

But all I wanted to do was sleep.

Vaguely, I saw the dot swing around the bend about 300 yards in front of us, growing rapidly all the time until it took the shape of a car. Hurtling ever nearer. Nearer. Nearer.

A single powerful and penetrating note launched a

vicious assault on my ears, drowning out the insistent words that were still trying to lull me to sleep. Suddenly I saw two beams of bright light flashing angrily and constantly.

Headlights. A car horn.

The car heading straight for us was no more than a few yards away, braking, swerving sharply.

In the split second when my senses returned and I hauled the wheel around, I caught sight of a man's malicious face leering at me in the mirror. It was a face of utmost evil but was gone before I had time to register its features. All that showed in the mirror now were Helen and Mark being jerked around by the car's sudden erratic spinning.

My feet jabbed at the brake and clutch, and with a protesting squeal of burning rubber, I somehow managed to guide the Nissan past the oncoming vehicle with half an inch to spare. We came to a halt with a body-lurching jerk, flinging my passengers into a heap against the nearside.

I whirled around, but there was no sign of anyone in the back except Mark and Helen.-

As I finished that episode I wondered how much more of that dreadful summer I should relate to Anna. There were so many more times the spirit we went on to believe was Jim Roberts, attacked us.

Until we attacked back. Helen's 20th birthday party was the final straw. The night the spirit killed our beautiful red setter, Titus, and electrocuted Mark.

I'd been sitting alone, moodily drinking beer and my thoughts were turning dark. Thankfully they were interrupted when a pair of arms flung themselves around my neck, almost making me spill my beer in surprise...

I looked into Janice Briggs' smiling face hovering only inches from mine. "Come on Simon," she purred. "You promised me a dance, remember?"

Oh, don't worry, there was no way I would forget that. The fact that she was an active member of the bring-back-the-mini-skirt brigade ensured she would linger in my memory.

"Hang on," I said, quaffing my pint in one go.

Her three-inch heels pierced the grass as soon as she led the way out of the marquee and stepped off the canvas floor onto the lawn. She slipped off her shoes and made her way towards the dancing. I looked at her rear, appreciatively, and couldn't help but wonder whether the hem of her pure white cotton skirt was nearer to her chin than her ankles. I wouldn't have liked to lay odds on it either way. Her red cotton jersey halter top was knotted at the front, exposing her midriff. Short raven hair tapered at the base of her neck, around which was slung a black necklace comprising large Perspex lumps, and her pierced ears each sported two red hoops.

She made her way to a bench and slid her shoes under the seat, then ran barefoot to the edge of the dancers where she turned and waited for me to catch up before pulling me into the throng.

The record on the turntable was not one I recognised but needed a fairly active step to keep in time. Ignoring that fact, Janice linked her arms behind my neck and started squirming sideways in a style more suited to a smoochy number.

Janice Briggs was sixteen and had just left school. Her father ran the village hardware shop and she was going to begin working behind the counter there full-time. I guessed that trade would soon be boosted by a stream of Meriton's boys popping in for a packet of nails, a ball of twine, and a chat. She was certainly a very attractive girl from whichever angle you viewed her.

The smell of herbal shampoo wafted up from her

shining hair and mixed with a none-too-delicate perfume giving the impression that she had bathed in it rather than dabbed it on.

After a couple more dances, during which she kept her arms firmly entwined around my neck, I managed to untangle myself and led her back to the bench where she had left her shoes. She sat down rather heavily, again draping her long willowy arms across my shoulders, and pulled my lips onto hers. Mechanically, I submitted to her kiss, but only half-heartedly returned it. I was aware of her tongue probing my mouth while her fingers twirled locks of my hair. Although my arms were around her waist, it could hardly be said that I was holding her. It was more by accident than design that my linked fingers rested on the bare flesh of her back between her shirt and her skirt.

Her own fingers moved back from my shoulders and made their way down my chest to my growing bulge. Slowly she began rubbing the front of my trousers, taking obvious delight as the swelling increased under her gentle touch. Gripping tighter, her tenderness disappeared. I squirmed slightly, trying to control my emotions.

Was this right with so many eyes around, including Mum and Dad's and, possibly, our nemesis? That final thought spurred me into action. Despite the continued stirrings of my manhood, I gently eased her hand away.

Suddenly she pushed me back and jumped up, her dark eyes flashing accusingly. "What's the matter with you? Don't you want me?"

"Sorry? I don't know what—"

"I've had a better reaction from litmus paper. What's bugging you? Is there someone else here tonight that you like better than me?"

"Er...no. No, there's no one else, Janice. You know I like you."

"It seems like it." Sarcasm twisted her words and made them ugly, almost to the point of bitterness.

"It's just that there's...look, I'm sorry. Come on, sit down." I smiled into those suspicious eyes and watched with satisfaction as they melted into the warmth they had shown earlier.

She sat back down. Her hand reached for my still-bulging crotch. I moaned at the touch, and...

Suddenly a blood-curdling howl pierced the night as the music stopped and the lights dimmed. Instinctively Janice squeezed with a vice-like grip, then scrambled up. I leaped off the bench and looked towards the dancers. The overhead fairy lights were still on, but the disco lights had gone off, and so had the linear rope lights.

In the immediate aftermath of the scream, a deathly silence and stillness descended on the party. One moment the dancers were twisting and weaving about the grass; the next they were immobile, rooted to the spot. Then the world came alive again, starting with a murmur from the disco revellers and then swiftly growing to shouts and then screams.

"What's happened?" I yelled, frantically sprinting towards them. Mass hysteria was sweeping Helen's guests.

"What's happened?" I cried again. One ashen-faced youth stood apart from the rest. I gripped him by the shoulders, but his eyes stared back at me blankly. I shook him fiercely; he felt like a rag doll. Then, beyond him, I saw the cause of it all.

The DJ was scrambling up from the shrubs behind and a little to the side of his disco unit. A violent crackling filled the air as blue sparks showered in a small fountain across the controls. Two shapes were sprawled on the grass and alongside them stood Helen screaming hysterically, her head shaking wildly and her bloodless lips drawn back as tight as they could go.

Frantically I swung my horrified gaze away from the still forms on the ground to Helen and back again. It was only then that one of the two figures registered in my mind as having four legs, one of which twitched uncontrollably, as if responding to the pull of a mad puppet master. It was Titus. And next to him, recognisable now from the unmoving profile, was Mark. Running through Titus's mouth was the electric cable connecting the disco equipment to the mains supply in the garage, and Mark's left hand was gripping the dog's head firmly.

I started forward but someone grabbed my shoulder, spinning me around. "No. Don't touch him. He's had an electric shock."

"We've got to get them," I insisted, not really understanding what I was doing. This didn't seem to be me. I was somewhere else, refusing to take all this in.

"Where's the power supply?" It was the same youth who had stopped me from touching Mark.

"In the garage," I managed to stammer, trying to break free from his grasp.

"Don't touch them," he repeated urgently. "Not until the power's off."

Vaguely I saw someone sprint across the lawn towards the garage door.

I didn't want to believe what was happening. Somehow, Janice's overpowering perfume and wonderfully exquisite grip on my manhood had made me delirious. Any moment now, I would wake up to a wet sticky mess in my pants.

Fuck, yes.

"Don't touch the machine." Again, words of warning hammered through my numbness. The DJ had reached out to within an inch of the disco controls, but now stood frozen on hearing the urgency of the command aimed at him.

I seemed to be detached, witnessing the scene from a great distance, only half seeing another figure haul the DJ away from the still-sparking turntables.

Then Dad's voice from behind me, close, yet a million miles away. I had no idea what he was saying. I looked at him helplessly, then turned away, tears in my eyes.

Mark and Titus lay unmoving on the grass. Titus's twitching leg stilled now.

"Not yet, Mr. Reynolds." This time it was Dad who had to be held back. All of a sudden the crackling stopped and the fountain of sparks died.

"Okay." A voice from the garage. "The power's off."

As I watched, dumbstruck, several people descended on Mark and Titus. Someone pulled the chewed and frayed cable away from the dog's mouth. I was still in a daze but Dad, who seemed to be in full control, pushed through, dropping to his knees beside Mark, pressing his right ear to the unmoving chest.

"Simon," yelled Dad. "Stop daydreaming and see to Helen."

His harsh tone snapped me back to reality. I would not be waking to an empty, spent manhood. This reality was more fucked up than that.

Focusing again, I realised exactly what was happening. Helen was still screaming hysterically and her guests crowded around to see why. As soon as I clasped her to me, the torrent of sound was silenced, replaced by a flood of tears.

"He's dead, Simon," she sobbed. "He's dead. I know he is."

I squeezed her tightly, trying to comfort her as best I

could, while Dad felt for a pulse in Mark's neck. He looked up sharply as if a thought had suddenly struck him.

"Has anyone phoned an ambulance?" he shouted. "Tell them his heart's stopped. And for God's sake, hurry."

Turning his attention back to Mark, he landed a heavy blow on the breastbone. A couple of Helen's friends disappeared towards the house while Dad gripped Mark's nose. Then he placed his mouth over Mark's and blew steadily. It seemed an eternity before the air forced into Mark's lungs caused his chest to rise; it fell limply as soon as Dad backed off.

Dad's face was ashen as he lowered his mouth over Mark's again.

"Oh, God," sobbed Helen, burying her head deep in my shoulder.

Sleep, sleep, sleep. That inner voice again. The same mocking voice I heard in the car that lulled me to sleep on the way back from Brighton. All control suddenly seemed to flee from me.

"Who are you?" I screamed at the top of my voice. "What do you want from us? Why don't you leave us alone?"

I was aware of all eyes swivelling from Dad's frantic life-saving bid to me. They must have thought I was crazy, but at that precise moment, I didn't give a flying fuck whether they did or not. Nor, indeed, whether I really was crazy. All I cared about, in an intense and sudden blaze of passion, was my family and Mark. I'd had enough of this being from hell tormenting us. I wanted it gone. I wanted the vicar to destroy it.

But first, Mark's heart.

Dad ran his hand along Mark's chest locating the sternum. He pushed sharply, rocked back, pushed again, rocked back, again and again, and again. Interspersed with mouth-to-mouth resuscitation, he kept up the relentless blows on Mark's chest seemingly for hours, but in this fucked up reality it was merely a matter of moments before he shouted triumphantly, "His heart's started."

Only then did Dad allow himself to sink back wearily onto the grass. Mum had been alongside him, watching the life-giving process through widened, terrified eyes. Now that Mark was breathing, she gently eased Helen away from me and led her, still sobbing, towards the house.

I didn't need to examine Titus to know our beloved pet was dead. Helplessly, I turned to the DJ. "What happened?" I asked in tones so quiet I could barely hear them myself.

"I don't know," said the DJ. "Someone suddenly shouted and the next thing there was a tremendous bang and I was blown off my seat."

A couple of teenagers stepped forward. "Titus was lying by the disco asleep, I think," said one of them. "All at once he leaped up and stared towards the house, growling. I couldn't see anything to upset him, but he'd certainly got his eye on something."

I groaned inwardly. In my heart of hearts, I already knew what had caused this mayhem.

"Then he howled and cowered up against the unit," the boy continued, pointing towards the disco's control box. "He barked then ran round the side and started to bite the cable."

The youth paused momentarily and cocked his head in Mark's direction, who was still lying unconscious on the ground but breathing evenly. "That chap tried to stop him, but the dog wouldn't let go of the cable. Then there was a bang and sparks everywhere."

"That's hardly surprising," said the DJ, peering down

at the cable. About a metre away from the unit, the cable's white PVC coating was torn away, revealing the wires inside. Poor Titus's teeth had gone straight through those as well. Shreds of copper glinted in the fading light. The electricity had surged through Titus into Mark.

I felt myself becoming detached as my mind wandered back to the thought of Titus growling at something unseen. I hardly noticed the ambulance crew rushing through the garden to lift Mark onto a stretcher. Dad's voice sounded distant and remote when he told me that Mum, Sarah, and Helen were going to the hospital and he and I would stay behind to clear things away.

Anna leaned forward in her chair. "How awful. Is Mark alright?"

"Yes, he's fine now. He's gone to stay with his parents until he goes back to university." He went to Helen's funeral, but I wondered if that would be the last we'd ever see of him.

"Helen's party really was the final straw for us. Dad said it wasn't safe to stay in the house anymore, and that night we moved into the Grenadier Hotel in the village. We'd already spoken to the vicar about what was happening at the house, and when we told him about the party he was extremely concerned about our safety. Even more so when we told him about the two attacks on us during our trip to Brighton."

I recalled to Anna that the vicar agreed to carry out an exorcism, and how we finally thought we'd won. He'd ordered us to make the sign of the cross with our forefingers, and I remembered seeing his own crucifix pulsate with a miscellany of vivid colours. One moment it was blue, the next red, then green.

A fierce pounding began on the stairs as if a giant hammer were being thrust up and down on the carpet. Its echo rang madly throughout the hall, vibrant and powerful, and a cloud of smoke somewhat reminiscent of the dying embers of a bonfire sprang up to mask the step beyond. The smoke was white and appeared to be taking on a definite shape. It was as if each shred of smoke knew its place and was becoming interwoven with its neighbour to take on a solid form.

As we looked on in absolute terror, the white billowing mass drifted up the stairs to the landing where it stopped dead. At first, it simply stood there, as if it were looking down on us, mocking, knowing its strength. More smoke seemed to grow from its very bowels, and before long a six-foot human form towered there. It was indistinct, without features, but where the eyes should be were two burning red holes, as if we were looking into hell itself. Those eyes mirrored all the wickedness and evil ever born on this earth—and yet, at the same time, I sensed a deep and bitter sadness that lay beyond. The smoke moved subtly, but without any real change. The sadness seemed to take over. The evil was replaced by a haunted, longing look from within those burning holes.

"You can't fool us." The Reverend McBeil's words were strong and majestic. The fierce pounding still hammered into my ears, this time from the top of the stairs where the entity stood. There was no movement, yet the noise grew in strength, pounding ever deeper into my head. I screwed my face up, trying to be rid of the hurtful, hateful sound, but it still persisted, driving onwards, deep and penetrating.

Behind me, Sarah screamed and I sensed, rather than saw, her withdraw her handmade cross to cover her ears.

"No," yelled the vicar. "Keep the sign of the cross. Don't weaken our power." But it was too late. The second Sarah dropped her hands from the position of the cross the white misty figure at the top of the stairs took the next step toward becoming solid. The bedroom door behind it became dimmer as the smoke thickened. The intolerable noise—the thumping, the banging, the hammering, the unholy sound of hell itself—drove on ever louder. My head pounded, pushing me to copy Sarah, to cover my ears in a feeble effort to drown the evil sound, but I knew I must resist.

The creature still stood there, mocking, as if daring us to let it live.

The inner voice, given life by our foe on the stairs, spoke to me again, doing its best to fight my efforts to resist it. *Let me come*, it cried. *Don't oppose me. Give me what's mine. Sleep. Sleep. Sleep. Let go of your cross.*

It was almost as if I could sense the creature's inner turmoil and its frantic attempts to defeat us. Its cry became a roar, battering the inside of my head as I held out against its power, and I sent back a defiant message of my own. "You're not going to win. Leave us alone!"

I don't know how long we persevered against it, but Mum was next to weaken. "I can't stand it anymore," she sobbed. "Please stop. Please, please, please." Her voice, shrill and loud, cut through the thunderous roar, and as I glanced around I saw her break the sign of the cross and clasp her ears.

"No" I cried. "Don't give in to it."

"Keep the sign of the cross." The Reverend McBeil's voice was harsh and insistent. "It's the only defence we have at the moment."

The creature's triumphant laugh was something that will be with me to my dying day, and something I never wanted to hear again.

The power of the smoky, white figure grew with the loss

of another of our defences. A further bitter, twisted laugh escaped from where its lips should have been. And then slowly a mouth began to grow in its face. Features began to form, vaguely, but they were definitely moulding.

White, wispy arms raised themselves in an all-embracing gesture. The noise became even more deafening and the lights flickered. Then, above the din, I heard the whistling of the wind in the distance. It was coming again. Slowly, like a breeze tickling the leaves on a summer's day, it wafted around my face before it was suddenly back, as strong and powerful as it had been moments earlier.

The candle flame blew and twisted, bending low under the force of the wind. Suddenly it shot up, mighty and high, fierce and bright, rocketing a good two metres into the air. That small and meagre half-inch wick burst into a wondrous flame, dancing madly between us and the source of its newfound power on the stairs, just for a second. Then the flame thinned to the thickness of a piece of string, and hurtled from the wick up the stairs, dividing itself into two as it went. Each strand of fire reached the outstretched hands of the monstrous being and plunged deep within them. As they did so, the creature grew in stature, strength, and power. The lights flickered again, then dimmed. Soon they'd be gone altogether, and we'd be in darkness, just us and this monster from the pit. It would be in its element.

Each time the lights faltered the white smoke grew thicker and the wind became stronger. We had to bend into it or be knocked backwards. In order to keep my sign of the cross I dropped to my knees and tucked my head onto my shoulder, but the wind still tore around me and still the hammering persisted, thumping ceaselessly and relentlessly. The lights gave up without warning as the power that was draining them finally won. Pure energy shot from the bulbs across the hall and up the stairs, finding their target in the outstretched arms. Sudden, intense darkness surrounded us; the only light came from the figure at the top of the stairs, which now radiated and glowed with the energy stolen from us.

The creature's lips split into a hollow grin as it finally started down the stairs towards us, its face becoming more distinct with every step.

"I command you..." The Reverend McBeil's voice strained above the wind that kept us bowed down. "Go back from whence you came, you creature of darkness. In the name of our Lord Jesus Christ, begone!"

Somewhere beyond the dreadful roar of the gale and constant hammering, I heard the crashing of our hall furniture as the wind picked it up like matchwood and smashed it against the walls. Yet still the vicar's words cut through.

The light shining from the creature grew brighter as it came closer, casting an eerie, almost moonlight-like glow across the hall. The vicar stood upright, his hair skinned back from his head in the blast of the hurricane. The creature took another step. Slowly the white smoke solidified. And there on the stairs stood a human man, as firm and real as any I have ever seen. Tall, thin, brown-eyed, with black hair cut short and swept back off the forehead. Behind me, Helen screamed. As I turned she, too, dropped her crossed fingers. Her eyes were wide and staring as she gazed upon the spirit's face. "You!" The single word tore from Helen's lips in a terrified shriek.

Something drew my eyes to the vicar's face that was contorting beyond belief as he shook his head, trying to pretend it wasn't happening. The next second the contortions disappeared and a determined look engulfed him. "Die, you monstrous thing. Die." The lifeless candle dropped from his grasp and he tore the crucifix from around his neck. With one movement, he hurled the Bible from his right hand and the cross from his left, straight into the advancing form. In an instant, the malicious smirk disappeared from the creature's face as, with an agonised cry, it thrust its hands up to where the makeshift missiles had passed through. The movement was accompanied by a blinding flash and deafening roar, and I was buffeted by this new power surge. Sprawling backwards into Mum and the girls, my last conscious memory was of the most dreadful scream coming from the thing on the stairs. I tried to look up to see what the creature was doing, but dropped suddenly into peaceful oblivion.

It must have been only a second or two at most before I awoke. Pitch-blackness surrounded me before the discarded candle burst into life, its flame rekindled. But the only thing going through my mind was that inhuman cry of pain and despair I heard before I passed out.

I struggled into a slumped position and looked around. The power of the candle's flame was now immense as it shone far and wide, illuminating the entire hall. I shook my head vigorously to clear it and found I could still hear the lingering throbs of that terrible cry. As the echoes died away, so did the flickering flame until it was nothing more than an ordinary candle again. The electric light found a new lease of life in that same moment, coming back and flooding the scene with brightness.

The creature was gone.

And with it, our torment. Or so we'd thought.

Now, sitting in front of Anna, the hardest part of the

story was yet to come. Telling her how Helen had died would be difficult. Not that I couldn't remember it, of course. That was the easy bit. Especially as I'd relived it again after COVID knocked me unconscious at home. It had all came rushing back during that strange, ethereal time until the paramedic brought me round.

No. I mean emotionally. Thirty-eight years may have passed but the flashback made it raw and jagged again. Instead of letting it all spill out, which was Dad's reasoning behind me seeing a counsellor, it had stayed bottled up inside, festering and growing because I'd not been there during that first session with Anna. Until now. Better late than never, I guess.

Does that mean I've definitely got to tell her now? What happens if I don't? What happens if I simply get up and walk out and don't tell her how Helen died?

I remember she'd said at the start of our second session how brave I'd been to tell her the whole story of that summer at White Pastures, and it emerged in the conversation that I'd explained about looking out of my bedroom window at events from the Second World War, and hearing Helen die at the same time.

If I don't do that now, will I change the future, which is also my past? Shit, this is confusing, and all the time Anna's holding me with that inscrutable look.

I'm expecting to wake up tomorrow morning with no memory of this, but I can't risk changing anything. I've no idea what would happen if I did. So, let's do it. Let's finally get it off my chest.

Which I did. Instead of it being 38 years since it happened, those scenes that I'd relived in my mind's eye were still fresh in my mind, so it was simple to pull them up and narrate them to Anna, like watching a film unfold before my eyes.

"How does it make you feel now?" Anna asked when I finally reached the part where Dad said Helen was dead.

Water tinkling around the copper wheel was the only sound for the next 30 seconds while I considered my words carefully. Even though I'd had many years to process those events, the answer needed to come from an 18-year-old mind and relate to something that happened just weeks ago.

"Everything's a little numb right now," I said. "So I guess I'm still in shock. I keep on thinking about all the things we did together."

"That's understandable," said Anna. "It's natural for our minds to protect us from pain, so you may find you'll be numb for a while. It'll help you process what's happened at a pace you can manage, and not before you're ready. Shock provides some emotional protection from becoming overwhelmed."

In those early days after Helen's death, I used to carry her photograph with me at all times, before Sarah claimed it. Did I have it today, I wondered?

Reaching into the breast pocket of my sweatshirt I retrieved my wallet and opened it. Yes. Here it is, captured just a few weeks earlier by the portrait lens of Dad's Pentax, showing Helen's silky blonde hair tumbling past her shoulders, her impish eyes, and smiling mouth. The cheeks displayed a trace of blusher, and the eyelids a hint of misty blue.

The second face, pressed tightly against Helen's, featured sad brown eyes, and a long tapering black nose, with the body below it entirely covered by rusty hair. Our poor red setter, Titus, had always posed beautifully when he saw a camera.

Silently I passed the picture over to Anna. "She's beautiful," she said. A slight smile played across her lips as she looked at it for a few more seconds before handing it back to me.

"There's just one more thing you need to know, which may help you to understand how we're all feeling," I said a little hesitantly, and paused again. I've just bombarded her with what many people would probably regard as an outlandish and highly improbable sequence of events, and she's not batted an eyelid.

Let's see how she reacts to this.

"You remember how I said Helen shouted 'You,' when the spirit's face became clearly visible?"

Anna nodded. "I do."

"The day after Helen died I went back to see the vicar."

Silently the Reverend McBeil pulled the bottom drawer of his desk open and brought out a frayed newspaper cutting. I took the proffered cutting, which was yellowing with age. The photograph and words on it were still plainly visible, though.

My heart leaped. It was a wedding report cut from the local newspaper, and the two happy, smiling faces staring up at me from across the years were those of my sister Helen and the apparition I'd seen at the top of the stairs. There was no mistaking the man. The short haircut swept neatly away from the high forehead, the deep brown eyes. Every feature was the same.

"James Roberts and Heidi Ryknield," said the vicar. "They were the first couple I ever married. It was just about the first church work I did here. Then she died a few days after that picture was taken and her husband disappeared."

My eyes were glued to the girl's face in the ageing photo,

unsuccessfully searching for something that would tell me it wasn't Helen.

"What happened to him?" I asked, trying not to let a tremor creep into my voice.

"After Heidi's funeral, he set off to walk home and wouldn't let anyone go with him. As you know, it's only a couple of miles from the church to White Pastures, but somewhere along that route Jim Roberts disappeared from the face of the earth and was never seen again. It was widely thought he killed himself, but his body was never found."

Oh, he has been seen again, I thought. Back at his house— our house—or at least what's left of him. His soul, his spirit, has been back to reclaim his bride.

"You'll probably think me a silly old man for telling you this," said the Reverend McBeil, "But I had a dream a few nights after Heidi's funeral, such a vivid dream that I've never forgotten it. I'd just gone to bed and must have been exhausted because it all seemed to happen as soon as I'd put the light out. I must have gone to sleep immediately. In my dream, I was sitting up in bed when a dark shadow appeared in the corner of the room. It grew from a shapeless mass to a vaguely human form. It became more distinct every second and I could soon see its face quite clearly. As I stared at it, it spoke to me. There was no mistaking either the face or the voice. It was Jim Roberts. At first, I thought I must be awake and he'd clambered up the vines outside my bedroom window. But as he spoke, the shadow dimmed and faded away before my eyes. I remember trying to snap myself awake, and the next moment I was sitting up in bed shivering with a definite chill in the air that hadn't been there before."

"You said Jim Roberts spoke to you that night?"

He nodded silently, almost as if he couldn't bring himself to tell me anymore. I was forced to ask what the apparition had said.

I could tell by the look on Reverend McBeil's face that he was thinking back in time. "I can remember his exact words." He paused again, looking me straight in the eyes, causing a shiver to emerge in the small of my back.

"He said to me, 'Reverend McBeil, you have married us in the house of the Lord. In the eyes of God, Heidi and I are one, bound to each other with a ring of gold. Nothing shall put us asunder. One day I will return for my bride.'"

"But if...?" Thoughts whirled irrationally through my muddled mind. "I don't understand. If James Roberts did kill himself, wouldn't he have been with Heidi again?"

The vicar shrugged. "I can't offer any explanation, Simon. I'm merely telling you what I know. One thing I might say, though, is that suicide is regarded as a major sin against God. If, in fact, he did kill himself, maybe his spirit has been condemned to wander in limbo all these years. Who knows?"

"But why take my sister? Unless...?" My eyes dropped to the photograph. "Do you believe in reincarnation?"

This time he smiled. "As a believer in the Christian faith, I must say no, I don't. I believe in the final resurrection of man, and until the final day of judgement is upon us the spirit dwells elsewhere, not in another body."

Clearly, though, his voice lacked sincerity, and his eyes clouded as if he knew the spark of truth had gone.

I had just reached the door when he called me back. "There is perhaps one more thing you should know, Simon," he said. "Heidi Roberts died the night after her twentieth birthday."

"So, you see, Anna," I said. "The spirit may just have

wanted its own true love back, and in its sad and misguided way saw in Helen the happiness it lost all those years ago.

"I don't suppose we'll ever know if Helen really was Heidi's reincarnation, or if she's an innocent victim of some dreadful spiritual mix-up. But, after what the vicar told me, I can sometimes see Jim and Heidi hand in hand, in my mind's eye, wandering wherever it is contented spirits go. Happy and peaceful, reunited across the years."

The pause seemed endless as Anna held silent eye contact with me.

I simply didn't know what to do or say. Here was 56-year-old me hitching a ride inside my 18-year-old body during the first of many blackouts throughout my life.

Is this Grandma's gift? Is it using me now, as Grandma said it would, sending me back to fill in the blanks? If it is her gift, and it surely has to be, how do I control it? She told me I'd begin to get answers the first time it used me. As a radio interviewer I've asked thousands of questions, and always got answers back. They weren't necessarily the truth, the whole truth and nothing but the truth, especially when it came to politicians, but they were answers, nevertheless. The biggest question I've ever asked isn't connected to my job, however. It's a personal one: 'What causes my blackouts?' I've asked it many times of many people, and while dozens of tests have been carried out and many theories put forward, I've never been any nearer to getting an answer.

Until now.

This has to be it.

Cause and effect. It looks as if I cause the blackouts by going back in time and into my body when I was younger. If this experience with Anna here in my past is anything to go by, it seems I'm now in control with older me guiding younger me, and older me's thoughts putting words into younger me's mouth. Am I going to live through these snippets in the past with hindsight and hopefully wisdom and experience? This begs two questions: is 56-year-old me having a blackout while my mind's here, and where's my younger self's mind while this is going on?

More questions suddenly take shape: what's the point of all this, why's it happening, what am I gaining from it? Then another thought materialises. Not a question this time, just a straightforward fact. Actually, it's an answer to my first question: I'm probably having a long blackout back in 2020, because the last thing I remember was seeing my unconscious body connected to all manner of machines and drips, being wheeled in bed along a corridor, and hearing the medics say they were taking me to intensive care.

My head's spinning with confusion, but I'm sure that was the last thing to happen before I found myself in the same white cavern where I'd met Grandma and Helen earlier, and then stepped into the summer of 1982 at the entrance to Merebrook Surgery and Medical Centre.

If I'm right, and the blackouts are caused by going back into my younger body, I've got a lot of trips into the past to make, because I've had at least four blackouts every year since 1982.

So, that being the case...

Anna's voice cut through my thoughts: "Are you alright, Simon?"

I nodded. For fuck's sake, this is hard. How do I get my head around it? She saw young me who's recently lost my sister, but the person replying to her lives 38 years in the future from this moment. Here's the paradox: younger me has several more meetings with her to come over the next few months, while older me remembers them all. Time has dimmed the details, but they'd been crystal clear at the time.

Maybe my nod had been a little premature. "Actually, no, I'm not," I admitted. "Do you think we could leave it for today?"

"Of course, Simon." She stood and crossed the semi-circle of chairs to me, placing her hand on my shoulder. For a second she didn't speak, and all I heard was the tinkling of the water wheel ornament.

I looked up at her, seeing the concern etched on her face before she broke the silence: "You've done very well. I wasn't expecting you to tell me so much at our first session. I feel as if I know you and your family already."

As I left the medical centre, the late summer sun dappled through the trees overhanging the path towards the car park where Dad was waiting for me, and I started to think about how to spend the rest of the day and evening. What would 18-year-old me have done? This is another paradox, isn't it, I asked myself? Would I change what's already happened if I tell Dad about it in the car on the way home or over dinner tonight, instead of during breakfast tomorrow?

No. I couldn't do that. I don't think Grandma or the universe gave me this gift to abuse it in that way. The flashback I'd had while lying on the spare bedroom floor waiting for the ambulance was still clear in my mind. In my past, I've already told Dad in the morning, and I just need to make sure I don't do anything to contradict that, before young me regains control and wakes up in bed tomorrow.

13

Proning

April 7th, 2020, Andrew

Andrew looked down at the ward's iPad, which was a little unnecessary given that they proned intubated patients every day. "Begin team and equipment check," he said, touching an icon. Everyone knew the procedure by heart and could have done it in their sleep. But, despite adding moments to the time taken to finish each procedure, they had to observe Maggie Bricknell's strict guidelines before starting to turn individual patients, without exception.

Doctor Douglas Moss glanced cursorily at the contents of a trolley behind him which were spread out so each one could be reached easily. "Three spare sheets, incontinence sheets, and three pillows; check," he said.

A second trolley, this one on the opposite side of Simon's bed, contained two red slide sheets and replacement ECG dots. Julian Marsh, from the ICU education team, confirmed their presence.

Emma had completed her checks a moment ago and now listed them for Andrew to tick the boxes on Bricknell's electronic form. "Aspiration of the nasogastric tube; check. ECG dots removed; check. Essential lines secured; check. Sufficient length of wires and pipes for turning procedure; check. Non-essential monitoring and infusions temporarily disconnected; check."

Andrew passed her the iPad for verification of his own pre-proning tasks—another aspect of the buddy system. As proning team leader, he couldn't be immune from the double-check. When Bricknell explained her thought processes she'd said it was all to ensure there could be no legal comeback for negligence, and to make sure they had what she called 'good PR optics.' He mentally shook his head at the time, clenching his fists as rage bubbled up inside him. *Oh, you've definitely got the modern jargon, haven't you? And the modern set of ethics. You really are all about the corporate establishment.* It always angered him that while front-line medical staff did everything to uphold the Hippocratic Oath for the good of their patients, everything the corporate wallahs did was in true never mind the quality feel the width fashion, to appease soul-less bean counters and maintain a good public image at all costs. Human collateral damage was a legitimate loss in their eyes, he thought.

"Endotracheal tube secured, and DuoDERM and sponge protection applied; check," he told Emma. She touched the relevant box to confirm the first of his required records. "Eyes cleaned, ointment applied, and taped shut; check," he said.

Andrew took the iPad back and looked at Karen Spencer. "Karen?"

"Urinary catheter in place between the patient's legs, exiting at the foot of the bed; check," she said. "Patient's arms by his side, palms facing inwards; check."

Once the checks were completed to Andrew's satisfaction and the procedure was ready to begin, he turned the ventilator up to 100 percent oxygen which would provide a margin of safety if something went wrong.

Doug placed three pillows on Simon—one on his chest, another over his pelvis, the last at his thighs—then covered him with a sheet. Poolswood Hospital medical staff never told induced coma patients or their families that they're turned naked, to preserve what little dignity they have left. Any form of clothing runs the risk of getting tangled in the essential wires and tubes, and Simon's Lapover hospital gown was removed when Emma disconnected the non-essential ones.

Now he lay naked on a sheet with the clean one on top. Doug, Jim, Julian, and Karen each took hold of the top one immediately in front of them and crimped it into the edge of the bottom sheet, twisting them so it resembled a Cornish Pasty, and gave name to the Cornish Pasty technique.

"Slide sheets at the ready," instructed Andrew. "Ready, steady, go." Doug and Jim pulled Simon to their side of the bed, away from the ventilator. "We will turn when I say three in a one, two, three count."

At the end of that manoeuvre, Simon had been half-turned while Julian and Karen pushed two flexible red slide sheets underneath him. Then they rolled Simon the other way, allowing Doug and Jim to pull the sheets completely through.

"Review all lines and tubes before the final turn."

Emma checked each of the connections. "All firm," she reported.

"Any preference on which way we're going?" asked Andrew. "Slide to the left and roll to the right, or slide right and roll left?"

"No, your choice," Doug told him.

"In that case, slide left, roll right. Ready, Doug?"

"Ready."

"Ready, Jim?"

"Ready."

Having gone around everyone, Andrew gave the next instruction: "Ready, steady, slide."

Another slide to the left and roll to the right put Simon

on his side. The next final half-turn onto the stomach would pose the greatest threat to the stability of the Endotracheal tube in his airway, so Andrew carefully checked it was still firmly secured to Simon's mask.

"Everything in place," he told the team. "Prepare to complete pronation."

"Ready," they replied together.

"On my mark. Take it slow. Ready, steady, cheers." They gently rolled Simon into the fully prone position, then removed the top sheet and covered him with his Lapover gown. Emma brought his right arm up as if he were swimming front crawl, and turned his head towards the ventilator.

While Andrew checked that Simon hadn't bitten down on the tube in his mouth, and confirmed there were no kinks anywhere in it, Jim placed new ECG dots on his back and quickly reattached all monitoring wires and infusion pipes.

The team removed the specialist slide sheets used in the process and carried out the remaining steps to make Simon comfortable for the 16-hour duration of his proning. They finalised the procedure by reviewing pressure points, turning the oxygen down again to its pre-proning level, and raising the head of the bed.

Doug confirmed that Simon's blood pressure was stable, and the ventilator currently provided an oxygen saturation level of 92 percent. The proning had been successful, and the team could move on to the next patient.

"Simon Reynolds pronation completed at 4.45 p.m.," said Andrew, logging the time into the iPad. "Setting reminder for the overnight shift to deprone at 8.15 tomorrow morning."

During the last couple of hours of his shift, after he handed over the ward reins to the lead doctor on the 12-hour overnight stint from 9.30 p.m. to 9.30 a.m., Andrew set about going through Simon's records with the proverbial fine toothcomb and found most aspects to be exactly what he'd expect for a coma patient.

But not the EEG results. Raising a hand while in a coma simply shouldn't happen. Neither should the eye flicker, nor saying "Grandma." While the general motor activity registered normal, several sharply spiking waves were far from normal.

He looked again at the data from yesterday's EEG and read the physiologist's conclusions about each wave. Andrew trawled back through his years of experience but failed to remember anything comparable to what the records in front of him showed, and confirmed his view that Simon was becoming a medical enigma.

He took his glasses off and laid them down on the desk, leaning back in his chair, deep in thought. While patients are in medically induced comas, their brains are quiet for up to several seconds at a time, punctuated by short bursts of activity. This 'burst suppression' gives the brain time to conserve energy, but looking at Simon's full readout it was clear something was happening that just didn't add up. The amount of anesthetic being dripped into him was strictly controlled, aiming for the optimum number of bursts as the EEG pattern streamed across the monitor, which needs to be maintained for days at a time.

Yes, he mused. The brain reacts when the body doesn't. He knew that a small percentage of coma patients—digging back into his memory a figure of around 15 percent sprang to mind—showed brain activity patterns similar to a fit and active person, but nothing along the lines of Simon's results.

Maybe COVID's turning what we know on its head, he thought. In the few weeks he'd been dealing with it, some patients had died in the most horrible way, and others were hardly affected by it. Who's to say that COVID doesn't keep the brain fully active in a coma, overriding the effects of the anaesthetic?

He scrolled down the screen, clicking on every file updated since Simon came into hospital. He needed to talk it over with colleagues, but the combination of his body's recovery and the EEG results told him it may be time to consider bringing Simon out of the coma.

Phone Call, April 8th, 2020, Andrew

"Oh God, what's happened?" The strain and panic in Janice's voice were all too evident down the 'phone line.

"There's nothing to worry about, Mrs. Reynolds," Andrew said. "In fact, it's just the opposite. I'm ringing to tell you we're going to start bringing Simon out of the coma this evening."

"What?" He sensed almost disbelief in her single word. "Is he alright, then?" Now she sounded lighter as if relief were flooding through her, but nothing he hadn't expected.

"He's been in the coma for eight days, which, in Simon's case, we're sure has been long enough for his body to recover enough to fight the infection naturally." Giving a ray of hope like this was his second favourite part of talking to patients' relatives, the number one being telling them their loved one was fully fit and ready to go home. Given his pessimism of a few days ago when he didn't think Simon was going to survive, he could barely believe he was passing this good news on to her.

"The longer someone's in a coma, the more dangerous it is for them," he said, "and the harder it becomes for them to make a full recovery. We've..."

"What's changed with him, though? When I spoke to the

ward this morning they said he'd had a comfortable night, but there was no change in his condition."

"He's been making slow but steady progress, in line with our expectations. We reviewed everything this morning and his heart and lungs both look considerably healthier than when he came in." *Now's not the time to tell her about the brain pattern anomalies. Let's get him out of the coma and see what he remembers of his time under, before we go down that route.* "We're very pleased with how he's doing at the moment, so we're going to gradually reduce the anaesthesia which is keeping him in the coma and see if he can breathe by himself, and assess his heart rhythm.

"If all goes as well as we hope, and indeed, expect, we'll stop his anaesthetic altogether, and bring him round."

"Will he be back to normal then?"

That was the 64,000-dollar question.

"We're hoping his body will have recovered enough to fight off the COVID infection, but everyone responds in a different way to coming out of a coma," he said. "As Simon's only been under for eight days, he could wake up relatively quickly. We'll keep you fully up to date with how he's doing, and we'll let you talk to him on a video call as soon as we can."

"When do you think that'll be?"

"The thing to remember is that waking up is, generally speaking, a process and not an event. This..."

"Sorry, Doctor Moore, I don't understand."

He paused for a second, collecting his thoughts on the best way to explain. "Well, by 'process' I mean it's something that takes place over a period of time and isn't a single event that gives you an instant result like switching a light on. In fact, if we were to follow that light switch analogy, it's like turning the light on slowly with a dimmer switch. He'll regain consciousness very slowly. And he may be confused when he starts to come round, but that's only to be expected."

"Does this mean he'll be coming off the ventilator, too?"

"It does. He'll only be able to tolerate the breathing tube down his throat while he's in the coma, as it would be too uncomfortable and painful to be awake during this type of mechanical ventilation with a breathing tube, so we'll take steps to wean him off the ventilator."

Another pause, while he wondered how much detail she'd want about this. "The medical term is extubation," he began hesitantly, and carried on when she didn't comment. "Initially, while Simon's still in the coma we'll continue with the controlled flow of oxygen delivering the required number of breaths every minute.

"When we start to reduce his sedation and painkillers to gradually wake him up, we'd expect him to start taking breaths himself, without the assistance of the ventilator."

"So you think he's ready for that now?" asked Janice.

"All the signs are that he's ready to give it a go, anyway. If he's not, we'll put him under again for a few days. But the sooner we can bring him out of it, the better it'll be for him.

"As he wakes up more and more, and we keep reducing the sedation, he should be able to take breaths with minimal support. Gradually, we'll bring what we call 'mandatory breaths,' provided by the ventilator, down to zero. Simon should then be making all the effort to breathe himself and can come off it."

Andrew thought how simple it all sounded, and he usually knew exactly what he was doing. Over the years he'd put many patients into induced comas and brought them out again with the full array of expected results. That was before COVID, though. So far, in the few weeks of the pandemic, he'd been involved in intubating 23 patients but none had recovered sufficiently to be brought out yet.

Except for Simon, and he was already feeling jittery at the uncertainty the voyage into the unknown of waking him, would bring.

"Once he's taking between ten and 30 breaths by himself from the ventilator, we'll consider that to be a sustainable rate. There are other considerations to look at, as well, to do with the amount of Carbon Dioxide in his blood, and Oxygen saturation levels."

He took his glasses off. Perhaps just a delaying tactic before going into the final phase.

"Because we're still in the early stages of fighting COVID, and the disease attacks the lungs, we're not sure how easily patients who've been severely affected, as Simon has, will be able to breathe by themselves when they come off the ventilator. That will be the crisis point."

He heard Janice try to stifle a sob and quickly continued with his train of thought before she could ask more questions which may take him down a side road. "But we firmly believe from the progress Simon's made, that he's come through the worst of it."

He leaned forward in his chair, resting his elbow on the desk, as if bringing his body closer to the telephone would put him closer to Janice.

"As his next of kin, we can't do this without you," he said. "Do you give us your permission to wake him up?"

14

Jigonhsasee

April 9th, 2020, Simon

It's as if time and space ceased to exist for me. I could be anywhere in the depths of infinity between the start of creation and the very end of time itself.

I'm coming up somewhere from a long way down, and as I emerge from the depths, I'm firing torpedoes from tubes, pipes, and wires which extrude from my body, like a warrior going onto the battlefield. None of the ammunition is indiscriminate, it's all aimed at Bob Appleyard, Poolswood Sound's station manager. Poor sod. What did he ever do to me to deserve that?

How do I know he's there, though? How do I know anything's there? My eyes are open but there's nothing to see except a yellowy-brown expanse above me, bisected by a thin strip of light, all of which was teetering in and out of focus.

Regular metallic beeps punctuate the stillness before I hear a muffled voice a long way away to my left. "Slight signs of him coming round."

I could feel a tightness in my throat and my teeth clamped down on something in my mouth. What the fuck was it? Panic hit as I tried to lift my right arm to my face, and couldn't. It simply refused to budge. Next up, I tried to expel the intruder in my mouth by getting my tongue behind it, but it was too long for my probing to find its end, either in or out of my mouth. It stretched away beyond my lips, and I guess its presence in the other direction was the cause of that tightness in my throat.

Of course, I could just be imagining it. I don't know what's real and what's not since COVID wrapped its obscene arms around me. Were Helen and Grandma real when I saw them by the white light? Hell, was the white light even real? What about the flashbacks to the events directly before my blackouts, and that weird jump I did into my own body in 1982? Everything started with COVID—has it done something to my mind, giving me hallucinations or random improbable dreams?

Wherever this was now, I didn't like it. For a few seconds, the yellowy-brown view flickered into focus. It's a ceiling, and the bisecting strip of light was exactly that: a strip light.

The voice came again: "Stabilise anaesthetic for the next hour." Perhaps it's a little nearer now. It's definitely less muffled. I tried to swallow but found it hard and almost ineffectual thanks to the obstruction in my throat.

Mentally I saw those torpedoes I'm firing at Bob take a detour to my lungs. Ah, now I know what the obstruction is. It's a tube in my windpipe. The torpedoes line up in my lungs and one by one ease their way into it, then fire in rapid succession, up the tube through my mouth and out of my body. I don't know if they hit Bob.

A large shape hovered into view right on the edge of my eye-line. I couldn't move my head to get a better look, but I could swivel my eyes to take in a person resembling an astronaut or deep sea diver in those old-fashioned movies. A plastic visor protected the entire face, and behind that, the eyes looked out through goggles, with the nose and mouth obscured by a blue mask. The rest of the head was covered entirely by a white cloth which reminded me of a balaclava.

The head started to swim out of focus before turning away, and its voice also lost clarity. "Some response, but..."

In an instant, the yellowy-brown ceiling with its strip light turned white. I'm no longer lying down and looking up, but standing peering into the depths of the white void, and I can move freely again. I start to walk towards the light's shining origin someway in the distance and find myself watching the coffin bearers gently lowering Grandma's casket into her grave.

The Vicar—I still couldn't remember his name—made the sign of the cross and bent to pick up a handful of soil from the large pile at the side of the grave, which he scattered onto the coffin.

As I was starting to gather my wits, Mum and Dad threw soil onto the coffin, too, and looked towards me, no doubt expecting me to do the same. I scooped some up and let it trickle slowly out of my hand.

How weird, I thought. Grandma's been gone for many years but here I am back at that time, and I've absolutely no idea what's going to happen next. And even weirder, I guess, is that I've been talking to Grandma recently. That was real, wasn't it? Of course it was, even if Captain Caveman wasn't.

This is definitely real, too. It's only recently that the flashback brought me to the cemetery, to the part I remembered. Here we go, into the unknown. What's about to unfold has always been one of the many blanks in my life. My heart pounded at the thought that I'm about to experience what happened during another blackout.

The funeral party started to walk back along the cracked concrete path towards the church, and I joined them alongside Sarah. I was just about to take her hand when a quiet voice penetrated straight into my mind: "Simon." It was Grandma's voice, and it set my heart racing.

I risked a quick glance at Sarah, but she seemed oblivious.

Grandma's voice came again: "Simon." I stopped mid-stride and looked around, not expecting to see her, of course. Not here. Not now. This wasn't that wondrous white realm pulling me in, where Grandma had seemed to be in her element so much.

"I'm just going back to the grave," I told Sarah.

She looked at me, concern etched across her face. "Why? Are you okay?"

"I just need to go and say a final goodbye to Grandma by myself." I doubt the younger me would have thought on my feet quickly enough to come up with that after hearing Grandma's voice, but older me was a different pan of potatoes altogether. "Tell Mum and Dad I won't be long," I said and sprinted back along the path without giving her time to quiz me further. Once beyond the avenue of trees bordering the graveyard I slowed to a walk.

"Grandma," I called in my mind. "I'm here."

What's that expression—the stillness of the grave? Everything was certainly quiet here now. I quickly looked around the area at the gaping hole in the earth with its soil piled up alongside. It had briefly crossed my mind that the funeral people or the gravedigger may still have been there, but they weren't. There was only me.

"Come to my grave, Simon," she said.

Excitement and caution each pulled me their way for a moment, as if I were a tug-of-war rope, then mingled into a single emotion. I could see why it had to be older me experiencing this. Younger me would have freaked out on hearing Grandma calling, quite literally, from beyond the grave.

I reached the edge and looked in. All I could see was the coffin with the loose soil that we'd thrown onto it scatted across the lid.

"Over here, Simon." It was all very well Grandma saying that, but her voice was only in my head. I've no idea where 'over here,' was. I slowly scanned the area. "Grandma," I projected mentally. "Where are you?"

Was that a slight movement alongside the Yew tree over by the hedge? Young me wouldn't have a clue what type of tree it was, or that Yews are often found in cemeteries and church yards, but I remember a vicar telling me about them during an interview in my early radio days.

He'd said the Pagan view was that Yews are associated with death and the soul's journey out of this life, and many churches were built on sites of pre-Christian temples where Yews were already planted. Christians went on to view the tree as holy because its heart is red and the sap white, symbolising the blood and body of Christ, and regarded its hardiness in being able to survive on infertile soil as suggesting rebirth and resurrection.

So it was no surprise when I saw Grandma step out from behind it. What did surprise me, though, was the girl who followed her into view and stood next to her. Just for a split second, I thought it was Helen, but as soon as I focused on her clearly, I saw, even from this distance, who it was.

It was the girl of my dreams. No, not like that. Perhaps I should say the girl of my nightmares. Her of the lank, greasy hair, of the dreadful white pallor to her skin, the deep ruby red lips, and black tongue. *No, surely this can't be*, I thought. *She doesn't exist outside my nightmares.*

The girl smiled. "And yet, here I am." Her words were thickened by an accent I couldn't place. As I stared at her, I got the impression that her appearance wasn't quite as shocking as I first thought. That wasn't it, though. She definitely had been deathly pale and her hair was thin and greasy just a second or two ago. Now her skin looked a shade darker and her hair was thicker, holding a richer tint and added glow. This was just as she'd looked before disappearing behind a tree in my nightmare of...well, however long ago it was, after stealing some of my life force in the two thin strands which had linked our bodies.

"Come on over," Grandma said. "I'd like you to meet Jigonhsasee."

As I approached the girl, I started to notice her clothes for the first time and tried to remember if they'd been the same in my dream. I couldn't recall if they were or not, but they certainly stood out today—her brown deerskin dress was decorated with porcupine quills and beading, along with a couple of silver brooches. A stunning blue overdress, fitted at the waist, fell to a flare between her knees and ankles, while beading and ribbons adorned the bottom of her leggings, which just touched the top of tanned deer hide moccasins.

A strikingly beautiful red velvet headband resembling a tiara, filled with beads and flower and leaf designs, completed the native American appearance.

What's she doing here? Does this mean it wasn't a dream but had been a real place, like the white cavern where I saw Grandma last time?

"All will be explained, Simon." Grandma's words rang out directly in my mind. D'Oh, I'd forgotten they would both be able to 'hear' my thoughts.

Jigonhsasee held her arms out to me. "Come, Simon," she said. "Embrace me."

A little concerned, I looked towards Grandma, remembering what she'd said about touching—that it would break the link holding my spirit to my earthly body.

She smiled. "No need to worry about that. This is different. The laws of Earth apply here, not the laws of the spiritual realm. You're still inside your body, so there's no link to break."

"But, Grandma, this is my body of nearly 40 years ago. Will I be able to get back to my older body in 2020?"

"Have I really been gone from you that long?" I sensed some sorrow in her tone. "Time doesn't mean anything to me now."

She reached over to me and took both my hands in hers. "Yes, you'll get back to where you belong. You just have to learn to use your gift first, and that's what we're going to show you. Now, embrace Jigonhsasee."

So the gift is this weird body jumping, sending me back to the time of my blackouts?

"Weird body jumping?" Again, Grandma picked up on my thoughts. "I like that. It's as good a name for it as the true name."

That kickstarted my journalistic instincts. "It has an actual name?" I asked. *Right, let's imagine I'm behind the microphone.*

"You won't need to imagine that." D'Oh, I'd done it again. I'll have to see if I can control my thoughts and restrict them to what I'd say out loud.

"Questions won't be necessary," Grandma continued. "Jigonhsasee and I will tell you everything you need to know."

She tightened her grip on my hands and swung me round to face Jigonhsasee, then released me as the girl put her arms around my shoulders. A spark of energy passed between us, but I couldn't say if it was from her to me, or me to her.

The hug felt absolutely right, as if I'd known Jigonhsasee all my life and we were greeting each other like old friends.

As the buzz of energy diminished, she eased me away slightly, clasping my left hand in her right. Grandma then took my right hand, before completing the circle with Jigonhsasee.

Instantly the spark returned, this time I felt it flowing in a constant anti-clockwise stream, passing from Jigonhsasee through me and into Grandma, its tingling sensation growing in intensity as it increased speed with each revolution. Not only could I feel it, but I began to see it after a few seconds as well, when a thin white strand of pulsating light materialised around us, just brushing the tops of our arms.

I'd seen this type of energy twice before. Once in what I'd thought was a dream, but now began to realise it may have been real, just on a different plane. That was when I'd first seen Jigonhsasee, and she'd absorbed it from me as it emerged from my body in two strands. The second time was when Grandma stepped out from behind a tree and it flowed from her to me, piercing my hands and entering my body.

"Grandma, what is this?" Even though my words were unspoken and telepathic, in my own mind they still sounded like a gasp.

The tingling felt almost electric as its power grew, flooding my body with raw spirit. I'd never felt so alive, thriving, and vibrant. It was almost as if I were being rejuvenated by the energy flow pumping its way through me.

I looked into Jigonhsasee's face and noticed subtle changes from a few seconds ago. It was as if someone was slowly turning up the colour saturation on a photograph. Her skin, which had already lost that awful deathly white pallor and taken on a darker hue, was now even further along the spectrum, reaching a smooth creamy brown. Her thick, jet-black hair shone with what was almost an internal glow and her eyes radiated warmth and love.

It was impossible for me to say how much time passed as we stood there—it could be a moment, it could be a lifetime, but a powerful thrumming filled the air throughout, while the white energy band continued its endless spinning, connecting me ever stronger to Grandma and Jigonhsasee.

However long it was, Grandma brought it to an end by releasing my hand and breaking the circle. The white strip of energy winked out of existence, and the only sound came from a pair of collared doves in the trees at the edge of the graveyard who seemed to realise it was spring and time to do what they and the bees are renowned for.

"You're now fully imbued with the power of Orenda," Grandma told me, "and your spiritual link to Jigonhsasee has been strengthened. You now see her as she truly is."

Grandma's words may have sounded logical in the context that one followed the other, but making sense of their meaning was an entirely different thing.

"Grandma, I'm a man of words, but you've flummoxed me with that one. What's Orenda?" I asked.

The reply came not from Grandma, but in Jigonhsasee's heavy accent. "It's my people's word for the spiritual energy inherent in everyone and the environment," she said. "Yours has been expanded, and we've given you the ability to control it."

"What?" My head seemed to spin faster than the white strip had.

"Everyone has Orenda, but only we Iroquois know how to harness it."

"Iroquois? Who?" I turned my attention to Grandma. "I thought you said I wouldn't need to ask any questions. Everything you're telling me leads to more questions."

"Patience, my boy, patience," she said. "The Orenda energy has heightened your senses and your inquisitiveness."

Then it was Jigonhsasee's words appearing in my mind: "If you quieten your thoughts, Simon, and let Orenda flow, peace and calm will fall upon you and your mind will be stilled, ready to take in and absorb the wisdom of the Iroquois."

"Who are the Iroquois?"

"My people," replied Jigonhsasee. "During my physical life in the 1700s, I belonged to a Cayuga tribe of Iroquois in northeast North America…"

"Seventeen hundreds…?" I couldn't help but interrupt.

"…and since my physical death I've been a spirit guide," she continued as if I hadn't spoken. "You're my latest charge."

"You're my spirit guide?"

"I am, indeed," she said, smiling at me. "I have been since the day you were born."

"What? I thought we'd only just connected?"

"We've had an unbreakable bond since your birth, but the energy of Orenda which Rosemary Paulina and I have just strengthened within you, tightens our connection."

"Why haven't I known about you before? Why now?"

"Jigonhsasee's been looking after you in more ways than you'll ever know," Grandma told me. "And more often than you can imagine. If she hadn't been at your side you'd have died several times over."

What? How can this be?

"Your Grandma perhaps overplays my role," said Jigonhsasee. "I've pulled a few strings when you've been threatened by spirits, that's all."

Grandma's gaze held mine firmly. "Twice in one day, when Jim Roberts came for you," she said.

This was getting too much. "Jim? But he was only after Helen, wasn't he? I wasn't in danger."

"You were, very much so. During those summer months at White Pastures in 1982 when the parallels between his bride and Helen were at their strongest, his grief led him down paths he shouldn't have taken, and he later bitterly regretted the steps he took along them. That's when Jigonhsasee was with you constantly."

"Let me show you," said Jigonhsasee.

Slowly the churchyard turned hazy as if I were seeing it through water. Wait. I *am* seeing it through water. The graves, the grass, the trees, and the church spire rising above them all appear to be on the seabed. Has my ability to decipher reality taken a raincheck? The next moment, in place of this quiet church setting, I was watching Mark and myself underwater. I looked on in horror as for the first time I realised we hadn't been alone that day on the Brighton coast when Mark had almost drowned. What I hadn't seen before was a figure holding Mark's right ankle, resisting all efforts to kick himself free. I saw him continue beating at his ankle as his eyes bulged in their sockets and his blond hair streamed upwards.

I watched myself arrive within a few inches of his writhing body and take hold of his arm, trying to steer him upwards. I recalled it felt as if I were pulling a ten-ton weight. I'd yanked for all I was worth until I was afraid I'd tear his arm from his shoulder, but now I knew why he'd remained rooted to the spot, and what had caused the vivid bruises on his ankle which we discovered later. How was it possible I hadn't seen Jim Roberts that day, holding him down, because I saw him now, as clear as a bell?

A shudder ran along my spine as I watched me grip his

ankle, right where Jim Roberts's hands were. Jim turned to me, an expression of pure rage and hate distorting his features. Then he looked beyond me, at something over my shoulder. Of course, the me in 1982 knew nothing of that. I'd been too busy trying to free Mark, but the me from 2020 now standing in the graveyard at Grandma's funeral (oh, for fuck's sake, could this get any more confusing?) saw Jigonhsasee arriving through the water. She barrelled straight into Jim, knocking all three of us several yards forward. Jim's hands lost their grip, and I saw Jigonhsasee grab my own wrists, pulling me away from Mark, then launching him towards the surface.

Jim Roberts turned in the water, locked his eyes on me, and moved towards me with outstretched arms. Thank God, I'd been totally unaware of any of this at the time. A second or two before he'd have reached me Jigonhsasee barged him again, wrapping her arms around him in a wrestling-style bear hug. He squirmed and writhed, trying to force his way out of her constricting embrace.

"That's what happened," said Grandma. "Now watch what he'd have done next if Jigonhsasee hadn't stopped him long enough for you to get out of the water."

I remembered spinning backwards as the watery void danced around me in a circle. My head and heart had been pounding and my lungs burning like fire, screaming for a fresh supply of oxygen. I saw that Mark had made it to the surface, and set off in his wake.

That's when things changed. Instead of breaking through into the air and gulping in a mouthful of salty water in the haste to replenish my lungs, which is what happened, I felt my ankles grabbed and I shot back down to the seabed.

As I hit the rocks, Jim released my feet and took hold of

my throat, snarling into my face.

Just as I'd seen Mark's eyes bulging, I now looked on in horror as mine did the same. There was no need for Jim to throttle the life out of me, my lungs were already empty from being underwater far longer than was comfortable. All he had to do was hold me there. Now, standing here in the churchyard with Grandma just moments after her funeral, I watched as I thrashed around in the water, desperately trying to free myself from his grip. I only had seconds left. I could imagine the blood rushing to my brain, and the universe exploding around me as my lungs strained to breaking point.

Those mere seconds were literally all it took before my frantic flailing became still. He let go of my body, and my arms spread out as if I were on a cross, while I floated aimlessly away.

The scene slowly faded and we were back by the trees in the churchyard. Stunned, I looked across at Grandma. "That...that wouldn't have happened, would it?"

"It most certainly would if Jigonhsasee hadn't given you time to get away."

For the first time in this conversation, I spoke aloud. "Thank you, Jigonhsasee. It looks as if you saved my life."

"It wasn't the only time that day," said Grandma.

Again, the landscape melted away and I found myself looking into our car on the way home from Brighton, with me at the wheel. The memory of how sleepy I'd felt came at me in a two-pronged attack. One, across the years, and the other from when it had stirred while relating the episode to Anna. The road was hurtling beneath the windscreen at a frantic pace.

Sleep. Sleep. Sleep. I remembered how insistent the voice in my head had been.

Vaguely, I saw the dot swing round the bend about 300

metres in front of us, growing rapidly all the time until it took the shape of a car. Hurtling ever nearer. Nearer. Nearer.

A single powerful and penetrating note launched a vicious assault on my ears, drowning out the unrelenting words that were still trying to lull me to sleep. Suddenly I saw two beams of bright light flashing angrily and constantly.

Headlights. A car horn.

The car heading straight for us was no more than a few yards away, braking, swerving sharply.

I caught sight of a man's face—who I now know to be Jim Roberts—leering at me in the mirror.

What I hadn't seen before, now played out in front of me. Mark and Helen started to wake up in the back, no doubt oblivious to the fact that Jim was there with them. But he seemed to be more focused on me than my sister and her boyfriend. As I started to haul the steering wheel around, he reached over the seat towards me.

Another pair of hands suddenly materialised out of nowhere, grabbing him firmly around the neck and pulling him away. It was Jigonhsasee. They struggled furiously while my feet jabbed at the brake and clutch, and with a squeal of burning rubber, I somehow managed to guide us past the oncoming vehicle with half an inch to spare.

Jim and Jigonhsasee flew up from the car, still locked together, and disappeared over the treetops.

"Now watch what would have happened if Jigonhsasee hadn't been there," said Grandma.

The scene in front of me returned to the moment I began to jerk the wheel around. This time when Jim reached out for me, he succeeded in grabbing my hands on the wheel and yanking hard in the opposite direction, keeping us partially across the white line. The car weaved crazily, and instead of narrowly missing the oncoming vehicle my offside wing clipped it. A grinding screech filled the air as metal scraped along metal, and the impact threw us up onto the two nearside wheels.

The other vehicle, which I now saw was a silver Jaguar XJ6, spun a full 360 degrees before coming to a stop safely, albeit diagonally straddling both lanes. But my attention was quickly held by Mum's Nissan as it dropped back onto all four wheels and careered off the road, tyres churning the grass verge, leaving deep ruts in their wake.

I was sure I must be desperately pressing the brake pedal to the floor, but the car's momentum carried it forward along the verge, edging closer to the deep ditch running alongside. But I realised with horror that we'd hit the tree looming up at an alarming speed, before we'd get far enough to topple into it.

When the crash came with its sickening Earth-spinning thud and deafening crunch, the tree stood firm and resolute against the invasion of the car's bonnet which flipped up as the catch came free of its housing. Time slowed as I watched the engine block push backwards into the car's interior, crushing my legs, while the steering wheel and column smashed into my chest. The whole framework of the Nissan crumpled on impact with metal grinding on metal—this time not Nissan against Jaguar, but Nissan against Nissan as components were smashed apart and gouged into each other.

I could only imagine the agonising pain other-me and Mark and Helen must be going through inside, unless we'd blacked out. From my vantage point just outside the car, I couldn't see any details through the tangled metal, but I don't think I'll ever forget the sight of blood sprayed across the windows and windscreen. With a slight whooshing, leaking petrol ignited on the hot engine and a row of flames sprinted all the way across to the dashboard. Within seconds much of the car was ablaze with plumes of black smoke rising from it.

"Can't we do anything?" I pleaded to Grandma and Jigonhsasee.

"I've already done it." Amidst all this carnage and destruction Jigonhsasee actually smiled at me.

"As we explained, Simon," said Grandma, "this is what would have happened if Jigonhsasee hadn't stopped it."

The next moment a heart-rending scream came from inside the car. The high pitch told me it was Helen. My sister was burning in there. The scream continued unabated, and although it wasn't real, the horror of it certainly was. Also, I shuddered at the thought that it could so easily have been authentic. But for Jigonhsasee, all three of us could have died in the fire.

Correction. Would have died, and if not in the fire, definitely in the explosion which followed. It felt as if my eardrums were shattering as the loudest sound I'd ever heard boomed across my world. Flames and smoke billowed out of the car in every direction and fragments of metal showered into the air, starting smaller fires on the dry grass wherever they landed.

Jigonhsasee waved her hand and the scene of annihilation faded. We were back in the churchyard, standing by the Yew tree in front of the hedge.

I stood immobile for a few seconds trying to process what had just happened. Or rather, what *hadn't* happened— what would have happened if Jigonhsasee hadn't saved us. I wanted to thank her again, but after seeing Helen, Mark, and me wiped out in that explosion and fireball I was stunned into silence.

Fortunately, Grandma came to my rescue.

"I know it seems a lot to take in, but we felt the time would never be more right for you to meet Jigonhsasee and learn of the link between you. Which takes us to our next question. Are you ready to take the final step towards enlightenment?" she asked.

I nodded, eager to move away from the image of Mum's Nissan, which I hoped would fade like a bad dream.

"Yes, please," I replied, perhaps a little unnecessarily.

"In that case, we'll move on to Orenda," she said. "Jigonhsasee will explain."

"Indeed I will," said Jigonhsasee. "The native Americans of my time discovered a network of sacred energy which they called Orenda." She held her hand out to me again and squeezed mine reassuringly when I took it. I stared at her broad brow and high, rounded cheekbones which chiselled a delicate beauty into her features. Love, with a backdrop of humour, seemed to flow from the dark brown eyes twinkling back at me, and before I could stop my thoughts from gathering and, no doubt, broadcasting straight into her mind, I remembered how scared I was of her when I first saw her—and her appearance at that time.

"Your thoughts there bring me nicely to explaining about Orenda," said Jigonhsasee, as she let go of my hand. "What did you think when I stepped out from behind the tree in the forest, and you saw me for the first time?"

That scene was still imprinted on my mind, how the dreadful white pallor of her skin contrasted starkly with the deep ruby-red lips, and the long black tongue snaked out to rest on her chin. She tossed back her lank greasy hair, and pointed her arms towards me, connecting to the thin white strands which pulled free of my body before worming their way over to her and disappearing down her throat.

"I remember feeling sickened and horrified by you, if I'm honest. And scared." Would 18-year-old me have been that honest? I'm glad it's 56-year-old me replying to her. Even so, I still felt the need to add: "Which just goes to show that first appearances can be deceptive."

"A natural reaction to the changing energy around you at that moment," she said. "While we've always been connected, the best way I can describe it is that the energy I took from you that day was the final piece of the jigsaw."

That was puzzling. "But what have we just done with Grandma, when the energy passed between all three of us? Wasn't that the last piece?"

Grandma laughed at that. "Always another question with you, isn't it, my boy? No wonder you're doing so well in radio."

I started to say something—*think something*—but Jigonhsasee cut across my mental words. "The thing to remember about Orenda energy is that it's not static. It's dynamic, and constantly adjusting, rather like a process. So, while we finished our energy connection on that day in your dreamscape, it's always evolving and developing. The Orenda of your forest dreamscape consisted of all emotions and experiences that were ever part of the forest, which is deep in your psyche.

"What we've just done with Rosemary Paulina links everything together so you can use it properly."

"Use it for what, though? Why've I got it? I don't understand; why me?"

"Some people would say it's your destiny," said Grandma. "But I suppose it all depends on what you mean by 'destiny.' Is it the hidden power to control future events…"

she emphasised *control,* "...or does it refer to the events themselves that will *necessarily happen* to you in the future?"

"The energy you've now inherited from us gives you greater control to go back into your younger body at the time of your blackouts," Jigonhsasee told me. "Orenda is coded and sacred, providing you with a specific way of handling emotions and experiences. I'm sure you've noticed in your daily life that your energy and personality are never static, but ever-changing."

"And many blackouts have been at important times of your life," said Grandma. This was getting like verbal tennis, with my head turning to look first at one, then the other—whoever was talking. "They were at key emotional milestones such as your wedding, the awful day we learned of Janice's cancer, your first counselling session after Helen's death, and even now, at my funeral."

Her words struck home. That was true.

"You may not be able to control where you go back to at any given time." My head turned from Grandma to Jigonhsasee again. "But wherever you go, you take hindsight with you, knowing how a situation turned out. That's what this gift of Orenda really gives you. You go to a past moment of your life and handle it with greater wisdom and maturity. Orenda is the inner wisdom that guides you on your journey. Not only does it take you to your destination in the past, but it serves to guide you when you arrive."

I thought back to my visit to Anna.

"Exactly," said Jigonhsasee, clearly reading what was going through my mind. "For a while, you waited to see what your younger self would do. Then you quickly realised he wasn't coming and that you were in control. You unwittingly evoked the power of your Orenda to carry you forward through that time."

"But I don't know how I got there, any more than I know how I got here, to your funeral, Grandma."

"Do you remember me telling you that your gift would use you first, before you could control it?" asked Grandma.

"I do. You said it would begin to give me answers."

"Just as it has. The first time it took you to Anna. That fledgling journey gave you the answer you've been seeking all your life—that you caused that blackout yourself by going into your younger body. That's set the scene for all future journeys. Your current mind takes full control every time you jump, and you stay there until going to sleep when you'll return to the present. Your younger self knows nothing about it, and wakes up the next morning with no recollection of what's happened."

The beginnings of three more questions started to form in my mind, perhaps not coherent enough for Grandma and Jigonhsasee to make any sense of yet.

"But...if...actually..." Which question should I ask first? "You said a few moments ago there's a name for these 'jumps'?"

"Indeed there is," replied Grandma, "but you already know it."

"I do?"

"Of course. The...what did you call it; weird body jumping, is simply the power of Orenda. Orenda is the force that lets your spirit transfer from your present to your past, and back again."

She stopped, as if that was the full answer. Which, in a way, I guess it was.

So, let's move on to my next question. She answered almost before I'd thought of the words to ask about where my younger self's mind goes when I barged in: "He goes into a deep sleep, rather like a hypnotic trance. He's still there, with you in your body, but he's completely unaware of your presence, or what happens while you're there."

Jigonhsasee held her hand up as my third question started to take shape in my mind. "And you want to know what happens to your body in your present while your spirit's back here in the past?" she asked.

"Yes."

"Things will be different in future, when you're home, and we'll come to that in a moment. But for now, you're slowly being brought out of the induced coma, so while you've been with Anna, and now here with us, the anaesthetic has kept you unconscious. When you..."

"Does that mean I won't remember any of this?"

"Not at all. Just the opposite, in fact. You'll actually remember it clearer than you normally would. As a spiritual energy, Orenda transcends consciousness by travelling through all seven chakras of the body to take you to a higher plane, and..."

"Sorry. The what?"

"Chakras." She paused, as if expecting another question, but I was still processing the word and stayed silent, waiting for her to continue. "You don't know of them?" she asked.

"I've heard of them, but I've no idea what it means or what they are."

"Very simply, they're spinning energy points in a straight line from the bottom of your spine to the top of your head. They connect your physical body to your spiritual being, which means they make a perfect channel for Orenda to flow.

"Orenda's at work all the time you're in your young body, so not only will you remember everything you do, you'll remember it with even greater clarity than normal and you'll be able to recall every action and every word of your time spent there, for the rest of your life."

"Oh, is it giving me a photographic memory? That'll be good."

Jigonhsasee started to reply, but Grandma's louder thoughts cut over her. "Hold your horses, young man. I realise that sieve you call a brain won't know what's hit it when you can instantly recall everything from your trips into the past. But it won't help you remember what happens in the present. Your own little grey cells will still be responsible for that."

"But still," I said. "It'll be pretty cool to remember word for word what I've never been able to remember at all."

"You may come to regard that either as a blessing or a curse," said Grandma, which made me laugh.

"I'm sure it'll be a good thing, Grandma," I said. "That's the whole point, isn't it?"

"It'll be whatever you make it," she replied. "Come on, let's start walking back. They'll be waiting for you."

She took my hand and started leading me along the path back towards the church. Jigonhsasee came alongside and took my other hand.

"So much for me not needing to ask anything." I never liked to ask stupid questions, as the answers could end up being quite painful. But is there such a thing as a stupid question, if you genuinely don't know the answer? "Grandma, do you know what this reminds me of? That Johnny Nash song that you used to like: 'There Are More Questions Than Answers,' because the way I feel now, 'the more I find out the less I know.'"

"But you'll know what's important, my boy, and that's enough."

"But you've not told me what'll happen to my body back

home when my spirit jumps to the past. Nor how I even get out of my body."

"Again, patience, my boy. Do you know what my mother, your Great Grandma, used to say? Patience is a virtue and a little won't hurt you."

My heart started pounding as we approached the side of the church. My family would be waiting just around the corner.

"They are, indeed," admitted Grandma, obviously picking up my thought. "There's just time for me to tell you, though, that you'll only travel back to your past body when you're asleep in bed in the present. On a night when you want to make a journey, wait until Janice is asleep and then simply mentally call for Jigonhsasee."

"I'll come for you straight away and guide you to your destination," the girl told me. "While you're there, you'll be asleep at home."

Another thought started to take shape, which Jigonhsasee either anticipated or had lightning-fast reactions to answer it. "You'll be in a very deep sleep, but if you do wake up, your spirit will return instantly."

"OK," I said. "But how do I leave my body in the past and get..." Suddenly, my hands were holding empty air, and my words faded on the breeze: "...back home?" Grandma and Jigonhsasee had gone.

15

Waking

Voices from afar, indistinct but getting closer all the time. I still couldn't make any sense of them. This was odd. The brain fog was a real pea-souper and I felt on cloud nine. No, wait. That's not what I meant, is it? Cloud cuckoo land. Yes, that's it. Or somewhere away with the fairies, anyway.

What made it all rather weird and crazy, was that while I struggled to pick my way through memories and feelings, including where I am right now—I appear to be in some sort of bed with railings along the side, surrounded by pale blue curtains and several machines which are beeping at me—some things are crystal clear.

For instance, I can remember talking to my therapist, Anna Goodchild, and Grandma and Jigonhsasee. Also, at some point, and I think it was fairly recent, Helen was there, too.

What else do I know? The fog's swirling through my mind obscuring my memories. I'm still firing torpedoes through a number of wires which are attached to various parts of my body, and through a couple of tubes, one of which appears to actually go inside my body. The other comes up to my face. Who was I aiming at? His name's on the tip of my tongue.

Swallowing tells me my throat's quite sore, which triggers another memory. A memory of something going down my throat. What the fuck? I frantically grab at the tube near my nose. I remember biting it before, and I try to bite down on it again. That's a good sign. I'm starting to remember things. But this time my teeth don't clamp down on it, because there's nothing in my mouth. Instead, I bite my tongue, which probably turns out to be another good thing, as the sharp pain cuts a swathe through the fog, bringing even more memories into view. The last time I tried to pull the tube out my arms refused to work, but there's no such reluctance this time.

I gripped it with both hands and tugged. It moved a few inches and then stopped, caught at the end of straps that went behind my head. I grappled with them and managed to unhook it from my right ear. The tube ended at the oxygen mask which now flapped to the side of my face, a strap still wrapped around my left ear. I hadn't noticed how easily I'd been breathing until suddenly I wasn't. My heart pounded, pumping faster, trying to get my oxygen-depleted blood to its many destinations.

"He's awake." The words were still muffled, but much more coherent. The same figure I remembered from earlier (I'd no idea *how* much earlier—it could be an hour, a day, a week—but it meant my jumbled memories were becoming clearer) rushed up to me. It looked like the same figure, but it may have been someone else dressed in a similar blue overall, whose face was protected by a visor, goggles and medical mask sporting a filter that looked rather like a plughole.

"Simon, you need help with your oxygen at the moment." His voice was more distinct now, penetrating stronger through the fog. "Keep still, we've got to get your mask back on." His fingers fumbled at it, pulling the strap back into place around my ear, and I felt the cool flow of air across my face restored immediately. My nostrils greedily sucked it in, then I opened my mouth to grab even more.

Slowly my heart returned to its normal pace. Now, if only

my head wouldn't feel like it's still stuffed with cotton wool.

The masked face swam into view above me again, and I looked up, imploringly, into his eyes. "What's happening?" I asked with difficulty, my words croaky and hesitant, each one jaggedly pulling at my throat.

"Don't try and talk yet. You've been in a coma for ten days, but we're bringing you out of it now."

A coma. Yes, I knew that, didn't I? Grandma told me at her funeral 20 years ago, which I've recently come back from. Even though the cotton wool's still filling my brain, it can't hide that.

"Your wife would be here with you normally," the figure was saying, "but we're having to isolate the ward because of COVID. There's some good news on that, though. We can still..."

"COVID," I managed to croak. "Captain Caveman..." I desperately wanted to tell him that Captain Caveman was racing through my bloodstream destroying all the COVID cells with his wooden club, but it was both difficult and painful to articulate properly. The brain fog hid the words I needed, and the ones I managed to unearth spitefully jabbed my throat with tiny little needles poking out of every syllable.

Bob Appleyard.

That's whose name had been on the tip of my tongue. But why would I be firing torpedoes at my station manager through the wires and tubes connecting me to drips and machines? It didn't make sense. What did make sense, though?

It felt as if the cotton wool was expanding in my head all the time, pressing on my brain and the inside wall of my skull.

"Bob," I said. That was easier. Such a nice, short word.

"No, I'm not Bob," said the face behind the mask. "I'm Doctor Andrew Moore."

Silly sod. I think he thinks I think he's Bob. I giggled

inwardly. At least I thought it was inwardly, but it sparked a fit of coughing, so maybe it had been out loud. I simply couldn't seem to get to grips with reality. The oxygen mask had steamed up from the first cough, and I felt warmth and moisture over my nose and mouth as Doctor Moore pulled my head up from the pillow and gently rubbed my back.

"Don't move or speak for a few moments," he said. "You'll be alright shortly. Let me do the talking, and tell you what's happened."

I squinted up at him as my coughing eased, and nodded. "Okay." Just that one word triggered another cough that jarred my throat. I'd learned my lesson. I'd be quiet.

I felt myself drifting again and my eyes closed, but the Doctor's voice cut through the approaching blackness, keeping me just on the right side of consciousness.

"We'll tell you everything in due course," said Doctor Moore. "For now, though, all you need to know is you've been in a coma to help you fight COVID."

I remembered Alan in the next bed asking if I was alright. Then things became clearer. I'd been out of my body above my bed when that happened. Visions of the rest of the Panters Club swam into my mind and I racked my brain to remember who they are. Jack was one of them, wasn't he? No, fuck this cotton wool, it's not Jack. Jock. That's it. Except a pressing voice told me Jock wasn't his name, either, that's just what everyone called him because he was Welsh. Fuck that as well. Not Welsh, Scottish!

Like in a cartoon, green nameplates suddenly flashed into existence above the other Panters. Ah, yes. Iain, Mohammed, and Adil. I wasn't going to let my brain fool me, though. The universe didn't conjure those little cards out of nowhere, they came from my own memory. A sure sign it's coming back. Hope those guys are alright. They're a good crowd. Made me laugh all the time.

"We put you into the coma to help you rest and give your body time to fight the worst of COVID," the Doctor said. "Your lungs are mending well, so yesterday we started very slowly to reduce the anaesthetic keeping you asleep."

The top corners of the medical mask behind the visor moved sideways slightly, and the skin alongside his eyes wrinkled. My brain was in gear enough to know he was smiling down at me.

"I was telling you the good news about your wife," he continued. "The national lockdown means she hasn't been able to be here with you to hold your hand and talk to you while you've been in the coma. But now you're coming round she can talk to you on a video link.

"Simon, we've got a lovely surprise for you. Your wife's here now, on WhatsApp." He motioned behind him, and a second figure came into view, holding up an iPad. My heart leaped at the sight of my wife on the screen, with a wide smile beaming across her face.

"Simon, dear heart. It's so lovely to have you back." She blew me a kiss, just as tears squeezed out of my eyes and rolled gently down my cheeks.

"Imogen, I love you so much." It took a lot of effort to get those words out, but at least I didn't cough, and there wasn't too long a pause between each one. I wasn't ready for the stunned silence that followed, though, or the way Imogen's face crumpled.

"What?" she said.

Doctor Moore snatched the iPad from his colleague and spun it away from me, turning the camera towards his own face. "Don't worry about that, Mrs. Reynolds. The anaesthetic drugs are still in his body, and that's making him very confused. This happens a lot."

Confused? Yes, I'm confused. What's wrong with telling Imogen I love her? "Doctor...?"

Tiny fingers appeared at the side of his face, gripping his shoulder, but he gave no indication of feeling them. I stared, as a second tiny hand appeared from behind his back and locked onto his upper arm. Seconds later its owner pulled into view and a baby boy swung himself up onto his shoulder and sat there, legs dangling, giggling at me.

"Simon. I want to see Simon," Imogen's voice came from the tablet. "Doctor, put him back on, please. Dear heart, it's me, Janice."

Janice?

The baby's mouth opened, to reveal two rows of razor-sharp, pointed teeth. This little bugger would be no good with breast milk. It would tear its Mummy to ribbons.

Doctor Moore turned the iPad back to face me. The bulk of the screen was taken up with Imogen's smile, and I saw myself in the little rectangle in the top right-hand corner. Or rather, some other version of me. My eyes looked red and half closed, and I'll swear my hair was a shade or two greyer than the last time I'd looked in a mirror. The oxygen mask covering the bottom of my nose and lower half of my face was fastened in place with straps behind my ears, and the tube carrying oxygen to me snaked away from it, disappearing towards the array of machines to my right.

Crap! Another memory's returning: my wife's name isn't Imogen. It's Janice. Imogen's my friend and neighbour. The author. She gave me a lift home the day I came down with COVID.

"Janice." Still croaky, so I cleared my throat and nearly

leaped off the bed as the needles expanded into knives. "I'm sorry. Confused."

"I know," she said. "You'll be fine soon."

The baby giggled louder, attracting my attention again. He was weeing down Doctor Moore's overalls, but that wasn't the worst thing. I saw a movement out of the corner of my eye, and when I turned to look closer, a spider was crawling up the tube towards my oxygen mask.

I recoiled in dread. While I don't like spiders, I'm not arachnophobic and don't mind getting close to them to trap them in our long-handled spider catcher and release them in the garden. Janice is petrified of them, though, and has run to a neighbour on more than one occasion, asking them to come and catch one when I've not been in.

This one was different, though. It was no ordinary house spider. For one thing, it was bigger. Much bigger. As big as a sparrow, with a black, hairy body; its legs quivering as it inched its way along the tube.

I batted it away with my hand, listening as it plopped onto the floor.

"Simon," called Doctor Moore. "What's the matter?"

Couldn't he see, for fuck's sake? A second plop, this time much closer, was immediately followed by a third, both coming from my chest. Two spiders sat there, near enough for me to stare deeply into their bluey-green eyes— two large ones in the centre of their faces, flanked by two smaller ones on each side.

Another plop heralded the arrival of a third spider dropping onto me. The ceiling was covered with them, all swarming to gather above my bed, before dropping one by one, their legs now hardly making a sound as they landed— it was as if their actions had evolved and they'd learned how to avoid the plop their predecessors had made during the first wave of their invasion.

The baby loved this. He was giggling fit to burst, a high-pitched shriek of laughter.

It took a second or two to realise the rising scream was coming from my own mouth as more legs appeared at the foot of my bed, levering obscene bodies up onto the sheet. The floor was covered with them, too, and they were climbing the bed legs.

Then came another.

Then another.

And another.

Instinctively I flipped my arms up to try and push them aside. It turned out to be quite a feeble attempt as my muscles refused to work properly and only succeeded in lifting them a couple of inches. I did manage to scramble the bed covers aside, though, which was probably the worst thing I could have done, as the spiders now dropped onto my bare chest. And, anyway, where would I go? I wasn't putting my bare feet on the floor with those things covering it. Jesus, they're everywhere, where the fuck are they coming from?

"Get them off me," I screamed. But the scream sounded puny and feeble. "Get the fucking spiders off me." Their furry legs produced an agonisingly exquisite tickling sensation as they ran the length of my body.

Doctor Moore and his colleague rushed to my side, gripping my arms and gently pushing me back. The rush of energy and strength which had momentarily taken over me went awol, and I felt too weak to resist. Limply, I flopped back down. "Simon, there's nothing there," he said.

"What spiders?" shouted Janice from the iPad. "What's happening? I can only see the ceiling. Doctor Moore, what's going on?"

If she could see the ceiling why can't she see the spiders? It's alive with black squirming movement, like a rippling sea. They're squeezing through the gaps at the top of the door and window and making their way to me.

The Doctor cupped my head in his hands and looked into my eyes. "There's nothing there," he said, softly. Yes, there was. That baby was still peeing down his chest, its mouth wide open with laughter, showing those rows of pointed teeth. "It's the effects of the anaesthetic. We've lightened the sedation and stopped the muscle relaxants to bring you out of the coma, but there are still some drugs left in your system."

"What about the baby and the spiders?" I asked, pulling my head free of his gentle grip. "They're there, look. The baby's on your shoulder." Somehow I found my voice now, still weak with every word jabbing at my throat, but I was determined to make him see what was happening. "It's peeing down your front."

A spider dropped lightly onto the baby's head, crawled down his face, and disappeared between his lips. He raised his tiny hand to his mouth, and I watched in horror as first his fingers disappeared inside, followed by his wrist, and finally his arm right to the elbow, rippling his skin as he reached deeper, before emerging holding a spider dripping with saliva and stomach juices.

I heaved noisily and scrunched my eyes tightly shut to close out the ungodly sight.

"Simon. Doctor Moore." Janice sounded almost hysterical now. "Somebody please tell me what's happening!"

"Everything's fine," the Doctor called to her. "He's experiencing mild paranoid hallucinations."

What? Mild? There's nothing mild about these spiders. They're the fucking lions of the arachnid world. They're not hallucinations, either, Doctor. They're as real as Captain Caveman coursing through my bloodstream batting my COVID cells into submission with that large wooden club of his.

The tickling from the waving hairs on their legs became unbearable as they swarmed across my chest and groin. I guess it was karma for what my fellow sixth formers and I put Sheena Parr through when we tipped itching powder down her cleavage and knickers, and into her running shoes, just before her big race on sports day. You should have seen her fly round that redgra track—she actually broke the school 400-metre record that day in the summer of 1982 just before our nightmare began at White Pastures— and heard her choice language after she'd shugged off her clothes and finally emerged from the sports hall showers.

The dry heaving and attempts to scream not only wrecked the scant protection my throat had left, meaning my feeble effort to tell the Doctor I wasn't hallucinating was barely legible even to me, but also sapped what little energy I'd had. I had no strength to sit back up or try to shake the spiders off.

I opened my eyes, bracing myself for the sight of the baby still sitting on his shoulder—half expecting it to be pooing now as well as peeing—and to see even more spiders squeezing above the door onto the ward ceiling.

The baby had gone. The spiders had gone. The Doctor's face, showing as much concern as his features above the mask would allow, looked down at me.

"There really is nothing here," he assured me, and it seemed he was right.

"Will somebody please let me see Simon?" called Janice

from the iPad. Doctor Moore's colleague picked it up from the table where it had been discarded in their rush to get to me when I thought the ceiling was raining spiders.

"Here we are, Mrs. Reynolds." A woman's voice. She angled the tablet so Janice's face filled the screen and I appeared in the small tile in the top right again.

Janice's eyes shone. Not like eyes do when their owner's happy, but with droplets of water that found their way out of the corners and down her cheeks. It reminded me of a game Helen, Sarah and I used to play as children, each picking a raindrop when it hit the window pane, and having bets on which one would roll furthest and fastest down the glass. I looked at Janice and chose the one on her right cheek.

She smiled and sniffed back the tears almost at the same time. "Dear heart," she began. "I've been so worried about you, but Doctor Moore tells me you're going to be fine now."

"You're doing remarkably well," said Doctor Moore.

Damn. Janice wiped away the tears on both cheeks, ruining my game. Perhaps it was just as well, though, the left one had been winning so I'd have probably lost the bet with myself.

"Do you mind your wife listening in on the video while I have a chat with you?" he asked.

I shook my head, thinking it wiser than trying to put into words that I didn't mind at all. Welcomed it, in fact.

The medic holding the iPad rolled the table crossing my bed up to my chest, and propped the tablet at an angle in its support cushion. "I'll check all the readings and drips," she said.

"Okay, Emma, thank you. Now, Simon, let me tell you what's happened."

I nodded, feeling a little less woozy now, but there wasn't a lot in it. The brain fog was perhaps a touch thinner and

I definitely knew Imogen was a friend and neighbour and not my wife's name. A memory of collapsing in the spare bedroom poked through the swirling strands, as did the ambulance journey to hospital and a few days on the ward with the Panters Club, but not too much after that. Just a hint of the doctors carrying out CPR on me and then firing torpedoes through these tubes and wires that the medic he'd called Emma was now fiddling with.

Fuck, what's she doing with them? The beep from one of the machines connected to me with a wire sounds angrier now, a bit like a nest full of wasps that's been prodded and poked with a stick. And she's changing a bag hooked over one of two arms on a stand, that's dripping some fluid into me.

"No," I said. *Croaked.* "What are you doing? Stop it."

She turned to face me, but, like Doctor Moore, her nose and mouth were hidden behind a mask and its built-in filter, with goggles and a full-length visor guarding her eyes, so there wasn't much for me to see and even less to betray her intentions. "I'm just replacing your saline, vitamins, and electrolytes," she said.

"No, you're not," I screamed. *Croaked.* "It's poison. You're poisoning me."

She looked across at Doctor Moore, who said: "Simon, let Janice talk to you about it."

Janice couldn't be in on the plot, could she? *Could she?* No, of course not.

"Mrs. Reynolds, could you tell Simon what we discussed?"

Discussed? So she is in on the conspiracy. *No, she's not.* Not my Janice, my dear heart.

I stared at her furrowed brow on the screen and saw the pain in her eyes, which shrieked out at me louder than any words could. But was there a hint of deception lurking there in the background?

"Simon, listen to me," she said. "Listen to me."

I looked back towards Emma who had removed the two exhausted bags from the drip stand and was replacing them with fresh, full ones. Full of poison, no doubt. "Stop that!" In my mind, I wanted to shout those words, and scream them at the top of my voice. As it was, the top of my voice was nothing more than a sibilant whisper now.

"Dear heart, please stop. You've been very ill, but you're getting better now."

In between those hazy memories of collapsing, the ambulance, the ward, and the Panters Club (Jock—not Jack—Iain, Alan, Mohammed, and Adil; I've not forgotten anyone, have I?) crystal clear images emerge like a lance through the brain fog. Images of me heading towards the white light, Grandma, Helen, Jigonhsasee, my jump back to Anna in 1982, and to Grandma's funeral several years later.

Yes, those memories had been here a few moments ago. Then they went. Now they're back. Let's hope they stay, this time. "Orenda's at work all the time you're in your young body," Grandma had told me. "So, not only will you remember everything you do, you'll remember it with even greater clarity than normal and you'll be able to recall every action and every word of your time spent there, for the rest of your life."

I looked at what I later realised was the pulse oximeter clipped to my finger, but thought at this moment was my smartphone. Weren't the numbers flashing up on it the next callers on the phone-in part of my show? If only I can find the keyboard I can phone for a taxi to come and take me home.

There was another tear on Janice's cheek. Only one,

though. I couldn't play our game. No fun in betting that it would reach her chin with no competition. Oh. If I had bet on it, I'd have lost, because she's just wiped it away again, like the others. Spoilsport.

She sniffed more tears back. "The doctors are very happy with how you've been fighting COVID, and they've been bringing you out of the coma slowly since last night. You're going to be very confused for a while, dear heart, but everything's alright."

I wanted to tell her everything was not alright. It's not alright if I could barely speak, barely move my arms, barely move my legs, barely remember anything (except things that seemed too unbelievable, anyway), is it? But I couldn't tell her that, because I could barely speak—did I say I could barely speak?

So I simply lay there looking into her eyes on the iPad screen and listening to her tell me what had happened over the last few days. How the doctors had originally been extremely worried, and how I seemed to start fighting back strongly when they put me in the induced coma.

Ah, I wanted to say, that's Captain Caveman and Grandma. They've been busy annihilating the COVID cells in my body and helping me recover. Yes, it's true, I'd have said to them. A cartoon character and a long-dead relative. What is there not to believe about that? Look, I'm here, aren't I, supposedly against all the odds? I've come through to this point, brain fog and muscle loss notwithstanding.

And now, all these spiders, babies, and trying to kill me have exhausted me. Even if they were hallucinations. And I'm not convinced they were. But, hey ho, whatever. The brain fog's numbing. Let me sleep, please.

Part Three
LONG COVID

16

Recovering

Boxing Day 2020, Simon

There you have it. That's how all this started. I've got answers to the great mystery of my blackouts, which I've been seeking for the last 38 years. As you can see, I wasn't wrong when I said the answer was a doozy.

It took my long-dead Grandma and Iroquois spirit guide Jigonhsasee to show me, though, where all those tests and expert head shakers had failed.

But at what cost? It seems my journey to enlightenment was triggered by COVID, and my brain and body have been battered and ravaged by the virus in a way no one could have foreseen at the start of the pandemic.

I still haven't recovered from yesterday, which had been quite tiring. We'd invited Hannah and Claire and their partners for Christmas dinner. Hannah wanted us to go to hers to give Janice a break, but I wanted to be at home in case my heart rate suddenly shot up as it's been prone to do, and I had to go to bed. Or if the lung and chest pain got too bad. I've definitely been on the mend for a few weeks, but the simple effort of contributing to family life still exhausts me, so we'd insisted on having Christmas at ours.

The girls helped in the kitchen. A lot. Janice told me in bed last night that they'd done almost everything in the way of preparing the meal while I'd sat in the lounge with Claire's partner Jacqui, and Hannah's fiancé Jacob.

They stayed over for Boxing Day lunch, too, only leaving a few moments ago, so here I am, scrolling through the Sky

TV menu at 6.45 p.m. on Boxing Day evening while Janice loads the dishwasher.

Christmas television's crap nowadays. The second series of The Masked Singer launches in a quarter of an hour. Definitely won't be watching that, although I did interview one of the celebrities from the first series on my show just after they'd been unveiled.

When the programme first aired, the name made me think of a PR stunt Poolswood Sound's marketing team dreamed up a few years ago which took off in a big way. One of our freelance presenters—she was a swing jock, standing in when the regulars were on holiday—Octavia Charles (that's her stage name) was given her own show called The Masked DJ. She never spoke. Just played back-to-back music four nights a week, from 8 p.m. to 10 p.m. Then she started doing live gigs, turning up at events in a hired limo (one of Poolswood Sound's directors ran a limousine company and let her use it for free) sporting a full-head black mask with eye and nose holes, which laced up at the back rather like some wrestlers wear.

I thought of this again as I scrolled down the channels. The Masked DJ ended after a year. Octavia didn't want to renew her contract as she'd been offered a residency in Ibiza. There'd been talk of another presenter stepping into her anonymous shoes, but, really, who wants to go on the radio and not speak? A year's stint with your own show probably looks good on a CV, but in truth how far would something like that, which doesn't feature your personality, help in developing your career? No, thank you, everyone said. There were no takers, so the show was replaced by a new rock programme which went on to win a radio industry award for its presenter, Fracto Fon, and our marketing team came up with some other idea to generate PR coverage.

At least I've been able to hold that train of thought together. Things have been getting better slowly but surely. Slower than I'd have liked, but less slow than I'm led to believe for many patients.

I'd hoped my worries about COVID were coming to an end after emerging from the induced coma back in April. Doctor Moore waited a couple of days for the hallucinations to stop *(the spiders returned three times during my first day back in the waking world, and the baby put in one more appearance, sitting on Nurse Emma Grassmere's head and resting his feet on her shoulders, giggling hysterically while she put more poison in the drip bags to feed into me intravenously)* before starting to talk seriously about what had happened to me.

"Have you ever watched a patient come out of a coma in a film or TV show?" he'd asked. Yes, I had, I told him. I was glad he didn't ask me to name any, because I couldn't remember what they were called. Or even their plotlines if I'm honest, but I did remember seeing them. Probably hundreds of them.

"Well, it's nothing like that," he said. "Not a bit like in the movies at all." He'd pulled up a chair and sat next to my waist. I realised I'd never seen his face properly, and wished I could gauge his full expression behind the mask, visor, and goggles.

"No one ever really knows how well a patient will recover from a coma," he said. "Sometimes it'll be similar to waking from a deep sleep, but that's quite rare if I'm honest. Mostly, I'm afraid it's not. It's more like an arduous journey through a foggy and tangled landscape."

Oh, yes. I knew all about that. My dreamscape...or was it my subconscious?...where I first caught sight of Jigonhsasee, had certainly been tangled.

He explained with quite a bit of medical jargon, most of which I understood, or at least got the gist of, that COVID started attacking my lungs and other organs, and they had to put me in an induced coma to help my body fight off the infection. I didn't think he'd appreciate me mentioning Captain Caveman had also played a part, so I stayed shtum about that.

"Coronavirus infected your body by entering your healthy cells," he went on. "Then it made copies of itself and multiplied all over you." Where it eventually met Captain Caveman, I thought. Okay, okay, I won't mention him again.

"The virus attached its spiky surface proteins to receptors on your healthy cells, especially those in the lungs." His words made me think back to biology classes when I used to listen to Mr. Carter droning on. At least I was paying attention now, though, as I was the lab rat under scrutiny.

"Once inside your healthy cells, coronavirus took command and started killing them. We found that your lungs were quite inflamed, which made it hard for you to breathe. The CT scan we took of your chest showed shadows which we call ground-glass opacity. In turn, the infection grew more severe, and the shortness of breath you were experiencing, known as dyspnea, progressed to acute respiratory distress syndrome, or ARDS.

"The high-flow oxygen was a great help during that time, but on the night you fell seriously ill your oxygen levels suddenly dropped considerably, which brought on a cardiac arrest."

"Was that when you put me in the induced coma?"

"Yes. At that time there was no alternative. You'd have died if we hadn't. But a few days after you'd gone under, COVID's attack began to slow down, and you responded well to treatment. So much so, that we felt we could extubate you, and..."

That was a new one for me. "Sorry, what? Extubate?"

"Ah, no. It's me who's sorry, Simon. I should have said it more simply. When you went into the coma, we put a tube down your throat to feed oxygen directly to your windpipe and lungs, which is called intubation."

I vaguely remember that pipe in my throat, and thinking I was firing torpedoes out of it at Bob Appleyard.

"On April the ninth," he continued, "we started to bring you out of the coma. Your lungs were surprisingly strong so we were able to remove the tube—that's extubation, taking the tube out."

"Ah."

"So, you were off the mechanical ventilator which had been breathing for you, and back on high-flow non-invasive ventilation while you were coming round."

Doctor Moore went on to tell me the coming weeks would be full of physiotherapy and recovery. Apparently, I'd lost a good proportion of my muscle mass while in the coma, and needed to learn to walk again. First of all, I was told to flex my ankles and then slide my legs up and down on the bed. I didn't have the energy to do it more than once every hour or two, but it gradually became more frequent. It took several days—I don't recall how many—to even be able to sit on the side of my bed without help. I was determined to get better, and in a few more days my physical therapist helped me walk to the door of my room. It was hard, but she told me there wasn't anything wrong with my legs other than muscle atrophy, which she said was significant.

The effort of putting one foot in front of the other left me completely exhausted, but I was apparently progressing quite quickly. It didn't feel like it at the time, though. Looking back now, I realise I may have been spurred on because Janice and the girls often watched on the iPad, encouraging me all the way. The therapist and nursing staff helped me practice the sequence of sitting, then standing, and then walking, and gradually I felt up to walking to the toilet and window by myself.

Once I gained more confidence from those early tottering footsteps my rehabilitation started in earnest and had been intense, with input from physiotherapists, occupational therapists, and psychologists, as well as doctors and nurses.

Clinical psychologist Doctor Ellie Cunningham's guidance was integral to improving my mental health and played an important role in my rehabilitation. Having gone through the scale of trauma I endured in hospital, knowing how close I came to dying and not being able to be with Janice and the girls had sent my anxiety through the roof and my mood plummeting.

Sleep was elusive, and a much-missed memory. The best I could hope for were a few scant hours of fitful tossing and turning. The rest of those endless nights, week after week, were filled with haunting, anxious thoughts about my health and recovery, often obstructing my progress.

I struggled to make proper sense of what was happening to me. In the very early days (probably around April 1st2th), Doctor Moore hoped my brain fog would clear like the sun burning away a shimmering mist in the moments after dawn, once the anaesthetic drugs were out of my system. (The simile of sun, mist, and dawn is entirely mine. He didn't use those words. I think what he actually said was: "You'll start to think clearer once we've flushed all the shit out of you." I remember thinking that was a funny thing for a doctor to say, but I went on to see more of his quirky humour in the days and weeks afterwards).

The thing is, that shimmering mist didn't burn away. I wasn't as spaced out as when I'd been firing torpedoes at Bob Appleyard, but after a few days I'd expected to be able to focus on my recovery, and concentrate on the physiotherapist's instructions. But they simply wouldn't stay in my head and wandered off moments after she'd told me what to do, and I had to ask her to repeat them.

I'd forget what I ordered for lunch, sometimes even forgetting that I'd seen the menu, and press the call buzzer asking the nurse to bring it for me.

The medical team allowed Janice to drop Imogen's latest novel off for me outside the hospital's main door, but I must have re-read the first page a dozen times without having the faintest idea what was happening. So I put When Crime Does Pay back in my bag and didn't take it out again except to clutch it to my chest with tears streaming down my face a few days into my recovery.

"Simon, dear heart, how are you doing today?" Janice had asked when she FaceTimed me at 11.30 that morning. She normally smiles when we start our video chats. I know she's just putting on a brave face for my benefit, and I think she knows I know, but neither of us says anything about that. I guess it's just a little unspoken secret between us. But that day was different. It was only a half-smile and didn't reach her eyes. Also, Nurse Emma was in with me. The medical staff normally make themselves discretely scarce when Janice and I are chatting.

Something. Was. Going. On.

Her lips straightened and I saw her jawline harden, the

result of tension causing muscle contraction, no doubt. I didn't need to glance over at the monitoring machine I was wired to, to know my heart was racing, I felt it pounding in my chest, and my thoughts ran wild. She was about to break bad news: I was deteriorating. I'd have to go back on the mechanical ventilator. Worse still, one of the girls was ill. Or both. They'd got COVID and were in hospital, perhaps just down the corridor or in the Intensive Care Unit where I'd spent ten days intubated in a coma. One of them was lying in the same bed I'd been in, with that tube going down their throat. And there'd be no Grandma or Jigonhsasee to comfort and guide them.

I felt a bead of sweat form on my forehead.

"Simon," she said gently, but with a hint of firmness. "I need to tell you something."

I knew it. Did the doctors think it would be better coming from Janice? Had she practiced any complex medical terms in case I asked questions? Was this why Nurse Emma was with me, waiting to come rushing over to comfort me as soon as the cat was out of the bag?

"I'm dying, aren't I?"

That prompted a quick shake of her head. "No. No, Simon, you're fine. You're making good progress."

"The girls, then? What's happened to them?"

"It's not the girls."

"Is it you? The cancer's not come back, has it?"

Nurse Emma moved into my eye line. "Simon," she said, "just let Janice tell you."

I nodded at the camera on the iPad. "Sorry, Janice. Go on. I'm ready." But what could it be if it wasn't me, Janice, or the girls?

"I'm so sorry to have to tell you this. It's about Imogen."

"What's happened? Is she alright?"

"I'm afraid not. There's no easy way to say this. She's dead." No hesitation. Straight in and direct. Her words rang out loud and clear, but they had to be wrong. The buffer of shock kicked in as I stared blankly at Janice, then at Emma who put her hand on my forearm.

Neither of them said anything, waiting for me to process what I'd just heard. "How?" I asked after a few seconds. "Was it a car crash? She always was a reckless driver." Was I babbling now? Is prattling how I'm going to cope with this?

"No, it wasn't a crash," said Janice. "She was ill."

"Ill?" No, she wasn't. She was fine when she drove me home from... Oh no. Oh, no, no, no. She drove me home when I had COVID. Except we didn't know it was COVID at the time. We learned that a few hours later.

My eyes widened as those thoughts ran to their logical conclusion. "COVID?" I asked, already knowing the answer.

"Yes. It was. She died several days ago."

"And you've only just thought to tell me?" I recalled that night when I collapsed at home, and how I'd phoned Imogen to warn her I'd got COVID symptoms. She'd laughed it off, saying she was made of stern stuff. That was the last time I spoke to her.

The enormity of what I'd done hit me. I'd killed her, as surely as if I'd stabbed her in the heart. It had been my COVID germs invading her body, attaching their spiky surface proteins to receptors on her healthy cells. The tears building in my eyes burst through the dam and ran free, prompting Emma to let go of my arm and hug me tightly. I'm sure that's against COVID rules.

During the weeks that followed, Doctor Cunningham's gentle technique helped me explore my feelings of guilt over Imogen's death and softly probed my own health worries. I learned about coping mechanisms and different thought pathways when faced with particular scenarios.

The day of discharge, June 15th, had finally arrived. I'd spent 82 days in hospital and was nowhere near back to my old self, either physically or mentally, by that date. Physiotherapy had been tough and prolonged—several hours every day once I could handle the exhaustion that came with it—but the doctors said I was as good as could be expected and was ready to go home. Poor Imogen was in my thoughts all the time and every painful step of the way.

In the run-up to my discharge, Doctor Moore suggested something which I'm still doing today, and I'm going to keep doing for a good while yet. His idea was that I keep a diary or journal, charting my recovery at home. The reason being, that since I came out of the coma, Janice had recorded everything I did and how I told her I felt. He said it would be cathartic for me to continue that, by cataloguing my progress myself, so I could see how much better I was getting on a daily basis.

Which sounded excellent in theory. It turned out differently, though. As my first days at home morphed into weeks and then into months, it started to look increasingly likely that the old Simon Reynolds had gone, and I may never fully recover from COVID-19. New symptoms manifested themselves during that time, and a whole new chapter of the virus began. What had begun as my journal of hope and recovery, turned into one of despair and continued impairment.

All these thoughts, all these memories, were brought on by simply seeing The Masked Singer in the TV guide. It shows how my mind works differently nowadays thanks to

COVID.

There's actually nothing on TV anywhere that I want to watch right now. Not free-to-air, not Netflix nor Amazon Prime. I guess I'll have to start subscribing to Britbox in the New Year. But for now, let's make use of this spare time and add today's entry to my diary.

The joints in my legs, ankles, and toes screamed as I eased myself off the sofa and slowly made my way out into the hall, the pain seemingly deep in my bones. "Just going to do today's diary," I called to Janice.

"OK. I'll be a few minutes yet," she responded from the kitchen.

"In that case, I'll write up December's monthly log now, too." As well as the daily entries, I've also summarised each month, as I thought it would be nice to plot the tremendous strides I'd been expecting to make in that way, as well as the smaller daily steps.

I tried not to let the pain define me, walking as normally as I could to my study at the front of the house, ignoring its malicious stabs.

Firing up the laptop, I opened the folder tagged 'My COVID Journey' to reveal a series of documents inside, comprising the daily diary and six monthly summaries, starting with June's remaining 15 days after my discharge from hospital.

As always, before creating a new monthly report I'd need to read what I'd written each day, along with going through all the previous summaries. What those six reports didn't show, however, were the jumps I'd made back into my younger body in the past. No way was I ever going to write about those. As Grandma had said, I remembered every detail about each one with crystal clarity.

I clicked on the daily diary icon to read about my triumphs and setbacks in December before turning my attention to the monthly reports, ahead of creating a new one for this month.

Cancer

My Journal

Monthly Summary June 15ᵗʰ to June 30ᵗʰ, 2020—Simon

"My sense of disappointment comes over loud and clear when I look back through my daily entries.

My breathing feels restrictive, almost claustrophobic, as I struggle to go up and down stairs and I get breathless in a slow walk around the garden. Physically, I'm exhausted, and I've lost a couple of pounds since leaving hospital. I daren't record how much weight I lost during my 82 days as an in-patient, but I'd hoped to be putting some back on by now, not losing even more.

I thought it would be sailing—perhaps not plain sailing, but sailing, nevertheless—with the worst behind me when I came out of hospital. But an emergency trip back to the hospital a week ago shows that wasn't the case.

What happened on June 23ʳᵈ was truly terrifying. I was sitting quietly watching Alan Bennett's Talking Heads on BBC 1, so it would be around 9.15 p.m. when a faint buzzing began in my head, and I was hit by a weird sense of panic. At the same time, my heart started racing. My health and fitness watch may not be as accurate as the hospital monitor that I'd been hooked up to for weeks, but I easily believed its readout of 120 beats per minute. It reminded me of that song about the guy's heart breaking out of his body and flying away like a bat out of hell. That's where the panic came from; I actually thought that may happen.

Pain ran from my neck down my left arm and chest. Cue a blue light trip back to the hospital! Tests for about four hours. All clear, pain subsided, and heart rate back to normal. They put it down to something called Post Viral Tachycardia and told me it's a complication for patients recovering from infections such as COVID. Couldn't decide if relief or frustration was my main emotion. The exhaustion hadn't gone, though. I barely had the strength to walk out of the hospital to meet Janice at 2 a.m.

Another memorable low spot was Monday, June 29th. Just finished the daily diary entry and was making my way back to the lounge when it literally seemed as if I'd been hit with a sledgehammer. Janice had to help me get straight to bed. If I'd felt I was at death's door with the Tachycardia incident, this time I was watching it creak slowly open. It was like when I'd been ill with a bad cold or flu in the past, but a hundred times worse. I could almost see my energy draining away through the sweat that poured from my skin.

A creeping darkness inched its way towards me from the bedroom wall, engulfing the foot of the bed before moving up the duvet. I knew sleep was coming, but I felt so ill I didn't know if I'd wake again. Grandma would be awfully pissed with me if I met her at the white light without doing whatever she sent me back for.

I did wake up, of course, and Janice said I'd only been asleep for three hours, but surprisingly I felt considerably better.

My internet research shows those symptoms could have been something called a Cytokine Storm. Apparently, it's an escalated immune response, where the immune system, which fights infection, goes rogue, wreaking more havoc than the disease itself. Cytokines are biological chemicals that tell the immune system to start doing its job, but it looks as if COVID can make the chemicals come faster and lead to our immune system damaging us.

I just want COVID gone and to get back to my old life, but it doesn't look like that's going to happen anytime soon."

Cancer Jump

I rolled my chair away from the desk at this point and glanced up at the "Merry Christmas" decoration on my office wall. What the journal doesn't record is what happened when I'd gone to bed on my first night at home after being discharged. The memory of it remained clear in my mind, just as Grandma had said. There was no brain fog surrounding my first controlled attempt at jumping back into my body in the past, which took me to the start of one of the most traumatic times of my life. Long before COVID claimed that title, of course.

I'd gone to bed about nine o'clock, absolutely shattered from the exertion of coming home in the ambulance. The plan was that I'd wait for Janice to go to sleep—again, that's what Grandma told me to do—but it looked unlikely that she'd come up anytime soon.

'Jigonhsasee,' I'd called mentally. I didn't know how long to wait before trying again, but it turns out I didn't need to worry about that. One moment I'd been staring at the bedroom ceiling, projecting her name into the ether, and the next I was back in that familiar white void with the light pulling at me from the distance.

"Hello, Simon," she said. I turned to see her standing alongside me. "I wondered when you'd come."

"I've been rather busy," I said. "Trying to recover from COVID."

"In this realm, you don't have COVID," she said. "You're

forever young, forever vibrant, full of energy."

I could have done with that energy in the earthly realm. Since reaching my 50th birthday, I've concluded that youth is wasted on the young. I daresay the same revelation hits everyone of a certain age when the odd little ache stretches out for a few days longer than it used to; when they start to wonder why they'd just gone into the kitchen; when they have to get up to pee in the night; and when they start going to bed at the time they used to leave home for a night out.

I'm saying 'they' here. What I mean, of course, is 'I.'

Yes, God messed up when he made Adam and Eve. Things would be different if I were running the cosmos. He should have bestowed the energy of youth upon the elderly, and the wisdom of the elderly upon the young.

And now, on top of all that, COVID was sure kicking my ass.

"Are you ready for your first controlled jump?" Jigonhsasee's words rang out in my mind.

"I don't know about ready," I broadcast back at her, "but I..."

I hardly had time to blink before the white cavern dissolved into Doctor Horton's office. Janice and I sat across the desk from her, and the words she'd said in the run-up to that moment flooded strongly into my mind. Not just from the dreadful time itself all those years ago, but from one of the series of flashbacks while I was unconscious on my spare bedroom floor back in March.

My mind whirled.

Okay, here we go.

"I'm very sorry, Mrs. Reynolds." Doctor Horton's words rang through my memory again, as I sat waiting to see how I was going to handle this. "Your tissue sample indicates the presence of cancerous cells in your breast." They were the last words I heard before waking up the next morning, and

I was about to find out what I'd missed.

I reached out to take Janice's hand and looked at her beautiful profile. A tear welled up in the corner of her eye. This was the news we'd been dreading. Before those words, there'd always been hope that the lump we'd found during a bout of bedroom foreplay was benign, but the doctor's stark phrase had just snatched that hope away.

As Janice gripped my fingers tightly, I realised I could spare her—spare *us*—the agony we'd been through. I was sitting here with powers that would stun a clairvoyant. I can speak with absolute authority in telling Janice she'll get through this. Do I have the right *not* to tell her?

But I didn't tell her, did I? If I do, though, that will change our future from this moment, and my past.

"What does this mean? How far has it gone?" Janice's words sliced through my thoughts and brought me back to what was happening now.

"It's in the relatively early stages, so with treatment, your prognosis is very good." The doctor didn't take her eyes off Janice. And neither did I.

"What will you do?" asked Janice.

"We'll carry out more tests in the coming days to determine the best course of treatment."

"What are the options, doctor?" I asked.

Doctor Horton turned her head towards me. "Treatment is primarily based on the type and stage of cancer. As I've said, we've caught this quite early on, so there's every likelihood of a full recovery."

She was right. Janice did make a full recovery, but only after having her left breast removed and a course of radiation therapy to reduce the risk of the cancer coming back. The journey from this moment through to her getting the all-clear a long way down the line was fraught and painful both for us and the girls. I recalled how the doubt and worry in the coming months would eat into our very souls. None of us deserved that, especially when I had the power at my fingertips to stop it.

A strong resolve engulfed me. I'm going to tell her. I love her too much to keep this knowledge to myself. I'll listen to what Doctor Horton says, but once we're home I'll explain to Janice how I've met Grandma and Jigonhsasee, and that the husband she's currently talking to is from the future when all this is over.

That didn't happen, but surely I could make it happen, couldn't I, just by simply telling her today?

Then my thoughts slipped to when I actually had told her about Jigonhsasee. It was the day after I came home from hospital on June 15th.

The sun was just peeping over the rooftop, catching the front edge of the patio sofa where we sat side by side having a late breakfast at around 10 o'clock. I took a sip of orange juice, wishing it were a malt whisky for Dutch courage.

I swallowed nervously. How can I be lost for words? Words have been my bread and butter, along with crab, cheese, and malbec, throughout my working life.

Janice is one of those people who gingerly tiptoes into the sea with her arms stretched out sideways on every step, while I sprint through the waves from several metres up the beach and dive headlong under the surface. So, here we go. Straight in.

Another sip of orange juice. "Janice, I've got something to tell you."

"Oh, God." Her eyes widened. "What now?"

"Nothing to worry about. It's all good."

"Thank God for that."

"At least I think it's good."

"For God's sake..." Another God hat trick. "Just tell me."

"It's about my blackouts."

She continued to look at me without saying a word.

"I know what's causing them."

"What? How?"

"This is going to sound complicated," I began. "And it's paranormal."

I'd gone in rather blunt about that aspect of it, but I knew she'd have no trouble believing it, as we've often discussed the horrific paranormal events at White Pastures from that long-ago summer.

She sat in silence as my story unfolded. I told her about the recent flashbacks, about Grandma and Jigonhsasee, and the jump to my younger self which triggered the first blackout.

I'd briefly wondered if she might think it was nonsense and put it all down to COVID delirium, especially after I called her Imogen while coming out of the coma, but she appeared to take everything I said at face value.

"So you'll finally get to see what happened during each blackout?"

"Yes, and it's more than that. I'm not just a passenger watching what's going on. It's me now—older me—in full control of what I say and do."

Those thoughts from June 16th flashed by in an instant as I sat holding Janice's hand several years ago. So, if I tell Janice today, what impact will that have on everything that's happened since this moment in Doctor Horton's office? I must tell her, though, to avoid the mental torture she went through during her treatment. But I can't, can I?

The next second Jigonhsasee's voice cut into my thoughts: "Quite right, too. You certainly can't." That took me by surprise, and my heart skipped a beat. Surely she can't hear my thoughts all the time?

Her response was instantaneous. "I can't when you're in your own time, but I can whenever you're in your younger body during a blackout. I'm with you every step of the way there."

For fuck's sake. Spying on me now.

She ignored that jibe. "You're getting into dangerous territory even thinking about changing what you know has already happened," she said. "It would have catastrophic consequences for you and Janice."

"What sort of consequences? They can't be any worse than the devastating effect the worry and uncertainty had on our mental health at the time. I can cure that at a stroke."

"But that's the way it happened, Simon. You can't change it. You've just been remembering the day you told Janice. It was June 16th this year. So you couldn't possibly have told her at any time before then. If you try, the cosmos will stop you."

Although Jigonhsasee was in full flow inside my head, I was vaguely aware of Janice talking to me in the world beyond. "...isn't that right, dear heart?" she was asking.

Now look what you've done, Jigonhsasee. My blackout meant I missed this the first time around, and now you've made me miss it again.

"Sorry, Janice, I was miles away. I'm just trying to take all this in and process it."

I was aware she was still holding my left hand as she squeezed my fingers gently. Her smile looked radiant as if this dreadful news had cast off the shackles of doubt. At least we knew what we faced now and could plan accordingly. "I was just saying you and the girls will be here for me and will help me through this."

"Yes, definitely." I nodded enthusiastically. "We're a

strong family. We'll support each other."

"That's going to be an essential part of your journey ahead," said Doctor Horton. "I know this must be difficult for you, but the oncology team will be with your family every step of the way."

I turned my head to face Janice. "You're going to be fine, dear heart," I said.

"Remember, Simon..." Jigonhsasee didn't seem to mind that she was interrupting one of the most awful moments of my life at a time when my wife needed me more than ever before. "...if you try to tell Janice she's speaking to a version of you from her future, and that you know the outcome of her cancer treatment, the cosmos *will* stop you." There was something in her voice that I hadn't heard before. Hard, menacing, made all the more intimidating by the thick accent.

The next moment I felt a slight tug in my chest, rather like the pull when I'd come out of my body in the hospital ward. Surely I wasn't having an out-of-body experience here, in my past, during a blackout? No. I couldn't be. Janice would have told me if I'd collapsed, and Jigonhsasee said we couldn't change what's already happened.

"Remember, the cosmos will stop you."

The doctor's office spun in front of me, and my whole perspective changed. I looked to my right. And saw me looking straight back. But my eyes appeared to be glazed over and I was completely motionless, sitting bolt upright and stiff. Glancing down I saw Janice's jeans covering my legs and her Nikes on my feet. But, no. I was still sitting next to me over there in my own clothes. So, where was Janice? Why was I wearing her clothes?

It's an understatement to say the Earth stopped spinning. My head was doing enough of that. Full of memories I'd

never had. *The agony and ecstasy of childbirth, and holding Hannah and Claire just seconds after giving birth to them, with Simon smiling down at me both times.*

I'd had my pick of the boys in Meriton and at school, but I'm feeling again that insane jealousy way, way, back at Helen's party when it seemed Simon was giving me the brush-off. How I'd wanted him that night. I'd slid my shoes under the bench at the edge of the grass and pulled him into the group of dancers. The DJ was playing a fast number which had everyone else gyrating in rhythm, but I had something else entirely in mind. I hooked my arms together around his neck and thrust my groin at the expanding bulge in his jeans, squirming from side to side. Come on, Simon, make a move on me. Whisper in my ear that you'll sneak me up to your bedroom. What's he waiting for?

He seems preoccupied with something. I feel his bulge getting stronger and push myself firmly against it, but he still seems oblivious, even after a couple more dances. I'm sure if I didn't have my hands locked behind his neck he'd have been away.

Oh. He's managed to duck under my arms. Now he's leading me by the hand across the grass. My heart's pounding. Is he taking me to his bedroom? No one would see us slip away. There's Mark and Helen. And that bitch Debbie Bailey from the lower sixth form. She's never forgiven me for screwing her boyfriend at the school disco last year, even though he made the first move. But it seems she's forgiven him. Her hands are all over him.

You've got to be kidding me, Simon. Why've you brought me back to the bench? If it's just to get my shoes, you needn't have bothered.

Well, seeing as we're here...I sit down rather heavily, pulling him alongside me, draping my arms around his shoulders, and clamping my lips firmly over his. My tongue probes inside his mouth and my fingers twirl his hair. I'm glad I've chosen my shortest skirt and tied my red cotton halter top at the front to keep my midriff bare. It meant when he linked his fingers behind my back his palms rested on my skin there, making it tingle. Bedroom, bedroom, bedroom, I kept urging at him, as if I could talk to him telepathically and get him to smuggle me in through the back door which was only a few metres away.

I slowly separated our lips and moved my hands away from his shoulders, my fingers tracing a path down his chest all the way to his jeans, where I felt a bulge stir again. Locking my eyes on his I got to work down there, rubbing my hand up and down along the zip. My tongue broke through my smile, gliding from side to side along my lips in perfect harmony with my hand movement.

As I gently gripped his rising member his head rolled back and his eyes closed. I instantly fell in love with the low moan escaping from his parted lips as he squirmed against the bench, and I vowed to make it stronger, even more intense. I gripped him tighter, squeezing mercilessly in the same way that had made bitch Debbie Bailey's boyfriend howl with a combination of pleasure and pain.

But it didn't have the same effect on Simon. He gently eased my hand away.

For fuck's sake, Simon. A mixture of anger and frustration flashed through me as I pushed him back and jumped up.

"What's the matter with you?" I shouted. "Don't you want me?" No one's ever done this to me before. I've done it to boys, either because their fumblings fell far short of what I wanted, or simply to tease them, but in this case, it was neither. No one could say I was fumbling at Simon. I'd made my intentions clear and was starting to give him the sort of pleasure he needed to repay me a thousandfold. And there's a difference between teasing and showing real indifference. This was definitely the latter.

"Sorry," he said, looking a little puzzled. "I don't know what..."

He didn't fool me, though. "I've had a better reaction from litmus paper." Oh, yes, that was a good one. Those chemistry lessons with Mr. Plant hadn't been wasted. "What's bugging you?"

The memory was lost in a maelstrom of other tantalisingly short glimpses of the past which whirled and eddied around my mind, including our first time together shortly after Helen's funeral, with Simon penetrating me and thrusting deep inside as the stars and planets fused together, just as our bodies merged into one; of my Dad walking me down the aisle; our honeymoon on Jersey; that time I wrote the Mercedes off by overturning it in the ditch. A lifetime's cluttered recollections printed indelibly on my mind which I simply sensed were there, rather than recalling them.

Doctor Horton reached across her desk and took my hand. Janice's hand. "Janice," she said. "I can see you're shocked by what I've told you."

My thumping heart showed that 'shocked' doesn't begin to cover it. All these memories, jumbled together incoherently, and yet completely logical at the same time

"I'm okay," I said.

In Janice's voice.

The reality of what Jigonhsasee had done hit me like a sledgehammer. She's taken me out of my body and put me in Janice's.

But this couldn't have happened. Or, if it had, Janice hadn't remembered it.

"Remember, the cosmos will stop you," Jigonhsasee repeated. The tugging sensation came again, along with the spinning room. And I was back in my own body with a jolt, looking across at Janice and still squeezing her right hand, with the doctor leaning over the desk holding her left.

"Sorry." Janice flicked her head slightly. "I felt a bit dizzy for a moment. As if someone walked over my grave."

"Remember," Jigonhsasee said again, "the cosmos will stop you."

"Right, all done." Janice's voice from the kitchen snatched me back to Boxing Day 2020. I shivered at the thought of those few seconds I'd spent in her body, marvelling at how so many of her memories flashed between us and were now part of me forever. That was one flashback experience I swore to myself I'd never tell her, though. It would create a whole new definition of the word intimacy.

"The dishwasher's loaded," she said.

"OK, I'll be a while yet," I called back. "Not even started writing today's diary or my December journal yet. Still reading the others."

"Don't be too long. I'll have a glass of Jack Daniels ready for when you've finished."

"I won't," I said. "Ta muchly."

I opened the next file, and started to read.

18

Conflict

My Journal

Monthly Summary July 2020, Simon

"Struggled to sleep most nights, probably averaging around three to four hours.

I can only describe what happened in the first week as being a phantom stroke. Unless it was related to the Cytokine Storm, of course. I sat on a stool at the kitchen island unit peeling the vegetables, which is pretty much all I can contribute to the household chores at the moment, when the cupboards alongside the oven and hob started spinning around my head. At first, I thought the strange dizziness was going to be a repeat of the Post Viral Tachycardia. But instead of arm, neck and chest pain, the symptoms this time were complete numbness in my face, jaw, neck, hands and arms. Rubbing my forehead felt like stroking a dead haddock. Janice rushed me to A & E in the car, but by the time we got there it was wearing off, and the hospital couldn't find any evidence of a stroke or neurological issues.

Towards the end of the month, I tried a short walk through the village, including the hill on Apollo Lane leading to the church, which pushed my heart rate up to 156 bpm. I felt dizzy and sick and was sweating heavily. I was sure I was going to faint, but it passed after sitting on a bench just inside the church grounds for a few moments.

Looking through my daily entries for both June and July, it seems that COVID's legacy to me is a gift-wrapped package of grinding migraine headaches, heart rate control issues, heart attack and stroke-like symptoms, breathing issues with a long-term cough, chest pains, and my throat swelling as if someone's digging their fingers into it behind my Adam's apple. And, of course, the awful, chronic exhaustion.

Surfing the internet showed me I wasn't alone in suffering a raft of debilitating symptoms after COVID, but doctors told me I didn't need any more tests and there was no magic pill to make me better. An accepted name for this new condition seemed to be making the rounds, apparently coined as a Twitter hashtag a couple of months ago by a patient suffering from similar extended symptoms. She called it Long COVID."

Jump from July 10th, 2020 to 2010

I fully intended to carry on reading the other months' entries and journals at this point. That glass of Jack Daniels was waiting, and Janice was by herself in the lounge watching Boxing Day television, which is something I wouldn't wish on anyone. So I just wanted to finish reading and get December written up as quickly as I could.

I'd made two jumps during July, and now, as I came to the end of the month's journal, the memory of my second jump—on the 21st—to the day I picked up my radio award in 2004, and the incredible revelation which followed it, resurfaced.

After calling Jigonhsasee I found her waiting for me in the white void. "Hello, Simon," she'd said both times. And I was instantly at the start of my voyage of discovery into my past.

The thing I found most frustrating was that I couldn't control where I went, but having said that, it was quite a thrill to see when and where I was and to take charge of the situation.

Thinking of that revelation powered up the thoughts

of July's first jump, which I guess set the scene for the second, even though that destination was six years earlier in my personal timeline. God, this is complicated. As my white surroundings dissolved during the first jump on July 10th, back to 2010, I found myself at my desk in the production office at Poolswood Sound, with Liv looking at me expectantly.

This was the only show I'd lost to a blackout, and I'd listened back to it many times, so I knew exactly what to expect once I went on air. This means that even though I'm about to make it happen for the first time, I don't need to carry out any research into the Council's controversial planning decision.

My head's whirling at this—it's a little different from the other blackouts in that I know exactly almost word for word and action by action what's going to happen when I start the show. But only because I've already listened to myself doing it.

Jigonhsasee's told me I can't change anything, so even though I'm in the driving seat does it mean I'm still just a passenger? As an involuntary time traveller of sorts, do my actions in the past change what would otherwise have happened, or is everything already laid down in a predetermined plan?

"Simon...?"

"What? Oh, sorry, Liv. I was miles away for a moment." Years away, would be more accurate.

"You're not kidding there," she said. "You were somewhere else entirely."

"Yep, I've just come back from the future..." never a truer word was said in jest. I remembered the moment in 2020 when she put that caller (was it John?) through to me on the day I collapsed with COVID, knowing mischievously that he's going to give me a run for my money. So here's my chance to get her back for what she's going to do. This is definitely complicated, and I laugh out loud but only in my head, confident it's for Jigonhsasee's mental ears only.

"And it's a future where you're quite grown up and not so irritating," I said to Liv, just a second before Jigonhsasee's thick Iroquois accent appeared in my mind, almost before my thought had dissipated: "Funnee, you should be on the stage. It left town an hour ago."

Jigonhsasee! How dare you?

"And you'll be even older and grumpier," said Liv.

Oh. I'm getting it on both fronts now.

"But until you get there, while I still like you, do you want me to tell you what Councillor Jacobs said or not?"

Ah. So that's why she'd been looking at me expectantly when I dropped in here. "I guess you'd better."

"I've lined him up to be your first caller in the open-line hour. As he led the rebellion at the meeting he's going to be pretty scathing that the application was approved."

"Okay, what do we know about it?"

"Are you sitting comfortably?"

"As comfortably as I can for your bedtime stories."

"Just don't fall asleep before I've finished."

"You could always try and make it more interesting. I'd do my best, then, to stay awake."

She glanced down at her computer screen. "And you could always try listening to Ayesha's report from Leo's show instead."

That made sense. It would provide a taster, and Liv could fill me in with anything else she'd found afterwards.

"Okay. Let's take a look."

I opened the same file Liv had on her screen, which was

the recording of Leo Goodman's breakfast show today.

"One hour 20 minutes in," Liv told me.

We both put earphones on, then I dropped the cursor over the button on the horizontal scrolling bar, dragged it across to just beyond an hour and 19 minutes after the show started and clicked on the Play icon.

"...will it still be number two next week, or can it take top spot?" the morning presenter was saying. "That was Love The Way You Lie, from Eminem featuring Rihanna.

"Okay, let's take a look at the Poolswood weather for today. Staying dry throughout. Early cloud giving way to long periods of sunshine, with a top temperature of 23°C, 74°F this afternoon, dropping to an overnight low of 13°C, 56°F.

"Now, you may have heard in the news that Poolswood District Council last night approved a controversial plan to turn part of Batchelors Farm, near Dagglethorpe, into a religious commune.

"Our reporter Ayesha Patterson was at the meeting."

The voice through my headphones switched to Ayesha's. "Batchelors Farm is a 208-acre site owned by the Reverend John-Luke Matthews, and run jointly as a farm and haulage company," she said.

"Reverend Matthews applied to convert three barns into residential accommodation and offices for a religious organisation he established last year. Before the planning meeting started, he told me what he wants to do."

The next voice was a rich baritone, and not altogether unfamiliar. "For several years I've given church sermons as a lay preacher, and lectures and talks at local colleges and organisations about returning swathes of the countryside back to a natural habitat." Where did I know it from? I think I'd have remembered if I'd interviewed him. Especially with a name taking in three of the four New Testament disciples.

"I'm fortunate to have inherited this farm and transport company from a distant relative a few years ago. It means I've been able to turn this little part of the county into my dream. A number of my fields have now become meadowland, and I've restored all hedgerows at their original, ancient locations. This planning application takes my dream to the next level."

"Tell me about that," said Ayesha.

"Last year I set up a religious charitable trust with the aim of creating a small commune here at the farm. We won't be completely self-sufficient, as part of the operation will be supplemented by my haulage company, at least in the early years.

"I'm asking through this planning application to convert three of my barns into sleeping accommodation for ten people, a communal kitchen and recreational area, and two offices. I discovered during my sermons and lectures that many people in Poolswood feel the same as I do about our countryside. Not only do we need to stop this planning blight of residential and industrial development swallowing up our green and pleasant land, but we also need to take a long, hard look at modern systemic farming.

"Six people have already asked if they could move on to the farm with me and help me return more of it to natural meadowlands while maintaining the rest to manage crops and livestock for food and selling."

"So a type of self-sufficiency, back-to-the-land set up?" asked Ayesha.

"Yes, indeed. But, as I, say, not completely. We'd need to use the whole farm if we were to fully withdraw from the outside world, and it's important for the long-term sustainability of our planet that natural growth is allowed to flourish wherever possible. So, whatever happens, a third of my land is returning to its natural state.

"The rest of it will be farmed entirely organically, with no diesel-driven machinery, and no chemical-based pesticides and fertilisers. I'll be working in the fields manually, along with six people who attended my sermons and lectures and want to become part of the bedrock of what we're looking to achieve here. That's why we need somewhere for them to sleep, eat and rest. They want to live here for the rest of their lives and protect the Earth."

His passion came through loud and clear, but I couldn't decide if the intensity was that of dedication or naked ambition. It was certainly packed with determination. The voice was almost hypnotic, and I suspect he may have had extensive coaching to perfect such a slow, rhythmic delivery which was sure to leave a lasting impression on all who heard him.

"The farm's now being run as a charitable trust, and if planning permission's granted, it'll become a small commune with our six friends joining me here permanently. We'll also be able to offer accommodation for four more believers to join us temporarily, anything from a weekend to a fortnight. I've lost count of the number of times people have come up to me at the end of my sermons and lectures, saying how much they'd like to experience life on the land, if only their busy lives would allow it.

"Alongside the six permanent bedrooms, I'm also asking planning permission for four more rooms where our temporary visitors can sleep.

"So, all in all, we have the foundation for a wonderful commune here, with the express purpose of protecting our environment, both in the short term and long term. We won't be harming anyone, no one will be inconvenienced, and my solicitor tells me it can't be refused purely on planning grounds."

I couldn't help but admire the simple, yet powerful way he'd conveyed his message, almost presenting the Committee with a fait accompli.

"The Committee agreed with that," said Ayesha. "Reverend Matthews' application was approved by 11 votes to seven. But it wasn't without controversy. The Leader of the Labour opposition on the Council, Councillor Noah Jacobs, organised a pretty powerful rebellion against the plan."

I listened to the remaining 90 seconds of her report which was enough to bring me up to full speed and prepared me well enough for Councillor Jacobs' phone call this afternoon.

After hitting Play on the last music track before the 1 o'clock news, I pulled the headphones down onto my shoulders while I stretched out to ease some of the muscle tension. Then I heard Liv's voice, tinny and faint, coming from them, and saw her waving through the glass to attract my attention.

My 56-year-old eyes looked out at her from my 46-year-old body. At this time—2010—she'd only been a production assistant at Poolswood Sound since the summer, joining us straight from university, but was already making her mark. She was full of innovative ideas, and I'd seen a certain something in her talent right from the start, so I was delighted when our programme controller assigned her to my show for a six-month stint. Which became a year, then two years, before she was moved to the breakfast show. After 18 months of working with Leo, she asked to come back to me. She gave the official reason as not wanting to carry on getting up at 4.30 every morning. But the real reason was she preferred the variety of my Lunch Break show. When I'd taken over the programme in 2008 it was in the doldrums, the previous host, Steve Chandler, having let it slide to become boring and untargeted, haemorrhaging listeners by the shedload towards the end, which was why Bob had suggested he took early retirement and moved me to it from the evening drive-time slot.

Under Steve's reign anything from music, a listener's call, or a news interview would suddenly turn up anywhere in the jumbled three-hour hotch-potch. Under my structured revamp, out went the old programme name of Steve Chandler's Roundabout, and from day one of the new-look Lunch Break With Simon Reynolds, the first hour was a mix of music and short, two- to three-minute interviews recorded by the news team, followed by an hour's phone-on, with the final hour dedicated to a full in-depth interview. My guests for this ranged from celebrities and politicians to local individuals, charities and other organisations working throughout the County.

It's fair to say listeners didn't flood back in their droves immediately, but Bob and his number crunchers were happy with the slow and steady upward trend. And they were even happier after 18 months when my figures started rivalling the breakfast show, eventually overtaking it. The sales team were able to charge advertisers a premium rate to market their wares on my show, and I even turned down an approach from one of the BBC's national stations.

I put the headphones back on and pressed the talkback key on the console. "Sorry, Liv, what were you saying?"

"Noah's on line one, ready and waiting."

"OK, thanks. Can you tell him I'll come to him during the news, please?"

"Will do."

I eased the headphones off again and glanced at the computer screen to check how long was left of the music track. That's good. Long enough for me to use the bathroom before I need to cue in today's newsreader.

Roger Buchanan wrapped up the one o'clock bulletin with the weather forecast a few moments later, and I was on air with the second hour of the show.

"Welcome back to today's Lunch Break with me, Simon Reynolds, as we move on to today's open line. As ever, you're in charge. You pick the topics you want to talk about. Just ring Poolswood treble eight, double two, one. First off, today, we have a caller who wants to discuss a story you may have heard in the news, about Poolswood District Council approving plans to allow a live-in religious commune to be set up at Batchelors Farm, near Dagglethorpe. It was a close decision, though, as seven councillors—all members of the opposition Labour Group—voted against it. The Leader of the Labour Group, Councillor Noah Jacobs, joins us now. Good afternoon, Councillor Jacobs."

I opened his line on the console.

"Good afternoon, Simon."

"Now, Councillor Jacobs, why did you lead a rebellion against this application?"

"It's hardly a rebellion," he said. "Just a different perspective on the effects this religious cult will have in Poolswood."

"Strong words, Councillor Jacobs: 'a cult'. The application was to convert barns into accommodation for a commune."

"A *religious* commune, and it's not a mainstream religion. What do we know about the Reverend John-Luke Matthews and his acolytes? I'll tell you what we know, Simon. Nothing."

"Wasn't everything made clear at the meeting? I mean, the commune will be partly self-sufficient and focus on sustainable farming, while reverting some of the land back to a natural state. What can you object to about that?"

"It's the religious aspect that bothers me," said Councillor Jacobs. "Not the farming, that's perfectly acceptable."

"But that's the reason for the application," I argued. "The Reverend Matthews needs somewhere for the farmworkers to sleep and relax, and two offices to run the farm from. You said the plans he'd got for the farm itself are acceptable, so what's wrong with a simple barn conversion, which was all the Committee was asked to consider? It was an application to change the use of the barns along with some associated structural work. None of these buildings can be seen from the road, they're in the middle of the 208-acre estate, so I'll ask you again, Councillor Jacobs, why did you lead a Labour Party rebellion against a simple application, which your own officers told you in their report, can't be refused on planning grounds?"

Over the years I've become an expert in gauging someone's tone of voice and how far I can push them before they clam up and start giving monosyllabic answers, which doesn't make good radio. When Noah Jacobs began his answer, the clipped words and short sentences hinted I may be reaching that point with him.

"The Labour Group just wanted to delay the decision. We needed time for our officers to find out more about this cult. There's a wider issue here. I want to know what religious principles they have. How will they interact with local people?"

"How do *you* think they'll interact?"

"That's what I'm saying, Simon, we just don't know.

They may try to convert people to their faith."

"Noah—Councillor Jacobs—you can't seriously be saying they'll come out of Batchelors Farm in orange tunics and sandals and rattle tins under everyone's noses, or brainwash people, based on a planning application to convert three barns?"

"Can't I? I think that's very seriously what I'm saying."

My eyebrows shot up at that. I needn't have worried about him clamming up, after all. This was great stuff. Completely unexpected and off the wall, but good radio.

A ping in my earphones told me Liv had just sent a message. Looking down at the screen I read: 'I'll try and get Matthews on. He needs a chance to answer this.' I nodded and gave her a thumbs up, then watched as she started to key something into her computer. Presumably his 'phone number.

"I must come back to my point about your officers telling you there weren't any planning considerations to warrant turning it down, and recommending approval," I said. "Eleven of your colleagues on the Committee accepted that. Why can't you? Why do you try to fudge the issue by looking at non-planning aspects which aren't part of your remit? Don't you think you were trying to exceed your authority last night, which could have left the Council open to the possibility of the Reverend Matthews launching a costly appeal?"

"But six members of the Committee agreed with me," he said. "We proposed a motion to delay the decision until the next meeting to give officers time to carry out further investigations."

"Which was rejected by the same margin as the decision to approve the application, 11 votes to seven."

"Indeed. I accept the planning matter's now closed, but I just wanted everyone to know that as Leader of the Opposition Group on Poolswood District Council, I and my fellow Labour councillors have grave concerns about a religious cult being established at Batchelors Farm."

"As you say, the matter's closed. The application's been approved and Reverend Matthews is going to start converting the barns. What else can you do about it?"

"The ruling Conservatives may not care about a religious cult moving into Poolswood, but we do. We'll be watching their activities very closely once the building work's finished. We're determined that the cult and its members won't be allowed to pose any threat to the people of Poolswood."

Another ping in my headphones. Liv had written: 'Matthews was already listening. He doesn't want to come on but he's given me a statement. Oh, and he says to say hi, it's been a long time.' That threw me. I've never met Reverend John-Luke Matthews, but why had his voice been vaguely familiar when I heard him in Ayesha's report? Hhmmm. I made a mental note to Google him after the show. I quickly scanned the rest of Liv's message and enlarged it on the screen to make it easier to see when I come to read it out.

"Would you be prepared to personally meet Reverend Matthews to talk about your fears, and for him to explain his plans for the farm?" I asked. He left a slight pause before responding, perhaps trying to pick his words carefully. I usually allowed politicians no more than five seconds of silence, which can sound like a lifetime on the airwaves, and leaves my audience in no doubt that they're struggling to find an answer.

Away from the microphone Noah and I were good friends, but he knew not to expect any favours during interviews. If he was batting on a sticky wicket he was always aware I would take out his middle stump at the earliest opportunity. I suspected he was now frantically trying to decide whether to bite the bullet and take responsibility for an investigation into Reverend Matthews' religious charity himself or delegate it to the Council officers, which he had said was the reason for tabling the motion to delay making a decision.

I was getting ready to prompt him with a stern: "Councillor Jacobs," when he replied.

"I doubt if Reverend Matthews would talk to us about the workings of his cult or its aims, but, yes, if he's prepared to undertake that, I'll meet him personally."

"Thank you, Councillor Jacobs. I think you've got yourself a date. While we've been talking I can tell you that Reverend Matthews has declined our invitation to come on the programme, but has issued the following statement, which I'll now read verbatim. *'I'm happy to meet Councillor Jacobs or anyone else from the Labour Opposition Group on the Council, the ruling Conservative Group, the Liberal Democrats, or the two independent councillors. I can reassure them that we're simply farmers. We have no intention of rattling tins or coercing anyone to join us. Please meet with us and we'll put your mind at rest.'*

"So, Councillor Jacobs, do you accept Reverend Mathews' offer to meet you personally, or, as he also extended the invitation to the ruling Conservative Group, will you pass it on to them?"

And there he had it. My job was almost done. I'd taken the story a few steps further along for my listeners. They'd been assured the religious commune did not pose any threat. Councillor Jacobs had demonstrated conflict in the interview between the two political groups, and personally between him and Reverend Matthews. And this stage of the story could be concluded when he replied. But which way would he go? How would he respond? The clock was ticking.

Another pause. This time I may let it run longer. Maybe seven or eight seconds.

As it turns out, I didn't need to.

"I'll meet him, Simon, gladly," he said after just a couple of seconds.

"That's good to know, Councillor Jacobs. I'm sure we all look forward to hearing how the meeting goes. Thank you for the call.

"It's just coming up to 12 minutes past one on today's open line. Ring now on Poolswood treble eight, double two, one, to join the debate. You're listening to Lunch Break, with me, Simon Reynolds."

Googling Reverend John-Luke Matthews after the show didn't throw up much. No Wikipedia entry and just a handful of newspaper reports, mainly about lectures he had given. He had no social media presence—I tried to think back to the popular platforms of 2010. Friends Reunited sprang to mind, and Facebook was growing in prominence, but the elusive clergyman didn't have an account on either.

Twitter's been running for four years, but a search there was equally fruitless.

It seemed odd, though, that his name didn't show up anywhere except in those few press reports. No photos. Nothing. It was almost as if he didn't exist officially. While widespread internet use was well beyond its fledgeling infancy back in 2010, a search was nowhere near as exhaustive as it is today, but I'd still have expected something, however small and insignificant.

And why was his voice familiar? That was more disturbing. Had we met sometime during one of my blackouts, and it was bleeding through from my subconscious? I'd have to ask Jigonhsasee if that was possible.

He said he'd inherited Batchelors Farm and the haulage company operating from it, a few years ago, but a quick dive into Companies House records showed the sole director and CEO was a 23-year-old named Frederick "Fritz" Chikatilo. There was quite a bit on him. He's an up-and-coming software engineer, but I couldn't see any other apparent connection with Matthews.

I looked up from my screen. "Liv, I can hardly find anything about Matthews. Did you look into him?"

"I only did a quick search, which mostly drew a blank. He seems to be the invisible man. I did take a look at his charitable trust, though, and that's all above board. Hang on a sec." She opened a folder on her computer and pulled up a document. "When he applied to launch the Trust, he said it was to take his own church to the next level, and..."

"His own church?"

"Yes, it seems so. He established the Church of Euvenity many years ago, specifically to safeguard the planet. The Trust has taken over running it. It complies with the requirements of charity law and is registered with the Charity Commission."

"Safeguard the planet?" My sarcastic snort told Liv what I thought of that. "Who does he think he is, David Attenborough?"

She laughed. "It does sound a little twee, doesn't it? But when you look at it, I think he's just a harmless crank who's doing his bit in the best way he can. The Trust has established a 'Green Charter,' promoting the need for environmental stewardship as caretakers of the Earth and its biodiversity. I'll read you a direct quote from their articles of trusteeship; 'We're arming society with knowledge about the damage we as humans are doing to our environment and how we can turn things around. It starts with what we're doing at Batchelors Farm—a fully organic philosophy, and natural, unfettered growth.' Actually, thinking about it, maybe Noah's right to be worried. That bit about arming society with knowledge doesn't sound as if they're going to be quiet and not venture away from the farm. They may not be going to rattle tins, but it sounds like they may be planning to convert people."

"But not to their faith," I said. "I guess it's not breaking any rules if they're just going to talk to people about the environment." With the hindsight of my 56-year-old brain, I knew that we don't hear a peep out of Reverend Matthews again. Whatever he does, it's not regarded as newsworthy.

And, of course, everything I found out about him that day was consigned to the bottomless pit of my blackout memories until I jumped back there on July 10th 2020 to reclaim them.

Would it have made any difference, I wondered, if I'd known what I'd just discovered in 2010, back at the time it happened? Or indeed, the startling revelation on my next trip to the past, 11 days later, which took me even further back, to May 2004?

19

Skelton Industries Radio Awards

Jump from July 21st, 2020 to 2004—Simon

My first waking thought on July 21st was that I must still be asleep. I can remember how heavy my eyelids felt, as if they were weighted down, and the joints in my arms and legs were frozen and rigid. My brain was equally uncooperative, pushing through the now familiar fog, seeking clarity and consciousness.

It was almost like a hangover after an alcoholic stupor but having missed out on the good, imbibing part the night before, with elephants stampeding through my skull, battering the soft brain tissue with their tusks. Then stepping aside so the one behind could have a go. There were maybe six elephants in there, on a mad merry-go-round with no end in sight.

It took a superhuman effort to prise my eyelids apart, but the blinding sunlight streaming in through the open bedroom curtains prompted me to screw them up again. The pounding went into overdrive and I moaned incoherently while rolling my head from side to side on the pillow, willing the elephants to slide down my ear canal and out through the pinna. At this point, I wouldn't have cared if they'd shattered my eardrums on their way to the exit. I just wanted them gone.

Not only did that fail to dislodge the elephants, it fired up the cough, lending speed and power to the ferocity of their assault, but at least it inspired movement, as I forced myself to sit upright, ignoring the thousands of pinpricks jabbing at every part of my joints.

A faint chill on my naked back as it peeled away from the soaking sheet beneath me, was a testament to how much I was sweating.

I wanted it to be a good day so much. To have four consecutive good days would be a minor miracle (fuck that, it would be a *major* miracle) but this start didn't look promising. Fighting back the cough was a little easier now I was sitting up, but each breath felt like it was emerging from molasses.

Yesterday and the weekend had been bliss. I'd almost felt normal again, which had tempted me to walk a couple of hundred metres further than maybe I should. Saturday's watchword was caution, only taking a stroll down the lane. Sunday had been a little more adventurous, as I'd taken the sit-on mower for a spin around our paddock, and yesterday I'd really grabbed the bull by the horns making it all the way up the hill on Apollo Lane to the church, and had half a bottle of Malbec with dinner last night. The first drink I'd had since coming home.

But the revolving door seemed to have turned from those days of hope, and spat me out on the other side, back to where I'd spent much of this month. Sitting on the edge of the bed I took stock. Headache: check. A slight drag to each breath: check. Lumpy throat: an attempt at swallowing showed that box had been ticked, too. But the real sickener was that today felt like a dark Tim Burton version of Ground Hog Day, and I couldn't wait for night to come so I could try to sleep again and hopefully wake up a little better.

A sliver of hope came when I was able to shower without needing to lie down afterwards, and actually took the stairs in my stride. Albeit, a slow and careful stride, putting both feet on each step and gripping the handrail firmly. I paused at the bottom, testing my shallow breathing, before making my way towards the kitchen on legs that felt as if they were wading through treacle, each pace taking more effort.

Janice made me a light breakfast of toast and yeast extract. Not that I could taste it much, but at least I managed to finish it, and then moved on to my high daily dose of Vitamin D supplement, and then my inhaler to help me reach the lounge.

I dozed for an hour, before listening to Liv hosting my show. She made a bloody good job of it, as always. At least, it's in good hands while I'm away, and if I don't recover enough to go back to work there's no one I'd be happier taking over permanently. But, let's not go down that road. Yesterday I could have thought I'd be back at the microphone by early Winter. Today, that seemed just another pipe dream. This was the awful psychological legacy of Long COVID. I was euphoric one moment, and the next I was bitter and angry, feeling old before my time and grieving for the life I used to have.

The thought about wanting night to come kept pushing from the back of my mind to the front all day, and each time another one accompanied it. It wasn't so much about sleep, but something Grandma had said about COVID not affecting me when I was out of my body and jumping back to my younger self.

Roll on tonight. Let's have another adventure in the past and fill in another blank space in my memories while feeling like a fully fit human being again.

Tonight did indeed roll on, but it felt like a lifetime of waiting as I sat in my chair for the afternoon watching Netflix. I'd dozed off in the middle of a film around 4.30

p.m. and found myself back in my forest dreamscape. This time it wasn't a nightmare, but a pleasant stroll along a trail weaving through the trees which bowed their tops towards each other overhead until they touched, creating a leafy canopy blotting out all but the most persistent rays of sunlight. Despite this, the sun's heat still permeated through, and I realised just how warm I was. A fleeting, jumbled dream-thought told me this cozy little world should be much cooler, but clad, as I was, in just navy shorts and a sky blue vest top, I felt as if I were walking in open countryside at the height of the day. To complete the sense of how off-kilter this was, the path was a mixture of dried holly leaves, stones, and twigs, and yet gave no discomfort to the soles of my bare feet. It simply felt like the softest deep-pile carpet.

A couple of deer looked up inquisitively as I passed by, before returning their attention to munching at the grass.

As I moved from under the tent of trees into a clearing, the familiar shattered Oak tree stood before me. How different from the last time I was here when I was being chased by COVID cells, desperately seeking sanctuary at the Oak. Now, I gently ambled towards it. Its bark looked faintly luminescent as if the light of hundreds of tiny fairy lights were seeping through from inside.

A slight hum infused the air, making me think of the electric pylon in the field on my favourite circular walk around the village. A narrow brook carved its way through the land immediately behind it, and I noticed the tree's roots dipping into the slow-moving water

"That's your Tree Of Life." The heavily accented words came directly into my mind, but I sensed Jigonhsasee was immediately behind me. I turned and looked straight at her beaming smile. "It's rather sorry for itself at the moment," she said. "COVID's not been kind to it over the last few months. But, look here, Simon." She indicated the tree's roots breaking through the banks of the brook.

"This tree was nothing but an acorn when you were born. During your lifetime it's drunk constantly from these waters of knowledge which give life and strength. Before COVID, it towered proud and firm, and will do so again. See how its roots quest out and take in the water, and hear the energy in the air as it replenishes itself. It shows you're recovering, Simon. It'll be a long, hard path, but you're well on the way."

What she had called my Tree Of Life stood bathed in blazing sunlight, which created an infinity of diamonds sparkling on the surface of the brook, rolling its way lazily past. I could almost sense the combined regenerative forces of sun and water and the rich goodness of the Earth which rooted the Oak to its spot pouring energy into it, offering recuperation and stability.

The ground here was an enticing mix of light soil and grass, with sunlight accentuating myriad colours of wildflowers that sprang from it in abundance—daisies, buttercups, lavender, bluebells, roses, and orange-petalled ones I didn't recognise—which all seemed oblivious to seasonal differences.

The hum in the air grew a touch louder and I felt an irresistible pull from the tree. Gingerly I stepped towards it, and flattened my palms against the bark, feeling a throbbing surge of energy, pushing through my fingers to the top of my head and the tips of my toes in the grass, filling me with a current of life and hope.

My Tree Of Life was returning from the doldrums, awakening in the Spring after a COVID Winter.

The thought popped into my head that I had to ask

Jigonhsasee if memories from blackouts could bleed through to me before I went back to live through them. "Jigonhsasee," I began. But she'd gone. I looked up at Janice smiling down at me in my chair.

"Dinner'll be ready in a moment," she said. "I hope you've not dozed too long or you won't sleep tonight."

I didn't tell her the reason I wanted 40 winks in the middle of the film was to speed up the clock until bedtime when hopefully tomorrow would be a better day, and to increase my chances of staying awake until she came to bed so my jaunt to the past wouldn't be interrupted. Grandma had said if I were awoken I'd simply return instantly to the present. I don't ever remember suddenly coming round from a blackout mid-stream so to speak. Every time I'd had one, I awoke the following morning with no recollection of what happened in the hours before going to bed. So it seems safe to say I'm not disturbed here, but I'm not taking any chances. My ploy worked, too. At around 10 o'clock I told Janice I was going up and she said she would be another half hour.

It was actually nearer 11 when I finally heard movement on the stairs, and turned to face away from her side of the bed in case she looked too closely and saw I was still awake.

Bless her, she was as quiet as a mouse, making sure to close the ensuite door before putting the light on to clean her teeth, and instead of switching her touch-activated bedside lamp on, even to the lowest setting, she left it off and edged her way round to her side of the bed in the dark.

As she got in, she gently kissed me on the cheek. "Night night, dear heart," she whispered, as she always did every night since I'd come home. "Sleep tight while you kick COVID's ass a little more." With the ritual words out of the way, I heard her settle down and felt her arm snake softly around my shoulder.

Her steady breathing slowly turned into a rhythmic lull. Just a few moments more, I told myself, to make sure she was in a deep enough sleep.

Then I silently called out to Jigonhsasee.

"Hello, Simon," she said on that night of June 21st, 2020 as I found myself in the warm and comforting white void once again. I looked way beyond her towards its source in the distance, which was almost vibrating with brightness. But it no longer called for me, tantalisingly offering what I knew I couldn't accept yet. That final journey would be for another day.

"Jigonhsasee," I began. "Is it possible for memories to start bleeding through from blackouts before I go back to them?"

I'd not been focusing on my surroundings while mentally projecting to her, and as I pulled my vision back together, I realised it wasn't Jigonhsasee standing in front of me now, but the British Prime Minister, his right hand outstretched towards me, while his left held an eight-inch-high silver microphone fastened to a wooden base with a metal engraving across its front.

The whiteness behind him wasn't the void, but a curtain at the back of a large stage. He stood at the front of the platform, next to a lectern that sported a blue shield with a microphone depicted diagonally across it. An image of headphones nestling up to either side of the shield completed the logo.

I glanced up at a cinema-size screen suspended halfway along the stage, which was briefly emblazoned with the words 'Skelton Industries Radio Awards,' before they changed to 'Best Evening Drivetime Show—Winner, Going

Home With Simon Reynolds, Poolswood Sound.'

Applause was ringing out behind me. I looked again at the Prime Minister and the trophy in his hand.

I was at the pinnacle moment of my radio career, which I'd missed in a blackout. Now I was about to experience it at last. Adrenaline coursed through my bloodstream as I mechanically shook hands with the Prime Minister, hoping my brain would slot into gear. And quickly.

"Congratulations, Simon," he said. "Very well deserved."

"Thank you, Prime Minister." My words were picked up by the microphone (the real one on a stand in front of him) and flooded out through speakers across the ExCeL Hall. He looked at me expectantly, and extended his hand closer, with the trophy. My temporary daze evaporated as I took it from him, turning to face the audience and holding it aloft.

I looked out at several hundred people sitting at circular tables. Where was mine? Who had I been sitting with? I frantically pulled back the years to remember the hours and moments before being called on stage to pick up my award, just ahead of the blackout.

Janice and I had been up with the lark that morning. We were catching the 9.05 train to London Victoria, and the cab was already booked to take us from there to the ExCeL Exhibition Centre, where the Skelton Industries Radio Awards 2004 were being held.

I heard the Sizzlin ringtone of her Nokia 7610 while she was in the shower, and saw from the screen that it was her Mum, no doubt ringing to wish us good luck. Not that I really needed luck today. The winners were all notified in advance, and I'd already been told I'd won the Best Evening Drivetime show, so it was just a case of Janice and me having a relaxing meal, washed down by a glass or two of champagne.

We'd decided to make a night of it, too. If we caught the 8.29 train from London in the morning we would be back in plenty of time for me to get to the studio.

"Hi, Beryl," I said after clicking to accept the call. "It's Simon. Janice is in the shower."

"Simon." That one word was clipped and anxious. The next six sounded as if tears were bubbling beneath the surface. "It's Dave. He's had a stroke."

"What? How is he?" Janice was very close to her Dad. "How bad is it?"

"We don't know yet," said Beryl. "The paramedics are just getting him in the ambulance."

"Where's he going? Poolswood General?"

"I think so, yes."

"We'll be right over." All thoughts of my award paled into insignificance. Dave was the best Father-in-Law anyone could have. We had to go to him.

"No you won't," she said. "I insist you both go to the awards ceremony. I'll be with him today. Come tomorrow when you're back. I'll keep you posted as to how he is."

"No, Beryl," I said. "I'll get Janice out of the shower now. We're coming."

"I can't argue at the moment, Simon. Can you get Janice, please?"

"Yes, of course, Beryl. Hang on."

My heart was beating faster as I took the phone upstairs. Janice would be devastated. If anything, she was closer to Dave than she was to Beryl—which I suspect was the legacy of working with him in the hardware shop for several years. This would knock her for six. I went into the ensuite and called her name loudly over the noise of the fast-running water.

"Janice. Can you come out? I need to talk to you." I

knocked on the shower door. Her face appeared, distorted through the steam, before she ran the squeezy which we kept in the shower to wipe water off the door, down the glass like a windscreen wiper, clearing an area about two foot square at head height. "What is it?"

"Can you come out, please? Your Mum's on the phone."

"Mum? Tell her I'll ring her back."

"I think you ought to take this, Janice."

The shower door opened a crack. "Can't it wait?"

"Not really," I said, and asked for a third time: "Can you come out, please?"

I heard an exasperated sigh as she turned the water off. The bifold door snapped fully open with more ferocity than usual, and she stepped onto the mat, dripping everywhere.

"What does she want that's so urgent?"

"Janice, let me..."

"Give it here." She snatched the phone from me before I could prepare her. "Mum, this had better be good."

I could hear Beryl's sobs from the phone's speaker above the hum of the bathroom fan.

"Mum?" Janice's anger and frustration crumpled away from her face, turning to numbed disbelief as Beryl spoke. Tears mingled on her cheeks with the droplets of water falling from her hair.

"I'm so sorry," I said, pulling her naked body towards me, ignoring how wet my dressing gown was becoming as I wrapped my arms around her.

"I'll be straight over," she said. Janice cut the call and reached for a towel. "Simon, I've got to go to him. I know how much today means to you, but you do understand, don't you, that I can't come with you now? I'll be with you in spirit, but Dad needs me there with him."

"Don't be silly," I said. "I'm not going to London now, I'm coming with you to the hospital."

"No, you're not." She pulled back and looked straight into my eyes. "You're going to receive your award from the Prime Minister. This is the high spot of your career, and such an honour for the station. You've got to go."

"Yes, but..."

"No buts. You're going. You can't do anything for Dad even if you come to the hospital. He knows it's your big day and wouldn't want you to miss it. I'll be there for him. I'll hold his hand and talk to him."

For me, there still wasn't a decision to make. Dave was my immediate family. I loved him like my own father and wanted to be there for him. Despite my protests, though, Janice insisted I carried on as planned and go to London.

The cab to the station, the train journey to London Victoria, and the cab to ExCeL all passed in a haze. My mind was on Dave all the way. As soon as I got to the centre I rang Janice.

"It looks hopeful," she told me. "He got to the hospital in time for them to start emergency treatment before there was irreparable serious damage. Although it's very early days they think he'll make a good recovery."

A wave of relief washed over me, and I literally felt that old cliche of the weight of the world being lifted from my shoulders.

"That's good news," I said. "How is he in himself?"

"As well as can be expected. A bit frustrated and a bit frightened. He's wired up to a lot of machines, and it's hard for him to talk. His speech is slurred, but at least he can still communicate."

"What about his movement?"

"His left arm and leg are numb, and his face has dropped

slightly on that side. It's such a relief, though, as it could have been a lot worse."

It was for me, too, and made it easier to focus on the awards lunch and enjoy the food. What great food it was: a starter of steak tartare with aged beef fillet, confit egg yolk, and game chips, followed by roasted cod with confit fennel, mussels, and white wine veloute. The dessert was banana and caramel tort with milk chocolate and banana sorbet.

I shared a table with groups from Radio Expressive, MusicStream Radio, and Vibrant Sounds, and even though we were all broadcasters, a glass or two of champagne with the meal and brandy with the coffee afterwards meant the conversation flowed with perhaps a little more fervour than it would have done otherwise.

Throughout the meal, the large screen showed a repeating loop of PowerPoint slides of the nominees at work. I'd been thrilled to see they used all five that I'd sent them—one sitting alone at my console, and the others with guests I was interviewing.

According to the table plan which we'd all hovered around at the entrance to the hall to see where we sitting, the Prime Minister was on the same table as Roman Schaeffer, the Chief Executive of Skelton Industries, who were sponsoring the awards. Now, they both stood up and made their way to the stage, climbing the four steps at the side, and moving to the two microphones and lectern at the front. Schaeffer called out the winners' names and picked each award up from the table behind them, giving it to the Prime Minister for him to hand over.

The last time I'd won anything was when I was Captain of the Sixth Form debating team and we'd beaten Chapham College in the South East of England Open Challenge. The team picture appeared in the local paper, and I was interviewed by the media about it. That was my first time on the radio, and the bug bit me. After that, all I ever wanted was to make a career on the airwaves, and now here I was, the host of the best teatime show in Britain (according to listeners who voted for me on Skelton Industries' website, anyway).

"The next category is the Best Evening Drivetime Show," Schaeffer said as he reached to the table behind him and picked up the award. "The three shortlisted programmes are Going Home, presented by Jay Elleridge, on Cadenza FM." The images onscreen changed to a shot of Jay below his show and station names.

Schaeffer waited until the applause died before introducing the second nominee. "Next we have The Teatime Slot, with Sofia Harding, on Rush Radio."

I suddenly wondered if he left the winner's name until last on purpose. I'd not been concentrating on the order he read out the nominees in the other categories. I'll take note of what happens next.

But, of course, I couldn't. Not at the time, anyway. After my name was announced as the winner and I climbed the steps onto the stage, walking towards the Prime Minister, the next thing I remembered was waking up in my hotel bed the next morning.

Now, for the first time, I heard the applause ring in my ears as I proudly showed my trophy. The Prime Minister indicated the second microphone. I'd prepared a humble, but witty, acceptance speech and practiced it on Janice so many times until it drove her to distraction. But that had been 16 years ago.

This shouldn't worry me, though. It actually means I've had 16 more years experience of winging life behind the microphone. Just another day at the office.

"Prime Minister, Mr. Schaeffer, ladies and gentlemen," I began. "I'm particularly proud to receive this prestigious award for my evening drivetime show. The reason it means so much is that it's been given to me by my listeners, the people I talk to between four o'clock and seven o'clock every day—those who invite me into their cars when they're driving home after work, and those who are cooking or eating dinner at that time."

I looked around the room. "This is a great industry. Radio's been my passion for as long as I can remember, ever since I was interviewed myself over 20 years ago. As presenters, reporters, DJs, and newsreaders, people get to know us from afar. We're the friends they invite into their homes day after day. We owe it to them to always look after them, and repay their friendship. I believe this is their way of saying, Simon, you're one of us, you're a member of our family, our circle of friends, our work colleagues, our team-mates.

"That makes me feel honoured and humbled. As radio professionals, we have a job to do, but we must never forget how privileged and lucky we are. We simply talk for a living and gain people's trust, love and affection. We're nothing without our listeners. We sit behind a microphone and hope that people are listening to us. And more than that, we hope they take note of what we say.

"Everyone of us who's ever been nominated for a radio award can say yes to those two points. People have heard us and they must like what they've heard, as they've taken the trouble to vote for us."

Where was this coming from? It's the gist of what I prepared 16 years ago, so must have been stored all this time in some easily accessible filing cabinet in my head.

How fabulous to feel 100 percent fit again in this body of 2004, and for my brain to be firing on all cylinders.

The applause sounded like heavenly music as I made my way down the steps and towards the tables. The euphoria quickly dissipated, though, as I realised the immediate dilemma was to find where I was sitting. I knew a couple of people at the table. I'd been on the same BA media studies course at university as Patsy de la Ray from Radio Expressive, and had met one of the guys from MusicStream Radio a couple of times, so I think I'd still recognise them after all these years.

The plan was to go to the back of the room and find out where I was on the seating plan, then when I get back to the table I'd tell them I'd had to go for a wee. Lady luck was smiling on me, though, because as I weaved my way through the tables, I saw Patsy, and hurriedly sat down.

While I was honoured, humbled, and privileged to win the award, I was also proud. After all, who wouldn't be? A national award, gaining more votes than any other teatime show presenter in the country.

Maybe I should use this as leverage to further my career. The question was, where would I go? I don't want to leave Poolswood Sound as I love living where I do, so the options are limited. The breakfast show is always regarded as the flagship of any radio station but I don't think I could cope with getting up at the ungodly hour necessary for the programme's six o'clock start. The mid-morning and afternoon shows were a possibility, but I've always found them to be a little nondescript on every station I've listened to. Which leaves the lunchtime show. Not much chance there. The jury's out on whether Steve Chandler has presented Roundabout since Moses parted the Red Sea or Methuselah was a child, so I can't see him being surgically removed from the seat for a while yet.

I guess I'm saying I'd better not let winning a national award go to my head. I'm still the same old Simon Reynolds, plodding along with a good show and wonderful listeners, at least for the time being.

Another mild stab of panic hit me after the ceremony finished and we all got up to leave. I couldn't remember the name of the hotel where I'd be staying the night. A quick look in my wallet resolved that, as I found the booking confirmation slip.

A few moments later I was on my way in a cab.

After unpacking and showering I heard a large glass or two of Malbec calling my name. Slipping my wallet into my back pocket I chose the stairs rather than the lift to take me down to the hotel bar.

If I'd booked the hotel myself I'd have avoided this type of chain and gone for something smaller and more boutique with individual character. There's nothing intrinsically wrong with this one, which Bob's assistant at the time, Andrew Hardy, had found for me through Booking.com. It was clean and comfortable, and I'm sure the food will be perfectly acceptable, if just standard fair, but if I were in Nottingham, Edinburgh, Manchester, or Torquay the style, layout, and menu would be identical. A little soulless, each one just a clinical clone of the original. Or even worse, a clone of a clone.

Following the sign to Reception and Bar adorning the pale blue wall, I pushed the door open and walked through into the lobby. No doubt an identical scene faced someone emerging from the stairwell in the Stockton-on-Tees, Bournemouth, or Sunderland clone.

The receptionist in their smart blue uniform which matched the walls—even the burgundy waistcoat coordinated with the border spool providing the finished edge where wall meets ceiling—would have looked up and smiled in the same way that Alan who'd checked me in 45 minutes ago, did now.

I followed the curved glass walkway which looked out onto a well-maintained courtyard enclosed inside granite walls more normally associated with a country hotel than one in the heart of London, and came to a light and airy bar.

It was only 4.45 p.m. but I'd have expected more people to be in there, such as businessmen unwinding after a draining meeting, or couples on a city break. Perhaps everyone's getting too health conscious and are in the pool or gym.

As it was, only one table, near the centre of the room, was occupied. A businessman sat at it scrolling through something on his laptop.

And I had the choice of all but one bar stool. A guy wearing tan chinos, brown slip-on shoes, and a short-sleeved flowery shirt with a strong black and red theme, was perched at the far end of the bar.

The barman, a lad aged about 19 with spiky black hair and a bad case of acne across his cheeks and the top of his neck, was standing by the cash register, looking bored. Don't knock the quiet lull, I thought, make the most of it, as this place will be packed to the rafters in an hour, probably sooner, and you'll be rushed off your feet, even with a colleague on duty helping you out.

The far-away look in his eyes dissipated in an instant, and a well-rehearsed smile took over.

"Good evening, Sir. Welcome to Shooters Bar. What can I get for you?"

"Good evening..." I peered at the name badge on his lapel, "Daniel, how are you today?"

"All good, thank you, Sir. And with you?"

"On top of the world, thank you, Daniel, and very much in a celebratory mood. Do you know what? I was going to have a glass of Malbec, but I think champagne's called for instead."

"Very good, Sir. Any preference?"

"I'm not a champagne expert," I admitted. "I'm more of a red wine man. But today's a bit special. What do you have? Can you recommend a mid-price bottle?" Extravagant, but why not? As Janice isn't with me I need to celebrate in some way.

Out of the corner of my eye, I caught a glimpse of Chino guy turning his head in my direction.

Daniel reached for the wine list from a rack on the bar and turned to the inside back page. "This one's quite popular." He indicated a bottle halfway down the selection. "Or this one's a touch drier." His finger moved to a second one, which was not only drier but was also £35 dearer.

I felt Chino guy's eyes boring into my profile. I flashed him a quick smile and returned my attention to the wine list.

"I'll go for this one, please." I couldn't justify the more expensive bottle, and the one I chose would probably taste just as good to my uneducated palate. Maybe I should have stuck with my favourite Malbec, but these sorts of days don't come along often.

"Good choice, Sir," said Daniel. "Would it be impertinent of me to ask what you're celebrating?"

I realised for the first time that my comment about celebrating must have sounded as if I were fishing for him to ask. Maybe subconsciously I was. After all, this had happened 16 years ago and I hadn't spoken about it for a long time. I'd missed not talking about it the first time around, even missed the thrill of receiving my award. So, while it's still fresh in my mind...

"Not at all," I said. "I've just picked up a national award from the Prime Minister." Daniel's eyes widened. "As my wife wasn't able to come with me at the last moment, I think I'm entitled to celebrate with champagne."

"Indeed you are," he said. "That's very cool. Congratulations. Do you mind me asking what the award was for?"

"I have my own radio programme, and was lucky enough for it to have been voted the best teatime show in the country."

More movement from Chino guy caught my attention and I turned towards him again. He raised his glass in my direction. It looked like whisky.

"Oh wow," said Daniel. "Are you a DJ?"

Returning my focus to him, I shook my head. "Not just a DJ. Although I do play music as part of my show, I also interview people and do a phone-in. We're called presenters nowadays."

"Wow," said Daniel again. "I'm talking to a star."

I laughed, but before I could say anything, a smooth low-pitched voice from my right broke into our conversation. "You are, indeed." I looked around sharply at Chino guy. "None other than Simon Reynolds, if I'm not mistaken," he said.

That shook me.

"Do I know you?" I asked.

"Excuse me, gentlemen, I'll just fetch your champagne, Sir," said Daniel, diplomatically. He disappeared through a door at the side of the bar, and I hoisted myself up onto the nearest stool.

As Chino guy swiveled his own stool to face me, I saw the shirt was fully buttoned to his neck, and he wore a clergyman's dog collar through it. I thought back to the Reverend Hubert McBeil in his black cassock as he stood in the pulpit at Meriton Church all those years ago, and to him battling the ferocious entity at White Pastures. He had been the very model of a clergyman. Chino guy looked the opposite. Almost like an aging hippy.

"Don't you recognise me, Simon?" he laughed "I knew you before you were Simon Reynolds. "Well, before you were *thee* Simon Reynolds, of Poolswood Sound fame, anyway. From way back in the old days."

I scrutinised the warm smile, the striking blue eyes, and the thick, overlong grey hair which cascaded in well-groomed waves over his ears to rest on his shoulders.

Yes. I did know him from somewhere. And there's something uncannily familiar about that laugh, too. Not recent, though. As he says, way back. Which is relative, of course. It wouldn't be as way back to the Simon whose physical body he was now smiling at in 2004, as it was for me hitching a ride from 2020.

His eyes sparkled with amusement as he paused for me to ask. Instead of giving him the satisfaction, I should have waited for him to volunteer who he was, but my radio interviewer's inquisitiveness wouldn't let me do that.

"You're right. I do know you from somewhere," I said. But where? If, as he said, it was in the old pre-radio days, it could have been at university. I tried to picture what this face and hair could have looked like around 20 years ago. Was he someone from my media studies course? As I stared at him, I became aware that my gaze may have been a little too intense and unlocked my eyes from his.

I shook my head and laughed to cover my embarrassment. "But for the life of me, I can't think where. No. I'm sorry, Vicar, you're going to have to tell me."

He threw his head back and outdid my laugh threefold.

"Sorry, Simon. I'm not laughing at you. Well, I guess I am, but only because you called me Vicar. That seems so far away from when we knew each other."

He took a sip of his whisky. "I've been in your debt for many years, ever since you saved my life."

His comment hit me like a thunderbolt, but I was still none the wiser.

"I've never saved anyone's life," I said. Wait, though, perhaps I had, during one of my blackouts. Yes, that had to be the explanation.

"Come on, Simon, I can't have aged that much, surely."

Suddenly in my mind's eye, I saw those eyes bulging, and his locks flowing upwards. They'd been blond at the time and a little shorter, swirling haphazardly through the sea at Brighton, with me desperately trying to free his foot when he had been held down underwater.

"Mark," I exclaimed.

He bowed his head and rotated his hand theatrically several times. "At your service."

"Mark Brody. I can't believe it."

"You'd better believe it, buddy. It really is me." Another sip of his whisky. "But I said goodbye to that name a long time ago. Nowadays I'm known as the Reverend John-Luke Matthews."

20

The Church of Euvenity

2004, Simon

I stared at him again across the four stools between us, no apology was needed this time. His words were worthy of my fixed gaze. The man Liv and I researched six years in the future from this moment, turned out to be Helen's boyfriend who we hadn't seen since her funeral.

He slid off his seat and strode over to me, reaching out to shake hands, before perching on the stool next to me.

"It's good to see you again after all this time, Simon."

"You, too, Mark."

His smile was almost intoxicating, the type of charismatic beam that would take over a room the moment he walked in. "There's no Mark anymore," he said. "That's the one of the Four Evangelists I've abandoned. He was the most insipid of the apostles, so I'm leading my life now in the footsteps of the other three, Matthew, Luke and John. I've put them all together, and here I am, John-Luke Matthews."

"And a Reverend, too. I had no idea you had any leanings towards the church. Didn't you want a career in the law when you were with Helen?"

He touched his dog collar and took another sip. "I did. But things change. Helen's death made me see the world in a different light."

The world had never been the same for me and my family since she died, but I hadn't thought it would have affected Mark—John-Luke—so much.

"You're saying you went into the church because of Helen?"

"Because I lost her, yes. I went back to university at first, but something new was calling me. Something intangible. It's still difficult to put into words, but the huge hollow space she left was growing with time, not lessening."

The door at the end of the bar opened and Daniel brought my champagne in.

"Two glasses, please, Daniel. This gentleman will be joining me." I hadn't asked him, but I assumed he would.

"That's very kind of you, Simon, I'd love to join you. Thank you. And I'd like to extend an invitation for you to join me for dinner later. I've got a short meeting here, but after that, I'd be honoured to buy you dinner."

There was a muffled pop as Daniel twisted the champagne cork free in a linen cloth wrapped around the neck of the bottle. The wine was lively and bubbled around the rim, but he caught it expertly in the glass.

John-Luke looked at his watch, and I noticed the elongated crown logo on its face. A Rolex.

"I'm expecting someone in around an hour and a half. We should be through by seven, and there's an excellent Italian restaurant nearby, where I've got a table booked. If you'll join me, I'll change the reservation to two."

It would be interesting to catch up with what Mark—John-Luke—had been doing since Helen's funeral and would be a welcome alternative to how I thought my evening was going to pan out—a solitary dinner and staring alone into a champagne glass.

"Thank you. I'd love to."

"Excellent." He reached into his back pocket and pulled out a mobile phone. Once he had amended the restaurant booking and taken his first sip of champagne he locked his twinkling eyes on mine.

"Now then, Simon, time for you to tell me how your family are, and how you landed this road to stardom you're on."

That didn't happen often. Normally I'm in charge of the conversation, asking the questions. He'd slipped that one over me. I was desperate to hear about his journey into religion, but I'd better quench his curiosity first.

"Well," I began, "I went to university where I got my BA in media studies..."

An hour later I'd brought him up to speed on Mum, Dad and Sarah, landing the Drivetime show at Poolswood Sound after joining the station as a production assistant, and the fact that I was now married. He couldn't remember Janice, but why should he? He only met her once, briefly, at Helen's birthday, where she'd just been one of many partygoers.

"Time for your story now," I said. "I'm intrigued to hear how you moved into religion."

He raised his champagne flute to his lips. He wasn't drinking fast, and still hadn't finished his second glass.

"Helen's death hit me really hard." His eyes bored into mine. The twinkle had gone now, replaced with a hint of sadness as he started to recall those long-ago days.

Just as Heidi's death had hit Jim Roberts hard when she was carrying Helen's soul, I thought. I wondered how one soul could bring so much love and yet so much heartache. Why didn't the cosmos tell everyone that death was just a portal to another plane of existence, that we move on to a higher level of consciousness, and our fear of black nothingness disappears as we leave our Earthly life behind?

"You could have stayed in touch," I said. "We'd have been here for you." The more I thought about that awful time, the more I realised we seemed to have cut Mark off. Not deliberately, but we hadn't made any effort to contact him after the funeral. He could have got in touch with us, but that didn't lessen our fault. We closed ranks as a family and helped each other through as best we could. As Helen's boyfriend, he had become part of our family, and we abandoned him at his greatest time of need.

"I know," he said, "but a clean break seemed better at the time. If I'd seen you again, or even phoned, it would almost have seemed she was still alive at White Pastures."

"What did you do after her funeral?"

He turned to look out of the window opposite the bar. I followed his gaze onto the granite-enclosed courtyard which housed a few tables and chairs. Without looking back at me he said: "I started the new term at university, but couldn't focus on my studies. By the following year, I knew the law wasn't for me. I needed to devote myself to something more spiritual, that may help me to cope better with losing Helen and understand why it happened."

"Have you?" I asked. "Have you coped, do you understand?"

He didn't answer for several seconds, but this wasn't radio, there was no dead air to worry about, I didn't need to push him. Eventually, he turned back to face me and said: "Yes. And no."

I briefly wondered if 40-year-old me here in 2004 would handle this differently from 56-year-old me talking to him now.

"What do you mean?"

"I quit my law degree and studied theology at Glasgow."

"Glasgow?"

"Yes, it's the oldest subject taught at the university there, dating back to when the university was founded in 1451. Being able to explore perspectives across a variety of faiths, and investigate contemporary religious questions, all helped to numb the pain of losing Helen, but the main thing is that it brought me closer to God and led to something much bigger for me."

"Bigger than God?" I asked.

He nodded while keeping his eyes fixed on me. "In some ways, you could say yes to that question." John-Luke drained his champagne and covered the glass with his hand when I picked up the bottle to refill it. "No more, thank you, not before my meeting. I'll tell you what, though, I'll drink you under the table with another bottle—on me—at the restaurant afterwards. And we probably won't remember any of it in the morning."

How true that was, I thought. At least for me, but not for the reason you think, John-Luke. I'll remember it tomorrow in 2020, but not tomorrow in 2004.

"It's a deal," I said as I filled my own flute almost to the brim, which left just a tiny amount in the bottle. "What can be bigger than God, then?"

"The fate of the planet," he replied calmly.

That froze the glass halfway to my lips. "Yes, I guess it doesn't come any bigger than that."

"Not that I saw it immediately, of course, but when I did see it eventually, I couldn't unsee it. I've never been a conventional clergyman. I don't belong to a mainstream religion such as the Church of England or Roman Catholicism. My faith and beliefs transcend all that."

"To be bigger than God, they must do."

"Don't mock me, Simon." The voice changed in an instant. The soft burr was replaced with a hardened edge, and the eyes now glinted like steel.

"I'm not mocking you, John-Luke," I said quickly. "I'm sorry. I didn't mean anything by it. It's just that this is a lot to get my head around."

"I suppose it is. Sorry for taking offence where none was intended."

That swift glimpse of another side to Mark Brody had gone. The soft, rich voice was back, as was the twinkle in the eyes, just as if it had never been away. But I'd seen something lurking there, not too far beneath the surface. Something that was quick to trigger. Something I didn't like.

"I'm passionate about protecting Mother Earth," he said, "and sometimes I get carried away."

A sudden impression of the world on Atlas's shoulders popped into my mind, but I kept the thought to myself and batted it away.

"I sensed way back that something was wrong with the Earth," he said. "Helen's death awakened many questions from deep within me about it all. Why should a beautiful, intelligent girl be snatched away before she had a chance to experience life or make her mark on the world? And I came across something even more worrying, with tremendous, almost evil, consequences. The deeper I delved into religions across the globe, the more I saw how they were responsible for conflicts. All of it man-made and much of it in the name of many gods and faiths. By that time, the biggest conflict of all was emerging, between humans and the wonderful planet beneath our feet which sustains all life.

"We were attacking it. This shining, sparkling jewel of the cosmos, was under a bitter and sustained assault."

I listened, enthralled by his passion and his way with words.

"Throughout the 20th Century mankind began its relentless offensive upon the Earth, as more and more of its resources, such as coal and wood, were stripped away. Whole species were being hunted to extinction.

"I created my own church in 1999, the Church of

Euvenity, to spread the message of the Earth's plight, and how we, as a species, are damaging it to the brink of being beyond repair. We're destroying our planet. We're murdering her."

Euvenity. I'd first heard that name 11 days ago in my personal past, and six years ahead of this moment.

"As we moved forward towards the end of the 20th Century and into the new dawn of the 21st, the Earth began to fight back with a vengeance," he said. "Droughts, floods, melting ice caps, forest fires. The list grows ever longer."

And the world will really sit up and take notice in just a few months from now, I pondered, with the Boxing Day earthquake and tsunami in the Indian Ocean.

"Make no mistake, Simon, the Earth is waging war on humanity. We're at the biggest crisis in history."

"Are you saying we need to defend ourselves against the Earth?" I asked.

"Absolutely not. That would be sacrilege, heresy and blasphemy rolled into one. We have to become the Earth's ally to soothe and comfort her. We need to stop raping her and pillaging her finite resources. She sustains the life of every creature that walks and crawls on her surface, swims in her oceans and flies in her sky. We, the human race, are putting that fragile sustainability at considerable risk. We've had a nuclear clock rocking backwards and forwards for decades, but the tick of the environmental clock is inching us closer to an apocalyptic event than any nuclear threat has ever done.

"That's where Helen's death has brought me to, Simon. It awakened my destiny, and that's why I answered your question 'Do you understand why it happened?' with 'yes and no.' I don't know why she died unless it was to set me on the path of saving the Earth.

"Her death hasn't been in vain and never will be. The Church of Euvenity will stand tall and proud in her name, as more and more non-believers start believing, and turn to us."

"Non-believers? What don't they believe in, and what happens when they turn to you?"

I could scarcely take in what I was hearing, let alone process it adequately. Who had Mark Brody become? What had he become? The Reverend John-Luke Matthews bore scant mental resemblance to Helen's carefree boyfriend who we took to our hearts so much during the two years they were together, and who had shared those terrible summer days with us at White Pastures in 1982.

"Just as religions the world over face a set of heathens who disbelieve the teachings and gospels of their contemporaries," he said, "so we in the Church of Euvenity have our heathens, our disbelievers, who choose to look the other way and deny that Humanity's actions are destroying the planet and putting us on the brink of extinction. They're our non-believers, Simon, the ones who refuse to see what's happening to the world around them."

We looked into each other's eyes, the windows revealing our souls. His were steely again, but not the hard glint of anger and suspicion I'd aroused in them when he thought I was mocking him. This was the steel of passion, of total belief in what he was doing, to the exclusion of all else.

What would he see in mine? Maybe the hint of mockery now, derision, perhaps?

"When they see the light and turn to us, they become a true ally of Gaia. We go on..."

"Gaia?" I interrupted. "What's Gaia?"

"Gaia is the Greek Goddess of Earth and the Mother of

all life here. In many ways, she *is* Mother Earth herself."

"So your followers side with the old Gods?" I hope I had succeeded in keeping full scorn out of my tone.

"Not in the way you're thinking. My followers, as you call them—I prefer to think of them as my congregation—pledge their allegiance to the Earth. We fight the causes of climate change, so, no, we don't defend ourselves against the Earth. We attack what's leading the Earth to defend herself against Mankind.

"We are God's wind, Simon, and when we blow, it's in defence of our planet. We need to help her heal by opposing extensive travel on the roads and in the air, and cutting back on harmful emissions which are destroying the ozone layer in the skies above us.

"The Earth is fighting back against us. We must help her by reversing the path humanity has taken. If we don't save our planet, what future does any of us have?"

"Forgive me, Mar—sorry, John-Luke—but what can one man, one church, do in the face of teeming millions around the world who neither believe nor care?"

"You may look at me as just one man, and my church as small because you haven't seen what we've done, what we're doing. When you know the truth, Simon, you may want my team to come on your show and proclaim our army to the world."

"Army?"

"Yes, army. We're waging a war against the road of greed and self-destruction. We have soldiers everywhere. In big business, in Governments around the world, and in schools. They're parents, teenagers, and the elderly. We're truly everywhere. In just five years since the Church of Euvenity was founded, we've come such a long way."

"How come people haven't heard of you?" I knew the

answer to my question before he replied. Because in 2004 these soldiers of the Church of Euvenity would still be regarded largely as tree-hugging, long-haired, sandal-wearing crackpots. The sheer cost of environmentally friendly policies deterred Governments from imposing them, and the cost to individual families of adopting cleaner, greener, lifestyles, was still prohibitive, and several years away.

"And keep it that way." Jigonhsasee's words vibrated in my head just as if she were alongside me, speaking directly into my ear. "Don't forget, the cosmos won't let you change anything."

"Go away," I projected mentally to her. "I haven't done anything about this, have I, so I'm not going to?"

"You're learning." With that, I felt her presence depart from my side, but I knew she was still close by, watching, and listening.

"Those of us who've heard the Earth scream in pain and seen her fight back know what's coming," John-Luke said. "We have to change the way humanity's going before it's too late. But you won't see me there, at the forefront. I'm not going to become a figurehead for this movement. I'll leave that to others. I work behind the scenes, planning, coordinating, making sure the army's in the right place at the right time."

He looked up as a striking young woman came into the bar, her jet black hair tumbling below her shoulders, and dark brown eyes above cheekbones that could have been finely chiselled from alabaster. Her jeans were skin-tight, and the Greenpeace logo on her T-shirt pulled across her chest, leaving no curve of her ample breasts to the imagination.

"Jasmine, over here," he called.

"Hi, John-Luke." She made her way to the bar stool on his other side and sat down. She looked at his empty flute and the bottle in the ice bucket. "Champagne? What's the occasion?"

"To celebrate my friend, Simon, here, getting a national award from the Prime Minister today."

"The Prime Minister..." She spat the words with such venom they almost froze in the air en route to my ears.

He laughed. "As you may have guessed, Simon, the Church of Euvenity doesn't approve of Government action— or should I say *inaction*—regarding climate change."

It certainly hadn't made its way to the top of the mainstream agenda in 2004. Although it was starting to make inroads into some people's minds, from what I could recall of the time, Greenpeace was a name that made many viewers groan "not again" whenever it featured in a television news broadcast. If only we had listened, if only we had taken notice back then, I thought, the world may not be facing the environmental collapse we are now, from global warming.

"Jasmine, this is my friend, Simon Reynolds. Simon, Jasmine Foster-Brown, a leading member of my congregation's inner sanctum. My right-hand girl. I guess you'd call her one of my followers."

She regarded me with large dark eyes for a few seconds before reaching across in front of him to shake hands. Her grip was firm and dry as she pressed her thumb a little too fiercely into the back of my hand.

"Hello, Simon. Good to meet a friend of John-Luke's." Her vowels indicated an upper-class childhood and teenage years. She was probably no more than 19 or 20 now.

"Jasmine, good to meet you."

"I was just telling Simon how we're defending Earth against humanity's attack on the environment," said

John-Luke. "He was asking why people join the Church of Euvenity and what they believe in when they come to us.

"Daniel," he called to the barman. Then to Jasmine: "What are you drinking?"

"There's a drop of champagne left," I said. "Not quite a glassful, but you're welcome to start with that."

"No thank you," she replied. "I don't drink alcohol." Of course, she didn't. "Lime juice and soda, please."

"As you've been part of my congregation since 2002, perhaps you could tell Simon why you came to us."

She smiled for the first time since coming in. "Of course." She settled into what came across as a well-rehearsed and often presented routine. I can usually tell when someone has had media training, and I'd have bet my house Jasmine had. The combination of her natural upper-class confidence and obvious knowledge of the subject formed a scintillating and powerful mix.

"The Church of Euvenity is here because we can't live without stable temperatures, reasonable sea levels, and sustainable biodiversity," she said. "It's about this interconnected web of life and beauty and the fact that the Earth is dying. We have a stark choice, as to whether we go on as we are and let the planet become a barren rock unable to support life of any kind, or do we stop the climate vandalism that's been going on for years and do what we can to let it stay a green and blue gem—a jewel cradled in the blackness of the universe? A jewel that, as a place where life can thrive, is one in more than a million."

Her eyes blazed with the same passion as John-Luke's, while her words flowed with energy and conviction.

"The Earth is only alive because of its lungs—the forests— and its veins, the rivers. The Church of Euvenity is about life because people are dying as a result of humanity's treachery to the planet. Animals are dying. Plants are dying. Governments are only just beginning to think about it, and that's because people in privileged, advanced, countries are starting to face a bleak future. Those in less privileged, less developed, countries no longer have to face the fear of it in the future, because it's hitting them now. The crisis isn't in the future for many people in many countries; it's in the present, the here and now of 2004."

I tore my eyes from her mesmerising face and looked at John-Luke. He smiled, and said: "See what I mean?"

I did. Maybe I needed to invite Jasmine and him on to the show. I was just one radio host of one programme on one radio station, but perhaps I could help make a difference in a small way.

"Don't you dare." Jigonhsasee's voice thundered in my head. "The cosmos will stop you."

"Yes, I know," I projected back at her mentally. "I didn't, did I, so I don't do it? I can't stop these thoughts, though."

"As long as they stay just thoughts and never become actions," Jigonhsasee told me.

"But that's the problem, isn't it? It's the same problem around the world here in 2004. We need action from people who matter, and all we have are thoughts."

"Not your problem, Simon."

"Yes, it is. It's everyone's problem."

"The cosmos will stop you."

"I joined the Church of Euvenity because it stands for everything I believe in," Jasmine was saying. "The youth of today, whether they're suffering at the moment or whether that's still to come for them, will face much worse if we don't turn this around.

"I know some people say it's hopeless, but I don't believe

that, because I've seen the hope in the faces of the people when they show their anger, when they realise their power. I've seen it in the figures that show how small a percentage of the population we need to get onside to achieve real change."

I realised I'd heard all this, years later. What a waste of time. Had the Earth's scales tipped beyond the balance in the intervening years? People like Jasmine and organisations like Greenpeace have been warning us for so long. And we've ignored those warnings. It's taken the fierce, emotional words of a girl younger than Jasmine—Greta Thunberg—to finally reach the hearts and minds of politicians. So many wasted years.

"I see this hope in people every day," said Jasmine. "But, a word on hope. We can't just sit here waiting for hope to come to us. We have to be the change we want to see in the world. We have to know what it is we hope for, and then do what we can to make it happen. We have to earn that hope.

"Politicians and business leaders don't deserve that hope if they continue to make decisions which they know are disastrous for the planet, for indigenous communities, for animals. Hope isn't their lies, hope isn't them saying everything's okay when it won't be.

"Hope is action. Hope is the fact that we still have time.

"That was a word on hope. Now a word on time."

I picked up my champagne glass, almost feeling I should toast this incredible young woman and her passionate speech. I'd noticed John-Luke had been dividing his attention between Jasmine and watching my reaction. How many times had he heard her deliver it, perhaps to audiences who were sceptical to begin with, or as a battle cry to the already converted to take up action, whatever that action may be?

"We don't have any more time for 'business as usual,'"

she said. "We ran out of time for that years ago. We don't have any more time for excuses or lies, no empty words, or 'greenwashing.' No, this isn't an excuse to keep pumping out oil, cutting down trees or mass-producing plastic.

"What I mean when I say we still have time, is that in the view of most scientists, we still have time until we reach the tipping point that will take us beyond the brink, when there's no coming back. And if we act, not in a year, not in a month, not even in an hour, but right now, then we still have a chance of turning this around.

"Even now we still have a chance to save the Earth, a chance for humanity to live." She took her first sip of the lime juice and soda which had sat untouched in front of her all the while she was speaking.

"There you have it, Simon," said John-Luke. "This is what my congregation believes."

All this because of Helen's death, I thought. The flutter of butterfly wings.

Jasmine took another swallow of her drink. A deeper one this time. And I drained the last of the champagne.

"Would you excuse us, please, Simon?" asked John-Luke. "Jasmine and I have some business to discuss. And then we'll finish our catch-up over dinner at The Venetian Gondolier."

"Yes, of course, I'll leave you to it." I started to dismount— those stools almost felt tall enough to be a small horse—but John-Luke put a hand on my arm.

"No, stay where you are. Jasmine and I'll decamp to a quiet corner."

The bar had grown considerably busier since I came in (I glanced at my watch, just a humble Citizen, not a Rolex like his) two hours ago, but a quarter of the tables were still free.

They moved away from the bar to a table by the window, where they engaged in an intense-looking conversation for about half an hour. I killed the time by playing Solitaire on my phone, with a large glass of Malbec, which sat quite heavy in my stomach after the champagne. I resisted the strong temptation of a second, as John-Luke had mentioned we would be having another bottle of champagne with dinner.

Which we did. And looking back to that jump to 2004 from the comfort of my office chair on Boxing Day night in 2020 I smiled at the thought that getting drunk on a trip to the past has the same effect as in the present.

When I awoke in the hotel bedroom the following morning I had the Great Grandmother of all hangovers, and the same was true when I awoke after the jump on the morning of July 22nd. The disturbing thing was that I couldn't remember the last part of the jump.

Things had started to get hazy after finishing the Malbec. I vaguely recalled Jasmine leaving and John-Luke putting his arm around my shoulder.

"Come on, Simon," he said. "Sorry to have kept you waiting. Time to head to The Venetian Gondolier." The floor started to tilt while I was easing myself down from the stool, and I lost my footing. I grabbed the bar, and he steadied me by tightening his grip on my shoulder. At the time, my befuddled mind put it down to the stool being high.

As we left the air-conditioned hotel lobby and ventured out onto the streets of London, the heat of the sultry summer night hit me. "It's like being in Greece," I giggled. "You know, when you step out of the aircraft door."

The restaurant was a 20-minute stroll from the hotel and I felt a little less merry by the time we arrived. A pre-dinner gin and bitter lemon attracted the mist again, ordering the food was a bit of a blur, and eating it even more so. John-Luke had ordered a magnum of champagne, and the last thing I remember of the night was him refilling my glass for the third time.

Grandma had said I would be able to remember everything about a jump with crystal clarity, word for word, action by action. I guess she hadn't taken getting totally rat-arsed into consideration.

21

Back to Work

Simon

Reading through my August 2020 journal still brings grim memories of struggling with my brain not working properly, along with headaches, and chest pains around my heart and lungs.

More grieving for my former life when everything had been easy and effortless. The battle to do things and contribute to family life made me so tired. Expectations that I should be getting better started to manifest themselves, but I could only go as far and as fast as my body allowed. I constantly took my frustration out on Janice, and I really didn't know how she put up with my bad temper and mood swings.

I still had to limit my activities. If I did too much, I could hardly get out of bed the following day. The strange thing was that my symptoms changed from day to day. Sometimes I just felt drained. Some days my joints simply ached, other days the pain appeared to be burrowing deep into my bones. This seemed to move around my body. One day in my elbows and knees, the next, my fingers and toes. At times I couldn't bend my arms or fingers. Occasionally my balance appeared to leave me completely, maybe due to the weakness and pain in my joints.

But things did start to look up a little by the time we moved into September. My summary for that month gave the first real glimmer of hope, after a typical poor start.

"Still struggling at the start of the month with the same symptoms. Long COVID seems to be here to stay.

Had a private appointment with a cardiologist on Monday

the seventh, who suggested more tests and prescribed beta blockers to control my heart rhythm. Getting somewhere at last! More help in one meeting than in five hospital trips. Ashamed to say it took me a whole week to pluck up the courage to start taking them. What was I afraid of? Was it that these may be my last hope of any form of salvation, and if they didn't work, was I doomed to this half-life of merely existing and struggling in pain day by day?

After six days of taking them, I started to regain some ability to function properly. My heart rate no longer reached 156 beats per minute while walking up Apollo Lane, although there were still a few breathing issues, tightening of my chest, and fluctuating Oxygen saturation levels. But my legs no longer felt like I was wading through treacle.

Enjoying a little normality for short periods of the day, which made me feel ecstatic, if only for a few hours. My six-month 'Coronaversary' was looming up fast towards the end of September—six long months that seemed like a lifetime, since I collapsed with the virus on that awful day in March—and I tried to put on a brave face. Normally anniversaries are for celebrating, but this milestone was to be commiserated.

So, yes, while Long COVID is here to stay with me, at least for the foreseeable future, I'm adapting and taking slow, gentle steps into the future. I don't have a clue what that future holds, but it sure as the little green apples that God made is going to be better than the last six months. Slowlee, slowlee catchee monkee.

But the big, BIG, step forward this month was that I felt up to discussing my return to the airwaves with Bob Appleyard.

I cupped my chin in my hands, elbows resting on the

desk, thinking how I'd worked so hard and come such a long way, to reach this final week of 2020. The world had truly changed during the last ten months, and there was no real way of seeing how COVID would pan out. Something was telling me the world may be on the cusp. But the cusp of what?

Enough for tonight. Although I hadn't written anything and hadn't even finished reading through my journals, it was getting late and Janice had said something about having a glass of Jack Daniels ready for me.

Christmas Day and today had been fun but tiring. We hadn't had visitors since I became ill. Strictly speaking, I don't think we should have had both Claire and Hannah and their partners in the house—something about it being too many households mixing, and for too long, but we'd made our plans a couple of weeks before the regulations changed, and just felt what the hell. Just what the fucking hell. I'm sure we weren't the only family who bent the rules a little. Christmas is my favourite time of year, and I'd been determined to share this one with my family, especially as there had been times when they wondered if I might not make it.

But look at me now. Back on the airwaves once a week throughout October, twice a week in November, and three days a week during December up to the 18th. Which wasn't exactly what I wanted at the time. I thought I'd be presenting the full three-hour show five days a week by Christmas. But Bob had different ideas.

"It's great that you feel up to it," he said when we set up a Zoom call on September 22nd, "but are you sure you're ready?"

"I thought I could start slowly, just one show, and see how it goes."

"It certainly is going to be just one at first," he said.

357

"And not a whole show, either. I'm happy for you to host the 'phone-in hour to begin with. Olivia's doing a great job, and I'm going to ease you back in gently."

"I want to try the whole show, Bob, not just part of it."

"No. It's not open for discussion, Simon. Just take your time. You've been very seriously ill. Janice tells me you're still quite weak, and your symptoms are unpredictable. So, at this stage, it's the 'phone-in or nothing."

"Sounds like you've thought this through. I wondered if it might be a surprise, me wanting to come back at the moment?"

He smiled back at me from my laptop. "The only surprise is that you haven't pestered me about it earlier. I knew you'd be champing at the bit, and I've already spoken to the directors about it. Yes, of course, we're anxious to have you back, Simon, but we've got a duty of care towards you."

"Duty of care, my arse," I said. "If I suddenly go queasy I'm sure Liv would take over mid-broadcast."

"I'm sure she would. And she'll be ready and waiting during your 'phone-in, just in case. But we're going to ease you back in gently."

I glanced at my face in the little rectangle at the top of the screen to see if it betrayed my disappointment. A little downward pull at the corners of my mouth clearly showed it did. "I'd like to try a full show and see how it goes. If I feel too tired after it, I could just do the 'phone-in on the next show."

"No," Bob shook his head. "I've told you, it's not open to debate. The directors have already taken medical advice on the best way to get you back in the saddle, and our plan's in place. All that was left was 'when,' which was always going to be down to you."

"OK, the phone-in it is, then, for the first few shows. Shall we start on Thursday, and then try for every day next week?"

"No, we won't," he said instantly. "Simon, it isn't as if you're trying to run before you can walk, or even walk before you can toddle. You're trying to toddle before you can crawl. You're only at the crawling stage at the moment."

"And wearing nappies, I presume? So, what does crawling entail?"

"Crawling entails one 'phone-in a week, starting next month. And, yes, there will be a nappy."

I knew it would be nugatory to argue, and he was probably right, anyway. No point in over-taxing my strength. Hosting the 'phone-in segment was pretty onerous, even when I was fully fit.

"So, what's the nappy?" I said.

"It's a straightforward precaution to catch any shit," he said. You'll be presenting from home."

"What? No, I want to do it from the studio. How will I do it from home?"

"Our working procedures have changed considerably," said Bob. "We've got special measures in place for COVID now."

"Are all shows coming from home, then?"

"No. Apart from Richard, everyone's still actually broadcasting from the studio, but they do all the prep at home and only come in for their show itself. We keep the studios just for broadcast-critical staff, with limited numbers in the production room, and everyone's masked, except the presenter."

"But Richard does his show from home?"

"He does. He's not been into the studios since March."

It made sense about Richard. The host of our 70s music show was in his mid-60s, and I guess the bone marrow transplant he had a couple of years ago made him particularly susceptible to COVID.

"And Jenni had to self-isolate for a while after coming into contact with someone who'd got it, so she broadcast from home for a couple of weeks, too."

"I've caught Jenni's show a few times since I've been home, but the ones I heard sounded as if they were coming from the studio."

"You honestly wouldn't be able to tell the difference, Simon," said Bob. "It's so easy to set up, and the creative use of pillows and duvets means we can produce a sound not too far away from a professional studio in someone's front room."

The following day Bob sent an email confirming the arrangements up to Christmas.

Dear Simon

First of all, everyone at Poolswood Sound is thrilled to hear you're recovering so well from COVID. We were extremely worried about you, and it's a mark of the love, respect, and affection your listeners have for you that someone rings the phone-in every day to ask how you are.

We're so glad that you'll be able to tell them yourself on Friday, September 25th. You'll host the phone-in on that day, and every Friday throughout October. That will increase to every Thursday and Friday throughout November, and for December you'll also present on Wednesdays, up to the 18th.

This work will be carried out at your home. We'll provide you with a company laptop, microphone and headphones.

Over Christmas and the New Year we will assess how your recovery is progressing and whether our doctor feels you are strong enough to take on additional days, and perhaps extend your duties to a second hour each day from January.

We have every confidence that you will eventually return to presenting all three hours from the studio when your health allows it.

Welcome back to the Poolswood airwaves. Both we and your listeners have missed you.

With best wishes,

Bob

September 25th could not come soon enough. I wasn't sure whether I should be conserving my wayward and fluctuating energy in the days before, or pushing myself a little harder. On the 23rd, I struggled a little with chest pain and some breathing issues, which I was worried could affect my voice. But the next day the symptoms switched to joint pain. Awkward for working the laptop, but at least I'd be able to speak properly if they manifested themselves during the broadcast.

As my excitement mounted, sleep eluded me for several hours on the night of the 24th, making me feel like a child again on Christmas Eve. Eventually, the rhythm of Janice's soft, shallow breathing in my ear relaxed me enough to ease into a light sleep at around 2.00 a.m. At first, my senses simply dimmed to that wonderfully warm and contented state mid-way between being alert and dozing. Thoughts of tomorrow, and the first thing I planned to say on air, tumbled around my head, becoming more haphazard and incoherent by the moment, as Morpheus's gentle arms wove their magic.

At some point, the light sleep must have deepened to take me through the rest of the night undisturbed. Which rarely happened since COVID invaded my body.

When I woke around half seven I lay still, hardly daring to move a muscle. There was no hesitancy or pain with two slow deep breaths and no hint of exploding into a cough. Gingerly I flexed my toes and fingers. Then raised my arms, lifting the duvet. Slight stiffness, but nothing more.

After swinging my feet off the bed I sat for a few seconds, half expecting to be engulfed by a wave of dizziness, which probably happened on four mornings out of seven. Again, nothing though, apart from the usual hint of a mild fairground teacup ride. Even my heartbeat felt regular, instead of its occasional morse code stacatto greeting to the day.

Was it too good to be true, I wondered, or was it one of those rare days when Long COVID teased me into thinking it had come to the end of its fun with me? At that moment, sitting on the edge of the bed, I told myself I didn't care if it hit me with a vengeance tomorrow, as long as it left me alone today, and every Friday throughout October. But, of course, I did care. I cared very much. I'd had three months of it since coming out of hospital, which was more than enough for anyone, and I know it was just mocking me, lulling me into a false sense of security. That was alright, though. Just get me through today. Or at the very least, until two o'clock.

I took the stairs almost jauntily, almost with a spring in my step. Almost, but not quite.

If I'd felt like Christmas Eve child last night, I was Christmas Day boy now, starting to open my presents, as I went into my office at around half past 12.

Janice had created a makeshift studio in the corner with a white plastic picnic table from the shed, surrounded by bedsheets, duvets, and pillows held aloft by a contraption of tent poles, a stepladder, and two clothes horses. It reminded me of being inside a tepee. I wondered if Jigonhsasee had lived in a tepee during her Earthly life, and made a mental note to ask her.

Liv had suggested we start a Zoom call at 12.50 p.m. I'd wanted to make it earlier to double-check the crazily-simple system which would enable me to present the 'phone-in from here. It all boiled down to a Zoom call, the studio-quality microphone plugged into the laptop's USB port, and Liv doing the rest. I'd said no, could we at least make it 12.40 p.m.? Liz had said how about compromising at 12.45 p.m., which we agreed on? It hadn't stopped me from settling into the tepee at half twelve, though.

We had already tested the internet link from the laptop to the studio three times in the last few days. Everything had been fine. The link worked, the microphone worked, the headset worked, I'd heard the production room and studio fine and they could hear me. Liv simulated an outside call by putting one from the newsroom through to me. I'd opened my mic and responded to Ayesha, who said how wonderful it was to hear me.

The dry runs were over now. I'd be going back live on the Poolswood airwaves in the next few moments. Yes, this excitement rocked the shit out of Christmas Day boy.

The glow of my desk lamp illuminated the ethereal gloom inside the tepee, casting weird shadows across the computer screen, but ensuring I could read my handwritten notes.

Janice sat outside the tepee at my desk, in case I wasn't as strong as I thought. I'll be fine, I told her. But, Janice being Janice, there she was.

The fact that I kept glancing down at the digital time readout in the bottom right-hand corner of the screen didn't make the minutes pass any quicker. It probably made them go slower, as it now showed 12.42. Surely at least five minutes had passed since I last looked at 12.40.

Eventually, it showed 12.44, and I clicked the Zoom link Liv had sent me.

"Hello," she said when her face appeared onscreen,

pushing my own face into a small rectangle at the top. Her short, pixie-style blonde hair and pale blue eyes which twinkled at me above her COVID mask, always made me think she could be a refugee from a fantasy tale such as Lord of the Rings or Game of Thrones.

"So are you up for this?" she said, "or do I ask Bob for a rise to carry on presenting the phone-in?"

"You cheeky mare. I've never been more up for it."

"Just don't fall asleep halfway through."

"It's alright. I've had my mid-morning nap. I'm ready to rock'n'roll until midnight now."

"Only midnight. Lightweight. When you're my age you can party until three in the morning. Can you remember that far back?"

"When I was your age I could party until six in the morning and then go straight to work."

Her smile behind the mask crinkled the skin around her eyes. "Well, you've only got to get through until two o'clock," she said. "This afternoon."

It was just as if I hadn't been away. "Come on," I said. "Let's check the connection and make sure my callers can have a decent chat for the first time in six months."

"I hope I don't forget you're there on the other end of the line. Wouldn't it be awful if I kept your link shut and just carried on like yesterday?"

"Do that, and I'll phone in instead. I could always swear and get you taken off the air."

"I've missed this," she said.

"I thought you would."

"Just like I missed the veruca I picked up at the national schools swimming championship when I was 15."

This could have gone on all day, but Liv had to cue in a

report about the hunt for a COVID vaccine.

"Right," she said when the file was playing. "Let's see if the tech works or if it's decided to throw a wobbly when it knew you were back."

A few moments later my heart was beating as fast as it was when I did my first live broadcast all those years ago fresh from university.

Tamsin Mcilroy was coming to the end of the weather forecast. Just seconds away, now. Liv looked up at her computer camera and winked at me.

"...that's all for now," said Tamsin. "The next news and weather here on Poolswood Sound is at two o'clock." I saw Liv draw down the fader disconnecting the studio from the news booth and hit a button on her console to play the station identity jingle. Then another jingle: "You're listening to Lunch Break, with Simon Reynolds." Liv pressed another key, and a greyed-out light on my Zoom screen turned red as she flicked her hand at me, pointing her finger. "And GO," she mouthed.

"Now, where was I?" I said into the microphone in front of me, its blue windsock proclaiming Poolswood Sound 97.1 FM. "What was I doing before I was so rudely interrupted by COVID? Whatever it was, it's irrelevant now. Everything's changed from what I was saying six months ago, and what I was doing six months ago.

"There comes a time in everyone's life when they need to step back and take stock. The time for that is now. For all of us. The pandemic has brought that particular clock to midnight for the whole human race.

"How has this dreadful virus affected you, your family, and your friends? Welcome to the phone-in hour, with me, Simon Reynolds. Call Poolswood treble eight, double two, one, and tell me what life's been like for you while I was in an induced coma and fighting Long COVID. I can't tell you how good it is to be back.

"What have you all been up to in the six months I've been away? I hope you've been keeping safe, because let me tell you, when COVID hits, it can really knock you for six. I'd like to thank each and every one of you who took the time and trouble to ring in to ask how I was doing. And a very special thank you goes out to the team of doctors and nurses who looked after me during my 82 days in Poolswood General Hospital. Thank you in particular, to Doctors Andrew Moore and Douglas Moss, and to nurses Emma Grassmere, Julia Hemphill, April Karinski, Jim Rice, and Karen Spencer. Your care and dedication are exemplary. Every single day you go far beyond the call of duty. You're very special people, indeed.

"I'm just one of the thousands of patients throughout the country. The care and treatment given to me is repeated across wards in hundreds of hospitals by thousands of doctors and nurses, day in, and day out. This is our NHS. The National Health Service is vital to us all, and something we must treasure.

"I have absolutely nothing but the highest praise for everyone I came across during my 82 days in hospital My message to the Government is hands off the NHS. No privatisation, just a high level of funding so they can continue to save lives and provide the urgent care so desperately needed when people fall ill. If we need to pay higher taxes to ensure that happens, then okay, bring it on.

"Long live the NHS. I owe you my life, and I'll support you throughout the rest of it."

A message from Liv flagged up in a box on the right of

my screen: 'Caller. Paul, from Meriton.'

I nodded at the computer's camera lens. "And we have our first caller of the day on the line. Paul, from Meriton, has called Poolswood treble eight, double two, one. Good afternoon, Paul."

"Afternoon, Simon. I'm just ringing to say how glad I am to hear you after all this time. We've missed you. So, welcome back buddy."

"That's very kind of you, Paul. Thank you very much. It's been a long journey for me since I was last here, and the world is a very different place. Your world's a different place. My world's a different place. Will anything ever be quite the same again, I wonder?"

My mind was crystal clear, my voice was holding up, there was nothing but a dull ache in my chest, and the joints in my fingers throbbed a little. It had only been a few moments, but so far, so good.

And that was the way it went for the hour's broadcast. And for my stints behind the microphone for the rest of the year.

The good days were interspersed with bad ones, of course. I knew I wouldn't be lucky enough to get through entirely unscathed. But from January 7th, 2021 Bob agreed that I could go back to five days a week, and run with the first hour of the show, as well.

"Just to see how it goes, though," he said. "I'm not committing to anything permanent, but if you feel up to it, you seem to be ready."

"I'm more than ready," I said.

From January 7th to the 28th I presented the first two hours of the show with very few ill effects. A little drowsiness when I came off-air a couple of times, and some pain in my fingers from the computer keyboard, but my voice held up, and I drowned out three coughing fits with an ad break and station ident jingles. I grew to love my little tepee, and Janice stopped babysitting me from outside it after the first week.

When I finished the phone-in on the 28th I saw Bob come into the studio, as Liv was getting ready for the third hour's extended interview. I'd trailed it for her a few times during my stint at the mic. It was with a local doctor talking about running a GP practice during the pandemic.

"Can I call you on Zoom from my office in a few moments?" he asked.

"Sure," I said. I'd been expecting it. It was time for a review after a month of running two hours of my programme. His face gave nothing away as he looked back at me from the screen.

"How would you feel about interviewing Noah Jacobs in the third hour tomorrow?" he asked after we hooked up again.

"What?" I thought I may have to fight to get the third hour back, and I definitely hadn't expected to be doing the first interview with just 24 hours' notice. That Christmas Day boy now had his birthday as well, all rolled into one. "That's great, Bob. Yes, of course, I'd love to."

"Thought you might say that." His smile probably didn't match the childish grin beaming out of my face in the little rectangle at the top of my screen, but it radiated genuine warmth and satisfaction. "I know how hard you've worked since getting back on air, and you seem to be managing it well."

"Is this just a one-off?" I asked, "or am I going to be doing them every day?"

He laughed. "I knew you'd want to run while you're still walking slowly. But, yes, let's see how you cope with doing them all the time now."

My heart pounded with excitement. But the nervousness,

and indeed, the raw fear that Long COVID brought, had sapped my confidence. The brave face I'd put on since coming out of hospital was more for Janice and the girls' sake, as I channelled my resilience to encourage them.

If I had to be realistic, I'd say that physically I was between 75 and 80 percent now, and around 80 percent psychologically. That mental counter had probably been at the halfway mark before getting back behind the microphone, but ever since that magical day in September when I'd hosted the first phone-in of my recovery, it had risen steadily. Each milestone—moving to two days, then three, then to four—was like manna from heaven, and sealed shut another passage from the past behind me. I only looked to the future now. A future when I was back behind the studio microphone, not the one in the comfortable tepee in my own little world. A future getting closer by the day. Small strides. Softlee softlee catchee monkee.

"Liv will send you some potential questions and the full running order," said Bob.

"Is there a particular reason we're doing Noah?" I asked. "Have we got a news peg to hang it on?"

"Sort of. We're angling it around the local vaccine roll-out. Noah's overseeing that as Chair of the Poolswood NHS Trust, and he's keen to let people know the arrangements and how everything's going to pan out."

I laughed. "Couldn't be a better interview to bring me back than a COVID vaccine story. Certainly a poignant one."

"I thought you'd like that," said Bob. "Noah was over the moon when Liv told him I was going to ask you."

I bet, but not as far over the moon as I was at that moment. This interview will be one small step for me, but a giant leap at the same time.

Which it proved to be. After a successful interview with Noah on Zoom, and then two and a half weeks of presenting three hours, five days a week, Bob suggested I might like to host Friday, February 19th[th]'s show from the studio.

Would I, fuck? If I'd been a dog, I'd be wagging both my tails.

22

Revelations

Friday, February 19th, 2021, Simon

This day has been a long time coming. After 11 months, I finally feel my world may be restoring some degree of normality. Perhaps a new, different normal, but normal, nevertheless.

"I'm so proud of you," Janice says as I get dressed. "But I didn't doubt for a minute that you'd make it back."

"I had rather more hope than conviction, especially in the early days," I admit. "But once I'd started broadcasting from home, I was determined it would only be a matter of time."

"Don't forget," she says, as I walk out to the car Bob sent for me an hour later, "I'll be listening to every second."

Settling into my studio chair, I pull up my headphones as the mid-day news starts. Ayesha Patterson has the lead story, about yesterday's awful double murder. Tamsin Mcilroy cues her in for a live report: "The victims, 34-year-old computer software engineer, Adam Hampshire, and his wife Hayley, who was 31, and a popular travel agent with Shrinking World, were gunned down on their drive in Clowes Road, Poolswood, shortly before quarter to three yesterday afternoon.

"They'd just returned home after their COVID vaccinations at Poolswood Leisure Centre. Both Mr. and Mrs. Hampshire had underlying medical conditions which made them particularly vulnerable to COVID and led to them being called for their injections ahead of their age group.

"Two gunmen fled the scene in a grey BMW. Detective

Chief Inspector Stephanie Ingram is leading the investigation, reporting directly on it to the Chief Constable."

A computer file of Ayesha's interview with Stephanie, recorded after the press conference, starts playing. "We're following several lines of inquiry to try to establish a motive."

"You don't know the reason for the killings, then?" asks Ayesha.

"Not at this stage, and accordingly, we're warning the public to be on their guard."

"Are you saying it was a random attack, and they may strike again?"

"I'm not saying it is and I'm not saying it isn't. At the moment we haven't established a motive, so we have to keep an open mind and consider all possibilities."

"What can you tell us about the gunmen's getaway vehicle?"

"It was a grey BMW 5 Series M Sport, with fake number plates of TBW 781. These are likely to have been disposed of now, but the car has a blacked-out windscreen and front windows, which makes it highly distinctive. If anyone sees a vehicle fitting that description, please ring 999 immediately."

"You said in the press conference that the victims were shot several times. Can you say how many?"

"At this stage, no."

"Were they shot with handguns or machine guns?"

"All we can say at the moment is the weapons were capable of firing several rounds in quick succession."

The bulletin cuts back to Tamsin. "DCI Stephanie Ingram ending that report from Ayesha Patterson."

"Almost there," Liv says in my ear. "Welcome back to where you belong. I've been keeping the chair warm for you long enough."

"Thanks, Liv. It's been a while, hasn't it?"

It feels good to be back in this seat, in this studio, after six months away. Presenting the show from home eased me back into the world of work gradually, but the slightly unreal soundproofed atmosphere of the studio can never be beaten.

After all these years of live broadcasting, I still relish my three hours with the screens in front of me, my control over the mixer units, and the playout system for scrolling through the programme's running order, music tracks, and jingles, with the small screen above showing indicator lamps, clock, intercom, and talkback buttons. This was my world where I piloted my listeners on the same flight from midday to three o'clock, but every flight had a different entertainment package.

A glance at the clock. A couple of minutes of the news left, and I'll be on.

One of the screens confirms the opening track of the show. I'd smiled to myself when I saw it in the office as Liv and I were going through the running order and live interviewees. You've walked into what's coming your way, Liv.

The sweep hand counts down the seconds and hits the 12 exactly as Tamsin ends the bulletin, "...and that's all for now. The next news and weather here on Poolswood Sound is at one o'clock."

I draw down the fader disconnecting her news booth and hit a button to fire the station identity jingle. A lyrical female voice rings through my headphones: "Poolswood Sound, on 97.1 FM." Then straight into my personal jingle: "Welcome to Friday's Lunch Break, with Simon Reynolds."

Microphone open. Red light on. Heart thumping.

"This chair never felt so comfortable. Nor so warm," I say into the microphone, glancing at Liv. "Good afternoon Poolswood, and the world beyond. Nice to have your company today. Hope you can stay for the full three hours, but if you can't, you know what they say: half a loaf is better than none, or a few minutes of me, Simon Reynolds, keeps the doctor at bay."

Liv's quizzical frown and a tiny shake of her head as she mouths 'what?' tell me I've surprised her. No, doubt, as long as she can remember, I have never come out of the jingles by saying anything. My style is always to start the programme with the first music track. But how could I resist this when I saw what track she'd chosen?

"During the months I was away with COVID, you looked after Olivia with all the love and care you've shown towards me over the years, and I thank you for that from the bottom of my heart. Liv is, and always has been, the driving force of this show. She makes it what it is, not me."

I swear she was blushing through the glass. Was that a tear I saw glistening in her eye?

"Although I've been back full-time, broadcasting from home, for a few days, Liv is still here, putting everything together, setting everything up, chatting to those of you who ring the 'phone-in before you go on-air. Basically, Liv has been the lifeblood of the programme for several years."

A click in my headphones, before: "Shut up. This is lovely, Simon, but you're making me cry."

"I'd like to make Liv a formal invitation live on air." I'd been thinking of talking to Bob about this, but a wild urge, brought on by the track I was about to play, makes me bypass Bob and go straight in now. If he disagrees he can have my resignation. But he won't disagree. The time is right.

Liv's quizzical frown is back.

"This show needs another regular voice, and having listened to Liv over the last few months, I'm in no doubt that it should be her. So, Liv..." Her pixie-style hair always accentuates her eyes, making them appear large. They are even bigger now, above her COVID mask, as she widens them in surprise. "...I'd like to ask you to become my permanent co-presenter."

Her mouth falls into synch with her rounded eyes.

"No need to answer yet," I tell her. "You've got until the end of our first piece of music this afternoon, which is dedicated to you, Liv. I predict great things for this up-and-coming young artist, who shares your name; Olivia.

"She came out of nowhere with an incredible power ballad, which topped the charts for the fifth week yesterday.

"Liv, you've driven this show all these years. You've now got a license to take it further along the road." I hit a key to fire the music track, slowly fading up the distinctive intro of a car starting, beneath my words. "Here's Olivia Rodrigo, and Drivers License."

She is on the talkback the instant I close my microphone. "What a lovely surprise. I don't know what to say. I'm speechless."

"Which doesn't bode well for a permanent role behind the microphone," I say. "Unless I'm having the Masked DJ for a co-presenter."

She laughs. "This COVID mask is the only one I'll be wearing," she says, pulling it down and blowing me a kiss.

A dull throb in my fingers grows more noticeable as the minutes fly past, but my voice sounds firm and powerful, and I feel as if I've never been away from this seat.

After I'd cued in Tamsin's one o'clock news bulletin, a light flashes on my console, and Bob Appleyard's voice comes through my headphones. "I think we need to talk." Clipped, authoritative.

"You needn't start on me, Bob. You know as well as I do that Liv deserves this. And the advertisers love her. You've told me yourself how great their comments were about her while she stood in for me."

"I'm not starting on you, but I'd have liked a heads-up on what you were thinking, instead of presenting me with a fait accompli. Don't forget I've got to find the money for her additional salary."

"Which you'll find easily, and you know it. I was going to talk to you, but it suddenly became the perfect time—my first day back here, and Liv setting up Drivers License from Olivia Rodrigo as the first track clinched it. I couldn't pass up that combination. It had to be today. It had to be now. It's fate."

As the phone-in hour progresses, with many callers saying how pleased they are to have me back in the studio as it shows I am truly kicking COVID's ass, I know we will need some production assistance for this part of the show in future. Liv and I could drive the first and third hours of a new-look double-header programme, but not this segment. She combines answering calls with typing their names into the system. All I have to do is look at my screen to see who is on which line, and open that channel.

Looking down at it now, I see Amos is on line three, and he wants to talk about COVID vaccinations. Liv has typed an additional note: 'Voice synthesiser. Sounds like Stephen Hawking.'

I come out of the commercial break with a station ident

jingle and open my mic.

"Welcome back to the phone-in hour here on Poolswood Sound, 97.1 FM, with me, Simon Reynolds. It's 25 past 1, and on the line now, we have Amos. Good afternoon, Amos."

"Good afternoon, Simon." The harsh, robotic tone of the words coming back at me through the headset doesn't sound out of place nowadays. We are all used to hearing artificial computerised voice synthesisers, but I detect that each syllable appears to be slightly elongated, producing an unnatural distortion, even for a synthesiser. It is an unnerving sound, almost a little sinister.

Come on, Simon, I say to myself, he's only said three words to you. No time to analyse it further. This dead air needs filling. Liv is already chatting to another caller and obviously doesn't appear to have noticed anything untoward.

"I understand you want to talk about COVID vaccinations," I say. "Have you had yours, Amos?"

"I haven't," is his metallic response. "And I'll tell you why. They're not safe."

I shoot a glance at Liv, but she is deep in conversation.

"Shall I tell you why I think that?" he asks.

"Please do. I'm intrigued to hear what you believe because I've had COVID. Very badly. And I'm still suffering from Long COVID, although I'm getting better now. I wouldn't wish what I've gone through on my worst enemy. Why wouldn't you take something that reduces the risk of catching it and falling seriously ill?"

"Two reasons, but I need you to promise me something first."

Liv is still talking on the other side of the glass. I don't like the way this is going. I flick the talkback button so she will hear a click. She looks up. I cup my hand behind the headphones, tilting my head slightly in what I hope she will interpret as 'listen.'

"And what would that be?"

"I want you to promise that whatever I say, you won't cut me off."

"I can't promise that." The uneasy feeling from earlier jabs at me again like a sixth sense. This is definitely not going in a good direction.

"Okay, I'll park that for now," he says. With just two notes in every sentence, it's impossible for me to read anything from his voice to indicate his mood. "But you may wish to reconsider shortly."

A veiled threat? "Let me save you the trouble," I say. "Let me valet park it for you." Humour is often my mainstay in diffusing potential flashpoints. As ever, I'll try and push him as far as I can without getting him riled enough to say something offensive, which would mean terminating the call. "Tell me why you don't think they're safe."

"Vaccines take years to produce from the first breakthrough to getting them on to the mass market. This has been rushed through obscenely quickly. Just a matter of months, really. Nothing more than weeks. I wouldn't let my dog have anything that hasn't been thoroughly and exhaustively tested. Who's to say they won't send you blind, make you sterile, give you a heart attack, cause blood clots, cancer, arthritis, brain seizures, accelerate Alzheimer's?"

"Yes, we all know the slight risks to a tiny minority of people, but the risk of catching COVID and dying from it is far greater."

"Don't be one of the sheep, Simon. You simply can't believe the science behind the vaccines. Governments around the world have absolutely no idea about the long-term damage these injections may cause, but they're still telling us to have them. The vaccine will alter your body, your mind, and your very soul. It's nothing but an experiment on a cosmic scale, and we're the guinea pigs."

How far do I let this go? He's entitled to his view, but I can't let him push propaganda.

"While I respect your opinion," I say, "we must consider many factors. I've got to stop you there..."

"Don't cut me off," he snaps. "If you do, you'll live to regret it. But Janice won't."

"What?" My world seems to implode in my head. Have I heard correctly? It feels as if an invisible hand is squeezing my heart. Blood pounds through the highway of my arteries and veins.

"Simon, do as he says, please." The voice now coming through my headphones isn't robotic, harsh, or metallic. It's human, female, pleading, and rising hysterically with every word. A voice I know as well as my own. Janice's voice. But, how?

It also yanks Liv's attention away from the caller she is dealing with. She looks at me, horrorstruck, through the glass.

"Janice, what...?"

Amos interrupts me. "Listen carefully. I'm only going to say this once. There are no second chances."

I hit talkback, cutting the mic and connecting me to Liv. "Get Janice on the phone."

"On it," she replies and turns to her keyboard.

"Amos, what's going on?" My breathing starts to drag, each intake pushing through molasses, as the pain moves from my heart to my lungs.

"I'm just bringing that thought back from your efficient valet parking," he replies. "I take it I have your full attention now? Janice, say hello to Simon and tell him not to cut me off if he wants to see you alive again."

The lights on all our phone lines flash insistently but are left unheeded now.

Bob Appleyard bursts into the production room and mouths at me 'keep him talking.'

"Okay," I say into the microphone, "where's Janice? Is she alright?"

"You won't cut me off?"

"I won't."

"Good. I knew you'd see sense."

"Put Janice on."

"I'm okay, Simon," she says. "At the moment. Please listen to him."

There is no point in Liv trying to ring her. The phone would go unanswered. And here's the reason.

"I'm listening." As are people spread far and wide across Poolswood. Bob is talking frantically on the phone, red-faced, circling gestures with his free hand.

The sobs coming through my headphones melt my heart, as Janice tries to get her words into gear. "He kidnapped me shortly after you left this morning," she says.

"Where are you now?"

"Don't ask such stupid questions," snaps the robotic voice. "Shut up and listen to her."

Adrenaline pumps long and hard into my blood, and every beat of my heart pulsates in my ears.

"You've got to listen to him," Janice says. "Let him finish. He'll kill me if you cut him off. He's got Noah here, too."

Noah Jacobs. What the fuck is going on?

"Councillor Jacobs has a most important job to do today," says Amos. "As Chair of Poolswood NHS Trust, he's responsible for the roll-out of these murderous vaccines. He needs to do something about that. And he's going to in a moment.

"As Janice has told you, I'll kill her if you cut me off. Do you believe I'll do that?"

He's a fucking madman. How do I handle this? I hope Bob's on to the police.

"I'm not going to cut you off."

"That wasn't my question. Do you believe I'll kill your wife if you cut me off?"

"The airwaves are yours. You're free to tell everyone whatever you like about the vaccines. I'm not stopping you."

A robotic laugh. Which really is sinister. A harsh, grating sound. Almost how I imagine the Devil would laugh. Totally without humour. Almost to the point of mocking. "You've missed your vocation. You should have been a politician. Never mind, I won't ask you a third time."

"Simon, he's got a gun!" Janice's voice is rising off the scale.

"Wait," I yell into the microphone, and notice Bob and Liv staring at me through the glass. "Please don't do anything stupid."

"I won't," replies Amos. "This is probably one of the smartest and most rational things I'll ever do. Noah, say hello to Simon."

"Simon, it's Noah. He's mad. Completely mad."

"Noah," says Amos. "Say goodbye to Simon. Simon, say goodbye to Noah."

Silence for a couple of seconds. The world freezes. I don't move. Liv, and Bob with the phone to his ear, are motionless behind the glass. I imagine people glued to their radios, Alexas, Google Homes, and phones across Poolswood.

Then an ear-splitting explosion rings through my headphones. Janice screams at the same point I realise what I'm listening to.

A gunshot.

My turn to scream, but only Janice's name.

"I'm alright," she sobs. "But he's killed Noah."

My vision blurs momentarily as shock pushes me back in my seat. This can't go on. I've just let my listeners witness a murder. My finger hovers above the fader, ready to disconnect the call. But what will happen to Janice if I do? My breath comes in ragged gasps now.

"No," snaps Bob through the talkback. "I'm talking to the police. They need you to keep him on the line. Liv's coming in. If you need her to take over, just say so."

"That was the important job I said Councillor Jacobs had to do," says Amos. "I hope he's been successful in proving to you that I mean business because he's not in a position to do it again. It was a once-in-a-lifetime job and the last of a lifetime's job. You're all going to listen to everything I say. Janice is going back to her room now. I'm afraid it's not quite the five-star accommodation she's used to. But know this…" the voice slows to an even more sinister pace, "…if anything makes me unhappy in the next few moments, I'll bring her back here and she'll come face to face with the barrel of my gun to meet the same fate as the unfortunate Councillor Jacobs, who lies dead at our feet, with his blood pooling on the floor."

I've been so consumed by what is happening that I didn't notice Liv until she appears in my eye line at the other side of the desk. She points to herself and then to me. I shake my head, indicating the chair by the semi-circle. The last person I saw sitting there was Imogen. I couldn't save Imogen, but I've got to save Janice.

Liv sits down and pulls on the headphones.

"There's a second reason why we shouldn't take the vaccines," Amos continues, "and this is much more important than them not being safe. It's the reason I'm doing what I am, and why my friends around the world will start doing it soon.

"COVID is the Earth's way of fighting back against the human race. We're polluting the planet, choking her, destroying her natural surface, clogging her seas. Mankind must face up to the inevitable. Our reign is coming to an end. COVID is ushering us into our final days as masters of the world. We must not resist its force."

I can barely believe what I'm hearing. These are similar sentiments to Mark Brody's which he told me way back in 2004, but I was only able to access those memories seven months ago. Surely Amos can't be one of Mark's acolytes? Can he?

COVID is no accident," he says. "God created COVID to cleanse the Earth and make way for a species who will live in harmony with its neighbours in the forests, the plains, the deserts, and the oceans.

"And this is where you'll laugh," he says. "Noah Jacobs died for his pathetic attempts to save the tiny, puny speck of humanity in this tired corner of the Earth known as Poolswood, by injecting chemicals into your bodies. His predecessor, the other Noah, did it with an ark. The biblical flood cleansed the Earth, just as COVID will now."

His choice of words tells me this is a man descending quickly into madness, despite the metallic flow continuing with just two notes. Neither the tone nor the pitch change to indicate the raging inferno that must be tearing his brain apart while he speaks.

I watch as a man and woman suddenly appear in the control room. I recognise her as Stephanie Ingram from Poolswood Police, whom I've interviewed a couple of times. It is probably safe to assume that the tall, bulky male is a colleague. They are accompanied a second later by our Chief Engineer, Ricky Simons.

"There's no fighting God's will," Amos is in full flow, with barely a pause for breath. "Know this. I'll stop anyone who dares to take up arms in the form of this vile vaccine to combat what God has ordained. Yesterday marked the beginning of our fight in Poolswood."

What does he mean by that? My breathing is less laboured now, returning to normal, but I still don't trust myself to speak yet.

"Let it be known that my reach goes far beyond this small county, and this small country. We are just beginning. The fightback has started against those who stand up to God's wind."

Another familiar phrase. What the fuck?

"Adam and Hayley Hampshire were randomly executed as punishment for trying to evade God's wind as it blows across the Earth, and serves as a warning to others who consider having the vaccine."

No fucking way. This is no coincidence. I must be talking to Mark Brody—the Reverend John-Luke Matthews.

"Mark," I gasp, but he gives no sign of hearing me as he ploughs on along his maniacal furrow. I hit the talkback button. "Bob, I think I know who this is. Check out the Reverend John-Luke Matthews. He runs some sort of religious commune at Batchelors Farm near Dagglethorpe. His real name's Mark Brody."

Stephanie Ingram and her colleague look at each other, then back to me.

Bob points to the studio clock. Almost the top of the hour. "Forget the news," he says. Keep going with this maniac."

I tune myself back into what 'Amos' is saying. "Two things are about to happen to show how serious I am. Firstly, two more people will be executed leaving a vaccination centre, and a drone carrying explosives will blow up a laboratory making the vaccine."

The two police officers frantically hit keys on their phones.

23

World Message

Friday, February 19ᵗʰ, 2021, Hertfordshire

The air above the Hertfordshire countryside begins to buzz as if a swarm of angry bees is getting closer. The small, unmanned aircraft responsible for the noise was described in the trade press as a 'wonderful feat of engineering.' If its corporate designers had ever considered it may become the type of weapon for which it was now being deployed in the UK, they turned a blind eye.

Almost impossibly lightweight, its carbon fibre and titanium fuselage allowed it to reach altitudes of around 5,000 metres. What really appealed to the Reverend John-Luke Matthews, though, was the AirCorpUAS SL-35R drone's 200-kilometre out-of-sight flight range with a payload of up to 36 kilograms.

The dark web sellers had been keen to push how the engineering team perfected a lightweight design while increasing rigidity and strength, and how the 3D printed landing gear components and titanium parts for its SL-35R rotor engine gave optimum durability and power output from the smallest possible size and weight.

"Every gram saved on the drone increased the payload and endurance," they said.

As the drone was only making a one-way trip, that was all he needed to hear, and $400,000 were transferred from an untraceable division of a shell company in the Cayman Islands to several equally untraceable accounts around the world via a random sequence of servers and VPNs.

He had no interest in how the aircraft was transported from

Afghanistan to Morocco and then into Spain. All that concerned him was that it arrived on time, which it did, for him to organise the final leg of its journey to Poolswood, fitted snugly inside a concealed 4x1.5x1.2 metre compartment in a Batchelors Farm Logistics lorry hauling a delivery of tile accessory products.

Now, while Reverend Matthews is telling Simon and the growing number of listeners from around the world who are tuning in via the internet, that two more people are about to be murdered, and possibly many more in an explosion at a vaccine laboratory, Fritz Chikatilo is in a windowless room at his isolated glass and concrete home, guiding the SL-35R Unmanned Air System vehicle to its target in Hertfordshire.

After taking off from the hillside behind his house, it quickly rises to a cruising altitude of 4,500 metres and flies the 95 kilometres to western Hertfordshire. A number of sensors relay high-definition views ahead and below to his computer, while an adjacent screen charts progress in the form of a red pointer on a rolling map.

He was tempted to test the aircraft's top speed, which the sellers claimed was 220 kilometres an hour, but with 34 kilograms of explosives in the main payload bay, he resisted and keeps it to a shade under the recommended cruising speed of 190 km/hour.

A third screen provides telemetry of the system in the drone's electronics bay which will detonate the cargo when the time comes.

And that time is approaching fast. The red pointer is almost over the Goldman Brackland Piers laboratory which had won a Government contract to manufacture one of the COVID vaccines. The multi-millionaire owner was a good friend of a Cabinet Minister in the UK Government and had long experience of turning his hand to whatever the

Government needed.

Chikatilo adjusts the zoom on one of the camera sensors and pulls the three-storey rectangular building on the edge of an industrial estate below into focus.

Responding to his deft touch on the computer, the drone reduces altitude as it flies over the lab and banks slowly to the right to begin circling for its final descent. On the third pass, it is down to just over 200 metres, and another wide circle puts it on a trajectory which will send it straight into the building.

He opens the throttle fully, and the powertrain responds immediately, pushing the maximum amount of AV gas into the engine for the last few seconds of the AirCorpsUAS drone's life.

At precisely 2.05 p.m. it hits a first-floor window at 170 kilometres an hour, shattering the safety glass into thousands of pieces. At the same instant, Chikatilo calmly presses a computer key that sends a signal to the onboard detonator via the equipment in the drone's electronics bay.

The explosion can be heard up to 15 kilometres away.

Poolswood

Just as they had yesterday, Jake McGlynn and Patrick Kirkbride clamber through the passenger door into the cab of the unbranded 44-tonne articulated lorry, while Greg Whitehouse walks round to the driver's side, climbs the two steps and sits down behind the wheel.

Fifteen other lorries stand side by side, backed up to the wall separating the haulage business from the Church Of Euvenity's farming commune.

Whitehouse wonders if his partners in crime—*literally* his partners in crime—are experiencing the same deja vu. He fires up the engine, which comes to life with a throaty roar, and slowly eases the anonymous vehicle out of its parking bay, and past the office block and connecting workshop. The large green sign with red lettering of 'Batchelors Farm Logistics' spans the brickwork above both doors and rolls by the cab window as the lorry slowly picks up speed.

While it may have been deja vu for Whitehouse, it isn't quite groundhog day. The plan is the same, but there are differences. The car, for instance, and instead of tracksuits, they each wear jeans and a dark fleece—Kirkbride's is black, and McGlynn's navy blue, with battleship grey for Whitehouse. Fortunately for them, the February day is crisp and bright again, so the sunglasses don't look out of place.

Whitehouse guides the lorry carefully along the country lanes leading away from the farm, eventually picking up Blackthorpe Road, the main arterial route between the motorway and the city. Shortly before the start of the average speed check, he turns left along a lane that is barely wider than the lorry. As it is, the passenger door mirror scrapes the hedge a couple of times while they inch their way along the next 200 metres.

Their elevated position in the cab gives them a view of the derelict cottage above the hedge before reaching its short overgrown drive, which he turns into. Broken windows, crumbling brickwork, missing roof tiles, and the front door standing askew on one hinge, scream that the building has been deserted for years. As do the surrounding grass and wild vegetation that Whitehouse has seen regularly in the countryside, but has no idea of names.

He swings the artic to the right of the cottage, then reverses in front of it, expertly turning the wheel to back up alongside it on the left, leaving the cab pointing the way they have come, towards the road.

They alight, and stroll unhurriedly to the back, swinging

the double side-hinged doors open. Whitehouse pulls himself up into the darkened interior and presses a large green button on a grey box fastened to the trailer wall. A motor responds, whirring as it pushes a concealed steel platform from beneath the floor. When it has extended three metres beyond the open doors, it slowly dips until its tip rests gently on the overgrown drive, forming a ramp.

Whitehouse moves further down the lorry and gets into a Quartz Blue Subaru Impreza, whose rear wheels abut a three-inch-high block running side to side across the base of the trailer.

The car's powerful engine could have matched the lorry in the noise stakes as he starts it and drives slowly down the steel slope. Once it is on the ground, Kirkbride presses the button to retract the ramp and closes the double doors when it is fully stowed away again in its slot beneath the floor.

He gets in the front passenger seat, with McGlynn behind him. Before setting off they all put on blue face masks. There is no need to check what lies beneath the tartan blanket on the seat next to McGlynn. He had put the clips in the two Kalashnikov RPKs before Whitehouse reversed up the ramp into the lorry back at the farm.

None of them speaks on their journey back to Blackthorpe Road, joining the other figurative corpuscles in the blood flow to Poolswood. The silence continues right through the maze of streets which take them to Broadhaven Road and finally Priory Road. Still silence as the Impreza turns left onto the leisure centre's driveway.

Whitehouse thinks the marshall pointing to a parking spot is the same one from yesterday, but he can't be sure. There is something about the way the guy's short hair stands up at the edge of his parting, which looks familiar, though.

A few moments later, a white Toyota Prius pulls into the bay alongside. Let's look at today's sacrifices, he thinks. They had studied the comings and goings at the vaccination centre all week before their first strike, and realised that most people were elderly, and came in pairs. It was a bonus that the couple they executed yesterday was young. "Far more poignant, and much better news coverage," Matthews had said when they got back. "No one really cares about old people nowadays—but a young couple mysteriously mown down in the prime of their lives; what could be better?"

The couple getting out of the Prius fit the bill of being elderly. In the short time before they don medical masks Whitehouse places the two men in their mid-70s. The driver is about five foot ten, with a stylish Italian look about him, both in the cut of his tan suit (who wears a suit for an injection, Whitehouse muses? What a palaver to take the jacket off and roll his shirt sleeve up), and in his dark complexion with a slightly acquiline nose, and thick, grey wavy hair parted on the right.

Their eyes meet briefly through the windscreen as the man walks around the front of the Prius to take his partner's arm. Whitehouse doesn't look away. Why should he? All the guy could see was a baseball cap, sunglasses and a medical mask. And he wouldn't be alive to tell anyone, shortly. In that quick glance, though, Whitehouse notices, even through his sunglasses, that the eyes are a creamy caramel.

I wonder how long they've been a couple, he thinks. Quite romantic that they'll be gunned down together. And maybe arm in arm, as they are now, when they walk up their drive for the last time.

The other guy is perhaps an inch taller but lacks his partner's easy elegance which Whitehouse notices isn't even marred by a slight limp as they make their way towards the path, to join the quickly dispersing queue leading inside.

Whitehouse had been one of the first to join the Church of Euvenity commune when the barn conversions were finished in 2010 and he worked with Matthews as an environmentalist. When the pandemic struck it hardly took a great leap of faith for him to agree with Matthews that COVID was indeed God's wind blowing across the Earth, and it was his duty to help swat humanity from her face, like the insects they were.

The contempt he feels for the blasphemous heathens who dare fight God's wind with unnatural and untested chemicals, is powerful and absolute. He could see the wonder in Matthews' simple and effective plan—kill a few of them just yards from their homes in full public view in broad daylight, and make it known that no one's safe, everyone's a target. Imagine the panic and chaos that will sweep the land. Repeat it across the globe—Euvenity disciples are, even now, monitoring progress and preparing similar action of their own in many countries. Destroying laboratories will slow down vaccine production and distribution. As more and more people refuse to have the shot in their arms out of fear of execution for their blasphemous crime against God, more people will catch COVID. More people will spread it. More people will die in the coming days, weeks and months as God's wind blows strongly across the land, withering humanity in its blast. *And I'm proud to be playing a role in this plan,* he thinks. Even if he isn't pulling the triggers like McGlynn and Kirkbride, this job needs his skills as a driver, both for the lorry and the cars.

His thoughts suddenly change tack as he watches Italian-Man and his partner disappear along the path. That suit won't look so dandy when it's filled with seeping red holes, and the hair won't be so immaculate when it's covered with brain matter. That's assuming there's anything left of the head at all. Round after round of bottlenecked 7.62 x 39 mm cartridges from the Kalashnikovs had disintegrated Ben and Hayley's heads like overripe watermelons yesterday.

Maybe I'll get to sit at God's left hand in the Kingdom of Heaven. John-Luke will be at His right hand, and deservedly so. Earth is sick, and humans are the virus. God and Gaia have sent COVID to rid the planet of that virus. And I'll be there as part of the team that destroyed the virus harming Earth.

Just over 25 minutes later both men stroll back into view. Italian-Man gets into the Prius's passenger seat this time, while his partner slots in behind the wheel.

One drives here, the other drives back, Whitehouse thinks. *Cool.*

The Impreza follows them down the drive and right onto Priory Road. Unlike yesterday when they went straight across the junction with Broadhaven Road, they turn there and head towards the more upmarket region of the city, known colloquially as the Cartier Quarter, where houses change hands for at least £4m.

"This may be a problem," says McGlynn from the back seat.

"I was just thinking that," Kirkbride agrees.

"What?" asks Whitehouse.

"Most of the houses round here stand in their own grounds behind walls with electric gates," Kirkbride tells him.

"Yeah," says McGlynn. "We may need to kill them on the road while they're still in the car."

Whitehouse twists his head to glance at him briefly in the back seat. This isn't one of their planned scenarios. "Perhaps we should just go back to the centre and pick different blasphemers."

"No time," says Kirkbride, pointing to the clock at the top of the centre console. 2.01 p.m. "We've only got a fifteen-minute window. You know John-Luke wants this done at around the same time as the lab goes up. We've got to do it with these two."

Brake lights appear on the Prius, and the left indicator starts flashing. The satellite navigation map shows the nearest side road is Newferry Avenue, more than half a mile away. "It looks like they're turning into a drive," Whitehouse says. "They must be home."

"Right. Get ready," snaps Kirkbride. McGlynn pulls the two Kalashnikovs out from under the blanket, and manoeuvres one forward to Kirkbride.

The Prius slows as it turns off the road, and Whitehouse drops the Impreza to a snail's pace across the entrance to the drive before coming to a stop. Double gates are swinging inwards just inches from the Prius's bonnet.

"Now," shouts Kirkbride. "Get them before the gates open." He and McGlynn spring out, and Whitehouse punches an icon on the satnav to calculate the quickest route to a pre-set destination—the derelict cottage.

Almost before he looks up from the screen, the combined staccato voice of the two light machine guns speaks its deadly words, making its meaning of death crystal clear. The incessant firing renders it impossible for Whitehouse to hear anything else for those few seconds, or to form rational thoughts.

The seatbelts hold Italian-Man and his partner firm, while round after round shatters the glass and pours into them. With both assassins initially taking headshots, McGlynn at the back of the car and Kirkbride by the driver's door, they were probably dead after the impact of the first three or four bursts. Then the aim goes lower. The shells barely slow as they slice through the steel panels and weaker aluminium hatch at the back of the vehicle. Even the special high-strength steel in the doors and pillars crumple under the onslaught, and they meet considerably less resistance from the Katzkin custom-fit, premium leather seats, on their way to the warm human flesh, tearing heart, liver, lungs and kidneys apart.

What was left of their heads slump forward onto their chests as McGlynn and Kirkbride jump back into the Subaru.

"Go, go, go," yells Kirkbride, as if Whitehouse needs telling. The engine roars as the car accelerates from its standing start to 60 miles an hour in a shade over nine seconds.

"In 200 yards, turn left," instructs the satnav's female voice, which reminds Whitehouse of a popular television newsreader and presenter. They are almost upon the junction, and he hauls the wheel around, fully confident that the responsive four-wheel independent suspension would anchor them safely to the road.

Once away from the scene, he slows to just above the speed limit to avoid attracting attention. The rolling map on the centre console shows they will be on this road for another mile.

Kirkbride switches displays for a few seconds, during which he scrolls the phone log and presses the green key. The call is answered before the first ring has finished.

"Yes." The female voice has a hint of an accent.

"Tell him it's done," says Kirkbride. "Two targets eliminated."

"Thank you." The line goes dead.

He switches back to the satnav screen. "In 200 yards, at the roundabout, take the first exit." The clock shows 2.03 p.m. Two minutes have passed since he told Whitehouse there was no time to select different victims.

Simon

"The police need you out here," I hear Bob say in my headphones. "Tell Amos Liv is taking over, and assure him he'll still be able to say whatever he wants for as long as he wants."

I nod. "Amos, I'm going to have to go. My co-presenter, Liv will be here with you now." My voice cracks, a combination of my dry throat and fear for Janice. Probably COVID, too, as my heart still pounds ferociously, and my lungs have trouble pulling in air. The knot in my stomach tightens, and I have to fight the urge to throw up at any moment.

Should I stay in control, here in this seat, to keep him calm? Images of Mark at White Pastures all those years ago flash before my eyes, in the company of a number of thoughts and questions: How good he'd been for Helen. Could grief really corrupt his mind enough to slaughter innocent people? Have I got it wrong, and this maniac isn't Mark or his alter ego? What has happened to his voice that he needs a synthesiser?

His harsh metallic tones cut into my thoughts: "I realise this has taken you by surprise, and you've done well to stay as long as you have. I look forward to chatting with Liv."

He killed a man in cold blood, threatened to kill my wife, and yet, is this a softer, more concerned side to him? Is it, fuck?

"But know this, Simon. I won't hesitate to kill Janice if I don't get what I want." Not only does the voice sound inhuman, but the words it spoke are, too.

"Please don't harm Janice," I plead. "Nothing will change. You've got the airwaves as long as you need them."

"And for as long as you need to keep me talking, no doubt,"

he says. "I have to tell you you're wasting your time there."

"What do you mean?" I'm genuinely puzzled.

"I'm sure you've been told to keep me talking while the police trace the call, but they'll find the trail goes cold quickly. I'm speaking through a computer which is routing the call via a network of servers and VPNs around the world. The police will tear their hair out being pushed from pillar to post as my digital footprint washes away as if it were a mark on the sand facing the incoming tide."

"Please don't harm Janice," I repeat. "We're doing as you ask."

Another voice can be heard from his end of the call, faint and unintelligible.

"What?" he says. "Give me a second, Simon." The sound through my headphones flattens almost imperceptibly.

Liv is alongside me now, urging me out of the chair. I cut my mic and stand. She drops into the seat behind the desk and says: "Get out there and help them. I've got this. We'll get Janice back."

Within a second of me slipping out of the studio door, I hear Amos through the production office speaker: "I don't need to detain you any longer. Our work is done for today. I've just been told a laboratory in Hertfordshire contracted to produce 100 million doses of the COVID vaccine has been destroyed, and two more of Earth's enemies have been executed on their way home after being vaccinated."

Horror and disbelief hang in the air in equal proportions.

"Where?" asks Liv.

"You'll find out soon enough," he replies. "Be ready to put my next call on the air, any time of the day or night, when I tell you about the next executions. These could be in Poolswood, London, Torquay, Paris, Madrid, New York, or anywhere. My disciples around the world are gearing up to come out of the shadows.

"My message to the world is clear and simple. These executions will continue, and increase in frequency. Four people tomorrow, six on Sunday, and eight on Monday. The numbers will grow until vaccine production ceases and all vaccination centres are closed. Existing vaccine supplies across the world must be publicly destroyed in front of television cameras broadcasting live on all national and local news channels, by noon on Wednesday, local times.

"I'll say farewell until then, but don't forget, you know what'll happen to Janice if you don't put my next call on air as soon as I ring."

"Amos. Amos, are you there?" Liv's question goes unanswered. He's gone.

"What do we do?" Bob looks at Stephanie. He turns the speaker volume down as Liv starts recapping what has happened during the last few moments.

"We don't negotiate with terrorists for a start," Stephanie tells him. "But it's out of my hands. This is well above my pay grade. The intelligence services will take charge now."

"We can't do anything to put Janice in any more danger," I say.

"I'm afraid we've got to look at the bigger picture now," says Stephanie. "We can't give him any more airtime. It'll cause panic around the world. We've got to find him, fast. Kit's spoken to the Chief Constable, and a squad of armed officers are already on their way to Batchelors Farm."

"Look, sorry," interrupts Bob. "What do we do on air now? Liv needs some guidance."

"Can your girl put music on, maybe back-to-back records for the time being?" Stephanie asks. "It's best not to say anything more at the moment. I'm sure we'll be told what to do by MI5."

Back-to-back tracks? I'd joked to Liv about the Masked DJ just before this nightmare started.

Bob presses the talkback key. "Liv, finish this thread quickly, and get back-to-back music on." She nods through the glass.

"Thank you," says Stephanie. "I'm beginning to think we shouldn't have let him go on as long as he did."

"Yes we should," I snap. "He'd have killed Janice if we'd cut him off. Have you forgotten that? And, yes, we're giving him more air time when he rings. As much as he wants. Or again, he'll kill Janice. Unless you don't care about my wife. Do you regard her as collateral damage? Expendable?

"Calm down," says Bob. "It won't come to that."

I am exhausted and defeated, and not just by COVID. Now the on-air adrenaline is easing off, the awful truth hits me like a combined punch to the stomach and head. I visibly sag and struggle to hold back tears.

Stephanie starts to reach towards me, aiming for my shoulder, then pulls away, as if remembering the COVID social distancing rules.

"Simon," she says, gently, "what makes you think he's the Reverend John-Luke Matthews?"

"Something Amos said triggered a memory of a conversation I had with Matthews a long time ago." It takes an incredible effort to keep the tears back as I speak, and my heart continues racing.

"If it's a while ago how can you be sure you're remembering correctly?" asks Stephanie's assistant, who I assume was the Kit she mentioned.

I can hardly tell them Mark said it in 2004 but I'd only heard it seven months ago. Best go in hard on what makes it memorable.

"He used the phrase 'God's wind.' Matthews used that same phrase."

"When?"

"A long time ago...sorry, Kit, isn't it?"

"Yes. Detective Sergeant Kit McGrath," he replies. "How long ago?"

"It was 2004," I admit, a little sheepishly.

"Simon!" snaps Bob. "That's 17 years ago. COVID could be playing with your mind."

Stephanie raises her hand. "Let him speak. Go on, Simon. Bob does have a point, though. How can you be sure?"

"Three reasons. Firstly..." I point my index finger in the air, "...it's a memorable phrase. Secondly..." I raise two fingers, making sure my palm, and not the back of my hand, faces them, "...it was used in a similar context of defending the Earth's environment."

His words had left a lasting impression when I heard them seven months ago. "I remember him speaking of armies waging war against the road humanity has taken, and changing the way humanity's going. He's committed to stopping environmental disasters which are harming the Earth, and said his soldiers are everywhere, in business, governments and universities."

"Soldiers?"

"That's the word Matthews used, Stephanie, and he said they attack what's causing the Earth to defend herself against Mankind."

As Grandma had told me, I recall word for word, action by action, everything that happened on my jump back to 2004.

"He said they were God's wind, and when they blow it's to defend the planet. Exactly what Amos said about COVID."

Everyone stares at me. "I know it's a lot to take in, but so's what we've heard over the last few moments." I hold up three fingers. "Thirdly, it may be a coincidence, but do you remember, Bob, when Matthews applied for planning permission to convert barns into accommodation and offices for his commune at Batchelors Farm?"

Bob shakes his head. "I've been to bed since then."

I smile, despite everything, even though it is more of a mirthless grimace. "Noah Jacobs opposed the application. We had him on the show, talking about it. He didn't pull any punches about Matthews."

"We'll know soon enough," says Kit. "The armed response unit will be at the farm in the next few moments."

"Actually," I say. "There's something else." They look at me expectantly. "It's not directly related to what he said. More with who he is."

"Yes," says Stephanie. "You said his real name is Mark Brody?"

"How do you know that?" asks Kit.

"Because I knew him nearly 30 years ago. Mark Brody was my dead sister's boyfriend."

Batchelors Farm

Whitehouse breathes easier once they are through the speed check on Blackthorpe Road and turn onto the country lane leading to the derelict cottage. Home and dry. Just got to get the car into the lorry and it'll disappear, as the BMW did yesterday.

Half an hour later the lorry pulls into the farm's 200-metre drive curving through an avenue of oaks. As the complex comes into view he takes the left fork to the logistics compound, stopping in the middle of the yard. They climb down and Whitehouse goes to the back, opens the doors and extends the ramp. Reaching into the Impreza, he retrieves the Kalashnikovs, handing them to McGlynn and Kirkbride, then reverses the car out of the lorry and takes it into the workshop, parking alongside the BMW which is in an advanced stage of being stripped down.

The sound of running feet and sudden cries of "armed police" stop him in his tracks as he approaches the door on his way out.

"Fuck." He darts back between the cars, frantically ducking out of sight.

Outside, McGlynn and Kirkbride stand rooted to the spot, staring at half a dozen police officers in full body armour pouring through the gate in the wall dividing the commune from the logistics yard, gripping guns with both hands, thrusting them forward.

"Armed police. Freeze. Do not move."

The yelled instructions come from at least three officers. In a split second, McGlynn swings his Kalashnikov up and opens fire randomly in the general direction of the advancing force. Two officers take the brunt of the onslaught as the shells tear through the many layers of high tensile strength fibres in their armour, knocking them backwards.

This time there is no warning shout. The other officers simply pull their triggers. Four shots ring out. Three smash into McGlynn's skull, the other straight through Kirkbride's left eye.

Whitehouse had heard enough. "Don't shoot," he shouts. "I'm coming out. I'm unarmed." He raises his hands above his head and walks slowly through the door, blinking in the February sunshine. Four more shots find their target. The third eye which opens above his nose adds to the surprised look in the other two. Whitehouse dies where he stands, a millisecond before three more 9mm hollow point bullets plough into his forehead, right cheek and Adam's apple. His body crumples to the ground, and silence descends once more over Batchelors Farm.

Simon

Stephanie disconnects her call. "Looks like you were right," she says to me. "There's just been a shoot-out there. Two gunmen with Kalashnikovs, in a lorry, have been taken down. There was a Subaru Impreza in the trailer. And guess what they found in the workshop?"

She answers her own rhetorical question before an educated guess would have given me the correct answer. "A BMW 5 Series M Sport."

"Any sign of Janice?" I ask.

She shakes her head. "I'm afraid not. Nor Matthews."

Panic starts to hit me. "Have they searched the place thoroughly?" Janice has to be there, surely. And Matthews. The commune was the Church of Euvenity's headquarters. Where else would they be?

"They're doing that at the moment," says Stephanie. "We'll keep you fully informed."

"What do we do now?" asks Bob.

"Don't put any calls about it on air. Keep playing music for the rest of Simon's show." She pauses, as if her thoughts are changing direction. Then: "MI5 are due at police headquarters, and I'm sure they'll want to talk to you, Simon, if that's OK?"

I doubt I have much choice.

"In any case, we'll need to take a statement about what you remember from your meeting with Matthews. Would you mind coming with us to the station?"

Again, it sounds more like a command than a request. "We'll take you home afterwards, and arrange for our

Family Liaison Officer to be with you. Do you have anyone at home at the moment?"

The question hits me like a thunderbolt. The girls. "Oh my God. My daughters."

"We'll send a car for them," says Kit.

"No, it's alright, they don't live with us. They've got their own homes. My phone's in my office. I need to see if they've been trying to ring me." They won't be listening to the show as they're both working, and I hope no one's alerted them. This is something I have to tell them myself.

No missed calls from them. That is something, I guess.

"It sounds like you have a photographic memory," Kit says after I'd signed my statement in Interview Room One at Poolswood Police Headquarters. He and Stephanie had been with me throughout, and I couldn't help but wonder who else is watching and listening via the CCTV camera in the top right-hand corner.

"Not really." I'd played parts of it dumb. For instance, pretending I couldn't remember Jasmine Foster-Brown's name. And I left out the amount of champagne Matthews and I drank, or they'd wonder how I remembered anything.

COVID social distancing regulations mean Hannah and Claire can't be at the house when the Family Liaison Officer drives me home at 7.15 p.m. But she, Sergeant Alison Decker, could be. "I can stay the night and sleep in a chair downstairs if you need me to," she says.

I shake my head. "No. I'll be fine. I think I'll be better alone." I can't stand the thought of a stranger in the house while Janice isn't here. Another thing, if Sergeant Decker stays, I'd have to wear a mask in her presence, and that's the last thing I want in my own home.

No. I'll be alone. Time to think. Time to reflect on the

monster Mark Brody has become. No one could argue with his environmental ideals. That clock's been ticking for decades, but humanity's snoozed the alarms and managed to sleep through them all.

They say the end justifies the means. Not in this case, it doesn't. So many innocent people dead already—two couples simply for having COVID vaccinations, 14 lab technicians at Goldman Brackland Piers, according to the news, and two police officers at Batchelors Farm. Then there are the not-so-innocent three members of Brody's hit squad. This is just the beginning. He's planning to murder many more. I'm not going to call him John-Luke Matthews. I'm calling him by his real name. Mark Brody. Someone I once called a friend.

Exhaustion creeps up as I sit on the sofa. The television is showing some talking head detailing the latest COVID deaths and infections, so I guess it must be the news, but I couldn't tell you anything I'd watched all night.

By the time I was halfway through the second bottle of Malbec, I could barely keep my eyes open. I'd set up a Zoom call with Claire and Hannah for half an hour not long after getting home. We'd tried comforting each other, but all three of us ended up crying uncontrollably.

"I feel so helpless, Dad," Hannah had said. If she was anything like me, anger, fear and frustration would be jostling to knock that off the top spot, but I knew what she meant. Not being able to do anything except wait was unbearable. The terror Brody instilled in me by murdering Noah Jacobs is unlike anything I've ever experienced.

The numb, empty hollow deep in my stomach is worse than anything COVID had conjured up in me, and in the dark early days of Janice's cancer the prognosis was always good, but even the nagging doubt that we could lose her at that time, paled into insignificance compared to what we know Brody is capable of with her.

I fall asleep on the sofa with that thought firmly in my mind. Which is why it latches on to my dreams, moulding them in its image: Janice screaming as Brody pulls the trigger; Brody smiling at me while his face melts into Janice's; Titus leaping up at him, snarling, before he shoots him, and when the body falls unmoving to the floor I see it isn't our beloved Red Setter, but Janice.

"You'll never find her," says Brody, as Liv and I look through computer files. "Janice is lost forever." She screams somewhere in the background. It takes a second or two to realise the scream comes from the computer, and I see two open windows side by side on the screen. One shows Janice in a dimly lit room, looking intensely into my eyes while her screams continue unabated.

"Oh, do shut up," says Brody from behind me. I turn, and he's making a two-finger gun. "Bang," he says, pointing it at the screen. Janice falls to the floor, and Brody blows imaginary smoke from the imaginary barrel at the end of his fingers.

"Game, set and match," he says. "Checkmate. You're all out for a duck. Six-nil. I win by a knockout." He clicks his fingers and disappears in a puff of theatrical smoke like the ones I'd seen in pantomimes as a child. The window showing Janice disappears, too, leaving the file Liv and I had been looking at. I don't have a clue what it is. Peering closer at the screen I see it's a record from Companies House.

Only now it isn't a dream. It's a memory. From 2010. Which I'd only accessed on July 10 last year during my jump to Noah Jacobs' interview about the Church of Euvenity's plans. The memory pushed its way out, showing itself on the screen. The memory was a name. The sole Director and Chief Executive Officer of Batchelors Farm and Batchelors Farm Logistics.

Frederick Chikatilo.

I awake with a start, completely disorientated by voices in the room. They don't seem to be talking to me, so what are they saying? Oh, it's the TV. I am in the lounge. I stand stiffly and rub the back of my neck to ease some muscle discomfort there. The clock above the fireplace shows 4.05 a.m. I'd slept most of the night.

Frederick Chikatilo. The name doesn't mean anything to me, but it's a link to Brody.

I walk through to the kitchen to get a bottle of water and see two business cards that I'd left on the island unit when I got home last night. Kit McGrath's and Stephanie Ingrams'.

I like Stephanie, but hadn't taken to McGrath, so he's the one I'll wake now. I dial his mobile, and can imagine him turning over in bed, reaching for the phone on his bedside dresser, not recognising my number.

"Detective Sergeant McGrath." He sounds half asleep.

"Kit," I say. "It's Simon Reynolds. Sorry to call so early, but I've just thought of something." Now I imagine him looking at the clock and sitting up. Perhaps a little more alert.

"Oh, yes."

"I remembered Googling Matthews and his company when he applied for planning permission. The Chief Exec is a guy called Frederick Chikatilo.

"What?" He sounds fully alert this time. "Steph and I saw him yesterday."

Now it is my turn to say 'what?'

"OK, thank you, Simon. I'll ring Steph immediately."

"Why did you see him yesterday?" I ask, but my words

fall into empty air. He has gone. I guess Stephanie is about to have an early morning call, as well.

It is still too early to get up. Let the police do their job. I go upstairs and climb into bed. The last time I'd got out of it, Janice was there, snoring gently.

Will I ever see her again? My heart bleeds and tears flow as I lie down, sobs filling my ears.

24

Prisoner

Saturday, February 20th, 2021, Simon

Strains of tinkling music begin almost as soon as my head hits the pillow. This isn't like the start of my normal jumps—if jumping into my body in the past could ever be classed as normal. I usually only have to mentally call to Jigonhsasee and I'm in the white void. This is different. The sound comes from the shimmering rugby ball-sized hole which appears in the air in front of the en suite. It sounds way off in the distance at first, almost seeping through the walls, but grows louder as the hole enlarges.

The portal expands quickly to become its regular three-metre-high oval, with the familiar pale blue strands of energy radiating from its edges. The enchanting music continues for a few seconds before the wind engulfs it, as the portal moves towards me. Wait. The portal's not moving. I am. But I can't be, surely. I look down at myself, sleeping. I float towards the entrance while my body rests peacefully below, and pass through into the muddy-walled tunnel, my feet dropping to the ground as the opening zips up behind me.

As before, the wind inside switches to the soothing rhythmic flow that I remember so well.

"Welcome, Simon." The voice, along with the wind carrying the musical chimes, and the feeling of pure love, engulf me as the small, glowing orbs materialise ahead, darting back to form their regimented guard of honour, guiding me towards the light.

Moments later I reach the cavernous threshold and

cross over without pausing. A number of indistinct figures are silhouetted against the distant source of white energy, forming an arrowhead. As I step nearer I see Jigonhsasee at the tip, with Helen, Grandma, and Janice's Dad, Dave, fanning out to my right behind her, and Mum, Dad, and Jim Roberts to the left. I start to rush towards them, but Jigonhsasee bores into my mind, stopping me in my tracks.

"Remember your Grandma's words. Any touch here breaks the link with your physical body."

"But why am I here?" I ask. "I didn't call for a jump."

"You're not jumping tonight, Simon." This was Grandma. "At least, not in the normal sense." She steps away from Helen and Dave, and stops around three metres from me. "Tonight you face your destiny. This is why your life was saved from COVID, and the culmination of why you were granted your special power."

"I don't understand. What do you mean?"

"The chain of events was set in motion many years ago. It was ordained the moment Jim claimed Helen, and sent Mark Brody on his path of evil and destruction."

Jim Roberts steps away from the arrowhead. How different he looks from his appearance in the smoke on the stairs at White Pastures. The red-eyed monster who was coming for Helen. The monster who plagued us during that long-ago summer. And yet, we'd had a glimpse of the real Jim Roberts that night. Not the monster who'd hurt us, terrorised us in our home and beyond. The monster who'd materialised out of the smoke had been a man. This man: tall, thin, short hair swept neatly away from the high forehead. Concern is etched deep in his brown eyes. At White Pastures they'd reflected rage and longing, borne of despair.

"I unwittingly created the monster Mark Brody has

become, so I'm afraid I'm responsible for the predicament Janice finds herself in, and for the murders of those innocent people," he says. "But all I wanted was my own true love. Heidi was reborn as your sister and living with your family in our marital home. Fate showed me a way of bringing us back together, and I grasped it with both hands."

There's another movement in the arrowhead as Helen steps out of the formation and I hear her voice for the first time on this side of the veil. "You can't blame him," she says. "Grief at losing me tore his heart apart, and the chance of reuniting with me clouded his spirit, just as grief tore Mark's heart apart and clouds his judgement."

I want to shout from the rooftops that I'd grieved, too. Mum and Dad grieved, Grandma grieved, but we didn't murder people. We didn't declare war on the people of the world.

"Which is why we've got to stop him now," Jim cut in on my thoughts. D'Oh. I've done it again. I've really got to stop thinking what I wouldn't say aloud in this realm. "What I did was bad enough," he says. "Dare I say, though, Mark is even worse?" And Grandma gives me one of her old-fashioned looks with raised brows and an amused twinkle in her eyes.

"Sorry," I flash back to them, hoping they don't think I meant Jim was the same as Mark, but he did do some pretty evil stuff in the name of grief.

"I know I did," Jim says. "The harm I caused you will haunt me through eternity. My anger was directed at you, your family, and Mark, who I saw as having stolen my Heidi." His voice sounds quiet in my mind. Can you whisper telepathic thoughts?

Mentally I put my head in my hands. For fuck's sake. Grandma smiles at me.

Mum and Dad break from the formation, just leaving

Dave Briggs behind Jigonhsasee.

"We forgave you long ago." Mum smiles serenely as she says this. "It's love that binds us now. Not hate."

"One more will be joining us, and then we're ready," says Grandma."

"Us?"

"Yes, Simon. We're coming with you. You can't do this alone."

I feel panic rising. "Do what?"

"Rescue Janice and stop Mark Brody." Grandma's matter-of-fact tone suggests I don't have a choice about this. "The wheels of time and destiny have been moving inexorably from the moment Helen died at White Pastures and her spirit returned home to Jim. Evil lost its host in Jim that day and targeted Mark, using his grief instead.

"All the major players from that event have passed over, apart from Sarah," says Grandma. "They've all come together now to help you bring Janice safely home."

Dave steps forward. "There's no way I'm being left out, either. Janice will always be my little girl."

"I still don't understand," I repeat. "How can we do this? How can we rescue her?"

"Under my guidance." A new voice in my head comes from a figure slowly breaking through the intense brightness. A figure I recognise, but can't instantly place, and yet I'm sure I've seen him recently. Mid-seventies, just about matching my height of five foot eleven. A thick mane of pure white hair parted on the right with a couple of locks reaching down towards his equally white left eyebrow.

Yes, I remember now. It comes back once he's close enough for me to take in the kindly features with a few laugh lines around the eyes.

The Reverend Hubert McBeil.

Although he's long dead—Poolswood Sound covered his funeral as he'd been the county's longest-serving vicar in one parish; 42 years at Meriton before retiring in 1987—I saw him just a few months ago. Not in a jump, but in one of the first flashbacks when all this started, banishing Jim Roberts, or so we'd thought at the time. "I was here to help you last time," he says. "I can help again."

Now, though, we had to banish a more dangerous foe, who threatened the stability of the world. No pressure, then, but how do we go about it? "We've no idea where she is."

"Not at the moment," Grandma admits, "but you can find her with the psychic link between you."

Grandma's not making any sense. "What psychic link?" I ask.

"Do you remember what happened when Janice was diagnosed with cancer?"

How could I forget the worst day of our lives up to that time? Events in Dr. Horton's office begin replaying in my mind. The news we'd been dreading, even though the doctor said the prognosis was good and the oncology team would support us as a family, my ridiculous and short-lived resolve to tell Janice how I knew she'd make a full recovery, Jigonhsasee telling me I couldn't change the order of events and the cosmos would stop me if I tried, how she'd put me in Janice's body for a few seconds which were filled with a lifetime of jumbled memories including that first fumble at Helen's party, Dave walking her down the aisle and the whispered oohs and ahs as our wedding guests caught sight of her Laura Ashley dress, the pain of the chest injuries she sustained in the Mercedes crash.

Those memories have lain dormant for a while, but resurface in response to Grandma's question, bringing the answer to my own question with them.

"This is the psychic link, then?"

"It is," says Grandma. "It was established when I sent you into Janice as a warning that you can't change the past."

"I never did understand that." I look Grandma straight in the eye. "I wouldn't try and put it into practice, though. I believe what you say about it being wrong and impossible, but how did going into Janice's body stop me?"

"I'd have thought it was obvious after the experiences of going into your own body." A mischievous smile plays across her mouth and adds a twinkle to her eyes. "Doesn't that tell you something?"

I guess my frown and shake of the head show her it doesn't.

"If you try to change the past by telling someone something they shouldn't know, the cosmos will always put you in their body. It stops you from telling them, and they won't remember anything about it when you leave them, just like you don't remember your visits to yourself. It's a simple, but perfect solution. An added bonus, or disadvantage, depending on how you look at it, is that because you've shared their innermost thoughts, memories, and desires, for however short a time, you forge an unbreakable spiritual bond with them."

"Are you saying I can use that connection to find her?"

"With the help of everyone here, yes. You'll be able to focus your energy on her and be transported to wherever she is."

"What happens after we find her? How can I rescue her and stop Brody?"

"Questions, ever more questions with you, my boy," says Grandma. "I can't always hold your hand. You'll need to think for yourself when you get there. But remember, there's always a way."

"I thought you said I couldn't change history, but isn't that what you're telling me to do now?"

"No, it's not. You're going to find Janice where she is now, in the present, not the past. It's not history, because it hasn't happened yet, so you can influence the course of events and play a huge part in the outcome. Success isn't guaranteed, but you're the only one who has a chance of doing this."

"We need to start," says Jigonhsasee. "Don't move, Simon, and whatever you do, don't touch us." The Reverend McBeil joins them as they form a circle surrounding me, and clasp hands with arms outstretched at shoulder height.

A spark of white energy ignites from Jigonhsasee's right hand, passing along the top of Helen's arm and through to Grandma. At the same time another spark shoots to Helen, then another, and another, until they become a thin white strand of pulsating light flowing through everyone.

I sense it's the same energy that connected Jighonsee to me the first time I saw my Iroquois guide, and later at Grandma's funeral when it passed between the three of us. Round and round it spins, vibrating as it rises and falls, growing in strength with every anti-clockwise revolution.

Is this the physical form of Orenda, I wonder? The thought is knocked from my mind, almost literally, as they break the circle in one fluid movement, stepping back a couple of paces and forming a line in front of me. Again as one, they raise both arms, pointing directly at me. Raw energy crackles from their fingertips, targeting a single spot in the centre of my chest.

My ears ring with its vibrant thrumming as the strands flow into me, infusing my blood with power and vitality.

Fleeting visions flash across my eyes, and full-blown sights, sounds, smells, and emotions merge with me; Dave cuddling baby Janice, Grandma cuddling baby me, Jim's horrified look into the night sky as the bomb falls, Helen (except it's not just Helen, it's Heidi, too) feeling intense, horrific pain as her body's torn apart in the blast, Mum and Dad's wedding, the intense onslaught of the unnatural wind and fierce pounding on the stairs through the Reverend McBeil's eyes and ears as he confronts our monster at White Pastures.

Now there's another one, isolated and strong, pushing the others aside. I'm seeing trees flash past through the eyes of a runner, and for a moment I think I'm being chased by the COVID monsters again, but it's not me. Panic engulfs this new me as heavy footsteps behind, and the sound of someone pushing through the trees, suggest I'm being chased, and my pursuer's close.

Who am I? Where am I? I don't recognise the landscape. With trees all around, it's hard to go any faster as I have to weave through them. My breath comes in short panting gasps, and a sharp stitch stabs my left side just below the ribs, but I know I can't stop. The forest floor is littered with twigs and stones which bite through my thinly-soled shoes, but I can't afford to slow down.

"Come here, bitch," a coarse voice shouts inches from my ear. That spurs me on, giving extra speed to my heels. I risk a half-glance around and feel my pursuer's hand brush my shoulder. A scream bursts from my lips.

In the few seconds of all this happening, more memories surface, giving me some context. I know the village isn't far, but I've ventured away from the path to try and throw the two white settlers off the scent. What are they doing out here, deep in our territory, anyway?

"Well, lookee 'ere," the first one had said when they

emerged from the trees a few paces from where I was picking berries. His plain shirt and tanned hide breeches were both stained with brown smears, and a strong scent of body odour lay sour in my nostrils as he came towards me.

"I know, I see it," said his companion. It came out more *ah* than *I*.

The first settler pulled a long-bladed knife from a sheath on his left hip. "I think we need to show this young squaw a good time."

"It'd be rude not to," said his companion.

"After all, we're on Iroquois land here, so the least we can do is repay their hospitality." He leered at me, showing a grin split evenly between yellow and missing teeth.

"You ain't wrong there, Billy."

"Sure I ain't, It wouldn't be gentlemanly otherwise, would it, Bobby?"

"It sure as shit wouldn't," said Bobby, spitting a glob of phlegm into his hands and rubbing them together briskly, "and we're nowt if not gentlemen."

"You ain't wrong there, Bobby."

"I sure as shit ain't." They looked at each other and guffawed. A raucous, intimidating sound.

I hurled my basket of berries at them and fled along the path, back towards the village.

"Why, shit me sideways," laughed Billy. "We'een got oursen a lively bitch 'ere." Then the voice changed from its mock humour to a harsh, menacing tone, which instilled pure horror in me. "Come 'ere, you filthy Indian slut, and take what's coming to you."

I heard their boots pounding the trail, and picked up speed. They looked to be a couple of years older than me, and I wasn't sure if I could outrun them. My mind's eye pictured the village, about a mile away, comprising three longhouses between the farmland and river which threads its way through the valley.

A new burst of speed takes me away from his flailing arm, and I turn to look fully ahead again, just in time to see the low branch immediately before it smashes into my forehead, bringing a bolt of pain that sends stars spinning around me, and throwing me on to my back in the dirt.

The settlers' whoop of delight is like a war cry when Billy drops on me, straddling my waist. As stunned as I am, I lash out, pummelling his face.

"Grab 'er 'ands. 'old 'em still, you shithead," he shouts to Bobby, who flops down heavily across my chest and neck, pinning my hands to the ground above my head. My scream startles a pair of birds who take flight about three or four trees away.

"Shut 'er the shit up," Billy shouts. "There could be some of them Indian boys lurking nearby."

Bobby lets go of my left hand and delivers a hard blow to my cheek, reigniting the stars which were starting to burn out.

Dazed, I hear Billy tearing my blue overdress, and feel it splitting in two at my waist. Next, he slashes my deerskin dress, and suddenly he's pushing inside me, hard and brutal, each thrust arching my back off the ground. Bobby's scrabbling to recapture my free hand, and my fingers claw the soil, finding a stone. He knocks it out of my reach and makes a grab for my forearm, but I draw it away from his grasp and brush against something cold and firm. Breaking my focus from the rhythmic thrusts inside me, I glance across and see Billy's discarded knife. My fingers surround the haft greedily, and suddenly I'm stabbing Billy's side, pulling the blade out and stabbing again. Then a third time.

A roar of pain erupts from him.

"What the shittin' 'ell 'ave you let 'er do?" he shouts at Bobby.

"You dropped it there, Billy."

I try to turn the knife against Bobby, but he's too quick and wrenches it from my fist.

Billy begins to stand, stumbling awkwardly, with blood pouring from three wounds. "Gimme that." He snatches the knife from Bobby and drives it deep into my groin, twisting fiercely.

There's no pain for a second or two, then it erupts in a violent cascade, setting the lower part of my torso ablaze with agony. My body's drawn towards him as he struggles to pull the knife out. The blade emerges, dripping blood, and I flop back.

"Get off 'er, you shithead," he screams, knocking Bobby away. The knife descends, piercing my already torn and tattered dress, and on into my chest. The pain sprints from my groin to my heart as my mouth locks in a silent O.

He withdraws the knife, holding its reddened tip to the side of my neck. "You fucking shithead bitch," he snarls, with blood-flecked spittle flying from his mouth. "You could've 'ad so much fun with us gentlemen." I feel the knifepoint penetrate my neck, and he slashes quickly across my throat to the other side. Blood instantly bubbles through the long gash, soaking my chest which rises and falls with my remaining half dozen breaths.

Terror and fear lend desperation to my efforts to hold the split skin, tissue and veins together before a quiet sadness fills my soul as I realise I'll never spend any more cosy evenings alongside my mother, father, and two brothers in the beautiful longhouse framed with bent saplings and covered with bark, that we share with ten other families.

Our space is the second room inside the Western door, three paces before the first firepit in the hall which runs its full 70-metre length. Without windows, it's always quite dark inside the longhouse, the only natural light filters in through the firepit holes in the roof. This image of home fades with each agonising beat of my failing heart as life ebbs away. Then the pain dims into nothing and peace envelops me in its cloak.

The memory stays strong as I look into Jigonhsasee's sad eyes, and shake my head in disbelief at how brutally my spirit guide lost her Earthly life centuries ago. "I'm sorry," I whisper. "I don't know what to say."

"Don't say anything," she tells me. "Think of Janice, long for her with all your heart, call for her, your soulmate, your best friend, your lover. Go to her."

"Janice, dear heart," I shout wildly, but silently, into the white void. "I'm coming for you."

Energy crackles around us again, this time the white strands emanate from me, flowing to Grandma first, then to the Reverend McBeil, and on to the others. The power of Orenda is almost palpable in the air, as it joins our souls in unity, connecting us all as one. Our combined energy shoots out across the astral plane seeking Janice, calling her name.

A small bare room, illuminated by a single LED ceiling light fades up into view about 20 metres away. A figure lies on a bed, its solitary piece of furniture, with her back towards me, and I readily take in Janice's white knee-length dressing gown with its irregular floral pattern. There's a long tear from the shoulder to the waist which hadn't been there earlier.

"We've found her," I start to say, but before I can fully form my words, a rush of wind pushes us on into the room in a split second. But I don't stop there and brace myself for a sickening collision with her. Which doesn't come.

Instead, my world blurs, and then I sit bolt upright with a gasp, surrounded by those four whitewashed walls no more than four metres apart, and a sturdy-looking solid metal door in the corner.

At first, it seems as if Janice has disappeared. Everyone else is here—Grandma, Dave, Mum, everyone. Janice isn't, though, and...

Memories explode, pushing everything else aside. I'm answering a ring on the doorbell half an hour after Simon left for work. So excited for him on his first day back in the studio and so proud of how he's kicked COVID's ass to get here. I don't recognise the swarthy skin and jet black hair of one of the two men standing there, nor the shaven head and crooked smile of his companion, who talks first: "Good morning, Mrs. Reynolds. Your chariot awaits." He half turns in the doorway and spreads his arm to indicate a grey Volvo SUV on the drive. I hadn't heard its wheels crunching on the gravel, but I'd been singing along to Poolswood Sound.

I look around the tiny room, then up at Jigonhsasee. It's a tight squeeze with us all here. There's a mattress on the bed, but no covers and no pillow. I swing my legs over the edge, planting my bare feet on the floor and standing up. The floor's stone, and cold. My short night dress is riding up my back. It's all I'm wearing apart from the dressing gown.

Janice's terror from yesterday hits me in an instant. The image of me trying to close the door to the two strangers bubbles away, submerged by waking up in this room. The memory's jumbled with the sight of them pushing the front door into me, and storming into the house. I turn to flee but feel a hand grab my dressing gown, pulling me back. I hear it tear as I tumble back against him.

"Not so fast, Mrs. Reynolds," he says. "Don't be rude." He spins me round to face him, and a needle and syringe plunge towards my neck. I struggle against the sharp prick and remember nothing more until waking on the bed yesterday.

I wonder if Jighonsasee, Grandma, and the others are sharing these memories.

"What's in your mind is in ours," says Grandma. "We're feeling Janice's pain and terror, too." The pain in my hands from battering on the door, the pain in my throat from shouting myself hoarse to be let out of this tiny room, the pain in the back of my head when swarthy skin man sent me sprawling against the wall after opening the door. My mind replays hearing bolts being drawn back and seeing the door start to swing outwards. I launch myself at the figure standing there, but he holds firm, apart from taking a couple of steps backwards as I crash into him.

"I've told you before, Mrs. Reynolds," he says, "don't be rude." His hands are on my shoulders and suddenly he thrusts me away. I stumble back into the room, past the bed, and smash into the far wall. He's on me in a second, spinning me around and forcing me to the floor on my stomach. I feel my right arm wrenched behind my back, my wrist gripped tightly in his fingers. Then my left arm is forced alongside it, and I hear the ratcheting of a zip tie securing my wrists together.

"Let me go," I scream as he hauls me to my feet. "Where are you taking me?"

The memory of being dragged down a short corridor into a room where two men were sitting at computer screens, triggers a new horror as I realise what Janice had gone through.

One man turns to me. Janice doesn't recognise him. But I do. The Reverend John-Luke Matthews. Mark Brody.

"Welcome, Mrs. Reynolds, or can I call you Janice? Please take a seat." He indicates a stool against a wall covered with a huge world map. The computers are on desks against the other three walls. Two screens seem to be connected to one keyboard at the desk facing the door, while each of the other keyboards has three screens arranged behind them.

The second man sits at one of them, his hands playing gently over keys and looking at each of the three screens in turn. The largest screen shows an aerial video of open countryside moving beneath an aircraft. The neighbouring screen displays a rolling map, with a red arrow presumably marking its location, while a series of figures and graphs cover the third. The ground gets closer on the video and tilts to one side as if the aircraft is banking.

"I'm bringing her back," he says, as the video picture shows the ground approaching fast. A large glass and concrete house sprawls into view, staying on the screen as the aircraft touches down. He swivels his chair to face Brody. Even seated, his frame looks tall and well-proportioned. "The test's fine, she's a dream to fly with that payload. Responsive to every touch, however small. She's good to go."

"In that case, Fritz, perhaps you wouldn't mind educating Mrs. Reynolds about what's going to happen." Brody looks up at me from his computer chair. "Janice, when I asked you to sit, it wasn't an invitation. Sit. Now."

The man who brought me in pushes me towards the stool. Caught off balance, and with my hands zip-tied behind my back I can't counter the stumble, and crash into it, sending it across the room while I end up sprawling heavily onto the tiled floor. He hauls me roughly to my feet and forces me down onto it. Then, bending, he quickly surrounds my ankles with a zip tie, ratcheting it cruelly tight, causing me to wince in pain.

"Next time, do as you're told. Straight away," he snarls.

"Thank you, Alec, that will be all." Fritz rises and turns my stool around to face him while Alec goes out, shutting the door behind him.

"Why've you brought me here?" I ask. "What are you going to do with me?"

"We don't want to hurt you, but it's out of our hands, I'm afraid. Here's what's going to happen, and you'd better hope Simon plays ball with us."

"What's Simon got to do with it?"

"Everything, Janice," Brody replies. "I'm going to talk to him in a moment."

"But he's at work."

"Exactly. I'm going to call his phone-in." He raises a forefinger, touching his lips. "And while I'm talking you're going to be as quiet as a mouse. Fritz will tell you why."

"Because if you make even the tiniest sound until you're told to, it will be very bad for you," says Fritz.

"Very bad," repeats Brody. He opens a drawer and pulls something out. At this stage, I can't see what it is, but when he stands a second later, my eyes widen at the sight of a gun. "This bad, in fact."

He lunges towards me, grabbing my hair and thrusting the barrel hard into my temple. I scream, and brace my bound feet firmly onto the floor, pushing the stool backwards away from him. His grip on my hair stays firm, and the stool flies into the wall without me.

Again, I smash painfully onto the tiles, but he wastes no time lifting me by my hair and dropping me back on the stool. "That rule about being quiet starts now," he hisses directly into my face, "and includes not moving." He shoves the barrel of the gun under my chin, tilting my head back. "Do you understand?"

Janice's memories burn into my brain, her pain and terror cutting me to the quick. I know I'll never be able to forget them. They'll bring me even closer to her. As long as I can get her out of this.

"Do you understand?" he repeats, pushing the barrel painfully higher.

"Yes," I gasp.

"Right." He slowly lowers the gun, and as my head comes with it, I see the dog collar for the first time.

"You're a vicar," I say, incredulously. "Why are you doing this?"

He sighs long and hard. "If you'll stop being stupid, Fritz will explain," he says, quietly.

I pull at the unrelenting zip ties around my wrists and ankles. Not being stupid is the only option. I'm going to get you out of this, Janice, I promise, without any idea how I'm going to keep it. I look around the tiny room and the bed I'm sitting on, as the memory continues.

Janice listens intently as Fritz tells her how Brody's going to ring me to claim responsibility for yesterday's double assassination, and two more incidents that will happen in the next few moments.

"When we tell you to talk, you're to instruct him to do exactly as we say, or we'll kill you. Do you understand?"

Adrenaline pumps around my bloodstream, quickening my heartbeat so much that it throbs in my ears. I nod, dumbly.

"Good," says Fritz. "If you behave, and Simon does as he's told, you could be home in a couple of days. Remember. Not a sound."

He returns to the three computer screens, and I watch the house drop away below the aircraft as it shoots straight upwards.

Brody puts on a set of headphones with a connecting microphone which he positions close to his mouth, before touching a computer key, scrolling through a menu, and clicking Enter.

"This is what Simon will hear when I start talking to him," he says. The memory of his words shows me how they chilled Janice to the bone. Not for what he says, but for what they sound like. Janice stares at him, the voice assaulting her ears through the computer speakers is two-tone, harsh, and robotic. Even though I'd been expecting it, it still shakes me.

"A simple computer program," he says. "Imagine Simon's surprise when he hears this." Brody's smile looks almost childlike as if he's getting a schoolboy's simple pleasure from it.

I need to put these memories to one side and focus on getting Janice out of here. Getting off the bed, I move across to the door. It's even colder to the touch than the stone floor. Solid steel. No window in it, and no handle on this side.

Another memory bubbles its way through; Noah Jacobs being pushed into the room where I was zip tied on the stool. He's disheveled, the knot of his tie has dropped around four inches down his chest, there's a tear on the sleeve of his suit jacket, and a large blood stain on his shirt. The blood is obviously a combination of a jagged three-inch cut on his cheek and whatever didn't clot on his top lip and left nostril, from what must have been a powerful punch to the nose. One eye is swelling up and closing, the skin beneath it turning a shade which, if it were paint, would be described as either plum or claret.

No, no, no...I know what's coming without having to relive Janice's memory. I'll never forget hearing the gunshot on air.

While that jostles for position amongst another maelstrom of Janice's recent and not-so-recent memories—for some reason the Mercedes spinning off the road and overturning in the ditch is climbing up there—the door swings open behind Grandma, Jigonhsasee, Mum, Dad, and the others, in the here and now.

This time it's not the shaven-headed man who's come for me, but the other thug with the swarthy skin and jet-black hair.

I jump off the bed, pulling my nightdress and robe as low as they'll go over my legs.

"Easy now," he says, with a smile showing expensively-perfect, straight white teeth, and holding up a zip tie. "You're needed again for another broadcast. A nice early morning one this time, into the breakfast show. You know the drill. Behave yourself."

I'm not sure how Janice would react, but I'm not risking this arsehole getting violent with her. I look helplessly at Grandma. Silently I turn around and place my hands behind my back, wincing as he ratchets the zip tie tightly around my wrists.

25

The Power of Orenda

Saturday, February 20th, 2021, Simon

He grips my right elbow, guiding me out of this small cold space, and down the corridor to the room where Brody and the man he called Fritz the day before, are poring over their computer screens.

Fritz turns briefly to me. "Good morning, Mrs. Reynolds."

So, this is Chikatilo, is it? I take in the muscle-laden physique clearly visible through a pale blue T-shirt with two vertical lightning flashes forming part of the V in "EV-Tech" emblazoned across the chest. Almond-shaped dark brown eyes stare malevolently from black skin so shiny it almost glows.

Underfloor heating gives a warm feel to the tiles, but my short nightdress and thin dressing gown are no protection against a chill from the stone floor and walls of my cell which has ingrained itself into my bones.

Brody swivels his chair and stands, coming over to me. "Ignore him, Janice. He's not a morning person. I hope you didn't have too uncomfortable a night." I stare at Brody, with Janice's memory of his gun jabbing painfully at her temple and then under her chin, bubbling to the surface. We've got to stop this psychopath, and quickly.

"I've had better," I tell him.

"And hopefully you'll be sleeping in your own bed again tonight," he says. "All you need for that to happen is for Poolswood Sound to put me on air again in a few moments."

He pulls the stool away from the wall and indicates for me to sit. "You're not going to give us any trouble today, are you?"

I perch on the stool and push my feet hard to the floor, propelling it slowly back to the wall. "As quiet as a mouse."

He runs his fingers through the flowing grey hair and scratches the back of his neck. "Very pleased to hear that. I take it I won't be needing this, then?" He pulls the gun from a drawer and places it on the desk next to the computer.

I shake my head. "You won't."

To me, the room looks crowded. But, of course, only I can see Jigonhsasee, Grandma, and the others, as they scan everything intently. Dave's peering over Chikatilo's shoulder at his screen. "Look at this," he says. Connected by our joint Orenda, I see a number of faces on Chikatilo's Zoom call, through Dave's eyes. An automated background behind each delegate shows a clock and country location. "They're from all over Europe," he says.

This must be a customised system as I don't remember my Zoom calls having a location tag, but this indicates callers from Paris, Rome, Amsterdam, Madrid, Berlin, and Brussels.

The face from Rome is talking. "I'm hearing that we should have some news in a few moments. They've stopped outside the market square in a village."

"Thank you, Agustino," Brody replies.

The background clock shows 9.30 a.m.—an hour ahead of us.

He looks at me. "It seems we're getting ready for our first executions of the day. Time to ring Poolswood Sound."

"Simon won't be there," I tell him. "He doesn't work on Saturdays."

"Doesn't matter. As long as I get on air." He picks up the gun, examines it silently, and puts it down, presumably to leave me in no doubt about his meaning, then turns his attention to the headphones and microphone which are fresh in Janice's memory from yesterday. He slips them over his ears, and I watch his fingers play across the computer keyboard, calling the radio station.

The ringing tone runs for a few seconds, before: "Poolswood Sound Production. Good morning."

"Good morning." Although I was expecting the robotic voice, the unnatural twin-tone words still ring vicious and menacing in my ears. "I spoke to Simon Reynolds on air yesterday. You're going to put me on air again, right now, please."

"What? Who is this?" The voice doesn't sound as surprised as he tries to make out. It's the weekend breakfast show's production assistant, Damien Jackson-Brind.

"You know who this is," Brody replies. "This is Amos." His words are slow and measured, designed to portray increasing menace. "It's the man who took responsibility for Thursday's executions of Ben and Hayley Hampshire, and the two men in the Cartier quarter yesterday. The man who took responsibility for the destruction of the Goldman Brackland Piers laboratory in Hertfordshire. The man who will take responsibility for executions in Rome, Amsterdam, Paris, Madrid, Berlin, and Brussels in the next few moments.

"And the man who will claim responsibility for the death of Janice Reynolds if I'm not on the air in the next minute."

"I'm afraid I can't put you on air, Sir."

"And why's that?" Brody's robotic question is constrained and quiet, but the glare in his narrowed eyes tells a different story, that it's just a mask, a barrier to the rage that's burning within him. A volcano that's going to erupt, devouring everything in its lava path. And that includes Janice. *Try not to think about it. Focus on keeping calm, and on keeping Brody calm.*

"I have a gentleman here who'd like to talk to you, Sir," Damien says.

"Will he put me on air?"

"You'll have to ask him, Sir. He's here now."

"Hello?" The newcomer's word rose in pitch at the end. A question, not a statement. "Is that Amos?"

"It is. But who I am is immaterial. You just need to know what I'm going to do. I, however, need to know who you are, and that you're going to put me on the air."

"You won't be going on air today."

"You do understand that you're condemning Janice Reynolds to death if I'm not?" Still cool and collected. The mask isn't slipping yet.

"I'm not negotiating with you. I'm telling you a fact."

"Permit me to know the name of the man sending an innocent woman to her death," snapped Brody. Now the mask's slipping, the restraint gone from his mechanised words. Chikatilo swivels his chair, but Brody holds up his hand. "Not yet," he mouths.

"I'm Commander Alexander Bennett," the voice at the radio station tells him. "From MI5. I'll be talking to you from now on."

"Unless you put me on air in the next minute, you and I have nothing to say to each other, and Janice Reynolds will be dead. Put me on air for ten minutes and she lives."

I look Jigonhsasee straight in the eye and project a thought to her. "What can we do?" Janice's heart pumps wildly. "Leave this with us," Jigonhsasee says.

Bennett's voice comes from the computer speaker. "Tell me what you're planning to do and perhaps we can talk about it."

"We're not going to talk about it. It's going to be done in

the next few moments, and if I'm not on air to tell the world about it, you'll hear Janice Reynolds executed as a direct reprisal."

"Can you postpone it, if only for a few moments, and…"

"No, I won't." The mechanical words are a little louder now and somewhat clipped. "My agents in cities across Europe are closing in on twelve executions. And I demand that you put me on air to tell the world about it."

"Is that absolutely necessary? If you're really going to do it, Janice doesn't need to die because you don't get to talk about it."

"Don't trifle with me, Bennett. The world needs to know why this is happening."

"The world does know. You made it clear with Simon Reynolds yesterday. You're not going on air on Poolswood Sound today, and that's final."

"You'll do as I say." Brody's words thunder back through the computer's speakers. It's almost as if there's a conflict between the program which can only reproduce the metallic words in two notes, and the anger he's trying to convey. The volume, however, is a different matter.

Chikatilo calmly picks up the gun from Brody's desk and strolls over to me. I push back on the stool against the wall, but he grabs my hair and hauls me off it, spinning me around. His brown eyes are hard and almost manic—wide to the extent that the whites entirely surround the pupils— no pity in them, just a doorway to an empty soul.

The gun goes under my chin, tilting my head back, and I recall Janice's raw and jagged memory from yesterday.

"Come on…" Jigonhsasee's words sound distant, maybe watered down by so many other minds crowding in on me, everyone's thoughts jumbling around with mine. She and the others rush over, forming a wide circle around Chikatilo and me. They link arms at shoulder height, just as they had in the void, Again, sparks of white energy cascade from Jigonhsasee's right hand passing into Grandma, and through to Helen, then Mum, Dad, Dave, Jim, and the Reverend McBeil.

"Get me on air," screams Brody. "Do it now, or she's dead. You have 20 seconds." The robotic distortion serves to increase the menace his words punch into my head. "I'm counting you down. I mean it, you fuckers. Janice Reynolds will be dead if I'm not on the breakfast show in 20 seconds."

My neck throbs as Chikatilo continues to push the gun against my Adam's apple. Then he pulls it away, and I take a step forward, but he hauls me back by the hair. "Don't run off, now, Mrs. Reynolds." He wraps his left arm tightly around my throat and pokes the gun into the side of my head.

"Nineteen."

The blurring strands crackle and fizz. Round and round they flow, increasing speed with each anti-clockwise revolution.

"Eighteen."

Janice's heart pounds wildly, giving a double drumbeat in my chest and ears. The sound of her blood coursing through her veins is like a rushing river. The Reverend McBeil's words are the first to break through the incoherent noise. "Focus on the gun."

What? How do I do that?

"Not you, Simon," Jigonhsasee's reply cuts straight across the intertwined clutter.

"Seventeen."

Chikatilo's arm tightens against my windpipe, and the gun barrel presses harder into my right temple. The lightning strands of Orenda encircling us change hue, from white, through a pale blue, then dark blue, and finally to a deep, vibrant purple.

"Sixteen."

Their shared thoughts merge into a solitary word: gun. They break the circle, and through their minds' eyes, we mentally approach the barrel, going straight through the side of the cold metal rod and sliding up to the tip of the bullet.

At least, some of us are. Some are still outside. With the combined Orenda from Jigonhsasee, Jim, and Dave, inside the gun, I also share Mum, Dad, Grandma, and the Reverend McBeil's view of Chikatilo and me.

"Fifteen. I'm not bluffing, Bennett."

More energy crackles from them, but this time, instead of encircling both, it leaves Chikatilo largely outside the ring. Somehow the strands work their way between the two of us. A bead of sweat forms just inside my hairline and trickles down my forehead.

For the first time, I notice there are no windows in this room. Where is it? Chikatilo's home, perhaps?

"I think you are, Amos," says Bennett. "You're not going to shoot her. You know you're not. Not without an audience. That's what makes you tick, isn't it? You don't waste your trump card when there's still half the game to play."

"Fourteen. That's where you're wrong. Completely wrong. For me, the game, as you call it, has only just started, and the world's my playground. Today, Rome, Amsterdam, and those other European cities where executions are scheduled in the next few moments. Tomorrow, America, Japan, and China. My campaign to save the Earth will be all over radio and television stations across the globe. I don't need Poolswood Sound. I want it. There is a difference. And I'll tell..."

"Thirteen." That comes from Chikatilo as he squeezes

my windpipe even tighter for a second or two. *He must be itching to pull that trigger. This isn't good. Come on, Bennett, put Brody on air. The news will be across the globe in a matter of minutes, anyway. Does it matter if he claims responsibility straight away? Isn't that a good thing?* My mind continues to race. We can't be heading towards the end of Janice's life, we simply can't be. Another droplet of sweat. And another.

"Janice Reynolds was never my trump card," Brody says. "On the contrary. She was yours. You just didn't know it. And if you don't play your hand properly, you not only lose Janice, you lose the game. The only card you can play, Bennett, is to put me on the fucking air now! Time's running out for you. Twelve."

Bennett stays silent. Is he considering his next move? Despite my thin nightdress and robe, I'm now sweating heavily. Nothing to do with the temperature, but more to do with my pounding heart and the fear that is giving rise to the burst of adrenaline pouring into my bloodstream. I pull at the zip tie around my wrists, but it holds unrelentingly firm.

"Mr. Bennett," I suddenly cry at the top of my voice, "this is Janice Reynolds. He means it. He's going to kill me."

Chikatilo yanks my head back even further. "Shut up."

"No, wait," instructs Brody. "Let her talk. Go on, Janice, tell Bennett what's happening to you right now. Tell him where the gun is. Oh, and Bennett, just in case you've stopped clock-watching, we're down to eleven now."

"Mr. Bennett, they've got a gun to my head. They mean it. They're going to kill me. Damien, please put him on air."

Brody nods appreciatively. "That's right, Bennett, we've got a gun to Janice's head. Remember what happened to Noah Jacobs yesterday? You've now got ten seconds before my associate pulls the trigger."

Bennett breaks his silence. "Amos, we can talk about this. You don't have to do it. Think about it. What do you gain by murdering an innocent woman in cold blood?"

"It's not murder," shouts Brody. "It's an execution. For fuck's sake, Bennett, use Janice as your trump card, play it now to save her. Put me on the fucking air."

"Maybe we can do that, after all." *What?* A ray of hope brighter than any sunbeam, and a combined sense of relief and elation, hits me with those words.

"Thank God, Commander Bennett," I sob. "Please put him on air now. Damien can do it in a few seconds."

"That's better," Brody's mechanical words are quieter now. "I'd advise you to do what Janice is asking."

"But not just yet. We need to talk first." *No, no, no.* I feel like screaming at Bennett. What's wrong with the man? *Just fucking do it.*

"Don't play games with me." Brody's finesse has gone again. *Please stop toying with him,* I silently plead to Bennett.

"Nine. Commander Bennett, I'm not fucking around here. Get me on air, *now*, or you'll be directly responsible for Janice Reynolds' death."

His words ring through my head, bringing sadness rather than anything else. Death isn't to be feared. I've been there, but Janice hasn't. It's just a portal to a different plane of life. Everyone in the circle surrounding me is proof of that. But I don't want to be parted from Janice. We've still got so much Earthly living to do together.

"You're not going on air at the moment." I think the note of quiet finality in Bennett's tone hits home with Brody. He stares straight at me, locking eyes. There's a glint in them that doesn't look natural, doesn't look sane.

The robotic words are equally as steely. "We're down to

eight, Commander Bennett."

"We can put you on air, Amos, and we will. Just not right now. All I'm asking is that you hang fire on this. We'll get you on air later with a proper interview. Give Janice a stay of execution, at least."

"No. But I'm glad you accept that it will be an execution and not a murder. Seven, Commander Bennett, seven."

I'm running out of time. Mentally, I project into the ether: "Grandma, Jigonhsasee. Do something to save Janice. Please." The pulsating strands of Orenda surrounding me continue to gain speed, but Jigonhsasee gives no sign of having heard my distraught cry.

"But, why, Amos? We'll agree to a full interview with you on Poolswood Sound this afternoon. What if we get Simon Reynolds in for you to talk to?"

Brody's reply is a single word. "Six."

"Amos, we can't stop you killi—executing—these people around Europe but please spare Janice. Why are you doing this to her and Simon?"

"Five."

Chikatilo increases pressure on my neck, making me arch my back momentarily to try to ease it. As I relax back against his body a second or two later, my bound hands brush up against his manhood. An insane thought hits me. If this bastard's going to kill Janice, I'll make sure she goes out with all guns blazing.

Taking a deep breath, I squeeze for all I'm worth.

Chikatilo lets out an unholy scream. I grip even harder, twisting and pulling. He suddenly releases my neck, which is good. But what's not so good is the involuntary flick of his hand holding the gun to my head. A flick that catches the trigger.

In the confines of the windowless room, the gunshot

is deafening. We both jerk violently. *This is it, then. I'm so sorry, Janice. I came here to save you, and I failed.*

My world stops. Dave's looking straight at me. His jaw's dropped and his stunned eyes reflect what I can only imagine he's feeling at witnessing his daughter's death in this horrific way.

Dave, I'm so sorry.

It's not just Dave. Everyone else is staring, too. They're all standing in a line, no longer surrounding me or focusing their attention on the gun. And I realise the purple strands of Orenda that were spinning around me have gone. *When did they disappear? What've they done? They must have gone when Janice died.*

I brace for the unspeakable, albeit brief, burst of agony which must surely accompany the bullet penetrating Janice's skull. I know nothing about guns—will the bullet have smashed her head to smithereens, scattering blood, bone, and brains every which way, or will there be a small, neat round hole in her temple with barely a trickle of blood alongside her ear? A sudden feeling of considerable wetness in my hair and down my back tells me it could be the latter. Either way, I expect to be floating free of her body now, on the same plane as Grandma, Jigonhsasee, and the others, and I instinctively look for her blood, perhaps along with bone fragments and globules of grey brain matter. But there's nothing. I'm still seeing through Janice's eyes, and my hands—Janice's hands—still grip Chikatilo tightly, still pulling, still twisting.

He's no longer screaming in pain. Or is it that I can't hear him, because a powerful ringing fills my head—a legacy of the gunshot that ended Janice's life—and any sound from outside is strangely muffled? There's a stronger resistance from him now as if he's attempting to pull away from my grasp. He's become a dead weight in my hands. *No, you're not getting away that easily. It may be Janice's death grip on you, but she's going to make you suffer as long as she can.*

Brody stands transfixed on the spot, eyes wide, mouth gaping. *What did you expect?* "Fritz..." he screams through the barrier still muffling my ears, and loud enough to drown the now diminishing ringing. He takes a step towards me, then stops mid-stride and retreats, his eyes fixed on something behind my right shoulder.

I hear Bennett's voice coming from the speakers, faint through the audible fog surrounding me, but I can't make out what he's saying. *Am I somehow managing to hold Janice's body together, simply by being inside her?* Grandma, what's happening?

Chikatilo's resistance changes. His arm around my neck flops down my chest, and the angle of his body behind me drops away to my right, his manhood pulling sharply against my grip. I let go, and he drops to the floor, pushing against my legs, the momentum making me stumble forwards. I manage to stay upright and turn around.

And gasp in horror and disbelief.

Half of Chikatilo's face and head is missing, replaced by a tangled wreckage of exposed muscle, bone, and sinew. I'll blame Janice's stomach rather than my essence inside it for the violent retch that erupted from me. It isn't helped by the fact that my eyes fall on the hand holding the gun, too. Or should I say stump where the hand used to be? As if copying his face, all that is left is a shard of bone protruding through a mass of blood and strips of shredded skin dangling limply like catkins from a willow tree.

The shattered remains of the gun lie on the floor by my feet, the barrel, magazine, and handle blown into twisted shards of metal. Suddenly I realise what's happened. The gun exploded in his hand.

"Exactly," says Jigonhsasee in my head.

Everything suddenly clicks into place. "That's why you sent our combined Orenda into the gun...?"

"You've got it, Simon. The power of Orenda not only held the bullet at bay in the barrel, but it also pushed it backwards into the magazine and detonated them all."

"...and the Orenda circling around me, leaving him outside, protected me from the explosion?"

"Yes, and as well as shielding you, it pushed the full force of the explosion onto...what's his name? Fritz? Otherwise, Janice would be in the same condition, instead of just having his blood and brains on her hair and back."

I squirm involuntarily, shaking my shoulders and head. Something flies off me to the side, dropping to the tiles with an obscene plop, and, looking down, I see a wet, glistening red ribbon of what just a few seconds ago had been inside Chikatilo's head.

During the silent conversation, I'd been conscious of frantic voices coming from the computer speakers. Some were from Brody's Zoom call. Chikatilo and I were in direct line with the camera, and they must have seen everything. The questions had been quickfire and in a variety of accents, but all added up to the same thing: "What's happened?"

A stronger, far more powerful and dominant voice rings out above the others. Bennett. "Amos, what was that? You haven't shot her, have you? Because if you have..."

Brody slings the headphones and microphone aside and starts to move towards me, his eyes completely insane. "You killed Fritz," he screams.

"No, no," I protest. "I didn't. How could I?" I step sideways, but my bare feet slip in a pool of Chikatilo's blood, and I slide awkwardly with my legs going in opposite directions to each other, before falling backwards on top of his body.

Just as Brody reaches down and grabs my hair, the door opens and a slim, dark-haired young woman comes through. High, prominent cheekbones dominate her face, and the bright LED ceiling lights throw a shadow across the taut skin below, which detracts from her prettiness. "Fritz, what was that bang? I..." Her eyes widen as she sees me sprawled across Chikatilo. Then she sees his shattered face and missing hand, and her scream comes long and loud.

"Aamina, don't come any closer," says Brody, rushing to her and pushing her back into the corridor.

"No," she screams, backhanding him across the face, and barges past him into the room.

Bennett's shouting from the speakers again. "Amos, what have you done? Talk to me."

"He's killed Chikatilo," I shout as loudly as I can from my prone position, hoping they'll be able to hear me at the radio station.

The girl turns to face Brody. "You did this?"

"What? No. Of course not. She did. I was talking to MI5 at Poolswood Sound."

I struggle to my feet. What did Brody call her? Aamina? "Aamina, listen to me. Look at me. How could I have done this? My hands are tied." I turn, so she can see the zip tie around my wrists, holding them securely behind my back.

She drops to her knees, ignoring the blood on the floor, averting her eyes from what's left of his head as she clutches Chikatilo's undamaged arm.

"It's about time," she whispers. "Payback for this." She points to two large purple bruises on her left forearm. "And this." She raises her skirt and her fingers trace a ragged cut from the side of her belly button which disappears inside her skimpy black Lexington knickers.

"And this." Now she lifts her black baggy crop top and pulls her bra off her left breast. I gasp at the sight of three cigarette burns scarring the mountain of flesh.

"Did he do that to you?" I ask.

Before she can answer, Bennett's talking again, his voice loud and clear from the computer. "Brody, I'm through playing games. This stops now. We're on our way to you at Larkwise Lodge."

"What?" That gets Brody's attention.

"We know where you are. You're at Fritz Chikatilo's home, Larkwise Lodge. We know your name's not Amos. We also know the Reverend John-Luke Matthews isn't your real name. You're Mark Brody. And we're coming for you.

"We're just minutes away from Larkwise Lodge. You need to come outside and surrender."

"Like that's going to happen," snarls Brody.

I don't like this. It could go either way. How will Brody react to the adrenaline that's surely surging through his veins right now? Which mode will it ignite? Fight or flight? Either way, it won't be good for me. I pull as hard as I can against the zip tie, but the bloody thing's too strong, and my hands stay just as secure as they were.

Voices now clamour from the Zoom call. "What's happening, Reverend Matthews?"

Brody turns swiftly to the computers, cutting both the line to Poolswood Sound and the Zoom call.

Aamina locks eyes with Brody "How could they know?" she asks.

"There's absolutely no link between the church, Fritz,

and me now." I can almost see his mind working as he says that. He stares back at her, a slight frown creasing his brow. "Fritz removed his name from all records, including Companies House, years ago when our activities started to get noticed and deleted them permanently. No one could have found out. And his donations are all completely anonymous through our Caymen Island accounts. Someone must have told them."

I sense his unstable mind is rapidly reaching a conclusion about this girl. Could I let her take the blame for me tipping off the police? Somehow I've got to get us both out of here. But how?

"Come on," he says to Aamina. "If the police are on their way we've got to get out of here. Time to hold an inquest into who the rat in our midst is later."

"Where are we going?" Aamina asks. Something tells me she doesn't seem all that upset about Chikatilo. I suspect those bruises, cuts, and burns may just be the tip of the iceberg.

"We'll take the Cessna to France, and move further afield later. And…I'm sorry, Aamina, I'll have to set self-destruct here. We can't have them getting these computers."

"That's no loss." She tilts her head towards Chikatilo. "You know I've always felt a prisoner here with that monster. "Talking of prisoners, what about her?"

"She comes with us. The police won't try anything stupid while we've got her as a hostage."

I look across, horrified, at Jighonsasee and Grandma. The stark thought hits me of Janice suddenly finding herself in this situation when I leave her body. Sometimes ignorance truly is bliss. I think back to all the times I've woken up with no recollection of the previous few hours, and realise what an appalling prospect is in store for Janice.

She went to sleep in that small cell, and will wake up God knows where with this madman.

"Don't worry, Simon. We won't let Janice get on that plane," Grandma tells me.

Brody presses a sequence of computer keys, and almost instantly a red light above the door starts to flash, and a disembodied female voice fills the room. "Self-destruct sequence initiated. To complete the arming process, enter audio personal ID and authorisation code."

He hits several more keys, and speaks directly into the computer's microphone: "Matthews. John-Luke. Reverend. Personal ID two two four oh eight oh nine oh eight."

The automated voice from the computer acknowledges his input: "Personal identification verified. Please enter Larkwise Lodge self-destruction authorisation code."

Again, he enters a combination, the red light changes to green, and the voice continues: "Self-destruct sequence confirmed. Ten minutes to ignition."

It's getting hard to follow what's happening. Self-destruct? Does that mean wherever we are is going to blow up? It sounds like something from a sci-fi or spy movie, and from what I've seen of Brody over the last couple of days he fits the role of supervillain perfectly.

How on Earth can he have come to this? While grief is a powerful emotion, I don't understand how it can lead to someone becoming so obsessed.

Brody touches another key. After a few seconds the voice of the man who brought Janice in here yesterday, comes from the speaker. "Yes, boss."

"Alec, you both need to get out now. The police are on their way. Larkwise will self-destruct in ten minutes."

"What? What's happened?"

"It seems we've got a traitor in our ranks." He looks pointedly at Aamina, who seems blissfully unaware of what's going through his mind.

"Jighonsasee!" I plead silently. "What can we do?

"Who?" asks Alec. "Not anyone in the UK, surely?"

"I've got a good idea, and, yes, I think they're close to home," says Brody. "But now's not the time or place. Get out now, and use the bottom gate. The police will be at the front soon. I'll be in touch."

"Thanks, John-Luke, I appreciate what..."

Brody cuts the connection. "Bring her," he instructs Aamina.

She indicates for me to follow Brody as he strides out of the room, and pushes me in front of her.

A dozen paces in the opposite direction from the room where I'd been held, take us to a door at the end of the corridor. As we pass through, the tiled floor gives way to concrete—quite smooth, but noticeably colder to my feet. Automatic lights flicker on, and I see we're in a triple garage. And what a line-up of cars: a Lamborghini Huracan, a BMW 5 Series M Sport, and an Audi SQ7.

Brody punches a code on a wall-mounted box and removes a key fob as soon as it opens. The hazard lights flash briefly on the Audi. "Get in," he tells us. "Janice, you in the front. Aamina, you're in the middle row."

Aamina opens the front passenger door and puts her hand on top of my head to stop me from hitting it as I struggle to get it.

"Wouldn't it be easier to release my hands?" I ask.

"No chance," snaps Brody as he settles in alongside me, slotting his phone into its holder on the dashboard.

Aamina pulls my seat belt from its anchor and reaches across me to snap it into place, before settling into the seat behind me. Jigonhsasee and the others had all floated down the passage behind us, and now swirl into the car. Except for Grandma. "I'm staying here for the moment," she says. "There's something I need to do here. I'll join you later," and she moves off back down the corridor.

The door rolls up as Brody inches the seven-seater SUV forward, and then we're out into the early morning cold February sunshine. I catch sight of the large modern glass and concrete house through the side window as we glide past. The drive sweeps up towards a set of ornate gates, but at a fork, he turns the car the other way and we go round the back of the house alongside a wide expanse of sloping lawn, heading down towards security fencing and a hedge bordering open countryside which stretches as far as the eye can see.

After a few hundred metres the gravel gives way to a rutted track that turns abruptly towards a gate at the side of the estate.

My hands press painfully into my back through the thin nightdress and dressing gown, and I wriggle in my seat, trying to get more comfortable.

"We'll get you out of this, Janice." His daughter can't hear Dave's words, but I understand why he tells her this. It must be strange for him, to see and hear her voice, knowing she's buried deep inside, but it's me in control of her body.

"She'll be fine, Dave," I fire back at him. "I promise." God knows how I'm going to keep it.

The gate starts to slide back as we crawl past a sensor mounted on a small pillar, and once the Audi's out on the quiet country road he floors the accelerator. The sudden jolt pushes me back in my seat as the car shoots forwards.

"John-Luke..." shouts Aamina from behind me.

"We need to get to the airstrip," he says, turning his head to glance at her. "If the police know about my connection to Fritz and Larkwise, they may know about the plane, too."

Suddenly the air is rent with a booming explosion, scattering birds from the trees all around us. "There goes Larkwise," says Brody. "Hopefully that'll keep the police occupied for a while, but I'm not taking any chances. We're getting to the plane as fast as we can."

The high hedges on both sides of the road flash past at breathtaking speed, but Brody seems oblivious to any danger. "Hey, Siri," he says, calmly, as thin branches overhanging the road by mere inches are pushed back in the car's wake. "Ring Blackwood Farm."

A second or two later Siri's automated voice announces: "Calling Blackwood Farm," before giving way to the ring tone through the car's speakers, and then: "John-Luke... good morning."

Brody eschews all pleasantries and gets straight to his point: "Paul, sorry for the urgency, but I need the plane immediately. Can you get her out and fuelled straight away?"

"Yeah, sure. Why the rush? Are you okay?"

"No. I'm not. We've been betrayed. I need to get out of the country. Fritz is dead, and the police are on their way to Larkwise. Not that they'll find anything there. It self-destructed a moment ago, so our network's safe."

"Christ on a bike, John-Luke. I'll get on it right now. She'll be ready to fly in 45 minutes."

"Thanks, Paul. I'll be with you in 20." He cuts the call and looks over at me. "Sorry about this, Janice. Hope you don't get air sick."

"Why are you doing this? You could just let me go here."

"If you're a good girl and don't give me any trouble I

may dump you in the French countryside when we move on somewhere else."

Tyres screech as the Audi takes a blind left-hand bend far too fast, and I'm pulled to my right, the seat belt straining to hold me in. "John-Luke, slow down," Aamina shouts again. I brace my feet firmly on the floor as our trajectory stabilises and we come out of the corner and back onto the straight. Right into the path of an oncoming van.

My thoughts shoot back to driving Brody and Helen home from our day out in Brighton along the A26 all those years ago. The time when Jim tried to kill us, and would have succeeded if Jigonhsasee hadn't been there.

A sudden, crazy idea floods my mind. Adrenaline surges. It's now or never. If I don't do this, if he gets me on the plane, he'll never let me go, despite his empty promise. He's a psychopath, a maniac, a mass killer. I can't trust a word he says.

Jim's in the back of the car again, just as he was in 1982. And, as before, an oncoming vehicle's bearing down on us. The others are here this time, though. Strength in numbers. Strength in Orenda.

I scream two silent words to Jigonhsasee.

"Understood," she sends back. Thin strands of Orenda instantly fly out from all six of them. Those from Jigonhsasee, Mum, and Dave stream between the front seats and encircle me, while the ones connected to Dad, Jim, and the Reverend McBeil wrap themselves around Aamina.

A single penetrating note assaults my ears as the van driver hits the horn long and hard. The Audi shudders erratically as Brody hauls the wheel to the left, and I can see we're going to miss the van by inches.

Do I have the right to do this? Brody's UK operation is

already destroyed, and I could kill the innocent van driver. That may be so, another voice in my head tells me, but Brody's global network is still alive and kicking. You need to cut off the Hydra's head if you're to save hundreds of innocent lives.

Which is the voice of my conscience, though? The one telling me to do it, or the one planting the seed of doubt?

There's no time to weigh up any options. In seconds we'll be past the van, and my chance will be gone. It's now or never. And that's assuming I'll be able to do it, anyway.

I brace myself hard in the seat, twisting my body as I swing my legs up and over the centre console. The safety belt digs deeply into my shoulder, sending a sharp stab of pain jarring through it.

"What the...?" yells Brody, turning to look at me.

I draw my knees tightly up against my chest, then kick my legs out as hard and fast as I can. My feet crash into his face, and I hear bones crunching, as blood spurts from his nose. He howls in pain and clutches his nose with his left hand.

The van's right on us. I aim my feet for the top of the steering wheel. My toes connect with it, and I push with all my strength, hoping to turn it enough for us to clip the van.

"You crazy bitch," screams Brody.

"What are you doing?" Aamina shouts from the back.

In that instant, I see I've failed. The car moves sharply towards the middle of the narrow country lane, but the van flashes harmlessly past the windows.

"Simon, do it again." Jigonhsasee reaches over and grips Brody's right hand, pulling it off the wheel. I draw my feet back and have a second stab at it. Brody looks aghast at his hand, seemingly raising itself, but I'm sure he can feel her invisible vice-like grip.

Aamina reaches over the back of the headrest, clamping

her fingers around my face. "Stop it, Mrs. Reynolds. What are you doing?"

My feet hit the wheel a third time, pushing it further to the right. The car shoots across the road, and because of its speed, the sudden change in angle brings its offside tyres off the ground. Brody makes a grab for the steering wheel, but now Jigonhsasee hauls both his wrists back. The car smashes through the hedge, showering wood into the air, at the same time that the offside tyres crash back to Earth. I brace instinctively while the car bounces, loosening Aamina's grip on my head, as she's flung back in her seat, the belt holding her firmly.

The earth slopes away in front of us, and metal crunches all around me as we roll, first onto the left side, then the roof, crumpling the ceiling and side panels. Shards of metal slash down inside the cockpit, narrowly missing my head.

The seat belt holds me firm as I'm suspended upside down for a second, before we roll onto our right side. Momentum continues our rolling, bringing all four wheels to rest on the ground, but only for a second, then we flip over a second time, and a third, as we pick up speed down the hill.

It's all over in seconds, but for me, trapped in my seat, that brief moment of time feels like aeons, filled with the birth of stars, their lifetimes of blazing in the heavens, and collapsing in on themselves in their death throes. I've no idea how many times we roll, from wheels to side to roof, over and over again. The sound of metal scraping on metal fills my ears, and the dizzy sight of the sky and ground turning cartwheels flashes by the windows.

Now would be a good time to find out if Jigonhsasee and the others managed to take action on the two words I'd called to them a few moments earlier: "Orenda protection."

It's a bit late, though, if it doesn't work.

Trees flash past. I imagine the one we hit has probably stood firm for at least 300 years and will stand for 300 more. It's certainly "no contest" when the driver's door thuds into the sturdy Oak. The crumpled metal shatters even more as the tree surges through it like paper, smashing into Brody and pushing him sideways towards me. I scream frantically, pulling my feet back, trying to make myself as small as I can against the seat, and as close to the door as I can.

A whooshing sound accompanies my airbag activating and ballooning out to within a few inches of my face, but doesn't come anywhere close to drawing my eyes away from Brody's head, which flops limply at an absurdly impossible angle, almost twisting right around by 180 degrees.

My heart leaps. He's dead! The impact of the tree must have broken his neck. Part one of my task is complete. I've stopped him, but I've still got to get Janice to safety, and I can't do that alone. I'm completely helpless, the belt still trapping me in the seat feels even tighter now the force of the rolling and the final impact has locked it in place. I squeeze deeper into the seat to try and free it, but it remains stubbornly unmoving, and with my hands tied I can't get to the catch to release it.

At least the sky's above us and the ground below—the car's come to rest on its wheels, so I'm sitting and not dangling.

Aamina moans behind me, but I can't even turn to see her. "Are you alright?" I ask.

There's a pause of several seconds before she answers quietly. "I think so."

"We've got to get out," I say, gently. "But I'm stuck. Can you get my seat belt off, please?"

Relief washes over me. I can't see how either of us could

have survived if Orenda hadn't formed a protective bubble around us both and held the framework of the Audi at bay.

A whiff of petrol, and the sight of smoke wisping from the engine, tell me we're not out of the woods yet, though. "Aamina." More urgency to my tone this time. "The car could blow up at any moment. Please help me."

"Coming." She scrambles through the gap between the seats, crouching on the centre console, and clicks my belt catch. Nothing happens for a heart-stopping moment, then the tension suddenly releases, and the strap winds in, disappearing into its housing behind my shoulder.

"Thank God for that." Free of the seat belt, I take stock of the car's condition to look for a way out of this metal trap, and it seems Orenda's coming to the rescue again. Jigonhsasee's now guiding the Orenda that surrounded Aamina and me, protecting us from the crash, onto the cracked and splintered windscreen which is now full of holes and crazed glass.

I watch, fascinated, as the frame starts to vibrate with a faint hum as it's working its way apart from the surrounding metal. Aamina looks at it in horror. "What's going on?" she asks, her voice rising and shaking at the same time.

"Kick it out quickly," I shout. "The roof may be collapsing."

"What?" She looks up at the crumpled wreckage.

"Kick it, please. I can't. I've got bare feet, you're wearing trainers. The smoke's getting thicker outside. It could blow at any minute."

"Okay." She sits on the centre console, gripping both seats for extra stability, and draws her legs back. The Orenda's homing in strongly on the top right-hand corner, where the frame's already flapping freely, and before she can strike out at it, the windscreen blows out, tumbling away across the bonnet.

We're free!

"What happened?" Aamina looks at me, stunned. "I didn't touch it."

"I think the whole framework's warped," I tell her while smiling inside at the power of Orenda. "That smoke's worrying, though. Can you help me out?"

She scrambles through the open space onto the bonnet, and I manage to manoeuvre out of the seat and onto the wide armrest over the centre console's storage compartment.

I shuffle my way forward, ignoring the myriad tiny stabs of glass as they dig into my bottom and the back of my legs, seeking blood.

Aamina reaches in and gently helps me out.

The metal of the bonnet feels hot. Too hot.

"We need to get away," I tell her urgently, and start to swing my legs over the side.

"Be careful where you put your feet," she says. "There's a lot of glass on the ground."

I pick my way gingerly away from the car for a few seconds, with Aamina gripping my elbow. A rumbling begins behind us and I turn to look at the Audi. The smoke's now puthering out, swirling up into the sky. And standing alongside the vehicle are Jigonhsasee, Mum, Dad, Helen, Dave, and the Reverend McBeil, which raises another thought—I wonder why Grandma stayed behind at Larkwise?

"Where's Grandma?" I send through the ether.

"Get away from the car," says Jigonhsasee. "The engine's going to blow anytime."

"But where's Grandma?"

"She's fine," says Mum. "She's been busy at Larkwise."

"Doing what?"

Mum ignores my question. "We have to go now, Simon. We won't see you again until your time comes to join us here." One by one they all raise their hands, like a Mexican Wave, and slowly fade into nothing.

The rumbling's getting louder.

"Aamina, run!"

We've barely taken half a dozen strides before the rumbling builds to a crescendo and erupts into an ear-splitting explosion, which sends a stream of searing heat across my back. We're both blown off our feet, sprawling into the dirt. Aamina uses her hands to cushion her fall, but with mine still firmly secured behind my back, my face takes the brunt. I roll over onto my side, spitting soil and grit out of my mouth, before trying to struggle to my knees.

Aamina stands, and gently takes the top of my arm, helping me up.

"It's over," she says, looking at the burning car. "We're safe."

"Thank you," I tell her. "You saved my life there."

She smiles. "And you've saved me."

"How? From what? I haven't done anything."

"Oh, you have. You've done far more than you know, whether you meant to or not, just by being here."

"I didn't kill Chikatilo if that's what you mean. He was going to kill me, but the gun exploded in his face."

She looks deep into my eyes for a moment, then suddenly pulls me towards her and hugs me tightly. "I know, I know," she says from over my shoulder. "If you'd not been here, my monster of a husband would still be alive. You've freed me from a life sentence. You've no idea what he's done to me over the years."

"Oh, Aamina, I'm so sorry."

"But now, thanks to you, I'm free of him. And this whole life with the Church. If I'm honest, John-Luke wasn't much better."

"Did he hurt you as well?"

"Not often. But sometimes the two of them would. Together."

I wish I had more time to find out what this poor girl had gone through at the hands of these psychopaths. I could barely imagine it.

"You're just as much their victim as anyone else. You'll be able to tell the police so much."

"Oh, no, no, no." She holds her hands up. "I've got to go. I can't talk to the police. Not after what they've done. All those people they've killed. The Church of Euvenity is a vile and evil cult, and I'm part of it. Although I never wanted to be."

I can see in her wide frightened eyes, how terrified she is at the prospect. "It's over now," she says. "I've got the freedom I've wanted for so long. Janice, promise me you won't tell the police about the plane. Please let me get away."

"Of course, I won't tell them. As I've said, you're a victim in all this, but where will you go?"

"I'll still go to France, as John-Luke planned, and then move on somewhere else. Fritz and I have a number of homes across the world. I'll flit between them. I'll be fine."

"The police know about Fritz's involvement, though. They'll freeze his assets and raid those homes."

"They won't." She smiles at me. "Most of our wealth and all the property isn't registered with us. Only Larkwise and £3-million are directly connected to us."

"You know, you really shouldn't be telling me this."

"After what we've both seen and been through this morning, we're soul sisters now," Aamina tells me. "We look after each other. But..." a slight narrowing of her eyes turns her smile from merely confident, into something a little more sinister, "...don't forget that you killed John-Luke. You deliberately caused the car to crash. If the police find me, I'd have to tell them that, now wouldn't I?"

"How do you know that?" I ask. "You weren't even in the car. It was just John-Luke and me. I clearly remember him telling those two goons to take you with them. I've no idea where you're going."

She flings her arms around me, squeezing me tightly again, then breaks away and kisses me full on the lips. A long, lingering kiss. My emotions run amok. What's stirring? Is it me or Janice?

I'm lost in those thoughts until she eventually says: "I think we understand each other."

I nod. "We do, but who'll take you to France now John-Luke's dead?"

"I'll take myself. He wasn't a pilot. I am."

That makes me smile. Talk about jumping to conclusions. "Of course you are."

She gives me another quick hug. "Let's see if we can get this zip tie off you." She spins me around and I feel her fingers exploring the strong plastic strip. A jolt of pain shoots through my wrists as she tugs hard on it.

"Ow."

"Sorry," she says. "We really need to cut it."

"Looks like I'm going to be stuck, then." Any one of those jagged pieces of metal around 20 metres from us would have been ideal if the car hadn't been burning fiercely.

Aamina starts looking on the ground. "I could try and find a sharp stone."

"No, don't worry," I tell her. "You need to get to that plane. He said it was still about 20 minutes away. And that's by car. You've got a long walk. Go. I'll be alright. I've just got to walk a couple of miles back to Larkwise."

"But you've no shoes."

"Can't be helped. Just make sure I get back onto the road, please. You might have to help me through the hedge."

She links her arm around mine and we trudge up the slope, looking at the swathes cut through the grass where the car had rolled its way down.

"One thing," she says. "That policeman or whatever he is, said John-Luke wasn't his real name. He called him Mark Brody."

"Did he? I didn't notice."

We get to the smashed hedge where the car had left the road. Aamina helps me navigate my way through the splintered wood, and I find myself standing on the rough tarmac.

"Good luck," I tell her.

"I don't like leaving you like this," she says. "Anything might happen."

"The worst that can happen is that I have to walk all the way to Larkwise. You never know, I might get lucky and a motorist comes along this deserted lane."

"You know what I mean." Tears are in her eyes.

"Yes, I do." Of course, I do. "Believe me, though, I'll be fine." I try to make light of it, but I'm a vulnerable female wearing just a tattered and torn nightdress and dressing gown with my hands tied behind my back. So maybe I won't be fine. It doesn't bear thinking about, but we both need to be on our way in search of safety.

"Goodbye, Aamina. I wish we'd had time to get to know each other better."

She smiles. "Yes. We could've been great friends. Soul sisters." She takes a step back and her eyes slowly scan me from my hair to my toes. "There's something about you. Something different. I don't know what it is. I guess I'll never find out.

"Anyway. Yes. Goodbye, Janice. Good luck to you, too,

and thank you, again. You've given me my life back after all these years." She turns and sprints away down the lane. I stare after her until she's just a dot in the distance, and disappears around a bend.

I pull futilely at the zip tie again and start walking barefoot along the rough tarmac lane. It's a slow and painful trek, as my feet find every sharp stone and twig in creation. Despite the morning sunshine, it's still cold, and I shiver in my thin clothes, thinking again of that long-ago freezing night when I had to walk naked from Orangebow Lake to the phone box at Blackthorpe Crossroads. I smile ironically as I remember that I never did get even with my Best Man, Trevor Aimes.

I've no idea how long it takes me to get back. When I reach the gate Brody drove us through, I catch a glimpse of the wrecked house up the hill, just a stark skeleton of smashed concrete standing in a sea of glass rubble. Blue police and fire service lights revolve close by, and jets of water from fire brigade hoses play over the shattered remains of what was once a multi-million-pound house.

Just a few more steps up this lane, then I turn right. A police car is parked at an angle that would stop any cars going past from my direction. As I approach, I see an armed policeman standing guard outside the gate.

"Help me," I call. He spins to face me, and although we're still around 30 metres apart, it seems I'm staring straight down the barrel of his Heckler & Koch G36C semi-automatic carbine.

"Halt," he yells at me. "Armed police. Stay where you are."

"Help me," I call again. "I've escaped from this house. I'm Janice Reynolds. They were holding me prisoner."

"Stay there," he shouts, then says something into his

radio. A few seconds later two other police officers—a man and a woman—sprint past him towards me, stopping around four metres away.

"What have you got behind your back?" shouts the man.

"Nothing. I'm..."

"Get on your knees and show me your hands," he screams.

"I'm tied up," I shout back at him, turning, and thrusting my bound hands towards him.

"Christ." The female officer is alongside me in seconds. "Mrs. Reynolds, are you alright."

"I'm not hurt. Just very frightened."

"You're safe now," she tells me, taking my arm and guiding me towards the gate.

Sweat pours from my forehead. as I sit bolt upright. Light's filtering in through the curtains, and it takes a few seconds for me to get my bearings. Then I recognise the familiar surroundings filling my vision. It's my bedroom. I'm back. Which means Janice must be in a state of total confusion right now. She'd have gone to sleep in that cold cell and now finds herself tied up outside, being led along the road by a policewoman.

It takes every ounce of my self-restraint not to reach for my phone and ring Stephanie or her young Sergeant, who must have acted on my phone call and set up a dawn raid of Chikatilo's home. No. They need to ring me to tell me Janice is safe. Surely it'll come any moment now.

Even after all this time, the unpredictable sweating is part of Long COVID's legacy, as is the dizziness on getting out of bed. I reach unsteadily for my dressing gown hanging on the door.

As I sit down at the kitchen island unit with a double espresso from the coffee machine, my mobile rings showing

Stephanie Ingram's name on the display screen. I hit the "accept" icon. "Stephanie? Any news?"

"Yes, Simon," she says. "Janice is fine. She's safe and well."

"Thank God for that. Where is she?"

"She's on her way to hospital, but.."

"I thought you said she was okay?"

"She is. She's got a few cuts and bruises, but nothing to worry about. Listen to me, though, Simon, she's suffering from some type of post-traumatic stress."

"What?"

"She's extremely disorientated, and can't remember anything after going to sleep at Chikatilo's house, until finding herself just outside the grounds a few moments ago."

"I don't understand." I have to make this sound good. Hope my acting skills are up to scratch. "How did she get out there? Where's Brody and Chikatilo? Did they get away"

"We've no idea what's happened. The house is destroyed. Looks like there's been a huge fire there."

"Fire? Janice isn't burned, is she?"

"No. As I said, Simon, she's just got cuts and bruises, but we're more concerned about her mental state at the moment."

"Can I see her?"

"Of course. She's going to Poolswood General. You can go to her there."

"Thank you. I really appreciate you letting me know so quickly. I'm on my way."

"One thing, Simon. Take her some clothes and shoes. All she's wearing is the nightdress and dressing gown that she was kidnapped in."

Part Four
AFTERWARDS

26

Rage

Simon

And we all live happily ever after.

But that's only true in fairy tales, and for someone else but not for me, as a popular song from the 1960s goes. Except that's about love, and everyone does live happily ever after in fairy tales. At least the good guys do. The baddies often meet some horrific fate, such as falling down chimneys and burning up in the three little pigs' fire, or tumbling to Earth after Jack chops down their beanstalk. And whether you believe the wolf in Little Red Riding Hood drowned or died after being filled with stones is up to you.

But this isn't a fairy tale. This is true life. The life and times of Simon and Janice Reynolds. Between us, we've come through COVID and cancer, and a terrible time at the hands of someone I once trusted and regarded as a friend.

So why can't we live happily ever after? Don't we deserve it?

I'd say we do, and for around two and a half years things returned to some degree of normality for Janice and me at a personal level. Apart from the occasional grinding headache and regular cough, along with heart rate control issues and fluctuating fatigue, I've shaken off most of the ill effects of Long Covid, for which I'm eternally grateful. While I know I've recovered far better than many victims, I've come to realise I'll never be 100 percent again, and the best way of describing it is to say I feel old before my time. Physically I reckon I'm somewhere between 75 and 80 percent of what I was, and psychologically probably around 80 percent.

My emotions about those hours I spent in Janice's body are pulling me every which way. I feel even more closely connected to her, which I hadn't thought was possible, before. Our love and bond to each other had always shone through every day of our marriage, but having been so inextricably intertwined with her—feeling everything through her skin; the cold of that small cell, the cruel pull of the zip tie around my wrists, Chikatilo's arm around my neck, his blood and brains running down my hair and back, the resisting force of Brody's face as my feet crashed into his nose, the sear of the heat when the Audi exploded, and every stab of the stones, twigs and rough tarmac during that long barefoot walk from the crash site back to Larkwise—brought me more as one with her.

That was sealed by the mental intimacy of her flashing memories spanning the years, some of which, I'd been privy to at the time while others were new to me. The strongest ones surrounded childbirth and the love that flowed through her as she bonded with our daughters. They all formed part of Janice's very essence as I glimpsed her soul during those two or three hours when I was part of her.

It brought me so much closer to Janice than I could ever have imagined. For me, our intimacy was complete in ways I can't possibly share with her.

At one point I'd been tempted to tell her everything—how I'd jumped into her body in the way I've been jumping into mine, but then realised it could do more harm than good. As soon as we get home from the hospital and I'd poured her a large gin and tonic she looks at me and bursts into tears.

After her physical checkup, they'd insisted she see a psychiatrist, who told us her amnesia of the last few hours was probably her mind's way of shutting out some awful trauma that happened in Larkwise. I shudder when I think back. Tied up and helpless, the gun to her head and expecting to die, that dreadful split second after it went off waiting for the bullet to tear her head apart, the shock of Chikatilo's mutilated face in death, being bundled into the car and being told I was going to France, then those terrifying moments when the car was rolling down the hill, and seeing Brody's dead body in the driver's seat. I'm glad I went through all that, and not Janice.

"I can't remember anything about today," she sobs. "I fell asleep in that horrible room, and the next thing, I'm being comforted by that policewoman."

"Perhaps it's just as well," I tell her. "It must have been horrific in there."

"Even so, I need to know what happened."

I put my arm around her shoulder as she takes a sip of her drink. "No, you don't," I say, gently. I managed all those years not knowing what happened during my blackouts, but I can't tell her she's experiencing the same. Can't even hint at it.

While I'm euphoric at having been inside her, mingling with her life force, I can see how it's violated her. My very presence in her is tantamount to mental rape. Tears well up in my eyes as that thought hits home. She'll never know I was in her body, and she'll never know what happened.

"You're okay now, you're fine." I drop to my knees and hug her tightly. But she's not fine, is she? I've interviewed enough military personnel to recognise Post Traumatic Stress Disorder when I see it. Janice is going to need tender loving care. A lot of it. For a long time to come.

Baby steps each day. Janice's therapy helps her tremendously, but that blank space in her data banks continues to eat away at her. Her counsellors tell her the memories will come when she's ready to handle them, but I know better. Her lost memories are safely tucked up in my head where they belong. Where they can never get free and open up what are becoming old wounds. Those sleeping dogs are best left where they lie.

I lay awake into the wee small hours for the first few nights, just looking at her sleeping, knowing how close I came to losing her. Her slow, rhythmic breathing sounds so peaceful, and her face in sleep looks happy and content. I can only guess what battles her subconscious is fighting. Is it aware, somewhere deep in her soul, of what happened? Did my presence inside her during those horrific hours merely suppress the sights and sounds in that windowless room in Larkwise, and the Audi? Will time erode the barrier protecting her conscious mind? Will the memories start to trickle through? Tiny, but probing and teasing at first, before finally breaking down the gates and coming in waves, sweeping her peace and happiness away in their wake?

Those are my nights. The days are a different matter. Bob insists I take a month's compassionate leave, and won't listen to my argument that I'd only just got back into the studio, and a week off would suffice.

"You need to be with Janice at the moment," he tells me.

Yes. I know. Of course, I did.

"And longer than a week," he says. You're not coming back until Monday, March 22nd, and that's final, Simon. The end of it."

During the month that follows, I spend as many waking moments with Janice as I can. The only time I'm not with her is during her twice-weekly counselling sessions, and it's then that my thoughts turn to anger. Who do I direct my anger at? The two bastards who put my wife through that agony are gone. They've escaped justice. Death is too good for them.

One thing about Brody's death makes me smile, though. He went to his maker thinking his worldwide terror network was safe from discovery, all computer records and links to cloud servers destroyed when Larkwise self-destructed, and his agents would continue to protect the Earth, keeping God's COVID wind blowing. Well, I've news for you, Mark Brody. Before the end of my month's leave, the police told me that every one of your team around the world have been arrested. They said by some miracle there was one tiny part of the house that hadn't been destroyed in the explosion. Neither the police nor the fire investigators could explain why three square metres around the computers in what had once been the room where I was so terrified for Janice's life, were unaffected by the blast and the fire that followed. The computers were completely unscathed, and the MI5 cyber team had eventually broken the incredibly sophisticated encryption.

Stephanie Ingram's visit to tell us this comes out of the blue, and is the first time I've seen her since that day in the studio. She sits in our lounge with a coffee on the table alongside her, and a smile on her face. "I shouldn't really be telling you both this, but after everything you went through, Janice, it's only fair to let you know."

She says the computers' hard drives and links to cloud storage had split Brody's network wide open. Names and IP addresses of all his agents, details of many millions of pounds in bank accounts in the Caymen Islands, and other generally untraceable financial havens were eventually uncovered, along with details of luxury properties on three continents.

Despite Fritz Chikatilo no longer being the CEO of the Church of Euvenity, and having no public connection with it for several years, the computers tell a different story.

As I'm taking all this in, my mind turns to Aamina. Not only did she save Janice's life, but I'm convinced she's every bit a victim of the Church as anyone. In a different way, of course. She's still alive. Many victims aren't. She said she and Fritz had properties and money which couldn't be traced to them. I hope with all my heart that she made it safely to France, and didn't go to any of Brody's properties en route to her own. I guess I'll never know.

One thing I do know...well, perhaps not KNOW for sure, but I'd take a highly educated guess...is that the computers weren't saved by a miracle. That must be the business Grandma had back in Larkwise when Mum, Dad, Jim, Dave, Jigonhsasee, and the Reverend McBeil were with me in the car. Grandma was in that computer room spinning a protective web of Orenda around the hardware, keeping it safe, ensuring the Church of Euvenity's ultimate downfall, and we're free to fight God's wind with vaccinations again, safe against Brody's global terrorist threat.

So, should my anger be directed towards God for either sending COVID to the world, or, if it was the Devil's handiwork, allowing it to take so many millions of lives and affect millions more?

Human resilience and determination shine like a beacon after the COVID darkness of 2020 and 2021, as the world emerges once more into the light.

Maybe, though, the Earth isn't finished with keeping humankind in check and shows us in other ways that while mortals think we're in charge of our destiny, in truth we're not. We're as rudderless in the greater scheme of things, as the flotsam and jetsam polluting the seas.

Even as the spectre of COVID fades with the less deadly Omicron variant, our trials start over with another icy wind blowing across the Earth from the East. Early in 2022, the Russian invasion of Ukraine brings fears of a third world war, again testing humanity's strength and spirit.

Then we had the severe financial crisis across the globe, harder in some countries than others, particularly in the UK, where an inept and incompetent Government created enormous issues with fiscal stability, and resulted in Prime Minister Liz Truss leaving office after just 49 days in the job and the country sinking dangerously close to a recession.

Yes, the Earth has many more lessons in store to teach us humans polluting her surface.

January 2024, Simon

One morning early in January 2024 while I am putting four slices of bread in the toaster for us, there's a hint that our personal world may be turning on its head again. Poolswood Sound's breakfast show presenter is just introducing an item about the local council being accused of ignoring the plight of the homeless in the cold weather when I hear Janice retching in the bathroom.

"Alexa, mute." There's no doubt about it. She's retching heavily. If there'd been anything in her stomach it would have come up. I go to the foot of the stairs and call out to her: "Janice, are you alright?"

I hear the toilet flush, and she appears on the landing. "I'm fine."

It may be the three soft-glow bulbs in the landing light fitment casting a strange yellowish tint over her face, but from where I stand on the bottom step, she looks anything but fine.

"Janice, you're not." I run upstairs to her, taking her face in my hands. Her complexion has the look of ancient parchment, and even the whites of her eyes have a faint yellow hue.

"This looks like jaundice," I say.

She nods. "I was sick in the night as well."

"Right, we're getting you into the doctors this morning. How long have been feeling ill?"

"When I weighed last week I'd lost three pounds, and I've been feeling drained for several days."

Our hopes are high over the next few days, but Janice's oncologist puts paid to that. We're in her consulting room at Poolswood General, the day after receiving her letter calling Janice in. A stark, white clinical setting.

"I'm so sorry, Janice," Doctor Caroline Horton tells us on that fateful day. "Unfortunately, your cancer's returned."

I squeeze Janice's hand. It's the news we've been dreading, but not particularly unexpected. What is surprising, though, is the doctor's next piece of news.

"I'm afraid it's not just in your breast this time," says Doctor Horton. "There's a second cancer which has developed independently."

Janice sits bolt-upright next to me.

No, no, no. This can't be happening.

"Where?" she asks, her voice a mere whisper.

"Unfortunately, in your pancreas, Janice. You now have stage four pancreatic cancer."

It's an understatement to say the bottom dropped out of our world that day. I'm definitely directing my rage at God now. I hope He exists so He can hear my silent rage. It's not fair. How could you bring my wonderful Janice through the horrors she faced at Larkwise just to give us only two more years together?

My nightly rants and pleading prayers don't make a

scrap of difference. Janice's condition worsens by the day, and my incandescent outpourings are like pissing in the wind, as the saying goes. My prayers remain unanswered.

Doctor Horton had told us it was a double whammy. Those weren't the exact words she'd used, but that's what it boils down to. The breast cancer is back, but would probably be treatable if it hadn't been for cancer developing in her pancreas and spreading to several organs including her lungs.

Three to five months, the experts said. That's all the time she's got. She refuses chemotherapy, but agrees to a gastric bypass as palliative surgery, in addition to the constant drip-feed of powerful painkillers.

My Janice is disappearing before my eyes.

June 12th, 2024, Simon

Hill Retreat Hospice is beautiful, standing in five acres of landscaped grounds. I've been here in her bedroom for the past hour making sure everything's perfect for when she arrives.

Her favourite Beatles album, Sgt Pepper's Lonely Hearts Club Band, plays quietly in the background. The next track starts, and I sob uncontrollably. It's "When I'm Sixty-Four," an age Janice will never reach. It's so fucking unfair. She's too young to be taken from me. Especially by this cruel disease that's robbing her of everything.

I stand at the window, breathing in the exquisite fragrance of Maison Francis Kurkdjian Baccarat Rouge, which I've sprayed liberally around the room, looking out across a small lawn leading down to a lake. It's a scene of peace and tranquility.

For what you'd think would be a sad place, gloomy and oppressive, Hill Retreat is quite the opposite. It's the most wonderful haven, full of love and peace, which I guess, is all that's left after hope and prayers have been cruelly extinguished.

Love seeps through its every pore, it's there on the faces of all the nursing staff, it's in every word they utter, in every look they give, and will soon be flowing into my beloved Janice once she settles in to face her final days.

A family is walking on the gravel path in front of the lake. An elderly lady in a wheelchair, with a tartan blanket across her lap, is being pushed by a middle-aged woman—her daughter, perhaps—and flanked by a man and two teenage boys. She looks to be in her late 80s or early 90s.

It's terribly sad. Of course, it is. A daughter saying goodbye to her mother. Grandchildren saying goodbye to their grandmother. At that age, she's had a good innings as the hackneyed cliche goes. My Janice hasn't. She should be facing many more balls in the coming years. But she won't. Just a few more sunrises to go before her final sunset. That's what's out of kilter here. Janice is far too young, and has far too many things to do in what should be many more years of life ahead of her. That would be the correct order. Janice or I shouldn't be in Hill Retreat for another 30 years. Maybe I will be, but Janice is here now, the rest of her life measured in days, hours, and minutes, pain control, oxygen tanks, and medical drips.

IT'S NOT FUCKING FAIR.

27

Journey

June 17th, 2024, Simon

"We've had a good marriage, haven't we?" Janice's voice sounds weak and laboured and she punctuates her simple sentence with a pause and cough. She finds words hard to come by now. Not because she has none to say; I'm sure there are millions more she wants to find, just as I did when hovering between life and death with COVID, but because every breath she takes becomes increasingly more strained.

"We have," I sob. "The very best." I really want to be strong for her during these final hours, these final moments, but now the time's here, that resolve goes out of the window. Which is perhaps for the best. Emotion, not stoicism, is called for now. She knows her time is fast approaching, and all we can do is be here for her. Strength isn't needed. We are past all that. I want my tears to show how much I love her—the love we've held for each other since that night of Helen's party all those years ago, and cemented many times over; including on our wedding day and the birth of our two treasured daughters.

"Remember that holiday in Ibiza the year after our honeymoon?" I ask her. A slight smile crosses her lips as she looks straight into my eyes and gives just a hint of a nod.

"What was that couple's name we went around with? Oh, I can't remember. But do…?"

"Bob and Sally," she says, in nothing more than a whisper. Her body might be failing fast but her mind is still as quick as ever. I'd have to do most of the talking now.

"That's right, I remember." I smile, gently squeezing her arm. "I also remember you and Sally trying to throw me in the swimming pool."

Janice's eyes mist a little, and I'm sure she's thinking back to that sun-drenched hotel in Santa Eulalia on the east coast. I'd probably been a little mischievous to her and Sally in some way, because I found my arms gripped tightly, being frog-marched towards the pool.

"Get ready for a dunking, dear heart," said Janice.

"Should we get his trunks off first?" Sally had giggled when she said that, but I wasn't sure if she was joking or being deadly serious. My pulse began to race. The terrace surrounding the pool was packed with sunbathers. Surely they wouldn't. Would they?

"I'd not thought of that," said Janice. "But I rather like the sound of it. What do you say, dear heart? A spot of skinny dipping?"

"You wouldn't dare," I said, which turned out to be a big mistake.

Before I knew it, Janice had released my arm, whipped my trunks down, and pushed me forward sharply so I involuntarily stepped out of them, leaving them behind. A roar went up from everyone around us, while Janice grabbed my arm again, and she and Sally rushed me stark naked to the pool. I told myself there was no way I could go in the water. Having to climb out naked would heighten my embarrassment. And by then the girls would have stolen my trunks and run off.

Right. We're almost at the pool. I felt them gripping my arms tighter, getting ready to push me in. It's now or never. I planted one foot firmly on the tiles in front of me and swept my arms forward as strongly as I could. The girls catapulted ahead of me and tumbled helplessly into the water with an almighty splash. I turned tail, snatched up my trunks, and cupped them over my modesty before fleeing for the toilets, with a loud cheer following me.

I smile at the memory and can see from the beam on Janice's face that she's recalling getting my trunks off with probably more amusement than being unceremoniously hurled in the pool. "You lost your trunks," she whispers. "Naked in front of all those people."

"What?" says Hannah.

"That's a story for another day," I tell her.

I gently take Janice's hand. "What about all those picnics at Grant's Rock when the girls were toddlers?"

She beams at me. "Lovely."

The hours slip by with Janice smiling up at the girls and me in turn as we each fill her waning time with beautiful memories together as a family, showing her how much we love her and how much she'll be missed: Claire's first dance show, Hannah's first County netball match, the caravan park holidays while the girls were still toddlers, our first foreign holiday when Hannah was five and Claire three.

At some point, those hours pass midnight unnoticed and cross into another day...

28

Light

June 18th, 2024, Simon

...until eventually: "My time's come," Janice whispers. Tears stream down my face. I squeeze her left hand, while Claire and Hannah hold her tightly on the other side of the bed.

I can see she is right. Her chest rises with a shuddering wheeze. Falls. Rises again. She smiles at me and silently mouths: "I love you."

"I love you, too, my Darling," I tell her. "You'll be in my heart forever."

Then her eyes turn to the girls. It looks as if moving her head is too much of an effort for her diminishing life force. "Love you, Mum," they both say.

Her eyes slowly flicker shut. When we were younger I used to love watching her sleep. She'd tease me about sitting up in bed and looking down at her while she was on the verge of dozing off. I'd sit for a while longer until sleep overtook her completely, just as I did in those first few nights after Larkwise. This was the same. I watch her close her eyes and fall asleep. Except this isn't the same. This time, I'm not going to drop asleep alongside her, and we wouldn't both wake up in the morning refreshed and ready to face the day, so full of life, so full of love. She's had a lifetime of my love, and now I have to be ready to face the rest of my lifetime with just the memory of hers for me, and a heart overflowing with it.

Tears become a river as my sobs break through, noisily. Her fingers release their grip on my hand, and her chest rises again, but not so far this time. Then it sinks heavily, almost as if it had flopped lifelessly. And I realise it has. It was her final movement on this Earth.

My Janice has gone.

Time stands still. Her face which had been far beyond thin for months, residing deep in gaunt and haggard country, is now calm, peaceful, and pain-free. Then I see her face in the sunshine. In the rain and the snow. Smiling, laughing, crying. I see Janice as that vibrant sexy teenager at Helen's party. Janice as Hannah's mother, holding our daughter for the first time. Then with Claire. That anguished look as Doctor Horton told us she had breast cancer. Finally, even worse, when Doctor Horton told us the cancer was back with a vengeance. This time, pancreatic cancer. Her face is there, in front of my eyes, lodged in my heart, to live in my memory forever.

"Mum," calls Hannah gently. "No, please, Mum."

I put my arms out to them, and both girls come around the bed and squat down on either side of my chair. I shuffle forward out of the seat and drop to my knees. The three of us grip each other tightly in a hug, sobs shaking our shoulders.

I sniff loudly as the tears flow faster, which accentuates the clean, sterile fragrance permeating the room. Then I swallow, grimacing as a stab of indigestion hits me—no doubt the result of a bag of salt and vinegar crisps Hannah had fetched for me from the vending machine an hour ago. Looking up, away from our hug, I contemplate the sights around me, seeing the bed with its head raised and the railings running halfway along both sides, the three comfortable armchairs, the TV on the wall, the white deep-pile carpet. Things which dear Janice will never see again. She'd never hear her favourite Beatles CD again, which continues playing quietly in the background.

Sunrise is still some way off, but the first faint hint of light breaking beyond the horizon creeps into the Eastern-facing window looking out onto the hospice garden. The first dawn on a world without Janice in it.

I glance over to the clock above the door.

Ouch, that bloody indigestion takes another stab. Perhaps I should see if the hospice has any medicine for it.

They say most people die naturally during the wee small hours when the body's resistance is at its lowest ebb, and my wife has just become one of those statistics. She died at 4.10 on the morning of Tuesday, June 18th, 2024. I guess I need to remember that time to tell the doctor.

Wait a minute. Why does 4.10 ring a bell? Oh, how can I forget? What an amazing coincidence, though. I've never told anyone except Janice of course—how could I?—but that's the exact time I died on April 1st, 2020. I remember that slurping and popping sound as I broke free of my body and floated above in-bed-me, looking across at Julia-not-Julia who turned out to be April ringing for help. The clock above her nurses' station had shown 4.10. Is this why Janice slipped away at the same time, to somehow stay connected with me through a shared time of death? But it hadn't been my time, had it? Grandma sent me back.

The important thing I'm remembering here, though, is that when I died *I came out of my body*.

Which means...

At this very moment, Janice should be...where? Just above her bed? I rack my brain trying to remember if I'd floated to the right or left four years ago. I'm not taking any chances—I'll cover both. I look to the height where I'm pretty sure she'll be right now, probably pretty confused like I'd been, but maybe smiling down at the girls and me.

Easing my way out of the hug I stand and wave slowly from left to right. "Goodbye, Janice," I whisper, hoping she catches my eye somewhere. Hannah and Claire stare at me before looking up, too, with puzzled frowns across their faces, then back to me.

"Dad?" That's Claire.

"Nothing." I shake my head. "Just saying a final goodbye before her spirit's too far away." 'Away' stretched out in a jerk: *awaaaay*, as the indigestion catches my breath sharply.

"Dad?" Hannah, this time.

"Indigestion," I tell her. "Those crisps."

Maybe I can cling on to Janice's presence for a few more seconds before the portal to the light opens for her. Now, where will that be?

The memory comes flooding back. It had been to my right, near the door. Does that mean it'll be in the same place for Janice?

"Janice," I call. "Where's your portal?"

Claire stands up. "Dad, are you alright?" She sounds worried, which is hardly surprising, as my behaviour must seem weird to the girls.

I rub my chest as the indigestion rises a little higher. Bloody salt and vinegar crisps.

Hannah stands, too, and reaches towards me, but I raise my hand. "I'm fine."

The air near the window shimmers for a second, like a mirage just above the road surface on a hot day, and Janice floats in front of it, her head half turned towards me, as if she'd heard me ask about it. And she's smiling.

Then she's gone and the air is still again. I close my eyes and an after-image depicting the tiny fraction of a second I'd seen her, lingers there, rather like looking at an object in bright sunlight which stays burnt on the inside of your eyelids before melting away. But instead of being an indistinct outline, this is a proper, full-blown image. No longer the skin-and-bone cancer-ravaged frame that could be picked up and carried aloft by a gust of wind, this had been my beautiful, shining Janice of old, at the threshold of her journey to the light.

A wave of relief washes over me. She is safely on her way to the afterlife, and I'm convinced Helen and Grandma will be there to greet her and guide her on the journey, along with her own Mum and Dad. The two cats we'd loved during our marriage would be there, too.

Even though she's leaving the girls and me behind, my heart rejoices, knowing that a feeling of pure spiritual peace and love will be enveloping her right now, drawing her in. After all, I've been there, I know there's nothing to fear from death. We'll be reunited someday, across the years. Eventually, in many decades, our family will be together again. The worst part will be the waiting. Her death will leave such a huge void in the lives of those who love her.

That thought stirs memories of Grandma's funeral during my flashback while being taken to hospital in a COVID delirium: 'There is still a very genuine sense of sorrow and loss that a loved one is no longer with us,' the vicar had said. 'We're no longer able to enjoy Rosemary's company, her friendship, her fellowship.' His words now applied every bit as much to Janice. 'There will be no isolation in heaven. We will not be separated from each other. Heaven, for us, will be a place of perpetual reunion.'

Tears continue to roll down my cheeks uncontrollably, but unlike my daughters' tears which are forged in grief, mine come from joy in the knowledge that Janice's spirit, her soul, will live on somewhere beyond the white light.

Maybe it's time to tell the girls the full story. They deserve to know their Mother is only parted from us temporarily, and they'll see her again one day.

I gently pick up Janice's hand. It feels fragile, brittle, and paper-thin, like an autumn leaf that has fallen from the tree two days before. "Janice, my love, we'll be together again one day."

Then I turn back to the girls. "Hannah, Claire, there's something I need to say. Your Mum..."

Without further warning, the indigestion pain goes nuclear in my chest, and the most intense agony I've ever experienced blossoms all over me for a tiny microsecond. I never see the floor coming up to hit me, but I guess it must have done because the next thing I know is I'm face down in the white deep-pile carpet. I try to turn over but a slight resistance softly pulls me back as if I am wallowing in a bath of molasses. They suddenly relinquish their grip and I float a few feet into the air, looking down at the back of my head below.

I remember this sensation and what it means. This time, though, I haven't been aware of any slurping and eventual popping sound as my true essence breaks free from its mortal shell. For a few seconds, I float upwards away from my body.

Both my daughters scream, and Hannah drops to her knees alongside me, rolling me onto my back. "Help me, Claire. I'll get him into the recovery position. Can you find the nurse?"

Claire runs from the room as Hannah removes my glasses. She straightens my legs and stretches my left arm out at a right angle to my body. I watch from above, fascinated. I have no idea she knows about any of this.

A strange detachment engulfs me. I've been here before, so I'm not scared or even worried in the least about what is happening. Where is that immense feeling of peace and love, though, and the longing to stay? I feel nothing. Should I go with Janice or stay with the girls? Why am I emotionless right now? This doesn't make sense. Also, how can I have thought that what is obviously the onset of a heart attack, was indigestion? That doesn't make sense, either.

Below, Hannah reaches across for my other arm, drawing it across my chest, and places my hand against my left cheek.

I think of Janice, somewhere close by, just on the other side of the portal. *Where's the portal? Come on, open up for me.*

What would I do, if it did? Would I stay here with the girls, assuming I survive the heart attack? Could I leave them, letting them think Janice and I had gone forever? Wouldn't it be too cruel for them to lose both their Mum and Dad within moments of each other?

The portal appears, just as it had four years earlier, with the shimmering air parting like the Red Sea under Moses' command, just in front of the window where I'd caught that tantalising glimpse of it with Janice. Those same pale blue strands of energy radiate outwards from the oval entrance to the tunnel, and the familiar whooshing emanates from it.

"Dad, come back to us," Hannah pleads. While continuing to press on my cheek, she hooks her other hand under my right knee and lifts it up, bending my leg until it stays there of its own accord, supported by my foot flat on the floor. She'd certainly got this recovery position technique down to a fine art as she gently pulls on my knee to roll me onto my side. She finishes the manueuvre by bringing my leg down into a comfortable right angle.

While I feel calm and peaceful, it's almost like an anti-climax, with no strong desire either to go with Janice or stay with the girls. I try to think back to when I'd floated in front of the portal previously. I'd simply been puzzled and intrigued then, but I remember the sensation of instantly belonging once I'd gone through it.

The sound intensifies as I float towards the muddy grey tunnel, and just as before, as soon as I cross the threshold I'm no longer floating. The rushing maelstrom flashes past me as if showing me where I have to go. No need for that, I know the way. The world lurches sideways as I drop down, and my feet plant firmly on the floor of this dimension running parallel to our Eathly domain. The familiar emotional tug immediately strikes, enticing me to forget my past life and sacrifice any possible further life I may be due on Earth. I turn to look out through the rift in the spiritual curtain separating the two planes of existence and see Claire run back into Janice's bedroom, followed by the hospice's duty night nurse who carries a green bag.

I recall seeing April break my ribs last time. I've no idea of the nurse's name who now pounds my chest rhythmically and relentlessly to the count of 30, before reaching into the bag and bringing out a defibrillator, not unlike the one on the wall in reception at Poolswood Sound that we'd all had training on.

Thanks to that training, I know exactly what's coming, so it's no surprise when she presses the green button to power it up, and opens the lid. Even from this distance inside the tunnel, I see the pads, eraser, and gloves inside, and watch as she peels the sticky labels off the pads and fastens the first one to the upper right side of my chest.

An irresistible pull means the light is calling me. With the same calm detachment I'd felt when I first floated out of my body, I take a final look at the nurse placing the second pad on my stomach below my left armpit, and start to slowly walk away from the portal, along the tunnel towards the pinprick of light in the distance.

Her voice floats faintly through the portal to me. "Clear. Shocking."

Another massive pain grips my upper torso and I hurtle backwards involuntarily, as if shot from a cannon or pulled on a strong cable, out of the tunnel and straight into my body, where my back arches, before flopping down flat.

The pain twists and turns in my chest, but I can't shout out in my agony. I can't move. All I can do is simply lie there staring up at the ceiling, and even that seems to be behind a growing mist.

The girls are sobbing and on the verge of hysteria. "You've got to save him," screams Claire. "We've just lost our Mum. We can't lose Dad, too."

The nurse pauses momentarily as she lays the defibrillator aside and prepares to resume pumping. "What?"

"Mum's just died," Hannah tells her. "Dad collapsed straight after."

The nurse glances up at Janice's bed then back to me and starts the second round of CPR. "One." A powerful push on my chest. "Two." Another downward thrust. "Three." If I'd thought the pain was bad before, it just went off the scale. It isn't as if I've been hit by an express train but more as if the engine has stopped right above my heart.

I can't even move my eyes, and now the mist clouding them starts to seriously obscure the ceiling. My body is useless. Do I really want to stay here? Janice is waiting for me. She is probably at the end of the tunnel now and standing by the white light. The light's call to me is even stronger, metaphorically even louder, but my daughters need me more than ever. How can I leave them? Anyway, I'm back here in my body, so I don't have a choice. It looks as if I'm staying, but it can't be like this, though. I can't move. I need that engine to start up and pull the train off my chest.

Suddenly the nurse looms into my sight through the thickening mist. Her name badge is right in my eye line. Jacqui.

Well, Jacqui, come on. Get my heart going again.

"Thirty," she says. For fuck's sake. The pain is so bad I haven't even noticed she's gone through another full CPR cycle, and probably bust a couple of ribs, into the bargain. "Clear. Shocking."

If I could have widened my eyes, I would. The power flowing through me from the defibrillator intensifies the giant hand's grasp on my torso and sends my muscles into full spasm, arching my back. All movement is involuntary and uncontrollable.

"One," Jacqui says. Here we go with a third round. "Two."

I wish I could have turned to the girls to let them know I am still with them, but no matter how hard I struggle, how hard I will myself to move, I simply can't.

Then, maybe I'm not with them anymore, because the pain winks out of existence as suddenly as turning off an electric light, and I am moving again, gently floating upwards. My vision is perfect now, the mist which had clouded my world dissipates with the pain, and I see Nurse Jacqui immediately above me, thumping down on my chest. She is up to six now. I pass straight through her and draw myself upright to look down on the scene below.

My heart breaks at the sight of Claire and Hannah sobbing relentlessly. I can't leave them. I just can't, it would be too brutal.

A faint musical tinkling, reminiscent of the wind chimes hanging from the side of my garden shed, wafts its way towards me from the portal, filling my senses with tranquility and urging me to go. An image of the pinprick of radiant white light at the end of the tunnel flashes into my mind. It's almost as if it's saying: "Your time is now."

That can wait. Remembering Grandma's words that my thoughts would be heard on this spiritual plane, I project an agonised mental call to Janice across the ether. *Janice, forgive me for not joining you when I had the chance. Our daughters need us. I'll see you again someday, but not today.*

Dropping down again I position myself immediately above my body, right where Nurse Jacqui is pounding that rhythmic life-saving procedure. Her arms pass straight through floating-me, banging relentlessly on lying-on-the-floor me. I shiver mentally—I don't think it is possible for me to shiver physically—at the thought of staying dead until spiritual me gets back in.

"I'm coming, girls," I say, looking into their broken-hearted, despairing faces. Why am I saying that? They can't hear me. "I'm not leaving you." *Sorry, Janice.*

The musical chimes grow a little louder, and as I look for what I resign myself will be one final time at the oval doorway into the next world, I see the familiar glowing orbs, three on each side, forming a guard of honor, waiting for me to pass through, so they can escort me to the light.

No way, Jose, not today, thank you. Today's not a good day to die. I've got two daughters to comfort and hundreds more radio shows to broadcast. *Come on, Jacqui.*

Her voice cuts through the music and whooshing maelstrom: "Twenty-seven."

I sink down, inching my way into my body, bracing for the constricting pain to squeeze my chest. Last time, I remember being dragged back to my body as if tethered by an invisible psychic cord. There's no tugging sensation now, though. I'm making all the running this time.

"Twenty-eight."

I will myself to fully inhabit my body, maneuvering my arms and legs until they are completely synchronised with the shell around me.

"Twenty-nine."

Come on, come on. When the defibrillator jolts its blast of electricity through my body I'll be ready. That's when the cosmos will let my spirit go and I'll merge back with my body.

"Thirty." I experiment with a quick wave of my hand. My spiritual hand moves, but my physical hand stays resolutely immobile. We aren't together yet.

Jacqui reaches for the button on the defibrillator. "Clear. Shocking." *Okay, here we go.*

I scrunch my face up, waiting. And there it is. My body arches involuntarily as 500 volts shoot through it. The anticipation fades, and I don't feel a thing, watching helplessly as my body drops around me.

No...this can't be happening. I'm here, ready and waiting. Why won't my spirit reconnect?

Nurse Jacqui's voice cuts through my daughters' sobs. "One." Another rib cracking push. "Two."

The musical chimes coming from the tunnel grow louder and more enchanting, and I have a sudden mental image of the Pied Piper of Hamelin being just inside, drawing me in, and leading me away from my girls to Grandma and Janice.

The girls need me more than ever at the moment. Why can't the cosmos see that?

By now Jacqui has reached 11. *Come on,* I plead, *get to 30 and another burst of electricity from the defibrillator.* Not only is the Pied Piper luring me in, but I feel a definite push underneath, forcing me up and away from my body. This pull-me-push-me combination weaves a strong spell as it drags me towards the portal.

I look despairingly at the girls and Jacqui. Claire has clasped her hands tightly together pushing them against her mouth, while Hannah's arms hang loosely at her side.

The spiritual chain draws me in slowly but relentlessly, as if I were an anchor being pulled up the side of a ship. The music and maelstrom increase in volume, drowning out Jacqui's counting as I arrive at the pulsating oval. I assume she's reached 30 because she presses the button on the defibrillator again and my body arches, but I guess it's a forlorn hope that I'll shoot back and merge with it.

Then I'm inside the tunnel, surrounded by its muddy walls. The glowing orbs rearrange their formation, orbiting my head and starting to move towards the white pinprick in the far distance, escorting me away from the world I'd known for 60 years. I cast one final look at Janice's hospice room on what is now the other side of the veil. Her face is at peace, and I guess I'll soon be reunited with her.

Nurse Jacqui had stood up and has her arms around Claire and Hannah, hugging them in the same way I'd been doing just moments earlier. The girls aren't mourning the death of just one parent now, though, they're mourning the loss of both.

The portal shrinks quickly, zipping its sides shut like a sleeping bag, and I realise there really is no way back this time.

Perhaps now I'm here, I'm happy about that, though, because the further I go along the tunnel, the stronger that wonderfully calm sense of peace and love envelopes me. The orbs hurry me along towards the light, which is increasing in size all the time, and it isn't long before the familiar formless dimly-glowing figures which I recall so well from last time, step from the walls and flank me on the short journey.

"Welcome, Simon." The rich baritone voice comes from all sides, even more soothing than I remember, wrapping itself around me and drawing me further into the ecstasy it promises.

Within moments I stand on the threshold of the cavern, looking intently at the light's origin a few hundred metres ahead. Both the orbs and figures may have sensed they don't need to guide me any further as they stay in the tunnel when I start to move forward into the white glow which radiates out from its source.

I look over my shoulder but the entrance to the tunnel has gone. Nothing but this pure white energy exists as it washes over and around me, drawing me ever closer.

The feeling that this whole realm is shaped by God bores deeper into me with every step.

Then, a couple of things happen simultaneously. Two figures suddenly appear immediately in front of me, silhouetted against the light, holding hands. And a stream of energy, even more powerful, brighter, and whiter than anything else in this realm, flows out of the shining source like a waterfall straight into my spiritual being.

Just as if I am breathing in pure unconditional love, well-being, vitality, and joy direct from the heart of the Creator, it cascades into the top of my head through my Crown Chakra, enlightening and nurturing me.

The two figures are becoming more recognisable as Grandma and Janice with each step.

But my focus stays with the corridor of light now connecting me permanently to the force of the cosmos, of which I am becoming an integral part. It feeds my consciousness with the knowledge that this isn't only the heart of humankind, this is the heart of everything that has ever been and ever will be. I see that despite the horrors of evil and inhumanity, this healing, restoring energy goes out to every soul, and is on the brink of pushing aside all that veils the truth of who I am.

This unified field of pure white light is converting each fibre of my being, releasing me from the separating and constricting imprints stored within, washing away everything less than infinite perfection. It calls on me to invoke the healing light to transpose the cause, effect, habit, and memory of every limiting thought, feeling, word or action I've ever expressed throughout my earthly existence, and to transform it into divine light and love.

It is rewriting my entire essence into a subroutine of the program of eternity.

Another step and Grandma is before me, her smiling face conveying the most wonderful feeling of love, telling me I am home. And Janice stands alongside. My beloved Janice has made it here and I've not been far behind. They release each other's hands and hold their arms out, beckoning me to them.

This is my beautiful shining Janice that I'd glimpsed at the portal.

Serenely, I move towards them and Grandma steps forward to greet me. "Now's the time for that hug you wanted." Her lips don't move, nor do her words come through my ears. They form straight in my consciousness. "The time to touch."

The instant she grips my hand a powerful tingling sensation encases my entire...I was going to say body, but this isn't a body. Is it my soul, my spirit, my essence? What exactly am I now? What are Grandma and Janice?

Janice.

I look beyond Grandma's shoulder. My darling wife closes the four paces between us and takes my other hand. More tingling loops around and within me, and I stare in wonder as a rainbow of colours brighter than any I've ever seen, and comprising vibrant new hues way beyond the spectrum visible to a human eye, weaves itself around us.

"No going back now," says Grandma. She hugs the two of us briefly, then pulls away and strides purposefully into the white light's blazing source.

"I wasn't expecting you." Janice's words tumble directly into me. "But I'm so glad you've come, dear heart."

The lure of the light is now completely overwhelming, beckoning us to merge with it. More than beckoning. Calling, insisting, demanding.

Three paces and we'll be there.

One.

Two.

We stop on the threshold, smiling widely at each other with the rays pouring over us as the universe offers its embrace, inviting us to become one with it.

My physical body's journey is over. It lays lifeless alongside my dead wife back in her hospice room, but our spiritual journey is just beginning. Hand in hand, Janice and I take the first step on that voyage of discovery and follow Grandma into the light.

About The Author

Stewart Bint is a former radio presenter and Public Relations writer, now semi-retired, focusing on his fiction, along with editorials and a regular column in a monthly magazine.

Married, with two grown-up children, he lives in Leicestershire, in the UK. When not at his writing desk, he can often be found hiking in woodlands and on countryside trails near his home

Stewart Bint is the author of five novels and a collection of short stories:

In Shadows Waiting
Timeshaft
The Jigsaw And The Fan
To Rise Again
Thunderlands
When God's Wind Blows

Connect with Stewart Bint online

Website:
http://www.stewartbintauthor.weebly.com/

Blog:
www.stewartbintauthor.weebly.com/stewart-bints-blog

Twitter: www.Twitter.com/@AuthorSJB

Facebook: https://www.facebook.com/StewartBintAuthor

Amazon: https://www.amazon.co.uk/
Stewart-Bint/e/B00D18IARS

www.ingramcontent.com/pod-product-compliance
Lightning Source LLC
Chambersburg PA
CBHW020459020726
47493CB00001B/97